THE FIRST MOUNTAIN MAN
PREACHER'S
HELLSTORM

THE FIRST MOUNTAIN MAN
PREACHER'S HELLSTORM

WILLIAM W. JOHNSTONE
with J. A. Johnstone

PINNACLE BOOKS
Kensington Publishing Corp.
www.kensingtonbooks.com

PINNACLE BOOKS are published by

Kensington Publishing Corp.
119 West 40th Street
New York, NY 10018

PUBLISHER'S NOTE
Following the death of William W. Johnstone, the Johnstone family is
working with a carefully selected writer to organize and complete Mr.
Johnstone's outlines and many unfinished manuscripts to create additional
novels in all of his series like The Last Gunfighter, Mountain Man, and
Eagles, among others. This novel was inspired by Mr. Johnstone's superb
storytelling.

All Kensington titles, imprints, and distributed lines are available at special quantity discounts for bulk purchases for sales promotions, premiums,
fund-raising, educational, or institutional use. Special book excerpts or
customized printings can also be created to fit specific needs. For details,
write or phone the office of the Kensington sales manager: Kensington
Publishing Corp., 119 West 40th Street, New York, NY 10018, attn: Sales
Department; phone 1-800-221-2647.

PINNACLE BOOKS, the Pinnacle logo, and the WWJ steer head logo are
Reg. U.S. Pat. & TM Off.

ISBN-13: 978-0-7860-4000-1
ISBN-10: 0-7860-4000-9

First printing: January 2017

10 9 8 7 6 5 4 3 2 1

Printed in the United States of America

First electronic edition: January 2017

ISBN-13: 978-0-7860-4001-8
ISBN-10: 0-7860-4001-7

THE JENSEN FAMILY
FIRST FAMILY OF THE AMERICAN FRONTIER

Smoke Jensen—*The Mountain Man*
The youngest of three children and orphaned as a young boy, Smoke Jensen is considered one of the fastest draws in the West. His quest to tame the lawless West has become the stuff of legend. Smoke owns the Sugarloaf Ranch in Colorado. Married to Sally Jensen, father to Denise ("Denny") and Louis.

Preacher—*The First Mountain Man*
Though not a blood relative, grizzled frontiersman Preacher became a father figure to the young Smoke Jensen, teaching him how to survive in the brutal, often deadly Rocky Mountains. Fought the battles that forged his destiny. Armed with a long gun, Preacher is as fierce as the land itself.

Matt Jensen—*The Last Mountain Man*
Orphaned but taken in by Smoke Jensen, Matt Jensen has become like a younger brother to Smoke and even took the Jensen name. And like Smoke, Matt has carved out his destiny on the American frontier. He lives by the gun and surrenders to no man.

Luke Jensen—*Bounty Hunter*
Mountain Man Smoke Jensen's long-lost brother, Luke Jensen, is scarred by war and a dead shot—the right qualities to be a bounty hunter. And he's cunning, and fierce enough, to bring down the deadliest outlaws of his day.

Ace Jensen and Chance Jensen—*Those Jensen Boys!*
The untold story of Smoke Jensen's long-lost nephews, Ace and Chance, a pair of young-gun twins as reckless and wild as the frontier itself . . . Their father is Luke Jensen, thought killed in the Civil War. Their uncle Smoke Jensen is one of the fiercest gunfighters the West has ever known. It's no surprise that the inseparable Ace and Chance Jensen have a knack for taking risks—even if they have to blast their way out of them.

CHAPTER 1

Moving slowly and carefully, Preacher reached out and closed his hand around the butt of a flintlock pistol. The night was black as pitch around him, but he didn't need to be able to see to know where the gun was. He had committed all his surroundings to memory before he rolled in his blankets and dozed off.

Another pistol lay next to the one Preacher grasped, and a flintlock rifle and a tomahawk were nearby as well. Both pistols were double-shotted and heavily charged with powder.

Let the attackers come. He was ready to cry havoc and let slip the dogs of war, as his friend Audie might say. The little fella had been a professor once and was fond of quoting old Bill Shakespeare.

On Preacher's other side, the big wolflike cur he called Dog growled softly. He knew enemies were out there in the night and was eager to tear into them, but he wouldn't attack unless Preacher gave him the go-ahead.

Preacher sat up and put his hand out, resting it on

the back of Dog's neck where the fur stood up slightly. He waited and listened, not knowing what had roused him and Dog from slumber.

Preacher's almost supernaturally keen eyes adjusted to the darkness well enough for him to see the rangy gray stallion known as Horse. He stood not far away, head up, ears pricked forward. He'd sensed whatever it was, too. The pack mule Preacher had brought from St. Louis stood with its head down as it dozed.

A breeze drifted through the trees and carried voices to Preacher's ears. He couldn't make out the words, but the tone was familiar.

The voices were Indian, but they weren't on the warpath. If they had been stalking an enemy, they would have done so in grim silence. In this case, they sounded amused.

Preacher was on the edge of Blackfoot country, which meant he didn't see anything funny about the situation. For more than twenty years, he had been coming to the Rocky Mountains every year to harvest pelts from beaver and other fur-bearing animals, and nearly every one of those years, he'd had trouble with various Blackfoot bands.

In fact, it was the Blackfeet who were responsible for the name he carried to this day.

Early on in his frontier sojourn, he had been captured by them and tied to a stake. Come morning, he would have been tortured and eventually burned to death.

However, something had possessed him to start talking, much like a street preacher he had seen back in St. Louis, and when the sun rose he was still going at it, spewing out words in a seemingly never-ending torrent.

Crazy people intrigued and frightened the Indians, and they figured anybody who started talking like that and wouldn't stop had to be loco. Killing somebody who wasn't right in the head was a sure way of bringing down bad medicine on the tribe, so they had scrapped their plans to roast the young man known at that point as Art, and let him go.

Eventually, word of the incident got around—the vast wilderness was a surprisingly small place in some ways—and other mountain men started calling him *Preacher*. The name stuck. He didn't mind. Eventually, he never thought of himself any other way.

His war with the Blackfeet had continued over the years. He had killed countless numbers of warriors, some in open battle, some by creeping with such stealth into their camps at night and slitting their throats that no one knew he had been there until morning.

They called him the White Wolf, the Ghost Killer, and probably had other names for him, as well. The Blackfoot warrior who finally killed Preacher would be the most honored of his people.

Preacher figured to keep on frustrating that ambition, just as he had for a long time.

As he sat where he had gone to ground to sleep for the night, more than a mile away from where he had built a small fire to cook his supper, he knew he didn't have any friends in those parts. The warriors who were barely within earshot would love to kill him if they got the chance.

For a moment, he considered stalking them, becoming the hunter, but he realized they weren't hunting *him*. He hadn't seen a soul in more than a week. They weren't looking for him. They were on their way somewhere else, bound on some errand of their own, and already their voices had faded until he could barely hear them.

"Wouldn't make sense to borrow trouble," he whispered to Dog. "Sooner or later it always finds us on its own."

Dog's fur lay down. Horse went back to cropping at some grass. The crisis had passed.

Preacher rolled up in his blankets and went back to sleep, confident that his instincts and his trail companions would awaken him if danger approached again.

The rest of the night passed without incident. Preacher slept the deep, dreamless sleep of an honest man and got up in the morning ready to press on. He was headed toward an area where he hadn't been in quite a while, hoping to have good luck in his trapping.

For more than thirty years, since a party of men under the command of a man named Manuel Lisa had started up the Missouri River in 1807, men had been coming to these mountains in search of pelts. After all that time, beaver and other fur-bearing varmints were becoming less numerous, and it took more work to find enough of them to make a trip to the Rockies profitable.

That was why Preacher was expanding the territory where he trapped. He didn't really care that much about the money. His needs were simple and few. He loved the mountains. They were his home and had been ever since he first laid eyes on them. He would be there even if he never made a penny from his efforts.

If a fellow was going to work at something, though, he might as well do the best job he could. That was Preacher's philosophy, although he would have scoffed at calling it that.

After a quick breakfast, he saddled Horse and set out, leading the pack mule. Dog bounded ahead of them, full of energy.

Snowcapped peaks rose to Preacher's right and left as he headed up a broad, tree-covered valley broken up occasionally by meadows thick with wildflowers. A fast-flowing creek, fed here and there by smaller streams, ran through the center of the valley. He hoped they would be teeming with beaver.

At the far end of the valley about forty miles away rose a huge, saw-toothed mountain. Something about it stirred a memory in Preacher. After a moment, he gave a little shake of his head and stopped trying to recall the memory. Whatever the recollection might be, it proved elusive.

It would come back to him or it wouldn't, and either way it wasn't likely to change his plans. He intended to make his base of operations at the upper end of the valley, near that saw-toothed peak. He would work the tributaries one at a time, down one side of the valley and then back up the other. That would take him most of the summer.

In the fall he would pack up the pelts he had taken and head back to St. Louis, unless he decided to pay a visit to one of the far-flung trading posts established by the American Fur Company and sell his furs there.

If he did that, he could spend the winter in the mountains as he had done many times in the past, finding some friendly band of Indians who wouldn't object to having him around—

He straightened abruptly in the saddle and peered toward the saw-toothed mountain in the distance. "Well, son of a . . . No wonder it seemed familiar to me." He grinned and shook his head. "Wonder if any of 'em are still around."

Maybe he would find out.

Preacher didn't get in any hurry traveling up the long valley. By the middle of the next day he was about halfway to the point where he intended to set up his main camp. He still hadn't seen another human being, although he had come across plenty of deer, a herd of moose, and a couple bears. He'd left them alone and they'd left him alone. From time to time, eagles and hawks soared overhead, riding the wind currents between the mountains.

When the sun was almost directly overhead, he stopped to let Horse and the pack mule drink from the creek. Hunkering down beside the stream, Preacher set his rifle down within easy reach, then stretched out his left hand and dipped it in the water, which was icy from snowmelt. He scooped some up and drank, thinking nothing had ever tasted better.

The current made his reflection in the water ripple

and blur, but he could make out the rugged features, the thick, gray-shot mustache, the thatch of dark hair under the broad-brimmed felt hat he had pushed to the back of his head.

A few feet away, Dog lifted his dripping muzzle from the creek and stiffened. Horse stopped drinking as well.

Preacher acted like nothing had happened, but in reality, his senses had snapped to high alert. He listened intently, sniffed the air, searched the trees on the far side of the creek for any sign of movement.

There! Some branches on a bush had moved more than they would have if it was just some small animal rooting around.

Preacher still didn't rise to his feet or give any other sign he had noticed anything. All he did was carefully and unobtrusively move his hand toward the long-barreled rifle lying on the ground beside him.

Two figures dressed in buckskin suddenly burst out of the brush and trees on the other side of the creek and raced across open ground toward him. Preacher snatched up the rifle and came upright with the swift smoothness of an uncoiling snake. He brought the flintlock to his shoulder and slid his right thumb around the hammer, ready to cock and fire.

He held off as he realized the two Indians weren't attacking him. One was a woman, brown knees flashing under the buckskin dress, visible above the high moccasins she wore.

The other was a young man who carried a bow and had a quiver of arrows on his back but wasn't painted for war. He probably could have outrun the woman, but he held back, staying behind her as if to protect her.

A second later, Preacher saw why. At least half a dozen more buckskin-clad figures raced out of the woods in pursuit and let out bloodcurdling war cries as they spotted not only their quarry but also the white man on the other side of the creek.

CHAPTER 2

Instantly, Preacher shifted his aim, cocked the hammer, and pressed the trigger. The hammer snapped down, the powder in the pan ignited, and the rifle boomed and bucked against his shoulder. The mountain man's aim was true. The heavy lead ball smashed into the chest of the man in the forefront of the attackers and drove him backwards off his feet.

Preacher dropped the rifle butt first on the creek bank so dirt wouldn't foul the barrel. His hands swept toward the pistols tucked behind the broad leather belt around his waist as he shouted, "Get down!"

The young Indian man tackled the woman from behind and bore her to the ground. Preacher's pistols came up and roared. Smoke and flame spurted from the muzzles as they sent their double-shotted loads over the heads of the fleeing pair.

The volley cut down three more of the attackers, although one appeared only wounded as a ball ripped through his thigh. Preacher dropped the empty pistols next to the rifle. Two more pistols were in his saddlebags, loaded and primed, but it would take too long to reach them.

He jerked his tomahawk from behind his belt and charged across the creek, water splashing around his feet and legs as he charged. Dog was right beside him, growling and snarling.

Like a streak of gray fur and flashing teeth, the big cur leaped on one of the attackers and took him down. The man began to scream as Dog ripped at his throat, but the sound was quickly cut short.

At the same time, the young man rolled up onto one knee, put a hand on the woman's shoulder for a second in a signal for her to stay down, and then plucked an arrow from the quiver on his back and fitted it to his bowstring. A loud twang sounded as he let it fly.

Following Preacher's example, he dropped his bow and grabbed his tomahawk as he bounded to his feet.

Four of the attackers were still on their feet, but one of them staggered as he clutched the shaft of the arrow embedded in his chest. Counting the five men down, the original party had numbered nine.

Preacher, Dog, and the young man had cut the odds by more than half, but they were still outnumbered.

In Preacher's case, that wasn't hardly fair.

He moved like a whirlwind, lashing out right and left with the tomahawk. The stone head crashed against the head of an attacker, splintering bone under the impact. The warrior dropped, dead before he hit the ground.

Preacher pivoted and launched a blow toward a second warrior, who managed to block the mountain man's stroke with his own tomahawk. As the weapons clashed, the man launched a kick at Preacher's groin. Preacher twisted and took the man's heel on his thigh.

A few yards away, the young man went after the uninjured warrior, but the man with the wounded thigh lurched into his path. The young man's tomahawk came down and split the man's skull, cleaving into his brain.

The dying man fell forward, tangling with the young man, and both fell to the ground.

Preacher whirled to the side as his opponent tried desperately to brain him. The mountain man's tomahawk swept around and slashed across the attacker's throat. Flesh was no match for sharpened flint. Blood spouted from the wound as the man choked and gurgled. He dropped his tomahawk and put both hands to his ruined throat, but he couldn't stop the crimson flood.

His knees buckled and he pitched forward.

Preacher turned in time to see the youngster struggling to get a buckskin-clad carcass off him. The last member of the war party bent over them, tomahawk raised as he looked for an opening to strike.

Preacher threw his 'hawk. It revolved through the air, turning over the perfect number of times for the head to smash into the Indian's left shoulder and lodge there.

The man staggered back a step and dropped his own tomahawk. He turned and ran toward the trees, obviously realizing he was outnumbered, and wounded, to boot.

The young man finally succeeded in shoving the dead warrior off him. He sprang to his feet, grabbed the tomahawk the fleeing man had dropped, and flung it after him.

The throw missed narrowly as the 'hawk whipped past the man's head. A heartbeat later he disappeared into the trees.

Preacher started after the man, not wanting him to get away. To do that he had to pass the woman, who reached up, grabbed his hand, and said, "Preacher!"

That stopped him in his tracks. He looked down at her, wondering how she knew him.

Of course, he was known to many of the tribes. Up and down the Rocky Mountains from Canada to the Rio Grande, he was an enemy to some but a friend to many.

The woman looked up at him with a clear, steady gaze. Since she was holding his hand already, Preacher tightened his grip and easily lifted her to her feet.

The young man who had come out of the trees with her picked up his bow and turned toward them. A frown creased his forehead.

Preacher didn't pay much attention to him. His attention was on the woman as something stirred inside him.

She was a handsome woman, close to his own age. He could tell that by the faint lines on her face and the silver threads among her otherwise raven-black hair, which was cut short around her head. The years had thickened her waist slightly, but her body was still strong and well-curved under the buckskin dress.

From her short hair and the beading and other decorations on her dress, he could tell she was Absaroka, a tribe with which he had always been friendly. The young man's clothes and the long hair that hung far down his back marked him as a member of the same tribe.

As Preacher looked back and forth between them, he noted an even stronger similarity. He could see the resemblance in their eyes and in the cut of their jaws. Unless he missed his guess, the woman was the boy's mama.

Something else about the youngster struck him as familiar, too, but damned if he could say what it was. He had never laid eyes on the young man before. He was pretty sure of that.

He couldn't say the same for the woman. He looked at her and wanted to call her by name, but he couldn't quite do it. The words wouldn't come to his tongue.

She spoke in the language of the Absarokas. "Preacher. It really is you."

"Reckon it is," he replied, equally fluent in her tongue even though he hadn't been born to it.

"I prayed to Gitche Manitou, the Great Spirit, that we would find you. When we fled from our home, it was to look for you, but I did not dare to dream fate would bring us together again."

"I know you," Preacher said as he looked down into her dark eyes. "But I can't quite remember . . ."

He saw what looked like a flicker of pain in those eyes and wished he hadn't said it. Clearly, whatever had happened between them had meant more to her than it had to him.

It had been a long time ago. The memory was too dim and faded. He knew he hadn't seen her in recent years.

But it had stayed alive and clear in her mind. A

faintly sad smile touched her lips as she said, "My name is Bird in the Tree."

Preacher drew in a deep, sharp breath as the memories flooded back. "I knew a girl named Bird in the Tree, but it was many, many years ago. I called her Birdie . . ."

"I am she."

He put his hands on her shoulders, looked her in the eyes, and remembered everything.

He wasn't much more than a boy but had already battled river pirates on the Mississippi and fought the bloody British at the town of New Orleans with Andy Jackson. He had traveled to the mountains, made friends with the trappers, and become one of them himself.

He had befriended some of the Indians as well, and as winter settled down a band of Absaroka had invited him to stay with them. He had come West to experience everything life had to offer. The experience would be new to him, and so he stayed.

He hunted with some of the Absaroka braves and brought in fresh meat for the village. They gave him his own lodge, small but comfortable enough, with a good fire pit and a couple bearskin robes. He was sitting next to the fire on his first night in the village when someone pushed back the deerskin flap over the lodge's entrance.

A young woman stepped into the lodge and let the flap fall closed behind her. She stood without saying anything until he asked her, "What do you want, girl?"

"I am Bird in the Tree," she said. "I have been sent to cook for you, care for you, and warm your robes."

His heart began to slug hard in his chest. He'd had a little experience with women—well, one woman, anyway, the girl called Jennie—and he knew what Bird in the Tree was talking about.

She was beautiful, with slightly rounded features, smooth, reddish-tinted skin, and hair black as midnight cut short in two wings that framed her face. Not many men would be able to look at her without wanting her, and he was no exception. He struggled to find words to say.

She must have taken his hesitation for indecision or even disapproval. She bent, grasped the bottom of her buckskin dress, and pulled it up and over her head.

She wasn't wearing anything under the dress. Fringed moccasins on her feet went almost to her knees. Her skin looked even smoother everywhere else than it was on her face. He wanted to touch it and find out. The curves of her body were enticing in the firelight. The dark brown nipples that crowned her small but firm breasts were hard and insistent.

His blood began to hammer in his veins.

Bird in theTree dropped the dress she held and moved a step closer to him. "Do you not find me to your liking?"

He had to swallow and lick suddenly dry lips before he was able to say, "Birdie, I find you very much to my liking."

Her solemn expression disappeared as she smiled. "Birdie," she repeated. "Will you call me this name when we are together?"

"If that's what you want."

"It is what I want," she said as she came toward him and he stood up to meet her. Her voice dropped to a whisper as she added, "And I want to warm your robes many times."

"I reckon that's mighty fine with me." His arms went around her and drew her to him.

Before the night was over, he found himself wishing the winter would never end.

Preacher gave a slight shake of his head to diminish the memory. Of course the winter had ended. Such things did, after all.

The next winter, after another trapping season, he had gone back to St. Louis instead of staying in the mountains.

Since then, he had been to many other places, but never back to the valley where that particular band of Absaroka lived. For several years, he had thought of Birdie from time to time, but gradually she had slipped from his memory.

It was hard to keep track of everything when a man lived such a long, full, adventurous life.

As he stood there looking at her, the time they had shared came back to him, and he smiled warmly. "Birdie, it's mighty good to see you again. I'm glad the Great Spirit has brought us together after all these years."

"I thought you would return . . ."

"Life took me other places," he said, knowing that sounded a mite weak, but it was the only answer he had. The only honest one, anyway.

"The memory of what we shared never faded."

"I remember it well," he told her. That was true. He had remembered it, earlier or not.

Drawing Preacher's attention, the young man stepped toward them, downright glaring at him for some reason.

Birdie laughed. "It is like one peers into still water, and the other gazes back."

Preacher's head jerked back toward her as he said, "What—"

"Preacher, this is our son, Hawk That Soars."

CHAPTER 3

Preacher's eyes narrowed at the revelation. He was surprised but not shocked. For years he had accepted the possibility, even the likelihood, that he had fathered children among the various Indian villages where he had wintered in times past and had always had a woman to warm his robes.

As many years had gone by since he had come to the mountains, he probably even had a few *grand-children* scattered here and there.

It bothered him a little to think about that. He supposed he didn't have the same normal yearning for offspring most men did—he had always valued his freedom too much for that—but the feeling wasn't completely lacking in him.

Even though he wasn't around to raise and protect them, he hoped any young'uns he might have gotten started were happy and healthy, leading good lives in the mountains. Logically, he knew that probably wasn't true in every case, but he didn't let himself think about that too much.

That way, as Audie might say, lay madness.

Birdie was looking at him like she expected him to say something. He did some quick ciphering in his head and cleared his throat. "That was twenty winters ago."

"It was," she agreed.

Preacher glanced at the scowling young man. Hawk That Soars, Birdie had called him. He was about the right age . . .

Preacher understood why the youngster looked familiar. It wasn't just that he resembled his mother Bird in the Tree. Some of those features were almost identical to the ones Preacher had seen gazing back at him from the creek a while ago. From time to time he had seen himself in looking glasses, too, so he knew the general outlines of his face. The resemblance was undeniable.

He turned back to Birdie. "You should have told me."

"Would knowing have made you stay with us?" she asked.

It was Preacher's turn to scowl. He knew the answer to her question, and so did she.

Even if she had told him she was with child, he wouldn't have remained in the Absaroka village when winter was over. He was too fiddle-footed for that. There were too many hills he hadn't seen the other side of, too many trails he hadn't followed to see where they would take him.

"Damn it—"

She shook her head to stop him. "I knew the sort of man you were. The sort of man you *are*. You grow older, Preacher, but you never truly change."

"I ain't so sure about that."

"I am. That is why, when Hawk and I left our village,

we came to look for you. I knew you would still be the same man, and if anyone can help us, it is you, Preacher."

"Hold on, hold on. Back up a mite. You said before you were lookin' for me. Did you really think you'd just run into me, out here in the middle of nowhere?" He leaned his head a little to the side to indicate the vast, sweeping wilderness around them.

She smiled again. "It was not a matter of trusting completely to the Great Spirit to guide us to you. I knew you were headed in this direction. One moon ago, I spoke to a man called Nafziger."

Preacher grunted. Otto Nafziger was another trapper, a friend even though Preacher saw him only two or three times a year and some years not at all. "I run into Otto down on the Cimarron a while back," he said. "Don't recollect for sure, but I might've mentioned somethin' to him about tryin' my luck in these parts this year."

"Yes," Birdie said, nodding. "He is a good man and has visited our village before. I asked him about you."

"Because you were tryin' to find me?"

A shadow passed over her face as she shook her head. "Not then. Not yet. I ask all the trappers who pass through our village about you, to make sure you are alive and healthy."

"Now hold on a minute," Preacher said. "You never married up with some other fella and had more young'uns with him?"

"Many asked me, but I always refused."

"Well . . . hell!" Preacher said as frustration welled up inside him. "I never meant for that to happen. You shoulda just forgot about me and gone on with your life."

"How could I do that when . . . ?" She turned and looked at Hawk, and the silence as her voice trailed off was eloquent.

Hawk broke that silence. "Is it not enough? You talk and talk and talk, while the Blackfoot gets away!" He was right about that.

The wounded man who had disappeared into the trees was probably a good distance away. Preacher had intended to go after him, catch up, and kill him, but he'd gotten distracted by Birdie.

His practical side rose up in him again as he said, "I reckon those fellas were part of a bigger war party?"

"At least four times as many as the fingers on both hands," Birdie replied. "They split up to search for us. Tall Bull's men must have seen us leaving the village, and he believes we seek help." She paused. "He is right about that. We sought you, Preacher."

"Tall Bull." Preacher knew the name.

Tall Bull was a Blackfoot war chief who'd been making some noise in recent years, gathering followers to him and becoming more powerful in the tribe. Preacher had believed his stomping grounds to be north of there.

As soon as he had laid eyes on the men chasing Bird in the Tree and Hawk That Soars, he had recognized them as Blackfoot. That was why he hadn't hesitated to jump into the fight, even though he hadn't known who they were pursuing. He had figured if the Blackfeet were after them, he was on their side, whoever they were.

That assumption had been borne out, in spades.

"What does Tall Bull have against your village?" Preacher asked.

"We are Absaroka," Birdie said. "Does he need any other reason to attack us?"

"No, I reckon not."

"Many bands of our people have left these mountains and have moved south and east. Gray Feather will not go. He says we will stay where we have been and that Tall Bull will not force us from our home."

Preacher remembered Gray Feather. The man had been a stalwart young warrior back when Preacher had wintered with the band of Absaroka. From what Birdie said, Gray Feather must have assumed leadership of the band and become their chief at some point in the time that had passed.

Preacher could believe that. "Tall Bull's tryin' to extend the Blackfoot huntin' grounds down here and push out all the other tribes," he guessed.

Birdie just nodded.

Hawk said, "We will fight him. We will kill him!"

Preacher looked at him. "You handled yourself pretty good in that fight, youngster. I was impressed. But you can't take on an entire Blackfoot war party by yourself."

Birdie put her hand on his arm. "That is why we want you to help us, Preacher."

"Just how many Blackfeet do you reckon I can kill at one time, anyway?"

Hawk made a disgusted noise. "I told you we were wasting our time searching for this man. We should have stayed in the village to help there. But you would not listen."

Preacher pointed a finger at the young man. "Hold

on there. You shouldn't be talkin' to your ma like that. She deserves your respect."

"Why?" Hawk's lip curled. "For lying with a white man and pining for him ever since?"

A swift rush of anger went through Preacher. He took a step toward Hawk and began, "You'd better hush that mouth o' yours—"

"Preacher, stop." Bird in the Tree moved between them. "Hawk, be quiet."

"I will not be told what to do by a woman," the young man said.

"You better listen to your ma," Preacher told him, tight-lipped. "She knows what she's talkin' about."

Again the youngster blew out a contemptuous breath. He turned away.

"Listen, Birdie," Preacher said, "I'll help you and your people. Don't think for a second I won't. Dependin' on how big that war party is, it may take a while to kill 'em all. That's all I was sayin'."

She laughed. "As I said, Preacher, you never truly change."

"Let's head back to your village."

"What about your trapping?"

"That can wait until after we've dealt with Tall Bull." He looked around and realized Dog was nowhere in sight. Knowing the big cur, he had gone after the wounded Blackfoot. Preacher smiled grimly. Chances were, the man hadn't gotten far if Dog was after him.

Preacher whistled, but Dog didn't show up. Since Dog could hold his own against any critter, whether it went on two legs or four, Preacher wasn't worried.

He waded across the creek to retrieve his rifle and

pistols and reloaded all the weapons. Birdie went with
him, but Hawk stayed on the other side of the stream,
standing with his arms folded across his chest and a
frown on his face.

"Does he always go around all wrathy like a possum?"
Preacher asked quietly.

"He has a young man's pride," Birdie answered,
her own voice low enough that only Preacher could
hear. "He wanted to stay in the village so he could fight
if Tall Bull and his warriors came back, but he knew I
was coming to look for you and would not let me
travel alone." She paused. "That is not all . . ."

"I reckon he holds a grudge against me 'cause I
wasn't around while he was growin' up. And because
I'm white."

"Both of those things have caused him pain."

"Well, I wouldn't wish for him to be hurtin' because
of me, but I can't do nothin' about what I am. I'm a
fiddle-footed white man, and that's all I am."

Birdie looked him in the eyes. "Perhaps not all."

CHAPTER 4

Dog came trotting back a short time later while Preacher was still getting ready to leave for the Absaroka village with Birdie and Hawk. The big cur looked satisfied with himself and had blood on his muzzle, so Preacher knew the chase had been successful. It had just taken a little longer than he had thought it might.

"Is the village still in the same place? At the base of that saw-toothed mountain up yonder?" he asked as they started off. He finally understood why that peak had seemed so familiar to him.

"No, we have moved several times since you stayed with us, but it is not far from where it was then," Birdie said. "We can reach it in three days. Perhaps two."

They walked side by side with Preacher leading Horse and the pack mule. He had told Birdie she could ride the stallion, but she had refused and he wasn't going to ride while she was walking.

Hawk started out following them but soon strode past and took the lead. That was the pride cropping up that Birdie had talked about. The young man didn't like being behind anybody.

Preacher didn't figure it was worth arguing about. Let the youngster go in front if he wanted to. He turned to Birdie. "Has Tall Bull raided the village?"

"Once. Before that he attacked some of our hunting parties and killed several of our men. When he came to the village itself, it was with a small war party. They killed a few men and stole some horses."

Hawk was listening to the conversation, even though he acted like he wasn't. He proved that by looking over his shoulder and saying, "He only raided the village to see how strong we are."

"You're probably right," Preacher said.

Hawk grunted as if there were no doubt of that.

Birdie nodded toward her son and said quietly to the mountain man, "He has a talent for war." She didn't add that Hawk had inherited such a talent from his father, but Preacher thought he heard the sentiment in her voice anyway.

"Gray Feather and the older warriors say Tall Bull will return with more men, now that he knows what sort of fight we can mount," Hawk went on. "My mother and I have delayed him by leaving, since he pursued us, but that will not stop him for long."

"You're right," Preacher said. "Once a fella gets an appetite for killin', it's hard to slow him down."

Hawk looked back at him again. "You have an appetite for killing. We have heard all the stories about you, about all the men whose lives you have taken."

Preacher rubbed the heavy beard stubble on his jaw. "I don't reckon I've ever sent anybody across the divide who didn't have the trip comin'."

Hawk had no response to that. He faced forward

again and increased his pace so the gap between him and Preacher and Birdie opened up even more.

"I am sorry," Birdie said as she looked at her son's back, which was stiff with anger. "I hope he is not a disappointment to you."

"Never knew he was around until today," Preacher said, "so I can't very well be disappointed in the way he turned out. Like me, I reckon he is what he is."

"A man wants to be close to his son, and proud of him."

Preacher didn't point out what he'd been thinking about earlier . . . the possibility he might have lots of kids scattered across the frontier, including sons. Instead he said, "From what I saw of the way he tore into them Blackfeet, I'm proud of him, all right. Looked like a mighty fine fighter."

Birdie put it plain this time. "He takes after his father."

Birdie had said the Blackfoot war party had split up into smaller groups to search for her and Hawk, but since Preacher was always on the lookout for trouble to start with, that didn't change things. He kept his eyes and ears open. By the time they made camp that evening they hadn't encountered any more trouble or seen any sign of Tall Bull and his warriors.

Preacher built a small fire, cooked some salt pork and flatbread, and shared his supplies with them. From the way they ate he guessed they hadn't had much in the way of food since leaving the Absaroka village. They had been on the move nearly all the time, ducking the enemy who wanted to kill them.

When the meal was finished, he buried the embers and smoothed out the ground so no one could tell anybody had been there, let alone cooked a meal. "We'll move on for a spell before settlin' down for the night. It's usually not a good idea to lay your head down to sleep in the same place you ate your supper."

"Are you trying to teach me something?" Hawk asked.

"No, I'm just sayin'—"

"Because the time for my father to instruct me in the ways of the warrior is long past."

Preacher kept his face impassive as he asked, "Maybe you'd like it better if I just didn't talk to you at all."

"Do as you wish. It means nothing to me."

Preacher didn't point out that Hawk had been quick enough to eat his food. He wasn't too good for *that*, even though he insisted he didn't need Preacher's advice.

Bird in the Tree didn't let it pass, though. "You should speak to your father with respect."

"If I had a father I respected, I would. I did as you wished. I came with you to find this man. I will fight at his side against our enemies. But do not ask me for more than that." Hawk stood up and moved off into the gathering darkness.

Birdie started to get to her feet, but Preacher put out a hand to stop her. "Let him sulk. He'll get over it or he won't. It don't make no never-mind either way."

"You are a patient man, Preacher."

He chuckled. "That may be the first time anybody's ever accused me o' that."

A few minutes later Hawk came back from the

woods, and they moved on to locate a place to camp for the night.

After a short time, Preacher found a clearing at the foot of a rocky bluff about twenty feet high. "A fella up there would have a good lookout spot. Hawk and me can take turns standin' guard. We don't want Tall Bull and his men tryin' to sneak up on us."

"I have watched over my mother every night since we left our village," the young man said.

"Well, now you won't have to do it by yourself."

They had been traveling light, with no blankets or robes and only a few supplies. Preacher offered his bedroll to Birdie, but she insisted she would be fine without it.

Preacher didn't like arguing with a woman, but he finally convinced her to take a blanket, anyway. The weather was nice, but in the high country, the nights were always chilly, even in the middle of summer.

Without asking, Hawk took his bow and arrows and began to climb the bluff.

Preacher let him go, muttering to himself, "Up you go, kid." If the boy wanted to take the first turn on guard duty, that was fine.

After tending to Horse and the pack mule, Preacher placed his rifle, tomahawk, and a pair of pistols within easy reach and crawled into his soogans, remembering how distant voices had awakened him the previous night. Those voices had been joshing with each other. He was sure they hadn't belonged to Birdie and Hawk. The business they were on was no joking matter.

That had probably been one of Tall Bull's search parties passing fairly close to him, Preacher decided.

If they had stumbled over him in the darkness, likely all hell would have broken loose. He had dodged that bullet, but he was sure there would be another.

Birdie rolled up in the blanket a few yards away. Preacher heard her breathing and couldn't help but think about those long-ago nights when they had shared the bearskin robes in his lodge. She had always come to him eagerly, clutching at him as she drew him ever closer. They had been good together, very good.

That time was so far in the past it was hard to believe it had ever existed. He knew logically it had, but the woman who lay across from him was a different woman, just as he was a different man . . . despite what she'd said about him not changing.

When you got right down to it, though, he wasn't *that* much different than he'd been back then. The more he thought about Bird in the Tree, the faster his heart beat. He would have been lying if he said he didn't want her.

Those feelings roiling inside him kept him awake as the night darkened. The moon had not risen, and the shadows were thick. He heard a whisper of sound and realized she had pushed the blanket aside. As he lifted his head, he saw her crawling toward him.

"Preacher," she breathed.

He opened the soogans so she could slide in next to him. It was foolish, he knew, but the impulse was so strong he wasn't going to deny it.

"I should not be here," she said with her lips close to his ear, her breath warming his skin. "My son . . . our son . . ."

"Is up yonder on top o' the bluff watchin' for Blackfeet." Preacher nuzzled his face into her thick raven hair. Her body was warm in his arms, miraculously firm yet enticingly soft at the same time.

"I thought . . . you could hold me . . . for a short time. It has been so long . . ."

"Yes," he told her. "Too long."

"I know there have been . . . many other women for you."

He wasn't going to talk about how many. He wasn't ashamed of anything he had done, but it just wasn't the time or place.

"But for me, there has only ever been one man."

"Then I am thankful we found each other."

"You will . . . you will save my people . . . and our son. This is why . . . the Great Spirit has brought us together again . . ."

"Yeah," Preacher whispered. "For that reason . . . and for this." His lips found hers in the darkness.

CHAPTER 5

After a while, Birdie went back to the blanket Preacher had given her, saying it would not do for Hawk to find them together.

"I don't see why the boy would have anything to be upset about," Preacher said. "He knows I'm his pa."

"He knows that . . . but accepting it may be another thing."

Preacher supposed she knew the youngster a lot better than he did, so he let her go and didn't argue with her. He slept for a few hours before instinct woke him and told him it was time to relieve Hawk on guard duty. "Stay," he told Dog, then he climbed to the top of the bluff.

From up there it was impossible to see the spot where he'd spread his bedroll, and he was glad of that. He wouldn't have wanted to think Hawk had been watching his reunion with Bird in the Tree.

Since Hawk stood several yards away from where Preacher had climbed atop the bluff, he didn't know if the young man had been standing there the whole time or if he had sat down to keep watch.

"Everything quiet?" Preacher asked in a whisper, wondering if Hawk got to his feet when he heard Preacher coming so he would appear more alert.

"I heard and saw nothing except some small animals."

"Good. I'll watch now. You can go get some sleep."

"I can guard all night."

Preacher heard the stubbornness in Hawk's voice. "I know you can. But there ain't no need. If we run into trouble, you'll fight better if you're rested."

"I can fight any time, whether I am tired or not." A bitter edge crept into Hawk's voice as he added, "I have fought much in my life, from the time I was a boy."

"I reckon you have. The other youngsters in the village probably gave you trouble because your pa's white."

"The Absaroka may be your friends . . . but you are still not one of them. That means half of me is not of their people, either. I had to show everyone that I am as much a warrior as any, no matter what my blood."

"From what I've seen, you were up to the challenge," Preacher said.

"I need no kind words from you." Hawk turned to the edge of the bluff and started to climb down. Preacher leaned on his long-barreled flintlock rifle and stood under one of the trees that topped the bluff, concentrating on watching and listening rather than thinking about the surly young man who was his son.

As Hawk had said, the night was quiet, and eventually Preacher's thoughts drifted, although his senses remained alert to any indication of a threat around their camp.

He thought about the sort of life Hawk must have led growing up, constantly having to prove himself worthy of being considered a member of the tribe. Preacher knew that by and large, Indians were better about accepting half-breed children than whites were. They didn't consider the difference in the blood to be as much of a taint as so-called civilized folks did.

Even so, the only way for a young man of mixed blood to overcome prejudices was to be stronger, faster, better than the others his age. Indians were supremely practical people. If a warrior could battle against the tribe's enemies, he was welcomed, no matter what else he might be. It wasn't just a matter of Hawk inheriting his fighting ability. He had to have honed his skills in order to claim his place in the tribe.

Life for Birdie must have been difficult, too. Preacher had never dreamed she would remain faithful to him all these years. Absaroka women tended to run everything in the tribe except for matters of war and hunting, and one as fair as Birdie could have had several husbands during her lifetime, by her own choice.

Since Preacher had been an invited guest, it was expected that one of the women of the village would warm his robes. No one would think less of her for doing so. Even if she had been married, her husband likely would have considered it an honor for her to be chosen for such a role.

Birdie could have gone on and done whatever she wanted with the rest of her life, and none of her people would have thought twice about her time with Preacher.

That she hadn't was an indication of just how deep her emotions for him went.

He pushed those thoughts out of his head. Birdie had made her own choices, and so had he. He wasn't the sort to waste time brooding or regretting the past. With the threat of Tall Bull and the Blackfeet looming over the Absaroka, Preacher had more important things to think about.

Like how he was going to defeat those sons of bitches when he was outnumbered forty to one . . . or more.

There was one way, he thought as a smile curved his lips in the darkness.

Whittle 'em down . . . one dead Blackfoot at a time.

When the sky was gray in the east, Preacher climbed down from the bluff to rejoin Birdie and Hawk. She was already up, gathering wood for a small fire. Hawk still slept, but he woke up as his parents moved around the camp.

He got to his feet. "No sign of the Blackfeet?" he asked Preacher.

"Nope."

"May the Great Spirit continue to smile upon us."

"I can't argue with that. Facin' the odds we are, I'll take all the luck I can get."

"You are afraid?" Hawk asked.

"Nope. But I ain't too proud to turn down help from the Great Spirit or anybody else."

Hawk frowned as if he sensed a reprimand in Preacher's words. He turned away.

Birdie caught the mountain man's eye and smiled. That was a lot more welcome.

Breakfast didn't take long, and then they were on their way. Hawk took the lead again. Since Preacher and Birdie were leading Horse and the pack mule, the young man could move faster than they could, and as the morning passed he ranged farther and farther ahead.

A worried frown creased Birdie's forehead. "He should not be separated so much from us."

"We can still see him," Preacher said. "Anyway, he's a grown man. He ought to be separated from his folks by now, in more ways than one. Shoot, I'll bet most of the young men his age are already married and startin' families."

"He soon will be," Birdie said as a smile replaced the frown on her face. "There is a girl he likes named Little Pine. I think before winter comes, the two of them will be joined. At least, they will be if the threat of Tall Bull is over by then." That reminder of the danger hanging over the Absaroka made Birdie fall silent.

Preacher didn't say anything, either, as they walked on tirelessly. He found himself thinking, though, what it would be like to hold a grandchild in his hands . . .

A sudden whoop from up ahead jolted him out of that pleasant reverie.

Hawk was a couple hundred yards away, passing between two stands of trees. Warriors leaped from behind those trees and surrounded him, closing in with tomahawks raised to strike. The young man turned, lifting his own tomahawk to try to block the deadly blows as they fell.

"Hawk!" Bird in the Tree cried. "My son!"

Preacher figured he could cut down the odds a little. He dropped Horse's reins and lifted the rifle he held in his other hand. Its curved butt socketed against his shoulder as he drew back the hammer, settled the sights on one of the attacking warriors, and pulled the trigger.

The rifle's booming report rolled across the valley. A cloud of powder smoke gushed from the barrel, so for a second Preacher couldn't see anything. As he lowered the rifle, the smoke blew away and he spotted the man he'd aimed at lying motionless on the ground.

Preacher thrust the empty rifle into Birdie's hands and leaped into the saddle on Horse's back—the quickest way he could go to his son's aid. Responding to Preacher's heels digging into his flanks, the stallion leaped ahead in a gallop. Dog raced along beside them, equally eager to get into the fracas.

Up ahead, Hawk That Soars whirled with blinding speed, his tomahawk flashing back and forth as he parried the attacks with the skill and grace of a European fencing master. It was no sport for dandies, though. It was a battle of life and death.

Preacher guided Horse with his knees and drew both pistols as he rode. He closed within range of the weapons but bit back a curse as he realized he couldn't fire with Hawk right in the middle of the melee. He jammed the pistols back behind his belt, pulled out his knife, and left the saddle in a flying leap that carried him toward the mass of struggling figures in buckskin. Twisting in midair, he drove both feet into the small of one man's back with such force the backbone snapped with an audible *crack!*

That kick propelled Preacher into another man and knocked him off his feet. Preacher landed on top of him. Faster than the eye could follow, the knife in the mountain man's hand lanced into the Blackfoot's back, pierced his heart, and darted out again. Preacher rolled, came up slashing, and ripped another warrior's throat open.

A few yards away, Horse's hooves thudded into the battered corpse of the man he had trampled to death after Preacher leaped from his back. Dog's muzzle was bloody again from the ruin of the Blackfoot throat he had ripped out.

The sudden, furious attack by Preacher and his trail companions scattered the attackers. They no longer clustered around Hawk. Preacher glanced at the young man, saw some bloody scrapes and scratches on him, but it appeared Hawk wasn't badly hurt. Preacher yanked out his tomahawk, whipped it back and forth, and opened a path to his son's side.

They would fight side by side, he thought, and he had just moved into that position when back down the valley, Bird in the Tree screamed.

CHAPTER 6

Preacher turned in that direction and saw Birdie struggling with several more Blackfoot warriors who had been lurking nearby. Fear the likes of which he never felt for himself leaped into his breast. "Dog, go!" he ordered, figuring the big cur could reach Birdie faster than either he or Hawk could. "Protect!"

Dog raced back down the valley, moving so fast he was low to the ground and little more than a gray streak. Preacher would have followed, but the surviving warriors he and Hawk had been battling closed in again.

With Bird in the Tree in danger, Preacher and Hawk fought with an added ferocity. Preacher waded into his enemies, splitting skulls and slitting throats as he lashed out right and left, again and again. He weaved out of the way as the Blackfeet tried to fight back, seeming almost like a phantom through which their weapons passed harmlessly when they tried to strike him down.

His knife stuck in a man's breastbone when he planted the blade deep in a Blackfoot chest. Instead of trying to wrench it free, Preacher just let go of it and used that hand to pluck one of the pistols from behind his belt. He thrust the barrel into another warrior's face as he pulled the trigger.

That close-range blast shredded flesh and turned the man's face into a red smear as the double-shotted load bored through his brain and made the back of his head explode outward in a grisly pink spray.

Preacher spun and used the empty pistol to crush another man's skull. Suddenly, there were no more enemies in front of him.

He looked to his left and saw his son smash his tomahawk into the side of a man's neck with such strength it sheared all the way to the spine. Hawk ripped it free as the last of the men he was battling collapsed to bleed to death.

Surrounded by corpses and dying men, Preacher and Hawk leaped over the bloody, mangled heaps of flesh and ran toward Bird in the Tree.

Dog had reached her side and brought down one of the warriors, ripping his throat out. He had hold of another's arm, powerful jaws and teeth rending flesh and crushing bone as the screaming Blackfoot tried to fight his way loose.

Horse had joined in the battle as well, knowing that Birdie was Preacher's friend. The stallion had reared up and lashed out, his hooves breaking one man's ribs and driving him to the ground, where Horse proceeded to stomp him into something barely resembling a human being.

But there had been half a dozen of the attackers, and even though Birdie had tried to fight them off by using Preacher's empty rifle as a club, three of them had managed to grab her, tear at her clothing, and strike her with their tomahawks.

One man stepped back away from her, which was a fatal mistake. Preacher yanked out his other pistol, took swift aim, and shot him through the body. The man staggered and opened his mouth, but only blood came out in a bubbling stream as he twisted around and collapsed.

Birdie tried to push the other two men away, but she was too weak. A tomahawk rose and fell, striking her in the head.

Hawk shouted, "No!" He lunged ahead of Preacher and barreled into the man who had just struck Birdie. Both of them spilled off their feet.

Preacher, a few yards behind, tackled the other warrior going full speed. The impact as they hit the ground jolted the pistol out of Preacher's right hand, but he still had the tomahawk in his left and raised it for a killing stroke.

The Blackfoot seemed to be stunned, but he recovered before Preacher could smash his brains out and jerked his head aside as the mountain man's tomahawk swept down. The flint head hit the ground an inch away from his ear.

He writhed and brought a knee up into Preacher's belly. The blow landed with enough force to make Preacher double over and gasp. The Blackfoot grabbed his throat with both hands and rolled over, taking Preacher with him so the mountain man wound up on the bottom. The warrior dug his thumbs into Preacher's throat in an effort to crush his windpipe.

Preacher grabbed hold of the tomahawk's shaft with both hands and rammed it up under the man's chin, forcing his head back. That loosened the Blackfoot's grip on Preacher's throat. Preacher jerked loose from him and kept up the pressure on the tomahawk. The man went over backwards, and Preacher lunged after him.

Preacher's knee came down hard in the man's belly, pinning him to the ground. The tomahawk rose and fell again, and there was no escaping it. The edge landed between the man's eyes and split his head open like a ripe melon.

Preacher pulled the tomahawk out of the wreckage of the man's skull and leaped to his feet. He looked around to see Hawk slamming his weapon again and again into the face of his defeated and already dead enemy. With each blow that fell, Hawk let out a savage grunt. Blood was splattered all over his chest and face in a grisly mosaic.

Looking past him, Preacher saw Birdie's slumped figure lying on the ground. He ran to her and dropped to his knees.

Her buckskin dress was dark with blood in several places, and she had a large gash on her head where the last blow had fallen. Preacher slid his hands under her shoulders and gently lifted her bloody head into his lap.

She was gasping for breath and he knew she was badly hurt, probably broken inside. Crimson threads trickled from her ears and nose and mouth, and that told him her skull was likely fractured as well.

"Birdie," he said in a low, urgent voice. "Birdie, can you hear me?"

Her eyelids fluttered a little and then opened. She

peered up at him without seeming to see him for a moment, but then her eyes focused on him.

"Preacher," she whispered. "Our son . . ."

"Hawk's all right," he assured her. The young man had been wounded in the battle, but as far as Preacher could tell he wasn't hurt seriously.

He glanced over, saw that Hawk had finally dropped the tomahawk, and was now sitting astride his vanquished enemy, sobbing.

"Hawk," Preacher said. "Get over here."

He had to call the young man's name again before Hawk looked around and saw the mountain man cradling Birdie's head in his lap. Hawk started to crawl toward them, then scrambled to his feet and ran.

He knelt beside them and said in a choked voice, "Mother."

She found the strength to lift a hand and rest it on his arm. "Do not . . . worry. Soon I will be . . . with the Great Spirit."

"No!" he cried. "No, this cannot be!"

"Take it easy, son," Preacher said softly. "There's nothin' we can do for her, so let's make her passin' as easy as we can."

"No! You do not love her! If you did, you would try to help her!"

"Hawk That Soars," she whispered. "Listen to me. When your father helps our people . . . when he helps you . . . he does this for me as well." Her eyes turned toward Preacher. "You will promise . . . to do these things? To protect the Absaroka? To protect . . . our son?"

"I do not need him to protect me!"

Preacher ignored Hawk's protest, bent his head so

his face was close to Birdie's, and smiled at her. "I promise, my beautiful Bird in the Tree. And I thank the Great Spirit for letting us see each other again after all these years."

Her lips curved in a smile, too, as she breathed, "Preacher . . . I go . . ."

"Go in peace, my love."

She had one more thing to say, though. Her head turned slightly as she said, "My son . . . love your father . . . as he and I . . . love you."

The breath of life went out of her in a long, gentle sigh.

Tears ran down Hawk's cheeks, but he didn't make a sound. He rose to his feet and looked down at his mother's body. His face was like stone. "She is gone. We must tend to her."

"Yeah," Preacher said. "I'll fetch the blanket she used last night and wrap her in it. Reckon you can go look for a good tree we can use."

"Farther up the valley. Closer to our home." Hawk glanced down disdainfully at the dead Blackfoot warriors. "Away from this carrion."

Preacher couldn't argue with that sentiment.

With a rag he'd soaked in the creek, Preacher carefully and tenderly cleaned as much of the blood from Birdie's face as he could; then he wrapped her body in the blanket.

Normally, a few trinkets or other possessions that meant something to her would have been placed in the shroud as well, but she had nothing like that with her.

Hawk found a suitable branch in a tree, farther up the valley toward the Absaroka village. They could have built a scaffold for her body, but a tree would work just as well if some of the branches were arranged right. He trotted back to where he had left Preacher and Birdie.

Together, they lifted her body and carried it wordlessly to the tree Hawk had selected. Dog and Horse followed, and the pack mule trailed along, too, without having to be led.

Hawk climbed into the tree and Preacher lifted the body so Hawk could take hold of it and raise it to the proper place in the branches. Satisfied his mother's remains were secure, he dropped lightly to the ground. He pulled out his knife, reached behind him, and grasped his long hair, gathering part of it so he could bring it around in front of him. While he chanted a song of mourning, he hacked off a long length of the raven strands. Given that an Absaroka warrior's most valued symbol of his manhood was his hair, cutting off part of it was mutilation of a sort and showed the depth of his grief.

Preacher took off his hat and gazed up at the body.

Hawk scowled. "Do not say a white man's prayer for her."

"Wasn't plannin' to," Preacher said. "I was just thinkin', she really is a bird in a tree now. She's gone home."

"I will return here someday, gather her bones, and return them to the earth."

"I'll come with you."

"There is no need for that. She spent nearly all of

her life without you. She can spend her time in the Great Beyond without you as well."

"Now, look here," Preacher began. "She wanted the two of us to get along—"

"Will you help me kill Tall Bull and as many of the Blackfoot as we can?"

"You know I will. I gave her my word, and I keep my promises."

"Then we will fight at each other's side to avenge her. But know this, *Preacher*." The emphasis Hawk added to the mountain man's name made obvious the contempt he felt. "She said for me to love you . . . and that will never happen."

"Fine by me. Somebody else can worry about that. You and me . . . we'll handle the killin'."

CHAPTER 7

"Do you know Tall Bull when you see him?" Preacher asked Hawk as they walked away from the tree where they had laid Birdie to rest.

"No. Do you think he might be among those we killed?"

"I reckon it's possible. Let's take a look and see if we can figure out whether one of 'em might be a war chief. If the varmint's already dead, it might take the wind outta the sails of the warriors who've been followin' him."

"I do not understand this . . . wind out of sails."

"You never seen a boat?"

"Like a canoe?" Hawk's chin jutted out defiantly. "I can paddle a canoe faster than anyone else in our band."

"I don't doubt it. But a sail is a piece of cloth you put up on a mast—that's a pole in the middle of a boat—and the wind pushes against it and blows you along."

"And if there is no wind?"

"Well, you don't go very far or very fast."

Hawk shook his head. "Foolishness. A paddle is better. All it depends on is a man's strength."

"I reckon that's one way to look at it."

"Do not try to *teach* me things," Hawk said. "I do not need instruction in the ways of the world, especially from a stranger."

Preacher's first impulse was to slap some sense into the boy, not to mention some respect. Hawk had just lost his mother. He ought to be mourning her instead of getting his dander up over things that meant nothing, like some damn sailboat.

Preacher knew he would have a fight on his hands if he tried to do that, and while he certainly wasn't afraid of Hawk, he didn't want to hurt the youngster. "Let's just take a look at them Blackfoot carcasses and see if we can tell anything about 'em."

The name *Tall Bull* didn't necessarily mean the war chief actually was tall. Indian names could be symbolic as well as literal. Preacher figured he might be able to tell from the beadwork and other decorations on the clothes, not to mention the painted faces, if any of the dead warriors had been the leader of the Blackfeet.

It was a grim chore, and when they finished Preacher had to admit they still didn't have the answer they had sought. He didn't think Tall Bull was among the dead warriors, but he couldn't be certain of that.

All they could do was push on toward the Absaroka village. The answer might be waiting for them there.

They made camp atop a brushy knoll that could be defended if it came to that. Even though Preacher and Hawk had killed many of the Blackfeet so far, still more were out searching for them.

Not only that, but Tall Bull could have had an even larger war party waiting somewhere in reserve. There was no telling just how many enemies wanted to kill them.

They made no fire and had a meager supper of jerky from Preacher's saddlebags. He noticed that Hawk winced and grunted in pain when he sat down.

"You might want to let me take a look at them wounds you got," he suggested.

"They are nothing. I do not even feel them."

"Could've fooled me. You looked like you were in a mite of pain just now."

Hawk scowled, which seemed to be his only expression other than one of cold disdain. "I said they were nothing."

"Suit yourself. You appear to have some pretty bad scratches, though. If some o' them fester up on you, they're liable to cause a problem."

"I suppose you know what to do about such injuries."

"Well, as a matter of fact . . ." Preacher said with a grin.

Hawk got to his feet again. "I know how to make a poultice of moss and herbs that will heal those wounds. I can find what I need."

"Fine. Just keep a sharp eye out for more o' them Blackfeet. I can send Dog with you if you want."

"Why would I want that beast to accompany me?" Hawk's lip curled. "Curs are best for the stew pot."

Dog growled softly as if he understood the implied threat. As smart as the big fella was, Preacher wouldn't put it past him.

The mountain man chuckled. "I wouldn't advise tryin' anything like that. Your intended meal might eat you instead."

Hawk grunted and walked off into the darkness.

"I swear, that boy's just askin' for a good hidin'," Preacher said quietly to Dog. "If I didn't feel so kindly toward his ma, I'd be just the one to give it to him, too."

Hawk came back a while later with an armful of moss and other plants. He ground it with rocks, used water from the creek to make poultices of the stuff, and plastered it on his injuries.

"Get some sleep," Preacher told him. "I'll stand first watch."

"I do not need—"

"Look, there are only two of us, and somebody's gotta stand guard first. It don't mean a blasted thing which one of us does it, so quit lookin' for things to argue about and get some sleep." The words came out sharply.

For a moment Hawk looked like he was going to argue anyway. But then he turned away and stretched out on the ground.

Preacher would have offered him a blanket, but he figured the kid would bite his head off and it just wasn't worth it.

Hawk seemed to be getting around a little stiffly the next morning, but that soreness loosened up as the two men prepared to resume their journey. He wasn't quite as surly, either. "If nothing happens to delay us, we may reach the village late this afternoon." He paused. "There will be great sadness when my people learn what happened to Bird in the Tree. She was a friend to everyone."

"I can believe that," Preacher said. "She was a fine woman."

"She did not deserve what happened to her."

"Most folks don't deserve what happens to 'em, be it good or bad. I'd say if everybody got what was comin' to 'em, there'd be a whole lot fewer people in the world."

Hawk glanced over at him. "You see the worst in people. Bird in the Tree always saw the best."

"Yeah, I reckon the way she felt about a couple o' rapscallions like you and me proves that." Preacher wasn't sure, but he thought for a second that Hawk almost smiled.

A long period of silence went by as they walked up the valley, Preacher leading Horse and Hawk grasping the pack mule's reins.

Preacher got so accustomed to the quiet that he was a little surprised when Hawk said, "Why did you not come back to the village and my mother?"

"I reckon I just never got around to it," Preacher answered honestly. "There were a heap of other places I wanted to see. The frontier is a mighty big place. But it was nothin' against your ma. I thought mighty highly of her and had only good memories of our time together."

"Not good enough to bring you back."

"I might've been better off if I *had* come back, but I reckon we'll never know."

Hawk was quiet for a few moments, then said, "I have

never been far from this valley. I am not sure I have ever been out of sight of Beartooth."

"Beartooth?"

Hawk pointed to the distinctive peak looming ahead of them in the distance at the head of the valley.

"That's a good name for it," Preacher said. "Don't reckon I ever heard it called that until now."

"That is because you did not come back."

"Well, yeah, I suppose so."

"Those other places and things you went to see . . . was seeing them worth it?"

"That's somethin' else I'll never be able to answer. You see, a fella's life is just a whole mess o' choices he makes as he goes along, and it's easy for him to say, well, if I'd just done this, then that other thing woulda happened, or if I'd done this, that thing *wouldn't* have happened . . . but how in blazes are you ever gonna *know*? The only things you can ever know for sure are the ones that actually happened, and all you can hope is that there's more good than bad among 'em."

"Are you through talking now?" Hawk asked. "I think I would like to see other places someday."

"No reason you can't. The whole world's out there just waitin' for you to have a look-see."

They kept moving all day, staying in the cover of trees and brush and ridges as much as they could, rather than leading the animals out in the open. They traveled slower than they might have otherwise, but it was safer.

Preacher had a hunch that the other Blackfoot search parties had found the dead warriors, possibly where both battles had taken place. They would be able to find the trail left by Preacher and Hawk. Trouble was behind them, probably to either side, and possibly ahead of them, as well.

All they could do was keep moving.

"You ever handle guns?" Preacher asked as they moved through a thick stand of trees.

"A few of the warriors have rifles they traded for with white trappers," Hawk said. "I have fired one now and then. They are loud and smell bad and it takes forever to make them ready to shoot again. A good bow and a quiver full of arrows are better."

"Depends on what you need 'em for, I'd say. And reloadin' gets quicker the more you practice it. When we get a chance, I'll show you how to use these pistols."

"I do not need to know—"

"If you're plannin' on explorin' the rest o' the world one o' these days, you do need to know how to handle a gun. It ain't the same everywhere else as it is in this valley."

"Perhaps I should just stay here after all."

"That's up to you," Preacher said with a shrug.

He knew that wasn't going to be the case, however. Now that Hawk had admitted he had something of a wandering urge, that restless nature was just going to grow stronger inside him until he couldn't stand to stay where he was. He would have to move on and see what was on the other side of Beartooth Mountain.

Preacher figured the youngster had inherited *that* from him, too.

The sun was low in the sky by the time they came in sight of several dozen tepees scattered along the creek bank with the peak looming darkly above them. Eager to be home again and probably anxious to see that gal he'd left behind, Hawk's pace grew a little more brisk.

Preacher frowned. What had Birdie said her name was? Little Pine?

"Where are the dogs?" Hawk asked.

"What?"

"The dogs should have smelled us and seen us and started barking."

"Maybe they're all asleep." Unease began to stir inside Preacher, as it obviously had in Hawk That Soars.

"No. People should be moving around. Smoke should be coming from the cooking fires. Something is wrong!"

"Could be." Preacher dropped Horse's reins and tightened both hands on the rifle he carried. "We'd best take it slow—"

He had barely gotten the words out of his mouth when Hawk promptly ignored them and broke into a run toward the village.

CHAPTER 8

Since Hawk was dashing forward into possible danger, Preacher had no choice but to bite back a curse and go after him. Leaving Horse and the pack mule where they were, he and Dog ran toward the village, too.

Hawk was fast on his feet, Preacher had to give him that. With the speed of youth, he pulled well ahead. He came to an abrupt stop, though, as he neared the village.

Preacher caught up to him a moment later and understood why Hawk had stopped. The stench of death filled the air, along with a buzzing that could only be a horde of flies.

"I . . . I do not see anyone," Hawk said.

"Neither do I, but I reckon we both know they're here." Preacher jerked his head back toward the spot where Horse and the pack mule waited. "Go on back yonder. Dog and me will have a look around."

Hawk swallowed hard and then shook his head.

"No. Whatever happened here, I must see it for myself."

Preacher had a pretty good idea what had happened, and it wasn't good. Like Hawk, he had to know for sure.

The two men and the big cur stalked forward. The hair on the back of Dog's neck stood up, and Preacher's hackles were raised, too. He had a grim hunch no one was left alive to threaten them but held the rifle ready to fire. Hawk drew an arrow from his quiver and nocked it.

When they came to the nearest tepee, Preacher reached out with the rifle barrel and used it to pull back the hide flap over the opening. Instantly, thousands of flies swarmed out, forming a black cloud. Hawk jumped back, then immediately looked ashamed of the startled reaction.

"I'll take a look." Preacher moved closer, holding back the flap with the rifle barrel. Through the opening, he saw four bodies lying on the ground, two women and two children. The corpses were sprawled haphazardly, as if they had been dragged to the tepee and thrown inside by someone who didn't care how they landed.

From what he could see, the Indians had been dead for several days. He backed away, let the flap fall closed, and said, "It's pretty bad. Two women and a couple o' kids, all dead."

Hawk turned and ran to another tepee. He jerked the flap open and then recoiled as flies swarmed around his head. He batted at them to clear them away, then looked through the opening and let out a howl like a hurt animal.

Preacher closed a hand around the young man's arm and tugged him away from the tepee. Hawk struggled, trying to pull free.

"Blast it, stop that!" Preacher said. "There's nothin' you can do for 'em, Hawk. You have to understand that. You can't help 'em now."

"Little Pine!" Hawk cried. "I must find her!"

"Chances are, you don't want to do that. Let me look. Where did she live?"

"There." Hawk lifted a hand and pointed shakily at one of the tepees.

"You wait here."

"But . . . but someone may still be alive."

"I doubt it, but we'll check the whole village. Right now just stay where you are."

Hawk stood as if too stricken to move while Preacher went to the tepee the young man had pointed out. With no guarantee the murdering Blackfeet had dumped the bodies back in the tepees where they belonged, he knew he might not find Little Pine there.

He had no doubt it was indeed Tall Bull and his Blackfoot warriors who were responsible for the massacre. Birdie and Hawk had believed most of the war party came after them, but clearly, that wasn't the case. Tall Bull had sent search parties after them, sure, Preacher had seen proof of that, but the war chief had evidently kept most of his force with him. Shortly after Birdie and Hawk had gone to look for help, the Blackfoot war party had fallen on the village and wiped it out.

Preacher wasn't sure why the bodies hadn't been left where they had been struck down. Most war parties had a shaman or medicine man with them; maybe there was some mystical reason for putting the dead Absaroka back in their tepees.

He opened the flap and let the flies out, then steeled himself to step inside and take a closer look at the corpses piled next to the fire pit. Two warriors, their bodies covered with arrow wounds and their skulls bashed in by tomahawks. An older woman, her throat cut.

And a young woman, barely more than a child. A terrible head wound showed that she had been struck down by a tomahawk, too. Between the flies and the ants that had been at her face, her features were distorted and probably not much of a reflection of how she had looked when she was alive.

Preacher saw a tiny half-moon-shaped scar on her upper lip, though, just above the right corner of her mouth. He made a mental note of that, then said quietly, "I'm sure Gitche Manitou welcomed you into the life beyond, little one."

Hawk was waiting outside when Preacher thrust the flap back. "Little Pine . . . ?"

"There's a young woman in there," Preacher told him. "She has a little scar . . . here." He touched his own upper lip where the thick mustache drooped over the corner of his mouth.

Hawk cried out as if his soul had just been ripped from his body. He started to rush past Preacher, but the mountain man caught him before he could plunge through the opening into the tepee.

"Ain't no need for you to go in there," he said as he exerted his great strength and swung Hawk around so the young man's moccasined feet came off the ground. "No need for you to see."

"She was to be my wife!" Hawk panted as Preacher walked away. The young man struggled to get free, but Preacher's arm was like a bar of iron around his waist.

"Then remember her the way she was. That's the best way you can honor her memory and what the two of you might've been. I reckon that's probably what she would have wanted."

"You did not know her! You do not know what she would have wanted!"

"I'm right anyway," Preacher said. "If you don't ever take my word for anything else, boy, you best take it for this." He hauled Hawk well away from the tepee where Little Pine's body lay. When he stopped, he kicked Hawk's legs out from under him and dumped him on the ground next to the creek.

Hawk would have sprung right back up, but Preacher planted a boot on his chest and pushed him back down. "Listen to me!" he said, trying to get through to the wild-eyed young man. "I'm gonna look in every tepee to make sure there ain't nobody left alive, but you and I both know I ain't likely to find anybody. Tall Bull and his men have been here. He wanted to wipe out this bunch of Absaroka, and he's damn near done it." Since the Absaroka tongue had no word for *damn*, he had to say that in English. "But he hasn't been successful yet. You're still alive, Hawk. You're the last of this band, but you're still here."

"I will kill him," Hawk said, breathless from the rage that gripped him.

"Maybe. If I don't kill him first. But he's gonna die,

you can bet a brand-new beaver hat on that." Hawk seemed to have calmed down a little, so Preacher took his foot off the young man's chest. "Now, you're gonna stay here while I finish havin' a look around. Then we'll figure out what we need to do next."

"They must be laid to rest properly."

"I agree. It'll be a big job . . . a nasty job . . . but I reckon it ought to be done. It'll take a while, too. We're not in a hurry."

"We must go after Tall Bull!"

"Yeah, but you can let vengeance simmer for a long time if you have to." Preacher grunted. "Sometimes it's even better that way."

Hawk sat on the creek bank with his knees drawn up and his forearms resting on them while Preacher searched the rest of the tepees.

It had occurred to the mountain man that Tall Bull might have had all the massacre victims put back in the tepees so the presence of a seemingly empty village would serve as bait for any more Absaroka who might come along. The war chief and his warriors could be lurking somewhere nearby, keeping watch on the place.

Preacher decided that was unlikely. As far as Tall Bull knew, he had wiped out the entire band except for Bird in the Tree and Hawk That Soars, and since he'd sent men after them, he probably believed them to be already dead.

If it had been in his mind to use the village as a trap, he had grown bored and abandoned the idea. No one bothered Preacher as he went from tepee to tepee, finding only more bodies. The village's dogs had been slain and tossed into the tepees, too.

The warriors all bore enough wounds to tell him they had put up a good fight. Preacher was sure they had inflicted some casualties among Tall Bull's war party, but the Blackfeet must have taken those bodies away with them. He found nothing except Absaroka corpses. They'd been no match for the Blackfoot raiders.

The children were the worst. Preacher saw wounds on the little boys that told him even they had tried to fight.

He had witnessed the aftermath of many such slaughters in the past, but he had never grown callous to the human toll they took. He hoped he never would.

Finally, he had checked every tepee and hadn't found anything except the dead. He stepped out of the last one and looked toward the creek bank. Hawk still sat there, staring pensively out over the stream.

Dog sat a few yards away, unobtrusively keeping watch over the young man. Horse and the pack mule were grazing at the edge of the village.

Preacher headed toward Hawk so they could get started on the grim task of wrapping all the bodies in blankets and robes and placing them in the trees, but he had taken only a couple steps when he heard a sudden rush of sound behind him. Before he could turn, something foul-smelling landed on his back with a staggering impact and screeched and squalled in his ear.

CHAPTER 9

Preacher's first thought was that he'd been jumped by a wildcat, but as he stumbled forward a couple steps, he felt bony human arms go around his neck and start choking him. Whoever it was kept up the shrill hollering.

Preacher caught his balance, planted his feet solidly underneath him, and reached back over his shoulders. He caught hold of what felt like a bunch of sticks in a rawhide bag and heaved as he bent forward. The screeching took on a terrified note as the attacker flew over Preacher's head and flipped toward the ground.

The old man landed with a pained grunt. His mane of long, tangled white hair shot out in all directions from his head. He wore filthy buckskins and was so scrawny he'd be almost invisible if he turned sideways. He weighed little enough he wouldn't have made Preacher stumble if the attack hadn't caught the mountain man between steps, when he was slightly off balance.

Hawk heard the commotion and ran toward them.

As Preacher reached for one of the pistols behind his belt, the young man waved his arms and shouted, "No! Do not hurt him! That is White Buffalo!"

The old man rolled over, scrambled to his feet, and looked around wildly as if searching for a way to escape. He was positively ancient, Preacher realized, his face just a mass of wrinkles surrounded by the frizzy white hair.

White Buffalo started to dart away, but Hawk reached him and caught hold of his shoulders. "Wait! We will not hurt you! I am Hawk That Soars. You know me, White Buffalo. My mother was Bird in the Tree."

The old man rapidly blinked his watery eyes and finally focused on Hawk. He said in a cracked voice, "Your mother . . . Bird in the Tree . . . was?"

Hawk swallowed. "She is with the Great Spirit now." He tightened his grip on White Buffalo's shoulders. "But I am alive and so are you. How is this possible?"

"The . . . the Blackfeet came . . ."

"We know this. They attacked the village."

White Buffalo opened and closed his mouth a couple times, peered around blankly, and licked his lips. "The Blackfeet came."

"He's out of his head," Preacher said.

"Give him time," Hawk said. "His thoughts are scattered. They have been ever since I have known him. He must gather them before he can tell us anything."

White Buffalo nodded eagerly and said yet again, "The Blackfeet came."

"And what happened then?" Hawk urged.

"Much crying. Much, much crying. The Blackfeet hurt the Absaroka." The old man pointed to a crusted-over wound on his head. Blood had dyed the white hair pink around it. "The Blackfeet hurt White Buffalo."

"I am sorry. What did you do?"

"Hid." White Buffalo nodded. "Hid under Big Boulder."

"He hid under a big rock?" Preacher said.

Hawk shook his head and explained. "Big Boulder is the name of a warrior."

Preacher began to understand. "The old fella hid among the bodies and pretended to be dead. I reckon with all the blood from that head wound, he *looked* dead. If he was still enough, the Blackfeet might not 've noticed he was alive."

"They did not notice, or he would be dead."

The old man nodded. "They hurt White Buffalo. They k-killed everyone. Everyone."

"I'm sorry, White Buffalo," Preacher told him. "They won't hurt you again, and neither will we."

"They went away . . . but White Buffalo was . . . was too frightened to move."

The old-timer had been lying under a corpse for two or three days and hadn't come out until he heard somebody moving around, Preacher thought. No wonder he looked pretty wild-eyed. Such an ordeal would be enough to make a normal man go insane, let alone an old codger who was weak in the head to start with.

On the other hand, White Buffalo's mental state might have something to do with why he wasn't even crazier after what had happened. As Hawk had said, the old man's thoughts were scattered. He might not have realized just how harrowing his situation really was.

"You do not have to be afraid now," Hawk told him. "Preacher and I will take care of you."

"P-Preacher?" White Buffalo looked at the mountain man. "You are the one called Preacher?"

"I am."

"No one has killed more Blackfeet than you! You are the Ghost Killer! You should kill them! Kill them all!"

Preacher nodded. "That's sorta the plan."

They led White Buffalo back down the creek several hundred yards from the village. After the old man drank deeply from the stream, they found a log for him to sit on.

Preacher gave him a piece of jerky and told him, "You should stay here, White Buffalo, while Hawk and me do what's got to be done."

White Buffalo took the jerky and attacked it hungrily. He didn't have many teeth left, but he made up for that lack with enthusiasm. After three days without eating, he was starving.

"Reckon he'll be busy workin' on that for a while," Preacher said quietly to Hawk. "Dog can stay here and keep an eye on him."

Hawk glanced at the sky. "It will be dark soon."

"Yeah, I know, but the situation's bad enough as it is. It'll only be worse by mornin'."

Hawk nodded grimly. He and Preacher left the old man sitting on the log and headed back to the village to take care of the chore awaiting them.

They worked long into the night, wrapping the bodies in robes and blankets and placing them in trees. Preacher made sure Hawk didn't have to handle

Little Pine's body, but he told the young man which resting place was hers so he could chant another song of mourning and cut off more of his hair.

Dawn was not far away and both men were staggering with exhaustion and the shock of the massacre before they finished with their work.

Preacher said, "Let's move on and make camp somewheres else, then try to get some rest."

"Not here in this place of the dead," Hawk said.

"No. Not here."

"We must take White Buffalo with us."

Preacher had been waiting for the youngster to reach that conclusion. Just so Hawk was clear on things, Preacher said, "You understand we're settin' off to wage war on those damn Blackfeet. You really want to take along an old man who can't think straight and may have trouble keepin' up?"

"We cannot leave him here. He could not take care of himself." Hawk frowned. "We have no choice but to take him with us, at least until we find a place where he can stay safely. There might be another village somewhere that would take him in."

Preached nodded. "It just so happens I agree with you, but I wanted to make sure you knew what we were gettin' into. Like I said, we don't have to get in a hurry about takin' our revenge on Tall Bull. If White Buffalo slows us down a mite, it probably won't hurt anything in the long run." The mountain man paused, then said, "Wonder how he come to get that name."

"Because he is a rare creature, just like the white buffalo. That is what my mother told me."

Preacher let out a grunt of laughter. "Reckon I can't argue with that."

They walked back down the creek and found White Buffalo still sitting on the log, but Dog was sitting directly in front of the old man, facing him, with an intent expression on his wolflike face. White Buffalo leaned forward, his gaze fixed on Dog with the same sort of expression.

"What in tarnation are they doin'?" Preacher muttered.

"White Buffalo says he can talk to animals," Hawk said.

"Well, shoot, most o' the time I figure Dog and Horse can understand what I'm sayin' to 'em."

"Yes, but White Buffalo understands what they say in return."

Preacher frowned. "That sounds a mite loco to me."

"I do not know if it is true," Hawk replied with a shrug. "All I know is what he claims, and what was said of him in the village as far back as I can remember. Once, a bear wandered up while the warriors were away hunting. The people were greatly frightened, but White Buffalo went out and talked to the bear and asked what it wanted. The bear told him it wanted to hear a song, so White Buffalo sang a song for it. And the bear went away." Hawk shook his head. "I was very little when that happened, but I have never forgotten it."

Preacher didn't know whether to laugh or figure Hawk had gone crazy, too. Before he could make up his mind, White Buffalo lifted his head and said, "My friend Dog says we should leave this place. He says it stinks here, not only of death but of evil, as well.

There is nothing left here for us but memories, and we cannot recall them with fondness until we put this place behind us."

"Dog told you all that, did he?" Preacher said.

Dog turned and looked over his shoulder at the mountain man for a second and then let out a sharp, short bark.

Preacher was taken aback for a moment, but then he grinned. "Well, all right. I guess he told me, too. You're comin' with us, White Buffalo."

"You go to war against Tall Bull and the Blackfeet?"

Hawk said, "They have much to pay for."

With all the dignity he could muster, White Buffalo rose to his feet. "White Buffalo will go with Hawk That Soars and Preacher and Dog and Horse and The Mule With No Name." He was so skinny Preacher expected his bones to rattle together when he moved.

"Well, that's just, uh, fine."

"White Buffalo will kill many Blackfeet," the old man said as he began to shuffle along the creek bank with them.

"Maybe you'll get the chance to," Preacher told him, even though that wasn't actually the plan.

When they had gone a few steps, White Buffalo looked over at him and asked, "You have more jerky?"

CHAPTER 10

Preacher knew more Blackfoot search parties still might be in the valley. The men who had been sent to look for Hawk and Birdie would be searching for whoever had killed their fellow warriors. The whereabouts of Tall Bull and the war party that had wiped out the Absaroka village was a mystery, though.

For the time being, the little group had to avoid the searchers while doing some hunting of their own.

Preacher intended to take the fight to Tall Bull, which meant invading the Blackfoot chief's territory. As they moved toward the looming mountain called Beartooth, he said to Hawk, "Tall Bull's stompin' grounds are still north of here, ain't they?"

"That is the Blackfoot land, yes."

"That means we got to go either over or around that mountain."

"There is a pass"—Hawk pointed—"up there."

To the left of Beartooth, the pass was high but not inaccessible. It might take several days to reach the other side, Preacher thought as he studied the terrain.

They stopped when they reached a narrow bench

covered with trees. It was a good place for him and Hawk to get some rest. They needed it. Both men were tired after a grueling, sleepless night and a long, sorrowful day before that.

White Buffalo was the one who dozed off first, however, falling into slumber as soon as he stretched out on the ground. Within moments, surprisingly loud snores began to issue from his mouth.

"Hope that racket don't attract too much attention," Preacher said with a wry smile as he unsaddled Horse. "Dog, you and Horse keep watch." He knew the big cur and the rangy stallion were the best sentries anyone could want. He reclined under a tree and fell asleep almost instantly as well, confident his friends would awaken him at the slightest hint of danger.

He didn't budge for several hours, and then when he woke he was instantly and fully alert again, a habit the long and perilous years on the frontier had ingrained in him. He didn't sit up right away but lay motionless, letting his senses reach out and search around him for anything out of the ordinary.

Satisfied that nothing unusual or threatening was going on, he sat up and looked around. White Buffalo was still asleep, although the old man had rolled over and wasn't snoring anymore, just breathing deeply and regularly.

Dog lay a few yards away, head resting on his front paws even though he was wide awake. Horse and the pack mule cropped at some grass nearby.

Hawk was nowhere to be seen.

Preacher frowned. It wasn't common for anybody to move around near him without him being aware of it, even when he was sound asleep. Hawk had quite a gift for stealth in order to do that.

Dog and Horse knew Hawk wasn't a threat, so they hadn't raised any ruckus when the young man got up and left. Preacher had no idea where Hawk had gone, but his disappearance was worrisome.

Preacher came smoothly to his feet with the flintlock rifle in his hands. "Dog," he said quietly, "find Hawk."

Dog padded through the trees, moving briskly along the bench. Preacher followed at a trot. He figured Horse could look out for White Buffalo for a while. If the old man woke up and realized he was alone, there was no telling what he might do, but Preacher hoped he and Hawk would be back before then.

Dog slowed down and growled softly like he was stalking something. Preacher eased his pace to a more deliberate one. When Dog came to a complete stop, Preacher knew Hawk was somewhere close by.

Someone else might be, too, judging by the way Dog was acting. Someone unfriendly.

Preacher heard voices up ahead, making him think back several nights to the moment he had awakened in the darkness and had his first hint trouble lurked in the valley. He motioned for Dog to stay and went forward slowly in complete silence, living up to the Ghost Killer name the Blackfeet had given him.

His keen eyes spotted something out of place. Hawk almost blended into the brush where he knelt, but not quite. Not to someone like Preacher who could see things where others could not. Hawk waited at the top of a slope, watching something—or someone—down below.

Preacher heard men talking again and knew Hawk was spying on somebody. Since the only other people Preacher knew of in the valley were the surviving Blackfoot search parties, he had to conclude that Hawk had found one of them, instead of the other way around.

Preacher made a faint noise that wouldn't carry more than a few feet. He could have reached Hawk's side and taken the young man by complete surprise, but he didn't want to startle him into doing anything that might give away their presence.

Hawk turned his head to look. He seemed surprised to see Preacher, but he made no sound. He pointed wordlessly to whomever was below.

Preacher motioned for Dog to stay, then crept forward to join Hawk. Through tiny gaps in the brush, he saw five Blackfoot warriors. They had stopped in the middle of the day to chew on some pemmican and were hunkered down on their heels as they ate and talked among themselves.

Preacher spoke and understood the Blackfoot tongue, the Absaroka language, and numerous others as well as he did English. He could communicate at least some with every tribe on the frontier, the Spanish down in the Southwest, and the French-Canadian trappers. He could even make a little sense out of that Dutch talk.

He knew what the Blackfeet were discussing as he and Hawk eavesdropped on them. Hawk seemed to understand, too. After a few moments, the warriors finished their meal, stood up, and trotted on.

Preacher and Hawk waited until they were out of sight to say anything, and even then, they kept their voices low.

"I woke and heard them talking and followed them," Hawk said. "I knew it had to be one of the search parties. They go to rejoin Tall Bull, who returns to the Blackfoot village with most of the war party."

"You ain't tellin' me anything I don't already know," Preacher said. "They're bearin' news of what happened to those other search parties we ran into. I reckon it'd be best if we didn't let 'em get back to Tall Bull. For as long as possible, we want him believin' your whole band was wiped out."

"The better to take him by surprise."

Preacher nodded. "Yep."

"And killing these men would be a good start on what we have set out to do."

"Yep, again," Preacher replied. "You reckon they're headed for that pass up yonder?"

"They take a different trail, but that has to be their destination. It is the only way around Beartooth without going so far out of the way it would take a week or more."

"They'll want to find Tall Bull sooner than that. You know of a good place where we can jump 'em?"

"That trail goes past a waterfall. If we could reach it before them and use it for concealment—"

"We'd take 'em by surprise and the odds wouldn't mean near as much," Preacher finished.

"But what about White Buffalo? We must hurry, and can we trust him not to give us away?"

"He was still sound asleep when I came to look for you. He can stay right where he is until we get back.

Dog can look after him." Preacher turned to the big cur. "Dog, go back to your new pard White Buffalo. Keep an eye on him."

Dog whined a little.

"I know. You want to go kill some o' them Blackfeet with us. But do what I tell you." The mountain man added, "And tell White Buffalo we'll be back later."

Dog padded off through the trees.

Hawk said, "You believe now that White Buffalo can talk to animals?"

Preacher chuckled. "I ain't sayin' he can . . . and I ain't sayin' he can't. Now lead the way to that waterfall."

The Blackfeet hadn't seemed to be in any hurry as they left the spot where they had paused to rest and eat. Preacher and Hawk, on the other hand, moved as swiftly as they could. They followed a course roughly parallel to that of their enemies but stayed up on the bench so as to pass the Blackfeet and get in front of them.

They came to the mouth of a steep canyon slanting up away from them. A narrow trail also led into the canyon from below.

Hawk nodded toward it. "That is the way the Blackfeet will come. We are here before them."

Preacher studied the ground for a moment. "Yeah, there ain't been nobody come along here recently. We're ahead of 'em, all right. You're sure they'll come this way?"

"It is the only way to reach the pass around Beartooth."

Preacher nodded. "Let's go, then."

They followed the canyon, which was narrow and twisting and choked with brush in places. After a while Preacher began to hear a low, steady roar and knew it was coming from the waterfall they sought.

A short time later, they rounded another bend in the canyon and spotted the waterfall up ahead. It plummeted some fifty feet down a rock face to form a small pool. As he and Hawk came closer, he saw that the stream flowing from the pool entered a narrow cleft between sheer stone walls with no path on either side.

"Is this the same creek that flows through the valley down yonder?" Preacher asked.

"Yes. It twists around like a snake and even goes underground for a short distance before it comes out again and becomes the creek we know. The creek that runs by—" The young man's voice choked off.

Preacher knew what Hawk had started to say. *The creek that runs by our village.* Except it wasn't his village anymore and never would be again. As the seasons passed, everything that had been left there would return to the earth, and in time no one would know that a band of people had ever lived there.

It was a shame, but it was the way of the world.

The thought had put the habitual scowl back on Hawk's face. He pointed to where the trail ran past the pool at the base of the waterfall on the left, then made a sharp turn in that direction before zigzagging up the slope toward higher ground.

"If we hide behind the waterfall, we can take them there."

"If we're behind that waterfall, I won't be able to

use my guns," Preacher pointed out. "The powder will get wet."

Hawk grunted. "One more reason the weapons of my people are better than those of the white man."

"I suppose you could look at it that way." Preacher glanced around, searching for some other place he could conceal himself but finding none. The area around the waterfall was rocky and the vegetation was sparse. Hawk's idea of hiding behind the cascade seemed to be the only practical one.

Preacher found a place in some rocks where he could leave his rifle, pistols, powder horn, and shot pouch out of sight; then he looked again at the waterfall. "Gonna be a mite chilly under there. I hope them Blackfoot come along 'fore we're too froze up to move."

"My hatred will keep me from freezing," Hawk said.

Preacher figured the boy had a point.

They waded out into the shallow pool and then stepped underneath the waterfall. The constant cascade had worn down the rock face so there was a small hollow area behind the torrent. It wasn't big enough for them to escape being drenched, but it would make it more difficult for the Blackfeet to see them.

Once they were in position, all they could do was wait. They drew tomahawks and knives and stood motionless. Preacher's hat provided his head with a little protection, at least. The water streamed unhindered down Hawk's long hair.

The stream was as icy as Preacher had expected it to be. It took a considerable effort of will not to shiver as a bone-deep chill began to spread through him. Like Hawk, he thought about the atrocities the Blackfeet had carried out, especially the murder of Bird in the Tree, and he felt the heat of rage kindle inside him. It didn't keep the chill completely at bay, but it helped.

After a time that seemed much longer than it actually was, Preacher caught a glimpse of movement through the water. He nudged Hawk with an elbow. The young man nodded, and suddenly his teeth chattered for a couple seconds before he was able to clench his jaw and silence them.

The heat of battle was going to be mighty welcome, Preacher thought.

The blurred figures moved closer. The trail was narrow enough the warriors had to go single file. Preacher counted five and knew it was the same group he and Hawk had seen earlier.

They waited until the last Blackfoot was beside the pool, then Hawk leaped through the waterfall and brought his tomahawk down in a swift stroke, crushing the back of the man's skull before he even had a chance to cry out.

The others heard the impact of the blow and the sound of their friend's body falling, and they whirled around instinctively to face the danger.

Preacher was already bounding past Hawk. His tomahawk smashed into the forehead of the next Blackfoot and sheared through bone and brain matter.

The battle was on.

CHAPTER 11

Preacher wrenched the tomahawk loose as the second man's knees buckled. He fell toward Preacher and for a second the mountain man couldn't get past him.

He caught hold of the dead man's buckskin shirt and flung him to the side and into the pool at the bottom of the waterfall.

That brief delay was long enough for one of the other warriors to get an arrow nocked and loose it as soon as he had a clear shot at Preacher. Twisting aside at the last second, Preacher felt the arrow's shaft slap against his side as it went past him.

Behind him, Hawk cried out in pain.

Preacher didn't look to see how bad the youngster was hurt. He knew he couldn't afford to turn his back on the three remaining Blackfeet.

He leaped forward and swung the tomahawk in a backhanded stroke that crushed the throat of the man who had just fired the arrow at him. The man dropped the bow and fell to his knees, gagging as he choked to death. Preacher kicked him aside.

A tomahawk swept down at Preacher's head. He blocked it with his own 'hawk and thrust the knife in his other hand into the attacker's belly. A swift rip to the side opened a gaping wound. A hot flood of blood and entrails gushed out over Preacher's hand as the Blackfoot screamed in agony.

Folks back east liked to say Indians were stoic, but not many men could have their guts sliced open without yelling some.

Preacher lowered his shoulder and rammed the dying man, knocking him back into the fifth and final member of the Blackfoot search party. Their legs tangled and they went down. The last warrior struggled to get out from under the dead weight, but just as he did, Preacher's tomahawk flashed down and shattered his skull.

Preacher had killed four men in about twice that many heartbeats. It had been a display of savage fighting prowess that would make civilized jaws drop in amazement and horror.

To him it meant nothing. At the moment, all he cared about was finding out how badly Hawk was hurt.

He straightened and swung around to look back down the trail. Hawk was on his feet, standing in the trail, the body of the man he had killed at his feet. Pink water dripped from his left hand as it hung beside his body as blood welled from the wound in his forearm.

"How bad is it?" Preacher asked as he walked back down the trail toward the young man.

"A scratch, nothing more."

"I'll take a look at it."

"It will be fine," Hawk said. "I will wash it and then put a poultice on it later."

Looking at the facedown body of the man he had thrown into the pool, Preacher grunted. "That pool looks a mite fouled right now. Best wash your arm in the waterfall." He wiped the blood from his knife blade on his leg and sheathed the weapon, then reached down to take hold of the man's shirt and hauled the corpse out of the pool.

Hawk held his arm under the cold water until the cut stopped bleeding. It was a clean one and not too deep. "We should get back to White Buffalo. I do not like leaving him alone."

"He ain't alone. Dog's with him, remember? And Horse, too, for that matter." Preacher laughed. "And The Mule With No Name."

"But if he tried to wander off—"

"Dog would stop him."

Preacher was cold from his wet clothes and knew Hawk had to be, too, but the sun was warm and not too far past its zenith. Their buckskins would dry fairly quickly. They left the dead Blackfeet where they had fallen, except the one Preacher had pulled out of the pool, and headed back along the bench toward the place where White Buffalo should be.

As they approached, Hawk paused and frowned. "What is that strange sound?"

Preacher had heard it, too. He listened for a moment, then said, "I think it's barkin'."

"It does not sound like Dog."

"No, I reckon it's White Buffalo barkin' *at* Dog, not the other way around."

A couple minutes later, they came in sight of the

spot where they had stopped to rest. It couldn't really be called a camp because they hadn't done anything except flop on the ground and go to sleep.

White Buffalo sat cross-legged with Dog in front of him again. The big cur glanced at Preacher and Hawk as they walked up but didn't come to greet them. He turned his attention back to White Buffalo, who leaned forward and barked in a solemn manner.

After a moment, White Buffalo straightened and turned his head to look at the newcomers. "Dog tells me you have killed Blackfeet. He smells their blood on you. And you did not take White Buffalo to dip his hands in the blood of the enemy." The old man seemed more coherent.

The rest must have done him some good, Preacher thought. "We ambushed another of those search parties. Don't know if it was the last one or not."

"They are all dead?"

"They are all dead," Hawk said. "I killed one. Preacher killed four." A note of grudging admiration was in the young man's voice.

"That's just the way it happened to work out," Preacher said. "Anyway, it was Hawk who got wounded."

White Buffalo climbed stiffly to his feet and looked at Hawk. "You are badly injured?"

"No." Hawk held out his left arm and pushed back the bloody sleeve to display the cut. "It no longer pains me."

"In my younger days, I was a healer. White Buffalo was known far and wide as a wise man who could cure many ills."

Preacher had a hunch White Buffalo was one of

those fellas who always claimed to be an expert on whatever subject happened to come up. In his experience, it was usually the folks who kept their mouths shut most of the time who really knew more about most things, but he didn't see any reason to argue with the old codger.

"Well, you take a look at that for Hawk, why don't you?" Preacher suggested. "Maybe you can whip up a poultice for it."

Hawk shot a frown toward him, but Preacher ignored it and went to saddle Horse. He wanted to get past the waterfall and the bodies of the dead Blackfeet before the afternoon was over, and climb higher toward the pass that would take them out of the valley of the Absaroka.

Now that White Buffalo had had some rest, he proved to not only have his wits more collected, he was spryer as well and moved along fairly briskly. Preacher and Hawk had to move at a slightly slower pace because the old man was with them, but he didn't delay them much.

In fact, when they reached the waterfall and White Buffalo spied the scattered bodies of the Blackfeet, he bounded forward with a speed and agility Preacher wouldn't have believed him capable of. He didn't know what White Buffalo was going to do, but he wasn't surprised when the old-timer began kicking and spitting on the corpses.

Hawk took hold of White Buffalo's skinny arm and said, "Come on. They cannot feel what you are doing to them."

"They know," White Buffalo insisted as he delivered a vicious kick to the ribs of one body. "And in the great beyond, their spirits burn with shame!"

After a minute, Hawk convinced him to leave off with his angry antics and go up the trail next to the waterfall. When they reached the top, it opened onto another bench that formed a shoulder on the side of the mountain. The grass was sparse, but there was enough of it to provide graze for Horse and the pack mule.

The three men spent the afternoon crossing the bench and then made an actual camp in some trees on the far side where the trail began to climb toward the pass again.

Before the sun went down, Preacher built a small fire under a tree where the branches would break up the smoke and keep it from being seen. Hawk scared up a rabbit from the brush and brought it down with a throw of his knife, and before nightfall they were eating the roasted flesh.

White Buffalo wolfed down more than either Preacher or Hawk did, and the mountain man wondered if the old man ate like that all the time. If he did, it was a wonder he stayed as skinny as he was. Maybe he was still making up for the long ordeal he had spent in the Absaroka village, too frightened to move as he pretended to be dead.

When they had finished eating, and before it grew dark enough for anyone to spot the flames, Preacher put out the fire.

White Buffalo had been warming his hands on it. "It will be cold tonight."

"I've got a blanket you can use," Preacher told him.

"A white man's blanket is never as warm as a good buffalo or bearskin robe."

"Happens I agree with you, old-timer, but that's what we've got."

White Buffalo sniffed. "If that is the best you can do . . ."

Even though they had rested until late in the morning, the men welcomed the prospect of a good night's sleep. Preacher and Hawk agreed to stand watch in shifts, with Preacher taking the first turn.

White Buffalo didn't volunteer to take one of the shifts, and Preacher didn't ask him. He wouldn't have trusted the old man to remain alert, anyway. He didn't know White Buffalo well enough yet to put his life in the man's bony hands.

Odd, though, he reflected, that he had trusted Hawk almost right away, despite the hostility the youngster had displayed toward him on numerous occasions. Instinctively, he knew Hawk would live up to the responsibility placed on him, and he trusted Hawk at his back during a fight. There wasn't a much higher accolade Preacher could give a fella.

Maybe that was because Hawk That Soars was his son, he thought . . . although to tell the truth, he didn't really have much of the feeling he thought would exist between a father and son. Maybe it was too early for that. Maybe that bond would never truly be there since the two of them hadn't been around each other while Hawk was young.

Preacher didn't know, and at the moment, such matters didn't seem worth pondering.

They were out to kill Blackfeet, and as long as they were doing that, family wasn't really all that important.

* * *

The night passed quietly. It was possible the five Blackfoot warriors they had killed were the only ones left on this side of Beartooth. If that wasn't the case, none of the others had stumbled across the camp.

The next morning they ate the rest of the rabbit, then resumed their trek. The trail climbed all the way to the pass. As they moved higher and the air grew thinner, White Buffalo began to struggle more. At one point he sat down on a rock beside the trail, huffing and puffing, and said, "Leave me here."

"We cannot do that, Grandfather," Hawk told him. "You know that."

"Leave me. I go to meet my ancestors."

"No, you don't. You're just tired, that's all. We'll give you a breather." Preacher smiled. "To tell you the truth, I could use a mite of one myself. I ain't quite as young as I used to be, you know."

"When were you born?" Hawk asked.

Preacher scratched at his heavily stubbled jaw. "'Twas either right at the tail end o' seventeen hunnerd and ninety-nine, or the beginnin' o' eighteen hunnerd. The date was wrote down in the family Bible, but it's been so long since I laid eyes on it, I sorta disremember. A friend of mine named Audie was tellin' me once about the centuries. He said either way, I was born in the eighteenth century, since the nineteenth century didn't start until 1801, no matter how it seemed like it ought to be. Didn't matter one way or the other to me, but Audie sets great store by callin' everything by its proper name and puttin' everything in its right place."

"You speak like a wind that never stops blowing," White Buffalo said.

"You're a fine one to talk, you old varmint. But you got your breath back now, don't you?"

White Buffalo glared at him but didn't say anything. After a moment, he stood up and pronounced with great dignity, "We can go on now."

Preacher made sure they stopped to rest more often after that. If White Buffalo knew they were doing it on his account, he made no comment.

Horse and the pack mule began to struggle with the slope. Preacher wondered if they would be able to make it to the pass. He didn't want to leave the stallion behind. If necessary, he would remove what few supplies were left from the pack mule and allow the animal to wander back down to level ground. With bears and mountain lions and wolves in the area, the mule might not last long, but at least he would have a chance, small though it might be.

Shortly thereafter, the pass came in sight again above them. The contours of the rugged landscape around them had prevented them from seeing it for a while. It didn't seem so far away any longer.

"Come on, Horse," Preacher said. "I reckon we're gonna make it."

Less than an hour later, they reached the pass. The upper slopes of Beartooth lay to the right and another, smaller mountain rose to the left, but the way ahead was clear. They paused to catch their breath again and Hawk turned to peer out over the valley that lay spread out behind them, visible in its entirety from that height.

"Sayin' good-bye to your home?" Preacher asked.

"Saying good-bye to many things," Hawk replied with a slight catch in his voice.

Preacher knew he was thinking about Bird in the Tree and Little Pine. He understood, feeling the loss of Birdie, even though he had been separated from her for many years and their reunion had been tragically short. It would be a while before he was over it, and he would never forget her.

"This was the place of my childhood," Hawk said, "but now I turn my face toward war." He suited his actions to his words, turning to gaze toward the mountains and valleys that stretched northward as far as the eye could see. It was a beautiful country, but somewhere in it were Tall Bull and the other Blackfoot warriors who had slaughtered the Absaroka.

Vengeance was coming for them.

CHAPTER 12

They made camp a short distance down from the north side of the pass. The country there was much the same as the valley on the other side of the mountain—rugged ridges, lushly carpeted meadows, and stretches of tall, proud pines, as well as swiftly flowing creeks bordered by cottonwood and aspen. Preacher would have enjoyed spending the summer in those parts, trapping and hunting.

He would be hunting, all right, but not beaver pelts. He had put those plans out of his head.

For the next several days, the three men and three animals worked their way northward, keeping to cover as much as possible, building fires and cooking meat only when it was safe to do so, and staying alert at all times. Preacher and Hawk continued taking turns standing guard at night.

White Buffalo seemed to withdraw more into himself, spending a lot of time muttering and frowning darkly. He didn't slow them down much, though.

Hawk didn't know where Tall Bull's village was, only that it lay in the direction they were traveling.

"He'll figure he's safe," Preacher mused to Hawk as they were walking along one day, "because he thinks all of your bunch was wiped out . . . although he's got to be wonderin' by now about all those warriors he sent out who didn't come back. He may have even gotten word that somebody killed 'em. I don't think he'll ever dream that somebody's comin' after him."

"You are saying he will not take any more precautions than usual in his village," Hawk suggested.

"Yep. If we keep our eyes open, we should be able to spot the smoke from the village's cookin' fires."

When Beartooth was almost a week behind them, Preacher spotted a small group of men crossing an open meadow in the distance. A couple of them carried an antelope carcass lashed to a pole between them.

Dog saw the men at the same time and growled. Preacher tapped Hawk on the shoulder and pointed. The young man's jaw tightened.

"A Blackfoot hunting party," Preacher said. "Eight men, from what I can tell."

"They are too far away from us. We cannot ambush them."

"We don't *want* to ambush them," Preacher said. "What'll they do if we leave them alone?"

"They will return to Tall Bull's village with that fresh meat . . . and lead us straight there."

"That's right. Let's give 'em a little more room. They don't act like they've spotted us, and we don't want 'em to. We ought to be able to follow their trail without too much trouble."

They waited under the shade of some trees until the hunting party was well out of sight. Preacher knew the Blackfeet hadn't gone too far. They hadn't appeared to be in any hurry, and they couldn't move very fast while they were toting that antelope carcass.

When Preacher judged it was safe, he and his companions approached the meadow where they had seen the hunting party. As the mountain man had said, they were able to pick up the trail where the grass had not yet sprung back up. The occasional splash of blood that had dripped from the antelope's body made it even easier to follow.

A hunting party like that might range for several miles away from its home village, but usually not much farther unless game was scarce. Deer, antelope, elk, and moose appeared to be plentiful. That year, anyway. Preacher expected the Blackfoot village would turn out to be pretty close.

By late that afternoon, he caught the faint scent of wood smoke and grinned as he said as much to Hawk.

"I smell it, too," the young man said. "The village is not far away."

"Let's look for a good out-of-the-way spot where we can make camp. We'll go look for Tall Bull later, after it gets dark."

They needed a place they could use as a base for their campaign against Tall Bull and the Blackfeet, a place where they could safely leave White Buffalo and retreat to after they made their strikes against the enemy.

They searched until they found a cave hollowed into the base of a ridge. Preacher sniffed and grimaced as he stepped inside the place. "Bear den, but ol' Ephraim ain't here right now. He's done woke up for the season and won't be back until fall."

"Waugghh!" White Buffalo said. "It stinks in here!"

"You'll get used to it," Preacher told the old-timer. "We'll get some brush and cover up the entrance as best we can. With any luck nobody'll be able to find us when we're holed up in here." He wrapped some dry grass around a branch and made a torch out of it, lit it with flint and steel, and explored the rear portion of the cave to make sure no unwelcome residents were lurking back there.

The cave was empty.

Horse and the pack mule didn't like the smell any more than White Buffalo did. They balked when Preacher and Hawk tried to lead them inside, but the two were finally able to urge the animals in. The ceiling was high enough for them.

Dog sat outside, but it wasn't as important to get him out of sight. Any Blackfoot who caught a glimpse of him would likely take him for a wolf.

Preacher used heavy rocks to hold down the reins attached to Horse and the pack mule. There was no graze, so they would have to cut grass and take it into the cave along with water. That sounded like a good job for White Buffalo, if they could convince the old codger to do it.

By the time Preacher and Hawk had cut some brush and arranged it in front of the cave mouth to look normal, night was falling. They had a piece of cooked deer haunch from the day before that made a decent supper without having to build a fire. Any cracks in the rock would allow smoke to filter out, but Preacher wasn't sure yet if any existed, so a fire would have to wait until he could explore their haven further.

He said to White Buffalo, "You'll have to stay here while Hawk and me do some scoutin'. We need to find out exactly where that Blackfoot village is."

"Stay here?" White Buffalo said. "You want me to sit in the dark in a cave that smells bad?"

"It don't smell as bad once you get used to it," Preacher said again.

"You are a white man. An Indian's senses are stronger."

"You must stay here, White Buffalo," Hawk put in. "It would be too dangerous for you to come with us."

"Too dangerous for the Blackfeet, you mean, for a mighty warrior like White Buffalo to hunt them down and slay them all."

"Yeah, we want some of the varmints left for us to kill, so we can't turn you loose on 'em just yet," Preacher said. "Ain't that right, Hawk?"

The young man glared at him. "Do not mock White Buffalo. His head may be weak, but his spirit is still strong."

"Who says my head is weak?" White Buffalo demanded. "This is a lie!"

"All right, look at it this way," Preacher said. "This cave, no matter how bad it smells, is mighty important to us. We need a place to hole up while we're makin' life miserable for Tall Bull, and I don't think we're gonna find a better one. It's important for somebody to stay here and guard the cave and Horse and The Mule With No Name. Hawk and I talked about it, and there's nobody we trust more to do that job than you, White Buffalo."

The old-timer folded his arms over his narrow chest and regarded Preacher imperiously. "White Buffalo will guard the cave and the animals. He will not fail."

"That's exactly what we figured."

"But White Buffalo needs a weapon," the old man said, slipping back into the pattern of talking about himself as if he were someone else.

"You can have my knife," Hawk said.

"I've got an extra one in my saddlebags," Preacher said. "Let me get that for him." He dug out the extra hunting knife. The blade wasn't as sharp as the one Preacher carried, but it would do. He gave it handle-first to White Buffalo, who took it and ran the thumb of his other hand along the edge.

Hawk caught his breath as if worried White Buffalo would cut his thumb off.

The old man barely slit the skin and then nodded approvingly. "It is a fine weapon. It will be better when it has tasted the blood of the Blackfeet."

Preacher agreed. "Maybe that won't be too much longer."

A short time later, he and Hawk left the cave. Preacher could tell Hawk was worried about leaving White Buffalo behind, but they didn't have a choice. They couldn't trust the old man not to give them away accidentally while they were spying on the Blackfeet. He was the only living link Hawk had to the people he considered his own, so Preacher could understand why the old-timer was important to Hawk.

The smell of wood smoke was still in the air. By

following it as the scent grew stronger, they were able to locate the Blackfoot village. It was a large one.

Preacher and Hawk knelt in some brush several hundred yards away. Fires burned here and there, casting enough light that Preacher was able to count forty-seven tepees arranged along a shallow bluff, at the bottom of which was a stream. He knew there might be more he couldn't see. He was sure paths wound down the bluff so the women could fetch water back to the tepees.

That creek also furnished a way he and Hawk could approach the village unseen. Preacher was already thinking about other Blackfoot villages and camps he had entered without anyone being the wiser until it was too late for those whose throats he had cut . . .

"There," Hawk whispered.

Preacher looked where the youngster pointed and saw a lone brave walking away from the tepees. The man was going out into the trees to answer the call of nature, and he believed himself to be perfectly safe. After all, he was only a few yards away from his home and all the other people who lived in the village.

Preacher thought it might be a good time to start disabusing the Blackfeet of the notion that they were safe.

Chapter 13

"Stay here," Preacher told Hawk, keeping his voice to a whisper as well.

"Why? What are you going to do?"

"If I can get around there in time, I'm gonna grab that fella."

"You mean to kill him?"

That was the first thing Preacher had thought of, but after considering for a moment, he had what he thought might be a better idea. "No, I'm gonna try to capture him. I'll kill him if it comes down to that, but I'd like to take him alive."

"What good is a live Blackfoot to us?"

"I ain't figured that part out yet, but you never know, he might come in handy."

Clearly, Hawk thought Preacher was mad, but he said, "I will come with you. Two of us will have a better chance of success than one."

"Maybe so, but if anything happens to one, the other'll be left to carry on the war. Stay here." He thought Hawk might balk just on general principles.

The boy *did* seem to have a broad contrary streak in him.

After a couple heartbeats, Hawk said, "All right. But if you do not return, I make no promises about what I will do."

"I reckon if I don't come back, it won't matter much to me." With that, Preacher moved off into the darkness, employing all the talent for stealth at his command. All the other times he had approached Blackfoot villages with killing in mind came back to him. He reminded himself he didn't intend to kill this warrior, just to capture him.

It might be possible to make the man talk. They could find out how many warriors were in the village and what plans Tall Bull had made to expand his power and influence even more.

Of course, the fella wouldn't cooperate willingly. They'd probably have to persuade him.

Preacher moved as quickly as he could without making any noise, circling wide around the village toward the area where the warrior had disappeared into the thick shadows under the trees. When Preacher thought he was getting close to the right spot, he paused to listen, honing his keen sense of hearing for any sounds that didn't belong in the woods.

After a moment, he heard brush crackle and a scuffing footstep not far away. The sound was louder than what a small animal would make. Whatever the Blackfoot had come to do, he was finished and was heading back into the village.

Preacher angled through the shadows to intercept him.

It turned out to be easy. Spotting the dark figure,

he eased up soundlessly behind him. He could have killed the warrior without any trouble, clapping a hand over his mouth to prevent any outcry, then cutting his throat or sliding the knife into his back to skewer his heart.

Instead, Preacher looped his left arm around the warrior's neck and jerked it tight, clasping that wrist with his right hand. He pulled back so hard and fast the Blackfoot lost his balance and his feet went out from under him. He began to flail around and struggle as Preacher choked him. He pulled at the mountain man's arm, but it was clamped across his throat like a bar of iron.

Preacher felt the man reaching down toward his waist and knew he was going for a weapon, probably a knife. Preacher let go of his own wrist and slammed his right fist against the side of the man's head, stunning him. The Blackfoot's struggles became weaker, and Preacher hit him again.

The blows to the head, on top of the lack of breath, made the man pass out and go limp in Preacher's grasp. Preacher walloped him again, just for good measure, then found the sheathed knife at the man's waist and removed it. He got hold of the Blackfoot under the arms and dragged him through the woods away from the village.

The warrior was still out cold when Preacher got back to the spot where he'd left Hawk.

"Is he—?"

"He's alive," Preacher said. "Help me get him tied up before he comes to."

They cut strips of buckskin from the man's shirt and used them to tie his hands and feet. Preacher forced another strip into his mouth and tied it behind his head. The man might be able to make some noise when he woke up, but he couldn't yell very loud.

Preacher took the captive's shoulders, Hawk grasped his ankles, and together they carried him through the darkness toward the cave. After a while the warrior regained consciousness and started thrashing around. Preacher dropped him so his head hit the ground hard, stunning him again.

If it kept up, the fellow's brain might be mush before they had a chance to question him. Preacher hoped it wouldn't come to that.

By the time they reached the cave, the man had come to again, but he didn't try to fight, evidently figuring out there was no point to it, trussed up the way he was. He made plenty of angry noises through the makeshift gag, though.

When they set the prisoner on the ground and started to move the brush aside from the entrance, White Buffalo leaped out, brandished the knife, and demanded to know who they were.

"Take it easy, old-timer," Preacher said. "It's just Hawk and me . . . and a fella from Tall Bull's village."

"He is alive?" White Buffalo asked, astonished.

"Yep."

"You brought him for me to kill!"

That wasn't exactly true, but it didn't hurt for the prisoner to hear the excitement and anticipation in White Buffalo's voice. Their languages were similar enough the Blackfoot had to know what White Buffalo was saying.

"Not just yet," Preacher said. "We want to talk to him first."

White Buffalo scoffed. "Why talk to a Blackfoot? They are all ugly and thickheaded and know nothing. Talking to a Blackfoot is a waste of time. Better to kill him and get it over with."

"We'll talk about that later. Right now, let's get him inside."

They carried the man into the cave and placed him on the hard-packed dirt floor. Dog came over, sniffed at him, and growled.

"That's right, Dog," Preacher told the big cur. "Guard."

Dog sat down beside the captive. If the man tried to get loose and escape, he would regret it.

"If you will not let me kill him, he should be tortured," White Buffalo grumbled. "I will build a small fire and put burning sticks in his eyes. I will cut his ears off and slice his stones from his body as well. He will be a long time dying, and in much pain."

Preacher figured the old man was serious, but White Buffalo couldn't have been doing any better if Preacher had told him what to say. The Blackfoot was probably courageous enough, but after listening to White Buffalo for a while, he had to be getting a mite worried about what was going to happen to him.

"No fires tonight," Preacher said. "Even with that brush in front of the cave, somebody might spot it. We'll wait until tomorrow morning."

"Then we can roast the Blackfoot, a little piece at a time?"

"We'll see," Preacher said.

* * *

All sorts of dangers lurked on the frontier. A mountain lion or a bear could have gotten the warrior, but that would have caused a commotion somebody would have heard. A woods rattler might have bitten him, but again, he would have lived long enough to yell for help. The same was true if he had tripped in the dark and broken a leg.

Preacher had no doubt that after enough time had passed, somebody would start looking for the fella . . . but they wouldn't find any sign of him or anything to indicate what had happened to him.

His disappearance would be a mystery.

And in some ways, mysteries were the most frightening thing of all.

By the next morning, exhaustion had claimed the prisoner. He was sleeping restlessly as Preacher knelt beside him and lightly slapped his cheek to wake him up.

The man opened his eyes and looked up, seemingly confused at first about where he was and what was happening to him. Then he glanced past the mountain man at something else and his eyes widened with fear.

Preacher looked behind him and saw White Buffalo standing there, a leering grin on his wrinkled old face that made him look like pure evil.

Preacher jerked a thumb at him. In the Blackfoot tongue, he said to the warrior, "He gets you unless you talk to me."

Preacher took out his knife and worked the point

under the strip of buckskin pulled tight in the man's mouth. The man's eyes flicked down toward the blade nervously, but Preacher was careful not to cut him as he slashed the buckskin. The warrior spit the stuff out and began gagging and working his aching jaw back and forth.

He tried a couple times before he was able to talk. Then he said, "You are dead, white man. I am Strong Bear, mighty warrior of the Blackfeet! I will crush your bones and rip your arms and legs from your body!"

"That's funny," Preacher said. "You didn't seem so strong last night when I caught you. Fact is, I reckon there's probably young maidens in your village who would've put up more of a fight if I grabbed them."

Strong Bear glowered at him but didn't say anything.

Hawk came over and hunkered down on the Blackfoot's other side. He pressed the edge of his knife blade against Strong Bear's throat and said, "You are one of Tall Bull's warriors."

Strong Bear looked like he wanted to swallow, but he didn't dare with the knife against his Adam's apple. "Tall Bull is our war chief," he managed to say.

"You were with him when he raided the Absaroka village in the valley south of Beartooth." It was an accusation, not a question.

Strong Bear didn't respond. He could probably tell from the look in Hawk's eyes that saying the wrong thing would get him killed . . . and whatever he said, it might be the wrong thing!

"Hawk," Preacher said quietly.

The young man glanced up at him, and Preacher met his furious gaze squarely.

After a moment, Hawk grunted and took the knife away from Strong Bear's throat.

Preacher looked at the prisoner again. "You can see both my friends are Absaroka. They have nothing in their hearts for you except hate. I'm the only chance you got to live a while longer, Strong Bear. To do that, you're gonna have to tell me how many warriors Tall Bull has."

Preacher saw determination come into Strong Bear's eyes. The man didn't want to betray his war chief and his people. Preacher couldn't blame him for that. Such resolve was admirable. Unfortunately, they needed information, and Strong Bear could give it to them. It was a bad situation . . . but worse for the Blackfoot.

"I'm not gonna let Hawk kill you," Preacher went on. "He's young. He'd let his hate get the best of him and cut your throat. That's too quick. I *will* let White Buffalo go to work on you. He's old. He knows how to go slow when it comes to killin' a man."

White Buffalo let out a cackle of laughter.

"It's up to you, Strong Bear. White Buffalo's been wantin' to kill himself a Blackfoot, and you're the unlucky fella who got caught. I ain't gonna ask you again."

Strong Bear licked his lips. "If I tell you what you want to know, you will kill me anyway, and then I will know great shame when I greet my ancestors."

"As for as killin' you anyway goes . . . more than likely. But if you cooperate, it'll be quick. Your ancestors know there's no shame in dyin' a quick, clean death, instead of what this crazy ol' varmint will do to you."

Preacher saw a mixture of hate, fear, and determination roiling around in Strong Bear's eyes. He'd figured all along chances were good they wouldn't be able to get any information out of the captive, even if they resorted to torture . . . which he hadn't yet made up his mind to allow.

He thought the warrior was beginning to waver a bit. Evidently just the prospect of being turned over to White Buffalo was enough to make Strong Bear think twice about being stubborn. If that was the case, Preacher was going to try to take advantage of it.

Before the Blackfoot warrior could crack, Hawk stood up suddenly and moved to the mouth of the cave. He stood there for a moment, listening intently, and then turned and hurried back to Preacher. "Someone is coming."

CHAPTER 14

Preacher said to White Buffalo, "Take your knife and guard this man. If he tries to yell, cut his throat."

White Buffalo's face lit up with glee and anticipation.

"But *don't* kill him as long as he's quiet," Preacher added. "You understand, White Buffalo?"

The old-timer's lips pooched out in a pout, but he nodded.

Preacher nodded to Hawk as he joined the young man. "Let's see who's out there."

They moved to the cave mouth and knelt down, hidden by the brush they had artfully arranged in front of the opening. Preacher heard the same thing Hawk had, the sounds of men approaching the cave. He figured they were from Tall Bull's village and were looking for the missing Strong Bear.

Since the Blackfeet hunted all over the area, Preacher wondered if some might be aware of the cave's existence and would notice that the entrance had been covered with brush, or since their attention would be focused on searching for Strong Bear, would they fail to notice?

The next few minutes would provide the answer to those questions.

Four Blackfoot warriors came in sight, moving out of the trees on the other side of the open area in front of the ridge. They weren't heading directly toward the cave. From Preacher's perspective, their path carried them at an angle toward the left.

Tall Bull wasn't expecting trouble on his own stomping grounds. Preacher figured Strong Bear's disappearance probably was considered more of a mystery than a potential threat. The four warriors crossing the open ground certainly didn't seem overly worried about anything.

"I can kill two of them with arrows before they know what is happening," Hawk whispered to Preacher. "Can you bring down the other two with your guns?"

"More than likely," Preacher replied, "but I ain't gonna. The sound of the shots would carry all the way to the Blackfoot village. We don't want 'em knowin' somebody with firearms is lurkin' around."

Hawk frowned. "They might believe it to be white trappers."

"Yeah, and the Blackfeet hate trappers. They'd come lookin', and they'd bring more than four men."

"I still think we should kill them. The more Blackfeet we get rid of, the better."

The youngster had a point there, but Preacher shook his head. "We'll let 'em go as long as they don't figure out we're here."

In theory, that was probably the best thing to do, but

it didn't prove to be possible. Before the four warriors had crossed the open ground, one of them pointed toward the cave and said something to his companions. They all stopped and looked in that direction.

"Dadgum it," Preacher breathed out. "They're gonna come take a look."

"We cannot let them go back to Tall Bull and tell him where we are," Hawk said.

"You're right about that," Preacher agreed as a grim cast came over his face. He reached down to his waist and pulled his tomahawk from behind his belt.

Beside him, Hawk slid an arrow from the quiver on his back and fitted it to the string on his bow. He put a little tension on the string and waited as the four Blackfoot warriors came closer.

The men were about forty feet away when a loud snore came from behind Preacher and Hawk, followed instantly by a shout of warning from Strong Bear. White Buffalo's hatred for the Blackfeet hadn't been enough to keep him from dozing off as he sat beside the captive. Strong Bear had realized that as well and let loose that bellow.

White Buffalo's head jerked up and he yelled, too. The knife in his hand flashed down and bit deeply into Strong Bear's throat. The warning shout choked off into a hideous gurgle as blood fountained from the wound.

At the same time, Hawk stood up and let fly with the arrow he had nocked. With a solid *thunk!* the flint head drove into a Blackfoot chest and rocked the man back on his heels. He pawed at the arrow's shaft even as life fled from his body.

Preacher was on his feet, too, as his arm flashed forward and the tomahawk whirled through the air. It landed with bone-crunching force on the forehead of another warrior and penetrated enough to lodge there. The man fell to his knees and pitched forward.

The two remaining Blackfeet charged toward the brush in front of the cave, whooping defiant war cries. One of them nocked an arrow and loosed it at Hawk, who had leaped from the brush to meet the attack. He dove forward to avoid the shaft, and the arrow flew over his head and struck the ridge.

Hawk somersaulted back to his feet, and as he came up, he thrust out the knife gripped in his hand and buried the blade in the chest of the startled warrior who had just fired the arrow.

A few yards away, Preacher closed with the other warrior. Both men had drawn their knives. As they came together, each free hand darted up and gripped the wrist of the other's knife hand. They grunted as they strained against each other.

Locked together, the two buckskin-clad figures resembled a sculpted statue of men at war. The faint trembling of their muscles and the grimaces that crossed their faces revealed that they were flesh and blood, not cold stone.

Suddenly, Preacher let himself give ground. It was a deliberate tactic and threw his opponent off balance. Preacher went over backwards. As he landed, he planted his right foot in the Blackfoot's belly and levered the man up and over him. The warrior flipped over in the air and crashed down with stunning force.

Preacher rolled over and was ready to leap after

the man and kill him, but Hawk beat him to it. The young man lunged. His knife rose and fell with blinding speed, once, twice, and then again, each time burying the bloody blade in the Blackfoot's chest and then ripping it free again.

Hawk's lips were pulled back from his teeth as he looked up at Preacher from where he knelt beside the dead man. "I killed three to your one this time."

"Mark it down, then, if you want," Preacher snapped. "I ain't keepin' count." He got to his feet and quickly checked the bodies. All four members of the Blackfoot party were dead.

He suspected the one in the cave was, too, given what he had glimpsed of White Buffalo's reaction to Strong Bear's shout. Preacher parted the brush and entered the cave.

A pool of blood had formed around Strong Bear's head. The man's eyes stared sightlessly at the stone roof above him. White Buffalo still sat beside him, although the old man had moved back a little to keep from getting blood on his buckskins.

"I did not mean to kill him." White Buffalo's eyes were downcast, and he looked a little like a kid who had been caught doing something wrong. "He startled me, and there was a knife in my hand."

"Well, I told you to shut him up if he tried to yell," Preacher said, "so I reckon it ain't your fault, White Buffalo. You shut him up real good. Just not in time to keep him from warnin' those other fellas."

"Are they—"

"All dead, Grandfather," Hawk said as he came into

the cave. "Four more Blackfeet who will never murder another woman or child from another tribe."

A good thing, Preacher thought. "Yeah, and we'd better do somethin' with 'em so nobody else will come along and find 'em."

"You cannot leave their bodies in here," White Buffalo said. "It already stinks enough of bear."

The same thought already had occurred to Preacher. Sharing the cave with five decomposing bodies was unacceptable. He told Hawk, "Let's drag 'em into the brush while we look for a more permanent restin' place."

With the bodies quickly and roughly concealed, Preacher and Hawk climbed the ridge and located a ravine about a quarter mile away. It was deep and thickly covered with brush. Once the corpses were dropped into it, they wouldn't be discovered easily.

They performed the grim task of carrying the bodies to the ravine one by one, swinging them out, and letting go so the corpses plummeted into the brush some forty feet below. Branches broke under the impact, but more branches bent and sprang back into place. By the time Preacher and Hawk were finished, it was difficult to see where the dead warriors had fallen.

"If we're lucky, the buzzards won't spot 'em and start circlin'," Preacher said. "That might draw more attention to the area than we want. Let the wolves and the other scavengers have the varmints."

"I am sorry Strong Bear died before you could find out what you wanted from him," Hawk said.

The mountain man shrugged. "It was a mighty

long shot that he was gonna talk, anyway. He was a stubborn cuss, and I ain't sure even turnin' ol' White Buffalo loose on him woulda done the trick."

"You would have allowed White Buffalo to torture him?"

"I wouldn't have liked it much," Preacher said, "but I reckon I could've found the stomach to do it, especially if I thought about what Tall Bull and his men left behind in your village."

"So would I." Hawk cast one more glance toward the dead men at the bottom of the ravine and then turned away.

When they got back to the cave, they found that White Buffalo had gotten some dirt from outside and spread it on the floor of the cave to cover the pool of blood from Strong Bear's slashed throat. The old man was muttering to himself and still looked pretty upset.

Quietly, Preacher said to Hawk, "The old fella talks about what a mighty warrior he was, but do you reckon he ever actually killed anybody before?"

"I do not know," Hawk replied, slowly shaking his head. "Not in the time I have been alive and can remember. I am certain of that. Perhaps his stories are just that . . . an old man's stories."

"Well, if that's true, he's done had his baptism of blood now," Preacher said. "And I suspect he's liable to be dunked in it again 'fore all this is over."

Chapter 15

One warrior disappearing from his own village in the middle of the night was odd. Four more vanishing in broad daylight would be downright alarming to the Blackfeet, Preacher knew.

"We'd best wait a few days before tryin' anything else," he said to Hawk later that day. "That'll let things cool off a mite. Soon as they realize those four fellas who went looking for Strong Bear ain't comin' back, they'll be on their guard in the village."

"I do not like to wait. The spirits of the slain cry out for vengeance."

"And they'll still be wantin' that vengeance later on," Preacher said. "If we do somethin' foolish and get ourselves killed now, we won't be able to take all the revenge we can if we're smart about it."

Hawk grunted and shrugged. "You are older than me, and you are a mighty warrior," he said, although the words had no hint of admiration in them. "My mother told me many times about what a fierce fighter you were, even as a young man. And we heard many stories about you from other trappers who visited our village from time to time."

"What else did Bird in the Tree have to say about me?"

Hawk stared coldly at him. "You could have asked her yourself . . . if you'd ever come back."

Anger welled up inside Preacher, but the boy had a point. Still, Preacher wasn't going to apologize for the way he had lived his life. Maybe every decision he had ever made hadn't been the very best, but it had seemed like it at the time. He wondered if he was ever going to feel toward Hawk like a father should feel toward a son.

It was all too clear that Hawk didn't feel like a son should feel toward a father.

For a few days, they kept a close watch in case any more search parties came along looking for the men who had disappeared. That didn't happen, which made Preacher change his mind about what the war chief was thinking. Tall Bull was keeping his warriors close to home. That meant he was thinking the village was in danger of being attacked.

The Blackfeet had to eat, just like anybody else. Preacher thought they might be getting low on fresh meat. It had been a while since the hunting party he and Hawk had seen had brought in that antelope.

"I reckon we need to go find a good hidey-hole where we can keep an eye on the village," he told Hawk. "If Tall Bull sends out a huntin' party, we might have a chance to do a little huntin' of our own."

"At last," Hawk said. "I had begun to think our war had come to an early end."

"I've done told you, don't get impatient."

White Buffalo said, "You will leave me here again?"

"That's right, old-timer. You got to keep an eye on things here for us. Can you do that?"

White Buffalo nodded. "No one will disturb our new home."

Preacher frowned. He certainly didn't think of this cave as home, and he figured Hawk didn't, either.

White Buffalo had lost everything he had known for a long time. His mental state was fragile and he had seized on the old bear den as the place he belonged.

When it was all over, they would have to find a better place for the old man, a place where he could live out the rest of his life in peace and comfort . . . assuming any of them lived through the bloody campaign they had launched.

As Preacher and Hawk were getting ready to leave, White Buffalo said, "Dog has told me he should go with you this time."

"I can have him stay here with you if that'd make you feel better, White Buffalo."

The old man shook his head at Preacher. "Dog is a good friend. He and I tell each other many entertaining stories. Horse is friendly but not as smart as Dog. He does not have many stories. The Mule With No Name"—White Buffalo rolled his eyes—"has no stories. It is a waste of time to talk to The Mule With No Name. But Dog . . . Dog wishes to go with you, Preacher. He says you will need his help."

"Well, it always comes in handy havin' Dog around, if you think you can do without his company for a spell."

White Buffalo nodded solemnly. "The rest of us will be fine. Go and kill many Blackfeet."

"We'll do the best we can," Preacher promised.

A short time later, he and Hawk and Dog set out toward the Blackfoot village.

The first time they had spied on the place had been at night, so darkness had hidden them. It was much different in broad daylight. They couldn't approach the village directly so they circled and climbed to higher ground that commanded a good view of the tepees scattered along the creek bank.

The pines were thick enough to keep them from being seen. Preacher made sure no sunlight reflected from his rifle or pistols. A glint of light would give them away and bring warriors looking for them.

He counted tepees again and saw he'd been off by one in his earlier estimate. Counting the young, unmarried men who still lived with their families, he figured as many as eighty warriors might be in the village. They were no less dangerous in a fight. Upwards of a hundred women and children who also lived there had begun to worry him. Preacher wasn't going to make war on them. Such a thing was just not in the way he conducted himself.

If he and Hawk accomplished their goal of wiping out Tall Bull and all the Blackfoot warriors, far-fetched though it might seem, it would leave the women and children and old ones with nobody to protect them and hunt for them. Some of them would starve, or they might fall prey to other enemies.

The Blackfeet had plenty of enemies, that was for sure. Many of the other tribes hated them.

"I've been thinkin'," he said quietly to Hawk. "If we kill Tall Bull and enough of his warriors, there's a chance the rest of the bunch will pull up stakes and light out. They won't want to stay around here."

"Every warrior who helped slaughter my people must die," Hawk said. "Since we do not know who was there and who was not, we must kill all of them to be sure."

"If we do that, we'll doom the whole band, includin' the ones who didn't have anything to do with that massacre."

Hawk looked sharply at him. "They are all Blackfoot." That was all the reason they needed to exterminate them.

Preacher might have argued the issue longer, but at that moment he spied deliberate movement in the village below. Warriors armed with bows and arrows had been moving around all along, and he'd figured they were standing watch over the place, spooked by the mysterious disappearances. This was different.

A dozen men strode out together and left the village, heading up the creek to the north. Every man had a bow and a full quiver of arrows.

Preacher pointed to the group. "That's a huntin' party, unless I miss my guess."

"Yes, they are going after meat." Hawk's hand tightened on his bow. "And so are we."

They stuck to the high ground as they followed the hunting party below. Preacher searched for a good place to attack them but didn't see anything that looked suitable. Outnumbered as they were, he and Hawk might not be able to wipe out the whole group, but they wanted to inflict as many casualties as possible before they had to fade away.

Just as Preacher was about to decide they might have to let the Blackfeet go, he spotted a steep slope up ahead with a number of large rocks at the top of it. The hunting party hadn't scared up any game except for a few rabbits. Since that wasn't enough to feed the whole village, they continued north along the creek. That course would take them right past the slope.

Preacher pointed it out to Hawk. "Come on. We got to get there ahead of 'em and get ready."

Hawk instantly grasped what Preacher planned to do. Along with Dog, they hurried through the trees, leaving the slower-moving hunting party behind.

"What if they turn back before they reach that spot?" Hawk asked.

"Then we're outta luck this time and we'll wait to do our killin' some other day."

"I will pray to the Great Spirit to keep them coming toward us."

"You do that." Preacher didn't know if ol' Gitche Manitou—who he figured was the same God the sky pilots hollered about—involved Himself that deeply in the petty affairs of men, but he'd take any help he could get.

They had to be careful not to dislodge any small rocks as they worked their way toward the top of the slope. They were in the open for the moment, but a bend in the creek protected them from the sight of the Blackfeet below. If by chance the hunting party came around the bend in time, they would be likely to spot Preacher and Hawk, and then the jig would be up.

They reached the top and scrambled behind the boulders. At the moment Preacher looked down the slope, the first of the hunting party came around the bend into view. The others followed, holding their bows ready in case they spotted any game.

Preacher studied the boulders and figured out which two looked like they would be the easiest to dislodge. The rocks were massive, maybe too massive for a man to budge, but he knew that if he and Hawk could start them rolling, they would tumble down the slope toward the Blackfeet and cause a pretty big slide.

He grinned. Something to be said for using nature itself as a weapon.

With hand signals, he indicated which boulder Hawk should push and set himself behind the other one. Preacher braced his feet, placed his hands and shoulder against the rock, and looked over at Hawk, who'd settled himself into the same position. With a nod to the young man, Preacher began to push, throwing all his weight and strength against the rock.

CHAPTER 16

Preacher's heart slugged heavily in his chest and his pulse hammered inside his skull as he strained against the boulder. A low grunt of effort escaped from his mouth.

Hawk was struggling the same way, but neither rock moved an inch.

Dog sat to one side and whined as if trying to encourage both men, but there was nothing else he could do to help.

Then, with a grating of stone against stone, Preacher's rock shifted slightly. He took a deep breath and redoubled his efforts, trying not to groan. A few yards away, Hawk did likewise, even though his boulder hadn't moved at all.

Preacher felt his give a little more. It tried to rock back, but he kept it moving forward.

With no more warning than a sudden cracking sound, Hawk's boulder gave way first and toppled from its perch. He sprawled forward, barely catching himself and regaining his balance. Preacher's went over a heartbeat later. He too, sprawled before catching himself. With an ever-growing rumble, the boulders turned over and over, taking smaller rocks with them as they rolled toward the creek.

Even over that racket, Preacher heard the alarmed shouts from the Blackfeet below.

He and Hawk scrambled to their feet and looked down the slope. The rock slide was raising enough dust that it was hard to see.

Preacher spotted one of the warriors dashing into the clear and called to Hawk, "There!"

Hawk had already seen the fleeing man and whipped an arrow from his quiver. He launched it in an arching flight that ended between the Blackfoot's shoulder blades and sent him forward onto his face. The warrior had never even seen the doom flashing down at him from above.

"Come on!" Preacher gripped his tomahawk as he started bounding down the slope after the tumbling rocks. He hoped the rock slide would crush the rest of the hunting party, but if any of the Blackfeet survived, he and Hawk and Dog would wipe them out. He had been prepared to let some of them escape, but with the way circumstances had worked out, he didn't want any of them making it back to the village.

The cloud of dust choked and blinded them, but as the rocks stopped sliding and the rumble died away, the dust began to thin. Preacher heard a startled shout and turned in that direction to see one of the Blackfoot warriors drawing a bead on him with an arrow.

Preacher dropped to a knee as the feathered missile whipped through the air just above his head, then he was up and leaping forward again. The warrior used his bow to block the mountain man's tomahawk stroke and then grabbed Preacher by the throat with his other hand. Preacher barreled into him, and they went down among the smaller rocks that had piled up along the edge of the creek.

Tearing loose from the man's grip, Preacher chopped with the tomahawk at the warrior's head. The warrior jerked aside from the blow just in time and pulled his knife out. Preacher reared back and avoided the slash that came within an inch of ripping open his throat.

He backhanded the tomahawk against the warrior's forearm and heard bone snap. The man's suddenly nerveless fingers dropped the knife. A second later, his skull caved in under the tremendous impact of Preacher's tomahawk.

Preacher pushed himself to his feet and looked around for Hawk. The young man was locked in a hand-to-hand struggle with another Blackfoot. Bigger and heavier, the warrior forced Hawk back a step and one of his feet came down on a rock that shifted underneath him. Thrown off balance, he fell and hit his head on another rock.

Preacher could tell the impact stunned Hawk. He knew he couldn't close the gap in time, so he flung his tomahawk. It struck the warrior on the shoulder and bounced off, but that was enough to knock the man back a step and keep him from braining Hawk.

As soon as Preacher made his throw, he leaped to the top of a boulder and launched himself in a diving tackle at the Blackfoot.

His shoulder rammed into the man's midsection and drove him backwards off his feet. They landed among the rocks, but if Preacher hoped the Blackfoot's head would hit one of the stones and crack open like an egg, he was disappointed. The warrior writhed and twisted, fighting like a wildcat.

Preacher blocked the Blackfoot's tomahawk with a forearm and shot a punch into the man's face. At the same time, he dug a knee into the warrior's belly. An instant later, the man brought the elbow of his free arm up under Preacher's chin and jolted the mountain man's head back.

They grappled and rolled over among the rocks. Preacher caught hold of the warrior's tomahawk and tried to wrench it away from his enemy, but the man had a death grip on it. His face contorted in a hate-filled snarl only inches away from Preacher's. Preacher could feel the hot breath against his cheek, like he was battling a wild animal.

He slashed a side-hand blow to the Blackfoot's throat and made the man gag; then the heel of his hand caught the man under the chin, and he returned the favor, bending the man's head back so far it seemed like his neck would crack.

The warrior continued to battle.

Preacher landed a knee in the Blackfoot's groin, making his grip on the tomahawk slip. Preacher tore it loose and whipped it across the man's face, breaking his nose. A swift follow-up blow cracked the warrior's cheekbone.

The fight was rapidly slipping away from the Blackfoot, and he knew it. He bellowed in rage and jackknifed his body. The top of his head crashed into Preacher's face. The mountain man fell back. The warrior tried to come after him, but Preacher drew both knees up and launched a double kick that smashed his heels into the middle of the man's face.

The crack as his neck broke was loud and decisive. The warrior went over backwards, flopped loosely among the rocks, and then lay still as his eyes glazed over.

Preacher had had his hands full with that varmint, so he didn't know what else was going on around him. He rolled over quickly and came up on one knee to look back and forth.

"It is all right," Hawk said. "That was all of them. The others are buried under the rock slide."

It was true. They had killed two of the Blackfeet, and the others were nowhere in sight, at least at first glance. However, Preacher didn't think any of them could have gotten away. They had been directly in the path of the tumbling rocks.

"How about you?" he asked Hawk, who stood on top of a small boulder a few yards away. "You whacked your head pretty hard on that rock. I heard it all the way over where I was."

Hawk lifted a hand and probed gingerly at the back of his head. "There is a big lump . . . like a turkey's egg. But I think I am all right."

Preacher clambered over to him. "Let me see."

"I said I am—"

"And I said let me see." Preacher's voice was sharper than he intended, sharp enough to make Hawk glance at him in surprise. Using just his fingertips and as gentle a touch as he could manage, Preacher explored the injury.

Hawk had a lump on his head, as he had said, but it wasn't bleeding and he winced only the normal amount somebody would after getting a wallop like that.

"Reckon you didn't break your skull," Preacher said. "How come you looked at me like that a minute ago?"

"Because when you spoke you sounded like my mother."

"I did, did I? Well, don't get used to it. I know I'm your pa and you're my young'un, but what's between us ain't like it is for normal folks."

"No, it is not," Hawk agreed immediately. "I will fight beside you against the Blackfeet, but we are allies against a common enemy, that is all."

"Damn right." Preacher wanted to believe that.

But he wasn't sure if either of them did.

The rock slide had covered up quite a bit of the creek bank and even caved it in in places. Some of the boulders had landed in the stream but hadn't blocked it, so it continued flowing. Eventually it would probably carve out a wider bed around the remaining small, rocky ridge.

Preacher and Hawk searched among the boulders and found a few grisly remains. For the most part, the Blackfeet were buried and would remain that way.

"Let's get those other two, drag 'em among the rocks, and cover 'em up," Preacher said. "They'll be so beat up, even if anybody finds 'em, they'll think the rock slide killed 'em like it did the others."

"How many of them have we slain since we met?"

Preacher shook his head. "I've lost count, and I ain't gonna go back and try to figure it up. I never been that fond o' cipherin'."

"But many Blackfeet have died because of us?"

"Yep, I'd say so."

"Not enough."

"No," Preacher said. "Not enough."

"Why do you not want Tall Bull to know we killed these warriors? Why make it look like an accident?"

"I'd just as soon keep him confused as long as possible," Preacher said. "With everything else that's happened, he'll regard the loss of this huntin' party as bad luck."

"And he will start to believe his medicine is turning on him," Hawk said, nodding slowly. "You would fight his mind as well as his body."

"Sometimes a fella's worst enemy is what's inside his own head," Preacher said, grinning wearily. "Come on. Let's get that chore done, then get back to ol' White Buffalo."

He turned and saw a Blackfoot warrior standing at the edge of the rock slide, aiming an arrow at him.

CHAPTER 17

A fraction of a second before the warrior loosed the arrow, a gray streak flashed through the air and crashed into him. That was enough to throw off the man's aim, and the arrow flew between Preacher and Hawk, narrowly missing both of them.

At the same time, the Blackfoot toppled into the creek with Dog on top of him, snapping and snarling furiously. The man tried to scream but sputtered as he gulped down water. Splashes flew up around them as they struggled.

Then the struggle subsided and the water began to turn pink. Dog climbed out of the creek, stood on the bank, and shook some of the moisture off his shaggy coat, filling the air around him with spray.

The Blackfoot warrior stayed in the creek except for his feet, which still lay on the bank. They twitched a couple times and then were still.

A grim chuckle came from Preacher. "Looks like White Buffalo was right. We needed Dog with us. He saved our bacon."

Hawk looked confused. "Where did that Blackfoot come from?"

"I reckon he was another one who didn't get caught in the rock slide. His buckskins were wet, even before Dog knocked him in the creek. He must've been hidin' in the water, just waitin' for a chance to take a crack at us. He might've been able to put an arrow in me if it hadn't been for Dog."

"If he had killed you, I would have killed him," Hawk declared.

"Well, I'm mighty obliged to you for that," Preacher said dryly. "We got one more carcass to cover up now, so I reckon we'd best get at it."

It took a while for them to carry the bodies into the rock slide, then cover them with stones. Preacher and Hawk worked together to pick up some of the larger rocks and drop them on the corpses. The sounds they made as they hit weren't pretty, but the damage would help conceal the fact these men had died from knife and tomahawk and arrow if their remains were ever discovered, which was unlikely.

With that done, they headed back toward the cave where they had left White Buffalo, steering well clear of the Blackfoot village. Preacher didn't think it was likely they would run into any more hunting parties, but there was no point in risking it.

Hawk wouldn't have minded, of course. That would have just meant another chance to kill more of his enemies, and he would always welcome that.

Preacher couldn't even remember what it felt like to be that young and full of piss and vinegar.

When they reached the cave, Preacher called out, "It's us, White Buffalo. Everything all right in there?"

There was no answer.

Preacher and Hawk glanced at each other, then Hawk called, "White Buffalo! Can you hear me, Grandfather?"

Still no response.

Preacher said, "I hear Horse and the mule movin' around, so they're still in there whether the old-timer is or not. Stay out here. I'll take a look."

"I can look, while you stay."

"You're just arguin' for the sake o' arguin'. Stay here, blast it, and that's an order."

That probably wasn't the best way to phrase it, Preacher thought as he saw a stubborn expression come over Hawk's face. Before Hawk could say or do anything else, Preacher parted the brush and stepped into the cave.

A couple possibilities had occurred to him when White Buffalo didn't answer his hail. The old man could have left the cave for some reason and wandered off, then been unable to find his way back . . . or he might have died of natural causes. At his age, there was always a chance his heart or something else inside him would give out without warning.

A third possibility existed. An enemy could have found White Buffalo and killed him. In that case, it seemed unlikely the killer would have left Horse and the pack mule behind.

Preacher's keen eyes adjusted quickly to the gloom inside the cave. Almost immediately, he spotted the motionless figure stretched out on one of the beds they had fashioned from pine needles and the blankets among Preacher's supplies.

"Well, hell!" Preacher said out loud. It appeared White Buffalo's destiny had caught up with him. He had dodged death back yonder in the Absaroka village, but the Grim Reaper couldn't be denied forever.

"What?"

The word that came from White Buffalo's mouth made Preacher frown. He'd been convinced the old codger was dead. He stepped closer. "White Buffalo? You're alive?"

White Buffalo still hadn't moved except to form the one word. His eyes were closed, and his ancient, wrinkled features were calm and peaceful. "I am communing with my ancestors," he said, still without looking at Preacher. "They have many important things to tell me."

"Didn't you hear me and Hawk hollerin' at you?"

"I heard some foolish noise but ignored it. My ancestors are teaching me all the secrets of the world and of life and death."

Preacher grunted. He had seen Indians down in the Southwest get like this, unnaturally calm and hearing voices in their heads after they'd been chewing peyote. He wondered if White Buffalo had gotten into something like that or if the old man was just plain loco sometimes.

"Well, you'd best tell your ancestors you'll talk to 'em again some other time. Me and Hawk and Dog are back."

White Buffalo held up a hand, palm out. "Wait." A few more seconds went by, then he sat up and opened his eyes. "Did you find a Blackfoot hunting party?"

"We did."

"Are they all dead?"

"They are."

"Then it is good. My friend Dog will tell me all about it."

Preacher called to Hawk and told him to come on in.

The young man entered the cave with Dog, and asked, "Why did you not answer us when we called to you, White Buffalo?"

"It's a long story," Preacher answered for the old man, who was already petting Dog and, for all Preacher knew, having a serious conversation with him. "White Buffalo can explain it to you later."

For the next couple days, Preacher and Hawk stayed close to the cave, venturing out only to hunt. They always checked the surrounding area closely before showing themselves but saw no one.

Preacher was willing to bet the Blackfeet were sticking pretty close to home, too.

If he was counting correctly, the band had lost seventeen warriors in the past week or so. That was a dramatic loss. Throw in the warriors he and Hawk had killed down in the Absarokas' valley south of Beartooth, and Tall Bull's forces had been significantly weakened.

Preacher figured some of the Blackfeet were muttering among themselves. If Tall Bull was supposed to be such a great war chief, how come so many of their men had either died or disappeared?

Tall Bull would hear that discontent, and it would

anger him. He would start to feel like he had to do something to impress his people again.

A man who was pressing and worrying like that often made mistakes.

After a couple days of rest, Preacher thought it was time to give Tall Bull something more to worry about. "I'm going to the Blackfoot village by myself tonight," he announced as he and his companions made supper of some meat from a deer Hawk had killed with an arrow the day before.

"If you go to kill more of the Blackfeet, I will go with you," Hawk said.

"Not this time," Preacher told the young man with a shake of his head. "You'll be stayin' here with White Buffalo."

"But why?" Hawk insisted. "Have I not proven myself to be a capable warrior? Have we not fought side by side and slain many Blackfeet? Have I not saved your life?"

"All that's true, right enough," Preacher said, "but it still don't change anything. When I said I'm goin' to the Blackfoot village, I mean I'm goin' *inside* the Blackfoot village."

White Buffalo stared at him. "They will find you and kill you."

Hawk's eyes narrowed. "No, old one. This is Preacher you speak to. The White Wolf. The Ghost Killer. The man no one sees unless he wishes it to be so." His lip curled slightly. "At least, this is what all the stories would have you believe."

Preacher controlled the brief surge of anger he felt. Hawk was being a jackass, but all youngsters were like that, some of the time. It didn't mean anything.

Without bringing up his previous exploits that had given birth to all the legends about him, he said, "That creek bank is high enough I can follow the stream all the way to the village without bein' seen. Once I'm there, it's just a matter of either avoidin' or disposin' of the sentries." He paused. "*Disposin'* of sounds better to me."

"You think I cannot be as stealthy as you?" Hawk asked.

"I *know* you can't." Preacher held up a hand to forestall the young man's inevitable protest. "I didn't say you can't sneak up on anybody. You're mighty good, Hawk. I know that even though I haven't been around you for very long . . . but for a chore like this, good just ain't good enough. It requires the best."

"And that is you." It wasn't a question, but the words held a certain challenge.

"That's right," Preacher said. "I'm the very best at what I do."

For a long moment, Hawk stared at him in the fading light, then abruptly grunted. "Very well. I will stay here with White Buffalo while you go to kill Blackfeet and strike fear into the hearts of those left alive. But I tell you, Preacher, someday it will be me."

"I don't doubt it for a second."

"Someday *soon*."

"We'll see," Preacher said.

Chapter 18

The moon was nothing more than a tiny sliver in the sky. The darkness was so thick around Preacher it seemed solid enough for a man to reach out and touch it.

He rested his hand on the creek bank where it dropped off to the stream that flowed beside him. He could hear the water bubbling along, even though he could barely see it. Only an occasional pinprick of light, a reflection from one of the millions of stars above, told him where the surface was.

He had followed the creek for more than a mile, slipping through the shadows, his high-topped moccasins soundless where he stepped on the grass growing on the narrow bit of ground between the stream and the almost vertical face of the bank.

He'd had to cross the creek in places to make his way around impassable thickets of brush. Some flash flood in the past had washed up a number of logs that got caught, piled up, and formed another barrier. Here and there he'd had to wade along through the creek itself.

That his feet were wet and cold didn't matter to Preacher. When he was on a mission such as this—a mission of death—physical discomfort was meaningless. The only important things were those that might interfere with his goal of killing more of his enemies.

As he rested his hand on the bank, he knew he was almost there. The day he and Hawk had spied on the Blackfoot village, he had committed to memory as many physical details as possible about the village's surroundings. Even though he couldn't see much, he was certain the tepees were close by.

The women of the village had worn a couple trails into the bank by going up and down to fetch water from the creek, but Preacher didn't take the time to search for them. Using the rough face of the bank and the roots protruding from it, he scrambled up the bank like a squirrel climbing a tree.

He paused at the top, clinging to footholds and handholds as he edged his head up until his eyes cleared the rim. He had left his hat back at the cave and smeared mud on his face to darken it. He didn't think it would be easy for anyone to spot him.

He had left his rifle behind, too. It wasn't going to do him any good tonight. He was armed with knife, tomahawk, and two loaded pistols. If he ran into any unexpected trouble, that would have to be enough to get him out of it.

If it wasn't . . . well, Hawk would just have to carry on their war alone except for White Buffalo, Dog, and Horse. Preacher had a hunch the boy might be up to it, especially if he had a little luck on his side.

He was getting ahead of himself, Preacher thought.

Nobody was going to die tonight except a few more Blackfoot warriors.

The fires had burned low. The tepees were dark. No one was moving around, not even the village dogs.

Making no sound, Preacher slid over the edge of the bank and stretched out full-length on the ground to wait and see if his movement provoked any reaction.

When it didn't, he crawled closer to the tepees. He proceeded slowly, checking every inch of ground before he pulled himself over it. He didn't want to disturb anything that might make a noise, and he certainly didn't want to crawl over a rattlesnake, although it was unlikely very many of them were moving around much so early in the season.

Gradually, he closed the distance between himself and the nearest tepee. So far he hadn't seen or heard any sentries, but he knew they were out there somewhere. With everything that had happened, he couldn't imagine Tall Bull not posting guards.

A soft step only a few feet away made Preacher freeze. He turned his head and saw the dark shape of a man walking through the night. The warrior was headed away from the village toward the creek, probably part of his regular route.

Preacher put a hand on the ground, came up on one knee, then pushed himself to his feet, all without making any sound. The sentry was almost at the creek.

Since Preacher had already crawled over this area, he knew it was nothing but dirt and grass. The whisper his moccasins made couldn't have been heard more than a foot away.

The guard paused at the edge of the creek bank to

look out over the stream and the woods and meadows on the other side. He had just started to turn back toward the village when Preacher's left hand closed over his mouth and nose, preventing any outcry, and the knife in the mountain man's right hand drove deep into the guard's back.

He was aiming by instinct, but as usual, it guided him well. He felt a slight scrape as the razor-sharp blade glided past a rib, and then the Blackfoot spasmed as the point reached his heart. Preacher pushed harder on the knife, just to make sure it pierced that vital organ. The warrior's back arched as his death throes gripped him.

Preacher pulled the knife out and eased the dead man to the ground, preventing the corpse from rolling off the bank and falling into the creek. The splash would be terribly loud in the quiet night.

Confident the sentry had been responsible for patrolling that part of the approach to the village, Preacher stayed on his feet and turned back toward the tepees. He stalked toward them in utter silence.

Often when he'd infiltrate a Blackfoot village, he'd have a chance to watch it long enough to have specific targets in mind . . . like tepees where he knew he would find a lone warrior sleeping.

That wasn't the case. He didn't want to wind up inside a tepee with a bunch of women and children who would start yelling if they found him there. He was after the sentries tonight, and if he was fortunate enough to find some other places to strike, so much the better.

He paused beside a tepee and hunkered down on his heels. His keen hearing detected the deep, regular breathing of several sleeping people inside. Knowing he wouldn't be going in there, he moved on to the next one, keeping alert for more sentries as well.

A few minutes later, a warrior moved around a tepee right in front of Preacher. The mountain man had heard him coming in time to get set to strike. The Blackfoot spotted Preacher, obviously didn't recognize him in the darkness, and mistook him for one of the other sentries.

The man opened his mouth to speak, but before a sound could come out, Preacher's knife slashed across his throat, cutting deep enough no words could escape the man's mouth, not even a gasp of surprise and pain. Hot blood spurted.

Preacher caught hold of the man's buckskin shirt and swung him lightly to the ground.

The coppery smell of all that freshly spilled blood rose to Preacher's nose. He hoped the dogs wouldn't smell it and start barking. He figured he could get away before the Blackfeet knew what was going on, but he didn't want to light a shuck just yet.

He hadn't done enough damage to them.

He left the corpse where it was and moved on. As he knelt beside the entrance flap of another tepee, he heard only one person breathing inside. Preacher eased the flap aside and went in.

If the tepee's sole occupant was a woman, Preacher figured on knocking her unconscious before she could raise the alarm. He had never liked hitting a woman—although he had run into a few who were evil enough to deserve it—but that was better than cutting her throat.

If it was a man in the tepee . . . well, he was out of luck, that was all.

Preacher couldn't see anything. It was pitch black inside the tepee. He had to work by feel and guesswork, his left hand stabbing down to close around the sleeper's throat and choke off any outcry. His right hand, the one holding the knife, brushed across the sleeper's body at the same time and felt the broad, muscular chest of a warrior.

The blade bit deep before the Blackfoot could even try to fight. He died in confusion, never knowing who had killed him or why.

Three dead so far. Preacher knew folks back east would consider what he was doing to be nothing less than cold-blooded murder. They were fools. Any of the warriors he had slain would have been more than happy to take his life. They would have laughed if they got the chance to kill him slowly and painfully. As far as he was concerned, his actions were completely justifiable.

He wouldn't lose any sleep over what he was doing, that was for damned sure.

He pushed the flap aside again, looked and listened, and stepped out of the tepee to resume stalking the village. With nearly fifty tepees scattered along the creek, he had plenty of them to check.

A short time later he found another that had what sounded like only one sleeper inside.

He repeated what he had done before, but when he touched the sleeper's chest, he felt the rounded mounds of a woman's breasts beneath the buckskin. The hand holding the knife rose and fell, but instead of the blade, the side of the mountain man's hand struck the woman's head and stunned her.

To make certain she wouldn't come to and give the alarm, he bound her hand and foot with strips he cut from the bottom of her dress and tied a piece of bearskin robe in her mouth to serve as a gag. She would wake up with a terrible taste in her mouth, he reflected wryly . . . but at least she would wake up.

A few minutes after that encounter, as he continued to explore the village, he came across another sentry. Preacher was able to take the man from behind, grabbing him across the mouth and jerking his head back so his throat was drawn taut.

The knife cut so deep Preacher felt the blade grind against the dying Blackfoot's spine. With the man turned away from him, he didn't get blood all over his hand and arm when it spurted from severed veins and arteries.

That made four dead, a couple in pretty gruesome fashion. He wouldn't have minded killing two or three more, but when a dog started to growl somewhere nearby, he knew his time had run out. Once the dogs began to stir, it would be only a matter of moments before they were raising a ruckus, and then the Blackfeet would start looking around to see what was going on.

Preacher moved faster. His feet barely seemed to touch the ground as he headed for the creek. Behind him, a dog barked, then another and another.

He slid over the edge of the bank, climbed down part of the way, then dropped the rest, landing lightly on the balls of his feet. He was running an instant later. No one in the village could see him down there.

They might hear him splashing if he had to cut across the creek, but more than likely all the commotion those curs were creating would cover up any sounds he made.

It wasn't the most successful such foray he had made—he had penetrated Blackfoot villages in the past, killed half a dozen or more men, and gotten back out with no one even knowing he'd been there until the next morning—but it had accomplished his purpose and he felt exhilarated.

Now Tall Bull knew he had an enemy who could strike at him and his people anywhere, any time, even right in the middle of their village. He would be convinced his medicine had turned on him, and he might begin to wonder if the mysterious adversary was even human.

He would have no choice but to look for the attacker. If the war chief remained in the village and didn't do anything in response to the killings, he would lose all the power and influence he had left.

And once the Blackfoot warriors were away from the village, they would be even easier to kill.

When Preacher was well out of sight of the village, he crossed the creek and loped through the trees and across meadows, running as tirelessly as a young man half his age.

Hawk was a little more than half his age, he thought.

People had young'uns early on the frontier, if they were going to at all. Life in the wilderness held too many dangers to take a chance on postponing anything.

A harbinger of the approaching dawn, the eastern sky had begun to turn gray by the time Preacher neared the cave where he had left his companions. He should have been well satisfied with his night's work, but something had started to nag at him. He didn't know what it was, just a vague sense something was wrong, but he knew better than to distrust anything his gut was telling him.

He didn't think anybody could have followed him from the Blackfoot village, but he didn't want to take a chance on leading an enemy right to the sanctuary he and his friends had found. He veered away from the cave and moved deeper into the woods. After he had gone a short distance, he reached up, grasped a low-hanging branch, and pulled himself into one of the pines.

Since it was too dark for anyone to see him, he balanced on that branch and waited. He could wait without moving for hours on end if he needed to, barely breathing. His life had depended on that ability numerous times in the past.

He didn't have to wait very long for his instincts to be vindicated. After only a short time had passed, he heard someone moving toward him. He could tell from the sounds the follower made that it wasn't an animal.

Maybe one of the warriors *had* trailed him from the village after all. It was unlikely but not impossible, he supposed.

What was certain was that he couldn't allow the man to escape. If he got back to the village and told Tall Bull he had trailed the intruder to this area, the war chief would know where to look. Preacher was too close to the cave to let that happen.

He and Hawk and White Buffalo could always shift their base of operations to somewhere else, Preacher thought, but he didn't want to move. The cave was just about perfect, and he didn't want to lose it just yet.

He slid his knife from its sheath and poised himself to leap from the branch as soon as whoever was on his trail had passed beneath him.

More seconds dragged by. Preacher heard soft footsteps, then the faint rasp of rapid breathing. He had been moving pretty fast, and the follower would have had to hurry to keep up with him and not lose his trail.

The fellow was good. Preacher had to give him that. Not many men could have followed him without giving themselves away sooner than that one had.

Preacher spotted a deeper patch of darkness moving through the shadows below. His lips drew back from his teeth in a silent snarl as the figure passed underneath the branch where he waited.

Then Preacher leaped, the knife raised high and ready to swoop down and end the life of his enemy.

CHAPTER 19

Preacher landed on the man's back and knocked him forward a couple steps. His left arm went around the man's neck while his right hand brought the knife around in a stroke aimed at the Blackfoot's chest.

Before the knife could find its target, the man bent forward sharply and dived to the ground. The swift move was meant to dislodge Preacher, but the mountain man was able to hang on.

His left forearm slid down a little from the enemy's throat as both of them rolled on the ground. The pressure of rounded flesh against his arm was unmistakable.

Preacher was so surprised he experienced an extremely rare moment of indecision. In that moment, the person he was struggling with lifted an elbow that cracked sharply into his jaw and rocked his head back.

The Blackfoot twisted free and rolled away.

Preacher leaped to his feet and said in the Blackfoot tongue, "Wait just a minute. I don't want to kill you—"

"But I will kill you!"

The voice confirmed what Preacher had already discovered a moment earlier. He was fighting a woman.

She surged to her feet and leaped at him. He didn't know how she was armed, but he heard something moving in the air and figured she was swinging a tomahawk at his head. He ducked and she stumbled into him, thrown off balance by the missed blow.

Since he was already bent over, he grabbed her around the knees and found she was wearing buckskin trousers instead of a dress. He heaved on her legs and threw her over backwards.

From the sound and the pained grunt that came from her he could tell she had landed hard. He went after her, hoping the fall had jolted the tomahawk out of her hand.

No such luck. The flat side of the tomahawk's head smacked his left shoulder and sent pain shooting down his arm. Still able to use it, he reached out blindly and closed his hands around the shaft of the weapon she had used to wallop him. A savage twist wrenched it out of her grip.

She struggled to get up off the ground again, but Preacher put a hand on her and shoved her back down, then leaned his weight on her to keep her pinned where she was. His hand was resting right between her breasts, which was a mite embarrassing for him, but it was effective at keeping her from moving around.

"Stop fightin'!" he told her. "I don't want to hurt you, but I will if I have to."

"Killer!" she practically spat at him. "You would murder a woman? Of course you would, the same way you murdered our warriors!"

If he'd had any doubt she had followed him from the Blackfoot village, it was gone. He muttered, "The hell with this!", and threw a punch that cracked across her jaw. She went limp underneath him.

It was astonishing to him that a woman had been able to trail him through the night, but for the moment her sex wasn't an important consideration. He was more concerned with figuring out what to do with her. He didn't want to kill her in cold blood. That went too much against the grain for him. But he couldn't turn her loose. He didn't want her to lead Tall Bull and the warriors back there to find the cave. Letting her go would mean that he and Hawk and White Buffalo would have to find some other place to hole up.

That was unacceptable.

Preacher could think of one more possibility, but he didn't like it much more than the other two. Still, he supposed it was the lesser of the three evils. He looked down at her, still out cold from the punch, then he hefted her up and draped her limp form over his shoulder. She was solidly built and not exactly light, but he handled her weight like it didn't amount to much.

Holding her tightly, he trotted off toward the cave as the eastern sky continued to lighten with the approach of dawn.

By the time Preacher reached his destination, the sky had a few streaks of rose and gold in it. He paused outside the brush barrier and called, "Hawk! White Buffalo! It's me . . . and I have a prisoner."

The woman hadn't budged. Preacher thought he hadn't hit her hard enough to cause any permanent damage, but sometimes he didn't seem to know his own strength.

He heard stirring from inside the cave, then Hawk pushed some of the brush aside and stepped out.

"You brought one of the filthy Blackfeet with you?" he demanded. From where he stood, he could see only the prisoner's buckskin-clad rump and legs and clearly didn't realize she was a woman. "Why did you not just kill him? Why waste the effort to bring him back with you?" Hawk paused. "Or did you bring him to ask him questions, like you tried to do with Strong Bear?"

"Not exactly." Preacher strode past Hawk, through the opening in the brush, and into the cave, where he bent and placed the unconscious captive on the ground.

"A woman!" White Buffalo said as his watery old eyes widened in amazement. "A *young* woman!"

It was true. The prisoner appeared to be about Hawk's age, maybe a summer or two younger. She was dressed like a warrior. Her black hair was done up in two braids.

Hawk had followed Preacher into the cave and stared at the woman for a couple seconds. "Why have you done this?"

"She followed me from the Blackfoot village. I ain't quite sure how. Reckon she must be mighty good at woodscraft and have a keen eye."

"So a woman . . . a *girl* . . . was able to follow the

mighty Ghost Killer without him knowing it?" Hawk's tone was mocking.

Anger surged inside Preacher. "Don't push your luck, boy. I said before that you were mighty good. It appears this gal might be even better."

Hawk glared at him. He reached for the knife at his waist and said, "We should cut her throat before she wakes up and drop her in the ravine with the others."

"I don't hold with killin' women in cold blood. Since she followed me almost all the way back here, I didn't figure it would be a good idea to turn her loose."

White Buffalo asked, "Then what are we to do with her?"

Preacher said, "I reckon we'll just keep her here until we're through with what we've got to do in these parts."

Hawk and White Buffalo stared at him as if he had lost his mind.

After a moment, White Buffalo said, "No. Kill her! She is Blackfoot."

After surviving the harrowing ordeal in the Absaroka village, Preacher couldn't really blame the old man for feeling that way.

The young woman hadn't taken part in the massacre—at least Preacher assumed she hadn't—but he had no doubt she was just fine with Tall Bull and the war party slaughtering all of the Absaroka.

"Have you forgotten Bird in the Tree, Preacher?" Hawk asked. "I have not. Nor have I forgotten Little Pine. They were innocent, and yet Tall Bull and his men slew them."

"I haven't forgotten them or anybody else from your village. I helped lay all of them to rest. Remember? It ain't likely I'll forget that any time soon, if I ever do." Preacher waved a hand toward the young woman. "If we kill her in cold blood, don't that make us the same sort of evil varmint Tall Bull is? He wages war on women and children, but I reckon I'd like to be better than that."

"You are a fool," White Buffalo said. "Hate must be met with hate. Death demands vengeance."

"Death demands justice. I ain't shyin' away from killin' Tall Bull or any of his warriors . . . but this is different."

Hawk said, "If you keep her, she is yours to deal with, Preacher. I will have nothing to do with her."

"White Buffalo?" Preacher said.

The old-timer crossed his sticklike arms over his chest and glared. "I will do nothing to help you with this Blackfoot devil."

She didn't look much like a devil, Preacher thought as he gazed down at the unconscious woman. In fact, she was sort of attractive, in a severe way.

Nearly everyone in Indian society, male and female, regardless of tribe, knew their places in that particular culture and accepted them.

Often there were a few who, in one way or another, just never fit in. The so-called contraries, the ones who did everything backwards, were the most prominent, but there were also men who acted like women and women who acted like men.

Preacher wondered if this was one of the latter. She had trailed him through the night as well or better than any of Tall Bull's warriors could have, and when he jumped her she had fought with the strength and determination of a man.

Despite that, Preacher knew she was a woman and so he would act accordingly. That meant not killing her out of hand.

"All right. If you two want to act like stubborn ol' badgers, there ain't nothin' I can do about it," he told Hawk and White Buffalo, not trying to keep the anger out of his voice. "I'll figure it out later. For now, if you want to keep your distance from this gal, I reckon you can have at it."

"That is exactly what I intend to do," Hawk said as he turned toward the cave mouth.

"And White Buffalo as well," the old-timer declared with a disdainful sniff.

He was standing too close to the prisoner, and suddenly she lashed out with her right foot and kicked the back of his left knee. She had been shamming and had done a good job of it.

White Buffalo yelled in pain and surprise as his leg buckled and he went down.

The woman lunged up and grabbed the handle of the hunting knife Preacher had given him. "Murderers!" she screamed as she pulled it from the waistband of White Buffalo's filthy buckskin trousers.

Preacher and Hawk spread out to close in on her. She slashed back and forth with the knife to keep them at bay. At the same time, she edged out of reach of White Buffalo, although it seemed the old-timer wasn't going to do anything except lie there, hold his knee, and howl in pain.

"Now hold on a minute—" Preacher began.

"Let me go!"

"Let her run," Hawk said. "I will put an arrow in her back before she has gone ten paces."

"Nobody's shootin' anybody with an arrow." Preacher nodded his head in a signal.

Dog was behind her, and at Preacher's nod he leaped at her back. Weighing more than a hundred pounds, he knocked her forward off her feet.

He could have torn out her throat with one swipe of his teeth, but Preacher said, "Dog! Back!" as he leaped toward the young woman.

Dog backed away. Preacher's foot came down on the wrist of the hand holding the knife, making her cry out in pain and let go of the weapon. In an instant he snatched it up.

"Now do you see why we should kill her?" Hawk said. "She is our enemy and will always be our enemy. She cannot be trusted. A Blackfoot can never be trusted!"

"Maybe not, but I don't make war on women or kids." Preacher knew he was being stubborn, and from a purely practical standpoint, Hawk and White Buffalo were probably right. Their best course of action was to dispose of the woman.

But Preacher wasn't going to do that, at least not yet. He tossed the knife to Hawk and told him, "Look after White Buffalo. I don't reckon his leg's hurt all that bad, but we'd best make sure."

Hawk caught it deftly, "What are you going to do?"

Preacher walked toward the young woman, who sat

up and scuttled backwards until Dog blocked her escape and growled.

"I intend on havin' a few words with her. I want to find out just who it is that can track me as well as this gal did tonight."

CHAPTER 20

With Dog beside her, watchful and seemingly eager to sink his teeth into her, and Preacher hunkered down in front of her, the captive couldn't go anywhere. Her dark eyes were big with fright, but anger and defiance burned brightly in them, as well.

"Who are you?" Preacher asked. "What's your name?"

For a moment she didn't answer, and he figured she was going to be stubborn about it. But then she said, "I am called Winter Wind."

"Because you blow fierce and cold?" Preacher guessed.

She seemed surprised. "How did you know that?"

"I've spent a lot of time with Indians. Not Blackfeet, mind you, because they're always tryin' to kill me, but some things are pretty common among all the tribes, like how they'll name somebody according to how they look or act. No offense, ma'am, but you don't exactly strike me as the warm and friendly sort."

"I am a warrior," Winter Wind snapped.

"You act like one, no doubt about that." He paused.

"But I'll bet ol' Tall Bull don't let you go out raidin' with the war parties, now does he?"

"That is his mistake," she said, her voice and face sullen with resentment. "I could kill the enemies of the Blackfeet as well as any man."

"I'm sure you could. What were you doin' prowlin' around the village tonight? You must not have been in one of the tepees if you spotted me."

"Tall Bull will not even allow me to stand guard over our people. But I do it anyway. When the dogs began to bark I saw someone running away, so I followed. I knew you had to be an enemy." She looked at him intently. "I did not know you were the evil Ghost Killer, the murderer of so many of our people."

"So you heard that while you were still pretendin' to be unconscious, did you?"

"You do not deny it?" she challenged.

"I deny bein' evil and a murderer. I reckon I've killed plenty of Blackfeet, sure enough, but I promise you, there's been a whole heap more of 'em who've done their best to kill *me*. Shoot, one time they were gonna burn me at the stake!"

Winter Wind's lip curled as she said, "A fitting fate for a man such as you."

"Back when that happened, the Blackfeet didn't have no special grudge against me yet—"

Preacher stopped. He wasn't going to waste time arguing with the young woman or explaining his past to her. History wouldn't change the way she felt about him, just like it wouldn't change the way Hawk and White Buffalo felt about her.

Preacher glanced around to see how the old-timer was doing. Hawk had helped him to his feet and taken him over to the far side of the cave. White Buffalo was sitting down with his back propped against the wall and his legs stretched out in front of him. Hawk probed at the knee Winter Wind had kicked, and the old man grimaced.

"How's he doin'?" Preacher asked.

"I do not believe any bones are broken," Hawk replied. "White Buffalo's knee will be sore for a time, but he should be all right."

"The woman should be killed!" White Buffalo said. "She attacked me!"

Preacher turned back to her. "You can see you ain't got no friends here. I reckon I'm the only thing standin' between you and death."

"If you wait for me to thank you, I will not."

Preacher shook his head. "No, I ain't expectin' no thanks. But if you want to show me you appreciate me not killin' you—and not lettin' those two kill you— you can tell me how many warriors Tall Bull has left."

"I will tell you nothing!" she said through clenched teeth. "Go ahead and kill me!"

"You should do as she wishes," Hawk said.

"Nope," Preacher said. "If she don't want to cooperate, we'll just go on without her help. It won't change a blasted thing in the long run."

"So what are you going to do with her?"

"Reckon she'll have to be tied and gagged."

"No!" Winter Wind cried. Despite the threat of Dog at her side, she launched herself at Preacher again. He could tell by the crazed look in her eyes she was determined to force him to kill her.

He met her attack with a swift punch that once again stretched her out on the floor of the cave.

Before her senses returned to her, he lashed her hands and feet and fastened a gag in her mouth. As he finished, she blinked her eyes open and looked up at him with such hatred, he was reminded of something Audie had said once. *If looks could kill . . .*

Preacher figured if there was any truth to that old saying, he'd be one dead son of a gun right now.

By that evening White Buffalo was hobbling around, complaining about his knee, but as far as Preacher could see, the old-timer was almost as spry as he'd ever been. Preacher kept an eye on him, knowing he might try to get rid of Winter Wind if he got the chance.

Hawk had brought down a nice fat grouse during the day, and they roasted it for supper. Preacher took one of the legs over to Winter Wind and removed the gag from her mouth.

"I'm gonna let you eat," he told her. "Give me your word you won't try anything, and I'll untie your hands."

"I give you my word for nothing except that I will kill you," she said, her voice a little hoarse and choked from having the gag in her mouth all day. She turned her head and spat a couple times on the cave floor.

"Reckon I can hold this, then, and you can gnaw on it."

He held the food up to her mouth, but she turned her head away and refused to eat.

"All right," Preacher said. "I ain't gonna squat here and beg you to eat. You had your chance. You want some water?"

"I will take nothing from you. I will lie in my own filth and die of thirst!"

"Well, that sounds mighty unpleasant. I figured you were smarter than that. But if you ain't, I guess there's nothin' I can do about it." He carried the food back to the fire, where he hunkered down and ate it himself.

"You should put the gag back in her mouth," Hawk said. "She might try to yell, and if any of Tall Bull's men are nearby, they could hear it."

"In a minute," Preacher said.

White Buffalo said, "You are too kind to her. You cannot befriend a Blackfoot. They are all like dogs with the mad sickness that makes them foam at the mouth. All you can do is kill them before they kill someone else."

"She ain't killin' nobody, tied up like that."

After he had eaten, Preacher went back over to the captive and put the gag in her mouth again. She tried to bite him, but he managed to get the gag in so all she could do was make angry noises.

They had been standing guard at night anyway, taking turns as usual, so that didn't change just because they had a prisoner. Before he fell asleep, Preacher wondered if Hawk would kill the woman during the night. He didn't think so, but he wasn't completely certain.

Winter Wind was still alive the next morning. Her resolve had weakened overnight, and when Preacher offered her food and water, she accepted. She wanted to visit the bushes outside, but he took her back into a dark corner of the cave and stood nearby, ignoring her muttered complaints.

After he had tied her up again but hadn't replaced the gag, she asked, "Why do you hate the Blackfeet so much?"

"They've killed people I cared about," Preacher said, "and like I told you before, they've tried to kill me over and over again. I've had more trouble with them than any other tribe out here on the frontier. You got to admit, they've got a reputation for not gettin' along with anybody, white and Indian alike."

"The Blackfeet kill our enemies. It is what we do. If we tried to kill you, you must have done something to become our enemy."

Hawk had been pretending not to listen, but he couldn't contain his reaction to Winter Wind's words. "My people did nothing to yours! My mother never harmed anyone, Blackfoot or anybody else. The girl who was to be my wife, Little Pine, never hurt anyone. And yet Tall Bull and his warriors killed them and everyone else in my village! Women, children, old men, all dead!"

"They were not Blackfoot," Winter Wind said. "They were not truly people."

Hawk snarled and reached for the knife at his waist.

Preacher moved to get between him and the prisoner. "I know it's a crazy way to think, but it's what's been drummed into her head, her whole life." He turned to the woman. "So that's why Tall Bull wiped out that Absaroka village?"

"The Blackfeet need more hunting ground, Tall Bull says. He will bring many of the bands together, and then we will take what we need."

The blind, unquestioning acceptance Preacher heard in Winter Wind's voice was discouraging. He hadn't been inclined to try to persuade her to change her views, and she was making it clear such an effort would be a waste of time anyway.

It was beginning to look like they could do only one thing about the situation.

Preacher extracted Hawk's promise he wouldn't hurt Winter Wind or allow White Buffalo to do so.

The young man wasn't happy about it, though. "Why do you do this thing?"

"Because it's what your ma would have wanted."

"Again, you know very little of what Bird in the Tree would have wanted. But what I mean is, why do you ask this promise of me now?"

"Because I'm leavin' the prisoner with you and White Buffalo today, and I want her to still be alive when I come back."

"Leaving," Hawk repeated. "Where do you go?"

"To look for another place for us to stay."

"That means you are going to let her live."

"I can't kill her in cold blood or stand by while somebody else does."

"So you would have us abandon this cave that suits our purposes so well."

Preacher shrugged. "Don't see any way around it."

"You will let her go back to Tall Bull and tell him there are only two of us, and an old man who cannot fight." Hawk held up a hand toward White Buffalo to silence any protest he might make. "She will tell him you are the one called Preacher."

"They're probably startin' to wonder about that anyway, after I slipped into their village and killed four men without bein' caught."

"Your heart is too soft. After all the stories I have heard, I would not have believed it of you."

"Now wait just a damned minute," Preacher said, angry. "You complain about how I don't kill every enemy I meet, just as soon as I lay eyes on 'em. You say I'm too softhearted. Well, sometimes there's a good reason for not killin' first thing. I ain't gonna apologize for not riskin' innocent lives when it's better to wait. There's more to livin' . . . than killin'." He blew out a disgusted breath. "Anyway, when the time comes, I don't reckon I'm all that softhearted. I've killed more 'n a dozen of those varmints here lately, and I reckon 'fore we're done with 'em, I'm liable to kill two or three times that many. How much more bloodshed do you want, for God's sake?"

Hawk just glared at him, clearly not persuaded. The mountain man had had his say, and that made him feel a little better, anyway.

"I have given you my word," Hawk said after a moment. "No harm will come to the woman. You can go on and do what you feel you must do."

Preacher gave him a curt nod and left the cave.

CHAPTER 21

The terrain became more rugged to the west of the Blackfoot village, as the pine-covered slopes rose higher and higher to some of the most majestic peaks in the Rockies.

When Preacher had first come to the frontier, most of the trappers had called those peaks the Shining Mountains because of the way the sun reflected off the snowcapped crests. *Rockies* suited them just as well, though. They were the biggest piles of stone he had ever seen.

The important thing for him at the moment was to find a good place up there for him and Hawk and White Buffalo to move their camp. They could abandon the cave and leave Winter Wind there to work her way loose from her bonds and return to her people.

It was possible they might see her in battle if she ever succeeded in persuading Tall Bull to let her join a war party. She was stubborn enough Preacher could believe that would happen sooner or later.

In that case, he wouldn't hesitate to put a rifle ball through her or go after her with his tomahawk.

Winter Wind considered herself a warrior, and he would treat her like the enemy she was determined to be.

First things first, he reminded himself, which meant finding a good campsite, one easily defended and hard for searchers to locate.

Through trees, brush, and gullies, he ranged up into the mountains, using his talent for stealth to stay out of sight. He never allowed himself to be skylighted on top of a ridge or get caught out in the open for too long at a time. As he climbed higher, he looked back down now and then, and one of those times, he spotted the creek on which the Blackfoot village was located. From that height, the stream was a winding, glittering silver ribbon of reflected sunlight.

He came upon a narrow cleft in a towering rock face that intrigued him. He investigated and found the passage led to a small canyon surrounded by cliffs. It had plenty of grass but no water, which meant he and Hawk would have to find a spring nearby where they could fill their water skins if they were going to move their camp there.

The canyon certainly fit the requirement of being easy to defend. The cleft that led to it was wide enough for two men abreast, but that was all. Preacher knew he and Hawk would be able to hold the place for a long time if they needed to, as long as their supplies, arrows, and powder and shot lasted.

It was miles away from the cave where their current camp was located, and if they were careful not to leave a trail, nothing would indicate they had gone up there. If Winter Wind escaped and led Tall Bull back to the cave, the war chief would concentrate his search in that area, at least to start with.

It would buy them some time, Preacher thought as he left the canyon and started back through the cleft.

He stopped short while he was still inside the passage, just before he reached the opening in the seamed and pitted rock face. He had heard something and his instincts set off warning bells in his brain. Whatever it was, he knew it didn't belong there. It wasn't a sound of nature.

A moment later he heard it again and recognized it as a voice. A second voice replied.

Hearing a couple men talking wasn't what caused Preacher's back to stiffen in surprise. The conversation was being carried on in English. He couldn't make out the words yet, but he heard enough to recognize the language.

That was just about the last thing Preacher had expected to hear in the savage wilderness not all that far from a village full of bloodthirsty Blackfoot warriors.

He shouldn't be that surprised, he told himself. Many times during his years as a trapper, he had penetrated into equally dangerous areas. When he was going after pelts, he never gave much thought to the Indians he might encounter or the other perils he might find himself facing. He'd always figured whatever happened, he would deal with it as it came.

Plenty of other trappers felt the same way, and evidently two of them, maybe more, were nearby. Preacher eased into the opening of the cleft to take a look.

Two men wearing buckskins and coonskin caps

and carrying rifles were moving slowly toward him, paying more attention to the rugged ground on which they were walking than they were to their surroundings, so they wouldn't trip and fall on the rocky surface.

Such inattentiveness was a good way to get killed, and it was something a veteran mountain man would never be guilty of. They weren't near the streams where beaver were to be found, either. As fur trappers, they clearly left a lot to be desired. Preacher would have bet the pair had never been to the frontier before.

"—mite hard to breathe up here in this high country," one of them was saying.

"That's because you're used to the tidelands back in Virginia. At least I've spent some time in the Appalachians."

"I'm not sure those are even real mountains, compared to these."

"You'd think they were real mountains, all right, if you'd tramped all over them like I have."

The two men were close to Preacher. He stepped out, cradling the long-barreled flintlock rifle in his arms. "You fellas lost?" He didn't expect any trouble from them, but he was ready if it came about.

He didn't have to worry. Both men stopped short and gaped at him with open mouths.

They were fairly young, in their mid-twenties. One was on the stocky side, with a brown beard and round face. The other was clean-shaven, which made his face look even more young and innocent. He had curly black hair under the coonskin cap.

"Who the hell are you?" asked the one with the beard.

"Reckon I could ask you fellas the same thing. But to save time, I'll tell you they call me Preacher."

"Preacher!" the clean-shaven one said. "We've heard stories about you. Some of the other men said they knew you. They seemed proud of that."

"Other men?"

Both trappers made faces. The bearded one said, "Yeah, we were with a group of six more men."

"Where are they?"

"Dead," the second man said. "Wiped out by Indians three weeks ago."

"We escaped by the skin of our teeth," the first man said, "and we've been wandering around out here ever since."

Preacher looked around. Out in the open wasn't the best place to be. "You fellas come on in here out of sight. I reckon we need to do some talkin'."

The pair looked at each other as if they weren't certain they ought to accept the invitation then the bearded one shrugged and said, "He's not a murdering redskin."

"No, but what if he's a murdering white man?" the other man said.

Preacher said, "If you fellas want to go on about your business by yourselves, have at it."

"We didn't say that," the bearded one replied hastily. "You're the first friendly face we've seen in three weeks." He looked at his companion. "I say we take our chances."

The other man nodded. "I guess you're right.

Anyway, from what we've heard about Preacher, if anybody can get us out of this mess we're in, it's him."

They stepped inside the cleft.

The stout fellow with the beard was Charlie Todd. The clean-shaven one was Aaron Buckley. Both were from Virginia and had come west to find fortune and adventure.

"We joined up with a party of trappers in St. Louis," Todd explained as they stood inside the hidden canyon with Preacher. "A couple of them had experience, but the rest were newcomers like us."

Buckley added, "The men who had been out here to the mountains before were named Samuels and Powell. They're the ones who said they knew you."

"Abner Samuels and Cy Powell?" Preacher asked.

"That's right. Were they telling the truth? Did you really know them?"

"We met at a rendezvous or two," Preacher said. "Wouldn't say we was friends or even that well-acquainted." He paused, then added, "To be honest, I never was too impressed with 'em, but I reckon they were honest enough."

"Well, they seemed to know what they were doing, at least at first. They certainly knew a lot more than the rest of us." Todd sighed. "But in the end it didn't really help them all that much, I guess."

"What happened?"

"Indians jumped us. They killed everybody except Aaron and me. We were lucky, I guess."

Preacher figured instead of putting up a fight, they had lost their nerve and run. It was a little surprising the war party hadn't tried to track them down, but maybe whoever was in charge hadn't considered the two greenhorns to be worth the effort.

"Where'd this happen?"

Buckley pointed. "Over there east of that big mountain with the saw-tooth top."

So, east of Beartooth, Preacher thought, but still in the area Tall Bull considered to be Blackfoot hunting grounds. It was a good chance the war party was from Tall Bull's village. It might have been led by the war chief himself.

"And this was three weeks ago, you say?"

"Well, out here it's kind of hard to keep track of the days . . . but at least that long, yes," Todd said.

Tall Bull's warriors had attacked the trappers *before* venturing south of Beartooth to wipe out the Absaroka village. That made sense to Preacher. Ever since he and Hawk had started their vengeance campaign, Tall Bull wouldn't have bothered going after some white trappers who didn't represent a threat to him. He would have been too busy trying to figure out who kept whittling down his supply of warriors.

"How in blazes have you two fellas managed to stay alive since then?"

"It hasn't been easy," Buckley replied with a wan smile. "For the first few days we hid in a gully, in the middle of some thick brush where nobody could see us. I don't mind admitting we were too scared to budge from it."

"I might mind admitting it," Todd said, "but yeah, that's pretty much true."

"We had some water with us but nothing to eat, and eventually we got hungry enough we had to go out," Buckley went on. "We didn't shoot anything because we figured the savages might be looking for us and would hear the guns. We've had to get by with what we could catch with our hands or in snares we rigged. It, uh, hasn't been much."

Todd swallowed. "So if you could spare any food, Mr. Preacher—"

"Just *Preacher*," the mountain man said. "No *mister*." He pulled a couple chunks of leftover grouse out of his possibles bag and handed them to the two men, who began eating ravenously.

After a few minutes, Todd gnawed the last of the meat off the bone, then used the back of his hand to wipe grease from his beard and mustache. "So what are you doing out here by yourself, Preacher? If it's all right to ask, that is."

"A friend of mine and I have been doin' some huntin'." It might be a bit of a stretch to call Hawk his friend, Preacher thought, but he wasn't sure he wanted to go into all the details of their quest, at least not yet.

"Hunting," Buckley said. "You mean for beaver? Or some other sort of game?"

"The most dangerous game," Preacher said with a faint smile. "Blackfeet."

CHAPTER 22

Preacher didn't see any point in taking Todd and Buckley all the way back to the cave where Hawk and White Buffalo were waiting for him. He told them, "My friends and I are gonna move our camp to this canyon from where it is now, so if you fellas want to throw in with us, you can wait here until we get back."

"You mean you want us to help you fight the Blackfeet?" Buckley asked.

"I don't know if that's a good idea," Todd added. "We didn't do so good about that the first chance we got, you know."

"Then maybe you'd like a second chance."

Neither of the novice trappers looked particularly excited about that prospect, but at the same time, they obviously didn't want to continue trying to survive in a hostile wilderness by themselves.

"I guess we can stay here," Buckley said. "We can, uh, guard the place while you're gone."

Preacher nodded. "That's what I had in mind."

As a matter of fact, that might wind up being their

full-time job once the camp was moved. Preacher wasn't sure he wanted to take them along on any of the raids against the Blackfeet. He was comfortable with Hawk's fighting abilities, but the two greenhorns didn't inspire any such confidence.

Allies who were inclined to panic and make mistakes usually were more dangerous than enemies.

But they could stay in the canyon with White Buffalo and hold off any Blackfeet who chanced to discover the camp. Preacher considered that possibility unlikely, so chances were, Todd and Buckley wouldn't have much to do.

Later, when war with the Blackfeet was over, Preacher could take the two men back to where they could find their way to civilization . . . if they all survived.

There was a lot more killing to do first.

"I just have one question," Buckley said, then waited.

"Go ahead," Preacher told him.

"What if you leave us here and then, uh, never come back?"

"You mean if somethin' happens to me so I can't make it?"

Todd said, "Well, you wouldn't go off and just, well, *leave* us here, would you?"

"Nope," Preacher said with a smile. "I ain't that heartless. If I was to wind up dead before I got back here, I don't reckon you'd be any worse off than you were before you ran into me, now would you?"

The two men glanced at each other and Buckley said, "I suppose not," but neither of them looked very reassured by Preacher's answer.

* * *

Preacher showed the two would-be trappers around the canyon, then told them, "It'll probably be tomorrow mornin' before I get back with Hawk and White Buffalo. You can build a little fire if you want to, but make sure it's far enough back nobody can spot it through that passage."

"Those friends of yours that you're bringing here . . . they're Indians?" Todd asked with a nervous expression on his face.

"That's right. They're Absaroka. Some call 'em Crow."

"They're not members of the same tribe that killed all the men with us?" Buckley asked.

"Not hardly. The Absaroka are friends with the white men. Not because they're that awful fond of us, I expect, but because they know the Blackfeet hate us, and the Absaroka and the Blackfeet don't get along at all. As long as we've got a common enemy, you don't have anything to worry about where the Absaroka are concerned."

"What if the Blackfeet are ever wiped out?"

"I don't figure that'll ever happen . . . but even if it did, I believe the Absaroka would still be our friends. They're just decent folks. Fact of the matter is, a lot of the tribes out here are like that. They're willin' to get along just fine, as long as the whites don't come in tryin' to tell 'em how to live their lives or pushin' 'em out of their huntin' grounds. You see, the Indians don't hold with the idea of the land *belongin'* to anybody. That's why they think they oughta be able to hunt wherever they please."

"I think we can learn a lot from you, Preacher, if we get the chance," Buckley said.

"Just keep your eyes and ears open. The frontier's a hard teacher but a fair one. All it asks is that you never let your guard down."

Preacher left the two men in the canyon and started back toward the cave. It was mid-afternoon, and he knew night would fall by the time he got back to Hawk and White Buffalo. First thing in the morning they could set off for the new camp.

As the sun lowered toward the looming mountains, Preacher used the same stealth he had employed earlier to stay out of sight, even though he was traveling fairly rapidly. Along the way he scared up a nice fat rabbit and brought it down with a throw of his tomahawk. He would take supper back to his friends, as well as the location of the new campsite.

Darkness had settled over the landscape when he neared the cave. He stopped outside the brush barrier and hooted like an owl, then again. That was the signal they had agreed to use whenever one member of the group returned to the camp after dark. He expected to hear the call of a whip-poor-will in return, since that was the countersignal.

Instead, White Buffalo's cracked old voice called, "Preacher! Is that you?"

Instantly, Preacher knew something was wrong. White Buffalo shouldn't have spoken up like that without being sure who was outside. Preacher pushed through the brush and hurried into the cave.

A tiny fire burned near the rear wall. The flames weren't bright enough to be spotted from outside through the brush, but they lit up the cave well enough for Preacher to see White Buffalo sitting with his back against the wall. He had his left arm cradled with his right. A bloody rag was tied around the forearm.

Horse and the pack mule were there, but Hawk and Dog were gone.

Preacher saw no sign of Winter Wind, either.

"White Buffalo, how bad are you hurt?" he asked as he moved swiftly to the old-timer's side.

"It is nothing. A cut. It bled enough to weaken me, since at my age I have little blood to spare."

"I reckon Winter Wind must've done it?" Preacher asked grimly as he knelt in front of White Buffalo.

"I told you she was a Blackfoot devil."

"You got too close to her again."

White Buffalo sighed. "Now is not the time for blame. What is important is that she got away."

The blood that had seeped from the wound into the rag tied around White Buffalo's arm wasn't completely dried yet, which told Preacher the incident hadn't happened that long ago.

"Hawk went after her?"

"He said he would find her and bring her back," White Buffalo replied with a nod. "And he said he would not kill her unless he was forced to, since you wanted her to stay alive."

"Not if it comes down to a fight to the death." Preacher grimaced at the thought of Hawk hesitating at just the wrong moment and winding up dead, all because he was trying to honor his father's wishes.

Maybe Preacher could prevent that, if he moved quickly enough. Hawk and Winter Wind couldn't have too big a start on him. If he caught up in time, he could help Hawk recapture the woman.

"He took Dog with him to help trail her?"

White Buffalo nodded again. "I am sorry, Preacher—"

"We'll hash that out later," Preacher said. "You can tell me the whole story then. Right now I'm gonna get after 'em."

He didn't have Dog to help him, so tracking them down in the darkness wasn't going to be easy. He assumed, however, that Winter Wind would want to get back to her village and warn Tall Bull and the others as fast as possible.

All he could do was start in that direction and hope he could find them.

As he trotted through the shadows, it occurred to Preacher that Winter Wind might have tried to throw off pursuit by fleeing in a different direction instead of heading straight back to the village. If that were the case, it would be a pure guess which way she would have gone. He decided trying to figure it out would be a waste of time. Sooner or later, unless Hawk captured or killed her, she would try to reach the village, so Preacher hurried in that direction to head her off and keep her from getting to Tall Bull.

The stars provided plenty of light for Preacher to see where he was going. Staying in the shadows, he paused from time to time to listen intently. He didn't really expect to hear anything, since Hawk and Winter Wind were both skilled at moving silently. Sure enough,

Preacher heard no sounds except the usual night noises and moved on toward the Blackfoot village.

It was early enough in the evening that the scent of smoke from the cooking fires drifted to him a short time later. He followed it until he was getting close to the village and stopped where he could get a look at the place from a wooded knoll about a quarter mile away.

Everything about the village appeared to be peaceful. The fires had died down, but their embers still glowed orange in the night. A few people were moving around. Preacher spotted them occasionally when they moved between him and the remains of the fires.

No commotion of any sort told him Winter Wind hadn't returned with the news of her capture, escape, and discovery of the hideout being used by the men who had been plaguing her people. If nothing happened by morning, Preacher would assume Hawk had stopped her . . . one way or another.

Preacher settled in to wait and watch. His position commanded a good view of several approaches to the village. Winter Wind might still get past him, but it wasn't likely. Once the moon came up, it would be even easier for him to spot her if she tried to reach the village.

He hunkered down to ease his muscles. He had traveled a long way to find a new camp and back again, and his journey wasn't over yet. He might have to stay near the village all night, then return to the cave in the morning. If Hawk had dealt with the problem of Winter Wind, Preacher would need to lead him and White Buffalo back to the canyon where Charlie Todd and Aaron Buckley were waiting.

Well, it wasn't the first time he had gone for a long spell without any rest, he told himself, and likely it wouldn't be the last. Out on the frontier a man did what he had to in order to survive . . . or he died.

No two ways about it.

Preacher had long since mastered the art of letting his mind drift into a relaxed state while his senses remained alert and his body was ready to move at an instant's notice. In that almost dreamlike consciousness, he wondered why the Blackfeet hated everybody so much, especially the white men who had come to the mountains to explore and trap.

Many years earlier, when he was just a young man, he had talked to an old-timer at a rendezvous who claimed to have been with Meriwether Lewis and William Clark when they went up the Missouri River on behalf of President Thomas Jefferson to explore what was then called the Louisiana Purchase. That veteran frontiersman had talked about an encounter between Lewis and Clark's party and a group of Blackfoot warriors.

The meeting had started off friendly enough. Probably the Blackfeet had never laid eyes on any white men before, and like all Indians, they were curious.

An argument had broken out, most likely over something trivial, and one of the explorers wound up firing his rifle at the warriors, killing one of them.

That was how it all started, the old-timer had claimed. Ever since, the Blackfeet had hated all white men and done their best to kill them.

Preacher didn't know if the story was true, but it seemed plausible enough. All he was really sure of was that the Blackfeet were his enemies, and the feeling was mutual.

Sudden movement down below broke him out of his reverie. A figure had bolted out of the shadows under some trees and ran across open ground, heading straight for the Blackfoot village.

Preacher didn't need a closer look to know that running figure was Winter Wind . . . and it seemed he was the only hope of stopping her before she delivered her news to Tall Bull.

CHAPTER 23

Preacher could have brought her down with a shot from his rifle, but that would have defeated the purpose. The Blackfeet would hear the shot and be roused in a matter of moments. Instead, he ran down the slope through the trees.

Her course took her close to the knoll, so he was only about twenty feet from her when he broke out onto the flat and angled to intercept her. She spotted him right away and veered away from him. He knew she was going to scream, and the Blackfeet might well hear that, too.

He jerked his tomahawk from behind his belt and flung it at her legs.

The weapon's long wooden handle got caught between her calves and caused her feet to tangle together. With a cry of startled dismay, she fell forward into the grass.

Preacher was on her in an instant, but even as fast as he moved, Winter Wind was able to roll over and meet his attack. She thrust her legs up in an attempt to kick him and lever him aside.

Preacher grabbed her ankles and pivoted sharply, hauling her around with him so fast her body came up off the ground. When he let go of her ankles, she flew through the air for several feet before crashing down again. Her landing was hard and knocked the breath out of her, leaving her stunned.

Before she could do more than gasp for air a couple times, Preacher was kneeling beside her with the tomahawk held high and poised for a killing strike. "You start to yell and I'll stave your head in before you can get more than a peep out," he warned her. "I've done my damnedest to keep you alive, girl, and I ain't real happy about the way you're tryin' to pay me back for that kindness."

"It . . . it is not kindness . . . to be spared by an enemy!" she said breathlessly. "It is . . . a humiliation!"

"Then I reckon you'd rather me go ahead and dash your brains out."

"It is what you would do . . . if I was a man!"

"Well, you're right about that," Preacher said. "I ain't too happy about what you did to White Buffalo, neither. That old codger coulda bled to death, the way you cut him."

In the faint starlight, he saw Winter Wind sneer.

"I did not cut the old man. He did it himself, trying to stop me. He tripped and fell on his own knife."

White Buffalo hadn't mentioned that, but to be fair, Preacher hadn't given him much time to explain. And a good thing, too, or else he might not have been able to head off Winter Wind and keep her from reaching the village.

"We can talk about it after we get back to the cave. You're comin' with me."

"You will have to kill me to keep me from crying out to my people!"

"You really do have a hankerin' to die, don't you?"

"A warrior can aspire to nothing more than dying in battle. Give me a weapon. We will settle this between us, and I give you my word I will not call for help."

"Forget it," Preacher said. "I ain't fightin' you."

"I will—"

"No, you won't." With that, he walloped her on the jaw again. He didn't know what she was about to say and didn't care. He figured her jaw was probably getting pretty sore, but there wasn't anything he could do about that.

He met Hawk and Dog on the way back to the cave.

"Again?" the young man said as he looked at the tied, gagged figure draped over Preacher's shoulder.

"Oh, she did her best to convince me to kill her, so she could die with honor at the hands of an enemy the way a warrior should, but I didn't feel like cooperatin'."

"I should have caught her," Hawk said in a surly voice. "Truly, she runs as fast as the wind." Grudging admiration sounded in his voice.

Hawk and Dog fell in alongside the mountain man as he strode along with the captive.

Preacher asked, "How'd she get away?"

"She must have found a rock with enough of an edge on it to saw through her bonds. I can only guess she worked at them all day while you were gone. She had no knife or other weapon, and White Buffalo and

I did not disturb her, as you wished. She got loose while Dog and I were out hunting. When we came back to the cave, we found White Buffalo there, wounded. She tried to kill him."

"Not accordin' to her," Preacher said with a faint smile. "She says White Buffalo tried to stop her when she was gettin' away, and tripped and fell on his own knife."

For a moment, Hawk didn't say anything. Then, "I suppose it could have happened that way. Whoever is to blame for the wound, I bound it up as quickly as I could and then went after her. Dog was able to pick up her trail right away, but she had a good lead on us." He paused, then added stubbornly, "We would have caught her."

"Maybe, but not in time. She would have made it to the village."

"She would have if she had gone straight there, too, but she tried to throw us off by circling around. That gave you time to reach the vicinity of the village before her."

"Reckon you could say she outsmarted herself."

"And now we are right back where we started, with a prisoner we do not need," Hawk said, sounding disgusted.

Preacher didn't respond. He didn't want to say anything about the canyon or where it was located. He couldn't be sure Winter Wind wasn't pretending to be unconscious. She was pretty good at that, he recalled.

When they got back to the cave, Hawk did the two owl hoots to let White Buffalo know it was them. A shaky whip-poor-will call answered.

"You brought that evil woman back with you," the

old man said in an accusing tone as they came in with the prisoner. "I hoped you would finally have sense enough to kill her."

"Our plans haven't changed," Preacher said.

"*Your* plans," White Buffalo said with a disapproving sniff.

Preacher placed Winter Wind on the ground in just about the same spot she'd been when he left that morning. She was awake, he saw, just as he suspected. Her dark eyes blazed with hatred.

He checked her bonds and gag and was satisfied they would hold, even though he had done the job hastily. He said, "Dog, guard," and then motioned with his head for Hawk and White Buffalo to follow him outside the cave.

He walked away in the darkness, far enough he was confident they were out of earshot, before he turned to the other two.

White Buffalo started to say something, but Preacher held up a hand to stop him. "If you're gonna try to tell me how everything happened, you can save your breath, old-timer. Fact of the matter is, I don't care. She got loose, but she didn't get away and she didn't tell Tall Bull where to find us. I reckon that's all that matters . . . and pretty soon, even that won't be important."

"You have found a place for us to move the camp," Hawk said.

"Yep," Preacher said with a nod. "It's a mite farther away from the Blackfoot village and in some ways it ain't as good as this cave, but in other ways it's better. Anyway, I never expected we'd stay in one place the whole time we were makin' ol' Tall Bull's life a livin' hell. I figured we'd have to move around some. The canyon's just our second stop."

"Where is this canyon?" Hawk asked.

Preacher explained where the canyon was located in general terms, then described the narrow cleft that led to it. "A couple men could hold off a good-sized war party for a long time," he concluded.

"Could not warriors climb to the high ground above the canyon and rain down arrows on any defenders?"

"Not easily. The cliffs are too tall and sheer for that. I reckon it's possible they might be able to work their way around and get above us, but they'd have to go a mighty long way around. Not only that, but they'd be exposed to get a shot at us." Preacher patted the stock of his flintlock rifle. "As long as I've got powder and shot, I could pick 'em off. It'd be rainin' all right . . . rainin' dead Blackfeet. After that happened a few times, they might not be so eager to try it again."

"This canyon sounds like it might be a good place," Hawk admitted. "We can still venture out to strike against Tall Bull, and White Buffalo can guard the place."

"Well, there's somethin' else I haven't told you fellas yet. We've picked up a couple o' unexpected allies."

"Allies?" Hawk repeated. "What sort of allies?"

"A couple greenhorn trappers who are all that's left of an expedition that came out here after pelts."

"White men, you mean," Hawk said in a disgusted tone.

"I'm a white man, you know."

"You are Preacher. You are different."

"Maybe. But these fellas are in a bind. They don't have the sort of experience they need to keep 'em alive out here. It's pure luck somethin' ain't killed 'em already. There's a heap of different ways to die out here, and they're bound to stumble over one of 'em sooner or later."

For the next few minutes, he filled his companions in on the story Todd and Buckley had told him.

White Buffalo said, "Waugghh! It sounds like an Absaroka infant knows more than these white men."

"You probably ain't far wrong about that. But they got rifles and powder and shot, and they'll be two more warm bodies in a fight. Reckon we can't ask any more than that from 'em right now, but you can't ever tell. They might turn out to be fiercer than we think they are."

"That would not take much," White Buffalo said haughtily.

Hawk nodded toward the cave. "What about the woman?"

"If she got loose as good as I had her tied up before, she can get loose from the bonds on her now," Preacher said. "In the mornin' we'll leave her there in the cave, just like we planned. Don't say nothin' in there about where we're goin' or even let on that we're leavin' for good. She'll get that idea after we've been gone for a while."

"Then she will go back to Tall Bull and tell him everything she found out about us."

"Which don't amount to much," Preacher pointed out. "She can tell him there's three of us, one white man and two Absaroka, and that's all."

"She can tell him that his enemy is the one called Preacher."

"That's fine. Some of those yarns that've been spread around about me are pretty exaggerated, but if he wants to believe 'em and they get on his nerves, then so much the better. I like the idea of Tall Bull bein' worried the Ghost Killer is gonna get him." Preacher chuckled. "I hope I come to him in his dreams and make his sleep restless. Then he'll know that when the two of us finally meet up . . . one of us is gonna die."

CHAPTER 24

With Dog standing guard over Winter Wind, the young woman didn't get another chance to try to escape that night. It wasn't long until dawn, only a few hours, but Preacher was able to get a little rest.

Anyway, his iron constitution always allowed him to bounce back quickly whenever he was exhausted or injured. Some people had said he wasn't made of anything except bone and rawhide, and the description wasn't far off the mark.

When the sun was barely up, he and Hawk led Horse and the pack mule out of the cave, but only after quickly scouting the area and determining there were no Blackfoot warriors lurking nearby, looking for them.

White Buffalo came out of the cave next, grumbling and looking back as if he wanted to kill Winter Wind before he left.

Preacher didn't blame the old man for feeling that way, but he wasn't going to allow him to indulge his hatred. He whistled for Dog, and the big cur bounded out. Sensing they were going to be on the move again soon, he was eager to get started. Horse shared that same sense of anticipation, prancing around a little as he waited with the stolid pack mule.

Watching all the movement, Winter Wind started to wonder what was going on. They had never all left her alone since she'd been captured.

Preacher didn't think it would take her long to figure things out once she realized they were gone, but she wouldn't be getting loose from those bonds any time soon. He thought it would take her until the middle of the day, at least, and by then he and his companions would be long gone.

White Buffalo was complaining of being tired well before they reached the canyon. "I lost too much blood from that terrible wound. It weakened me."

"The cut was not that big," Hawk said. "I bandaged it, remember?"

"When we get to where we're goin', we'll see to it you get plenty of good red meat," Preacher told the old man. "That'll have you back on your feet in no time."

"I am on my feet now," White Buffalo said. "That is the problem. I want to sit down and rest. And why must we always be skulking through trees and behind brush?"

"Because Tall Bull could have scoutin' parties out lookin' for us. He can't just hunker down and do nothin' after everything that's happened. That'd make him look small and cowardly in the eyes of the other warriors. He's got to try to find us and kill us."

Preacher paused, then added, "When we get ready, we're gonna let him find us, but it ain't the time yet."

"What do you mean, let him find us?" Hawk asked.

"We can't fight all those warriors in their own village. We need to get them out of there and into the open where we can get to 'em easier. In order to do that, we got to keep harassin' Tall Bull until he's mad enough to come after us with every able-bodied man in the village." Preacher shrugged. "We'll whittle that number down some more first."

Hawk considered what the mountain man had said, then slowly nodded. "So that is your plan. Do you really think we can kill them all, even if we lure them away from the village?"

"We can sure make a good try at it."

"As long as Tall Bull dies, I suppose I could live with some of his warriors getting away."

"Not White Buffalo," the old man declared. "All Blackfeet must die!"

Preacher grinned. "You're a bloodthirsty ol' savage, ain't you?"

By mid-afternoon, they hadn't encountered any Blackfoot scouts or other threats and were close to the isolated canyon. Their route had been long and circuitous, and they'd had to travel slowly due to the necessity of staying in cover as much as possible.

Preacher figured they would be at the canyon in another few minutes. "Remember, I'm expectin' you to treat those two fellas decent."

White Buffalo looked down his nose at the mountain man and said, "The white men, you mean?"

"Yeah. Charlie and Aaron. That's their names."

"I will not be friends with them, but I will not kill them."

"Nice of you," Preacher said dryly.

They came in sight of the cleft leading to the canyon, and Preacher hailed Todd and Buckley, though he wasn't completely sure they would answer. He had told them to stay there and wait for him, but as greenhorns they were capable of doing almost anything, even things a veteran frontiersman wouldn't anticipate.

Charlie Todd came strolling out of the cleft and called, "Preacher! Hello! Are these your friends?"

Behind Preacher, White Buffalo made a low, disgusted sound in his throat.

"That is not a cautious man," Hawk said quietly.

"He'll learn," Preacher said, then added as much to himself as to the others, "if he lives long enough."

They walked up to Todd, who cast suspicious glances toward the two Absaroka. Even though Preacher had explained to him about how they belonged to a tribe that was friendly to white men, seeing the two Indians clearly made Todd a little nervous.

"Charlie, this is Hawk That Soars and White Buffalo," Preacher said, nodding to each of them in turn as he performed the introductions. He didn't explain about Hawk being his son. It didn't seem relevant at the moment.

"Do they, uh, speak English?" Todd asked.

Hawk said, "I speak . . . little English."

White Buffalo scolded him in their language. "Do

not use the white man's tongue. It sounds ugly and stupid."

Todd nodded to Hawk and said, "Then I'm pleased to meet you, Hawk That Soars. I hope we'll be friends."

Hawk just grunted.

"Where's Buckley?" Preacher asked.

Todd pointed over his shoulder with a thumb. "He's back in the canyon cooking a rabbit we caught. I've gotten not too bad at rigging a snare, if I do say so myself. We weren't sure when you fellows would get here, but we thought you might be hungry when you did."

White Buffalo might not have understood what Todd was saying, but the old man sniffed the air suddenly and asked Preacher, "Is that the smell of meat cooking?"

"It sure is," Preacher told him, grinning. "They got a rabbit roastin' in there. Still think white men are so bad?"

"One rabbit does not change things . . . but White Buffalo *is* hungry."

"What's he saying?" Todd asked.

Preacher chuckled. "Lead us to that rabbit."

When he met Hawk and White Buffalo, Aaron Buckley was just as nervous as Todd had been. Preacher thought for a second the young man was going to offer to shake hands but then he changed his mind and nodded and smiled pleasantly. He repeated what Todd had said about hoping they would all be friends.

"Rabbit," Hawk said, pointing to the carcass roasting on a spit over a small fire.

"I, uh, don't think it's quite done yet—"

"Rabbit!"

"But of course if you want to go ahead and eat it, that . . . that's fine," Buckley stammered.

"We're hungry," Preacher said. "That means we ain't quite as persnickety about our vittles as some folks might be." He took the spit away from the fire, let the rabbit cool for a few minutes, and then cut it up with his knife and shared the pieces with Hawk and White Buffalo. They hunkered down on their heels while they ate. Preacher tossed a few bits of roasted rabbit to Dog, who ate them but wasn't all that enthusiastic about them. The big cur preferred his meat raw and freshly killed.

"Is that a wolf?" Todd asked.

"You ain't the first one to wonder about that," Preacher told him. "No, that big fella's a dog. I ain't sayin' he don't have some wolf blood in him, somewhere along the line, but he's mostly dog."

"What's his name?" Buckley said.

"I call him Dog."

"Really?" Todd said. "What's your horse's name? Horse?"

"As a matter of fact—"

"I'm sorry." Todd held up his hands and said quickly, "I meant no offense. Dog and Horse are perfectly fine names. And no one ever wonders who you're talking about."

"That's sort of what I figured."

Buckley said, "I guess that means . . . the mule's name is Mule?"

Preacher couldn't resist translating the question for Hawk and White Buffalo.

The old man cackled with laughter and slapped a gnarled hand against his buckskin-clad thigh. "Crazy white men!" he said between cackles. "The mule has no name!"

Todd and Buckley were clearly confused and wanted to know what was going on.

Preacher told them, not unkindly, "White Buffalo calls it the Mule With No Name. He claims he can talk to animals and they can talk right back to him."

"Do you believe him?" Buckley said.

"Let me put it this way . . . I don't *dis*believe him. He's a mite touched in the head, but sometimes it seems like he knows what he's talkin' about."

Todd turned to the old man. "Thank you, White Buffalo, for telling us about the Mule With No Name."

Preacher translated.

White Buffalo nodded and said around a mouthful of half-chewed rabbit, "These crazy white men may not be so bad after all. At least they know to respect their elders."

"But can they really help us get our revenge on Tall Bull?" Hawk asked.

Preacher looked him in the eye. "I reckon we're liable to find out before too much longer."

CHAPTER 25

The two trappers volunteered to take shifts at standing guard, but Preacher didn't have enough confidence in them yet to entrust all their lives to the greenhorns. He solved that slight awkwardness by saying, "You and me can take one turn, Charlie, while Aaron and Hawk take the other."

If they knew why he made that decision, they gave no sign of being offended. Hawk and Buckley stood the first watch, while everybody else turned in once night had fallen.

Preacher roused from sleep without anyone having to wake him when the time came. That ability to wake up whenever he wanted to was one he had developed quickly after leaving the family farm and coming to the frontier.

Charlie Todd was wrapped up in a blanket nearby, snoring softly. Preacher reached over and shook his shoulder, saying, "Time to get up, Charlie."

Todd came out of slumber flailing and sputtering.

Preacher tightened his grip on the young trapper's

shoulder. "Take it easy," the mountain man said in a low, urgent voice. "Nothin's wrong. It's just time for us to stand guard."

The calming words seemed to get through to Todd. He settled down, then pushed himself to a sitting position, raked his fingers through his tangled brown hair, and scrubbed his hands over his face. "Sorry. I was, uh, dreaming that Indians were chasing me."

"Blackfeet?"

"I guess. Although to be honest, I can't really tell any difference in them, no matter what tribe they're from."

That sounded strange to Preacher, who could tell at a glance which tribe a warrior belonged to. Their clothing, the way they wore their hair, the sort of decorations they sported, the paint on their faces . . . all those things were distinctive and indicated a man's tribal affiliation.

No point in explaining that to Todd. He would learn if he survived long enough.

Preacher said, "Right now, all you've got to remember is that if you see an Indian who ain't either Hawk or White Buffalo, chances are he's an enemy and you need to avoid him."

"You mean I shouldn't shoot him?"

"Not until you're sure what's goin' on. He might have fifty friends with him, right around the bend, who'll come tearin' after you."

"I wouldn't want that."

"No," Preacher agreed, "you wouldn't. Best to avoid trouble, if you can."

"Is that what you do?"

Preacher chuckled. "Well, no. Most people would say I go out huntin' trouble. But I've had a heap more experience dealin' with it than you have."

"The only way to gain experience is to live life to the fullest. That's what Aaron and I were trying to do when we decided to come out here. We met and became friends in college, you know. We were students at the University of Virginia, the school President Jefferson founded."

"I've got a friend who taught at some college back east, but I ain't rightly sure which one. He gave it up to come west and be a trapper, like you fellas."

"A professor turned fur trapper. He sounds like a fascinating fellow."

"Oh, he is," Preacher said, smiling to himself as he thought about the diminutive Audie and his friend Nighthawk, a towering, laconic warrior from a branch of the Crow tribe different from the Absaroka.

The mountain man picked up his rifle, climbed to his feet, and motioned for Todd to follow him. "Come on, Charlie. We'd better let Hawk and Aaron get some rest."

They moved into the passage where the sentries were keeping an eye on the mouth of the cleft. Not wanting to startle them, Preacher made enough noise so Hawk would hear them coming, whether Buckley did or not.

"No sign . . . of trouble," Hawk said in English when Preacher and Todd came up to them.

"Hawk and I have been talking about everything that's happened with Tall Bull and the Blackfeet," Buckley said. "Charlie and I will be glad to help you any way we can, Preacher. Tall Bull needs to be stopped. He can't just go around the country killing anyone he thinks is in his way."

"He'll get what's comin' to him," Preacher said. "It may take a while, but fate usually catches up to a fella."

Buckley yawned. "We can go get some sleep now?"

"Go ahead," Preacher told him. "Charlie and me will keep our eyes and ears open. Ain't that right, Charlie?"

The question caught Todd in the middle of a yawn, too. He recovered hastily and said, "Sure, that's right, Preacher."

Hawk grunted and stalked off.

Buckley lingered for a moment and said quietly, "I get the feeling he'd like to be friends, but he doesn't quite know how. Not yet, anyway. He's never spent much time around whites much, has he?"

"Nope, I reckon not, just a trapper every now and then," Preacher said. "He's like any young fella, no matter what color. He's still got a lot to learn in this world."

Preacher had to poke Charlie Todd's arm a couple times during the night to wake him. Like a horse, Todd possessed the ability to sleep standing up. Preacher wasn't sure whether to be annoyed or amused by the young man.

Nothing unusual happened while they were standing watch. He was confident the Blackfeet had no idea where the men who had been bedeviling them were holed up.

As the sun began to appear over the eastern horizon, the fiery orb sent rays of garish red light through the cleft and into the canyon. It was beautiful in a way, but it also gave the place a sort of hellish air, like the canyon was actually a gateway to Hades.

Luckily, he wasn't the sort to believe in omens, Preacher thought.

Their breakfast was what was left of the rabbit Todd and Buckley had snared the day before. As they ate, Preacher said to Hawk and White Buffalo in the Absaroka tongue, "By now, Winter Wind has gotten back to the Blackfoot village and told Tall Bull everything that happened to her. He'll probably send a search party out to have a look around the area where that cave is."

"He will not expect us to still be there," Hawk said.

"Probably not, but he's got nowhere else to start looking. That means there'll be fewer warriors in the village today."

"So you can go there and kill all of them," White Buffalo said.

Preacher laughed. "I reckon Hawk and me would still be outnumbered by a whole lot, but maybe we can improve the odds a mite."

"You mean to go into the village in broad daylight?" Hawk asked.

"That's what I've got in mind. We might get a crack at Tall Bull himself."

Hawk stared steadily at Preacher as he said, "Tall Bull is mine to kill."

"I understand why you feel that way, and I don't blame you . . . but I can't make you any promises."

"Gitche Manitou will see to it that I kill Tall Bull."

"I hope you're right, if that's what you want."

The two novice trappers had listened to the conversation with great interest but no understanding at all until Preacher gave them a quick summary of what was said.

Buckley asked, "So you're leaving us here with White Buffalo?"

"And Horse and the mule, that's right. It ain't likely any of the Blackfeet will find this place, but it's your job to protect it if any come along. Don't start a ruckus if you don't have to, though. Stay out of sight. If they don't come all the way into the canyon, they'll never see you and the animals. If they do . . . that's when you'll have to fight."

Buckley nodded in understanding.

Todd just looked nervous. "We can trust White Buffalo, right?"

"He gave me his word he wouldn't kill you," Preacher said with a smile. "I don't think you fellas have anything to worry about. I wouldn't say he's all talk, but he ain't exactly in any shape to be ferocious, neither."

Preacher and Hawk departed from the canyon a short time later, taking Dog with them.

When they had gone a short distance, Preacher commented, "Aaron said you and him talked quite a bit last night while the two of you was standin' guard. Practicin' your English, were you?"

"It is the tongue of my father," Hawk said. "I should know how to speak it."

Hearing that made Preacher feel surprisingly good. "There's some folks who'd say I don't speak it none too good myself. Audie claims my grammar is positively shameful."

"Do people understand what you tell them?"

"Mostly they do, I reckon."

"Then there is nothing wrong with the way you talk."

"That's one way to look at it," Preacher said. "I'm glad you and Aaron got along all right."

"He was . . . interesting. He said he studied to be a . . . lawyer. I do not know what that is."

"Well, white folks have all sorts of rules about what they can do and how they treat each other. Lawyers are the ones who explain those rules to everybody and sort things out when folks go to arguin'."

"It would seem to me the fewer rules people have to remember, the better things will be. And when two men disagree, there is a simple way to settle the matter."

Preacher grinned. "Now you're makin' too much sense. You could never be a lawyer or a politician, Hawk. Those are the fellas who make the rules."

Hawk looked horrified. "Why would I ever *want* to be?"

Preacher just laughed. "That's a mighty good question."

CHAPTER 26

Knowing that Tall Bull likely had an idea where the cave was, Preacher and Hawk circled wide of the village so they could approach it from the opposite direction. The Blackfeet would be alert for trouble from any direction—that was just their nature—but they might not be expecting it quite as much from that way.

It was late morning by the time the two of them drew near to the village on the side opposite the creek Preacher had used to sneak up on the tepees a few nights earlier. He and Hawk paused on top of the long, rugged, wooded ridge that overlooked the village. Invisible in the undergrowth, they studied the collection of dwellings.

Dogs barked and women moved around, going about the usual tasks of day-to-day life. Young children played, but the older ones worked at various chores. Preacher saw a couple old men sitting on a log, not doing much of anything except possibly reliving better days.

Half a dozen warriors were in sight, but he didn't

believe they were the only ones in the village. Others were likely in the tepees. Tall Bull would not have left his village so apparently defenseless.

Hawk thought the same thing. He said quietly, "It is a trap."

"Yeah, I reckon he thinks he's one step ahead of us," Preacher said. "I don't doubt he sent a search party to check out what Winter Wind told him about the cave, but the rest of the warriors will be somewhere close by, waitin' for us to think they're all gone so we'll try to slip into the village."

"Which is exactly what you intended to do," Hawk pointed out.

"But now that he knows what I was thinkin', I know what he's thinkin'. He thinks he knows what I'm gonna do."

"And he was right. So you must do something else."

"Nope," Preacher said. "I'm gonna do just what I set out to do."

"But that means walking right into Tall Bull's trap!"

"And when I walk right out again, how do you think that's gonna make him feel?"

Hawk stared at Preacher for a long moment, then said, "We have barely started to avenge the deaths of my people. I will not throw away my life so soon."

"Ain't askin' you to. You're gonna stay here while I go down there."

"I do not like that idea, either," Hawk said with a frown.

"It ain't as risky as it sounds. Those reinforcements Tall Bull's got hidden somewhere close by will be waitin' for a signal from the warriors left in the village.

All I've got to do is make sure they don't give that signal."

"How will you do that?"

"By killin' 'em all," Preacher said.

Again Hawk looked at him in silence as several seconds passed. Then the young man said, "You do not lack for courage and daring."

"Sometimes that is a way of tellin' a fella he ain't got any good sense." Preacher chuckled. "Whether it's one way or the other usually depends on how everything turns out." He rose to his feet. "You stay here while Dog and me go visitin'."

"I do not like this, Preacher."

"It's all right. If we don't come back, you'll carry on. I got faith in you, son." He meant every word of that, and it felt good saying it. He had called Hawk *son* before, but he was finally starting to mean it. He reached down and squeezed Hawk's shoulder for a second then started down from the ridge, moving with his usual stealthy expertise. Dog followed him like a gray shadow. No one was likely to see them unless Preacher wanted them to.

The slope was rugged, forcing them to zigzag as they descended, but there were enough rocks and hardy brush to provide cover for them. He knew better than to get in a hurry. He took his time and made sure it was safe before he moved. He also kept an eye on the village and picked out one of the warriors. Burly and broad-shouldered, he kept looking sharply in one direction and then another as he moved around the village. Clearly he was on guard against something . . . or *someone*.

Preacher smiled to himself. The broad-shouldered

warrior, like the others who had been left in the village, was serving as bait in a trap, but he wasn't very good at it. He was on edge, and that would warn anyone trying to sneak up on the place that not all was as it appeared to be.

Some of the brush and trees had been cleared away between the tepees and the bottom of the ridge, to make it harder for an enemy to approach unseen that way, but Preacher didn't intend to move all the way in on the village just yet. He whispered, "Dog, stay," and glided a little closer. Crouching in the brush, he waited until he saw the broad-shouldered warrior glance in his direction and then gave the branches a good shaking for a second before moving several feet off to the side without disturbing any of the growth.

The Blackfoot started to look away, then turned his head back sharply toward Preacher's position as he realized he had seen something out of place.

Preacher waited, motionless. He knew the lack of movement would be intriguing to the warrior. The man might try to convince himself he hadn't really seen anything, but the tension gripping him wouldn't allow him to ignore the possibility.

Even from that distance, Preacher could practically see the warrior's mind struggling to decide what to do.

He could get some of the other men in the village to help him investigate, but if it turned out nothing was there, he would look foolish. Or he could take a closer look himself, which was riskier but also held the promise of more reward if he captured the predator who had been stalking his band of Blackfeet for days.

After a minute or so, the warrior started toward the brush where Preacher waited, unmoving. The mountain man grinned as he watched his quarry come closer.

The warrior's hand went to his waist and pulled his tomahawk from the loop that held it there. He tightened his grip on it. He paused a few feet away from the spot where Preacher had shaken the brush.

Through a tiny gap, Preacher watched as a puzzled frown creased the warrior's forehead. The man couldn't see or hear anything moving around, but he was sure something had been there a few minutes earlier. Cautiously, the warrior parted the brush and stepped into it with his tomahawk held ready to strike.

Preacher crouched in the thick growth, so close he could have almost reached out and touched the Blackfoot's leg as he moved past. Preacher let him keep going, though. The warrior stalked deeper into the brush, making it more difficult for anyone to see him.

Preacher cast a quick glance toward the village. No one appeared to be paying any attention to what was going on in the brush. No one seemed the least interested in the warrior poking around in it nor curious enough to come find out what it was about.

Easing out of his hiding place, Preacher became the hunter instead of the hunted.

The warrior was half a foot shorter than him but probably weighed as much or even more. His buckskin shirt bulged with muscles. He might not be the brightest fella in the world, Preacher thought, but he was willing to bet the warrior was a hell of a fighter.

Because he didn't want a big commotion that would alert the village, Preacher figured he would strike hard and fast and put the warrior down before the man knew what hit him. Silent as a wraith, he moved closer and lifted his tomahawk for a killing blow.

Before the weapon could flash down, the warrior stopped short, made a disgusted sound, and started to turn around, deciding he'd been seeing things after all and nobody was out there. That gave him just enough of a chance to spot Preacher from the corner of his eye as the tomahawk fell. The warrior flung up his own weapon, and while it couldn't completely stop the terrific force of the blow, it was enough to turn Preacher's tomahawk aside slightly. The stone head struck the warrior's left shoulder instead of crushing his skull.

The man opened his mouth to shout in a combination of pain and alarm, but Preacher lunged forward and barreled into him. His left hand locked around the warrior's throat before any sound could come out. They lost their footing and fell onto the carpet of old pine needles under the trees. Sharp branches in the brush around them clawed at their clothes and skin.

The Blackfoot swatted at Preacher's head with his tomahawk. Preacher jerked aside from the blow and launched another strike of his own. The warrior blocked it. His left arm seemed useless from the wallop on his shoulder, but he was using his right arm with desperate speed and fierce determination.

Preacher kept his left hand clamped around the man's throat to prevent any outcries as they wrestled in the brush. A shout of warning would ruin his plans. He was confident that he, Hawk, and Dog could get away from any pursuit, but that would mean he hadn't taken full advantage of this opportunity.

The Blackfoot rammed a knee into Preacher's side

with bone-jarring force. The impact knocked Preacher to the side, but he didn't lose his grip on the enemy's throat. As they rolled, the warrior's tomahawk clipped Preacher on the side of the head.

The world spun crazily for a second, but Preacher recovered quickly and turned aside another blow that would have split his face open if it had landed. He backhanded his tomahawk to the warrior's jaw with enough force to break it. The man's eyes widened in agony, but still no sound escaped from his mouth.

With pain slowing the warrior's reflexes and sapping his strength, Preacher drove a knee into the Blackfoot's belly and pinned him to the ground. The mountain man's tomahawk rose and fell again, and the warrior couldn't turn it aside. It crunched into the middle of his forehead, shattering bone and pulping the brain underneath. He bucked and writhed in his death throes, then fell back limply.

Preacher waited until life had faded completely from the man's eyes before letting go of his throat and standing up.

Instantly, he turned toward the village and moved back to his former position to see if anyone had noticed what was going on. Everything looked just as it had before, with one exception. A warrior was walking back and forth and looking around as if puzzled. He lifted his voice and called out a couple times.

Preacher couldn't make out the words, but he was willing to bet that warrior was looking for the man he had just killed and probably calling his name.

Preacher whistled too softly for anyone in the village to hear, but Dog heard and came up beside him. The big cur growled a little.

"You scoldin' me for gettin' into a fight without you?" Preacher asked, smiling. "Don't worry, I reckon there'll be work for you to do pretty soon." His eyes narrowed as he saw the warrior talking to another man.

Then they turned and started toward the trees.

"In fact," Preacher told Dog, "it looks like we've done hooked ourselves another couple o' fish."

CHAPTER 27

Preacher and Dog eased back deeper into the brush as the two warriors approached. It wouldn't do to jump the Blackfeet at the edge of the growth where the ruckus would be easily visible from the village.

The men wore wary expressions. Like the missing warrior, they held their tomahawks ready for action. With everything that had happened in recent days, they were expecting trouble, and who could blame them?

Caution wasn't going to help them, Preacher thought. Not if he and Dog had anything to say about it, and they did.

The warriors entered the brush at a spot different from where the first man walked in.

Preacher wanted them to find the body, figuring the sight of it would shock them into immobility for a second and give him a better chance to jump them. He picked up a broken branch and flipped it in the direction he wanted the warriors to go. It didn't make much of a sound when it landed, but it was enough.

Both men stiffened and jerked around in that

direction. They crept toward the spot, tomahawks lifted and poised to strike.

Preacher and Dog stayed where they were and let the warriors go right past them. Dog was crouched low, ready to spring, but he wouldn't move even a fraction of an inch until Preacher gave the command.

Preacher heard one of the men let out a sharp, surprised grunt and knew they had stumbled upon the body of their fallen fellow warrior.

It was time!

"Go!"

The whispered command unleashed Dog and turned the big cur into a leaping, lethal gray streak. He tore through the brush and slammed into one of the warriors from behind, knocking the man to his knees and then driving him forward on his face. Dog's powerful jaws locked onto the side of his neck and began crushing and ripping.

The other man was barely aware something was wrong before Preacher's left arm encircled his neck from behind and yanked him back onto the knife in the mountain man's right hand. The blade went deep into the warrior's body. He died without a sound as it sliced his heart open.

Dog's victim let out a gurgle as blood sprayed from his ravaged throat, but the grotesque noise couldn't have been heard more than a few yards away, certainly not in the village. Dog bit down again and shook hard, and with a crack of bone, the warrior's head separated from his body and rolled a couple feet away.

The warrior's eyes were still wide and uncomprehending. He had died without ever understanding what was happening to him.

Preacher lowered the corpse he held to the ground. Three more Blackfoot warriors were dead, a good day's work by anyone's accounting.

He wanted more, though. He thought about Birdie and Little Pine and everyone else back in the Absaroka village Tall Bull had wiped out. The scales of justice weren't as unbalanced as they had been, but they weren't even yet.

He reached down, picked up the head of the warrior Dog had decapitated, and looked around until he found a sturdy branch in a suitable position. He stuck the head on it and made sure it would be visible from the village.

It was a pretty raw thing to do, he thought, but Tall Bull had brought it on himself by slaughtering the Absaroka.

"Come on, Dog," he whispered. "Let's get back to Hawk."

The young man jumped slightly as Preacher and Dog eased up next to him. He controlled the reaction very quickly, but not in time to keep Preacher from noticing it. Hawk hadn't known they were there.

Preacher didn't see any point in mentioning that fact. It would just embarrass Hawk needlessly. Anyway, there was no shame in having Preacher and Dog sneak up on him. It had happened to plenty of other fellows over Preacher's long years on the frontier.

He said quietly, "We got three more of 'em."

Hawk nodded. "I saw those warriors go into the

brush and not return. Thought you must have killed them."

"Yep. Dog tore the head right off one of 'em, in fact. I stuck it up on a branch so they'll see it in the village if they look very close."

Hawk's eyes widened. "That is . . ." He gave a little shake of his head as he failed to find the words to describe what he was feeling.

"Yeah, I know. I ain't sayin' I feel all that good about doin' it. But it'll shake 'em up, and that's what we want. Let's back off, head downstream a ways, and then cross over so we can come up the creek again on the other side of the village."

"Why should we do that?"

"Because once they spot that varmint's head, they'll all be lookin' in this direction instead of watchin' the creek. I figure all the warriors Tall Bull left behind will come tearin' out here to see what's goin' on."

"Leaving the village unprotected," Hawk said.

Preacher inclined his head in agreement.

They moved as quickly as possible without drawing attention to themselves as they went back up the ridge and then hurried along its crest. Preacher listened for any outcry from the village, but there was no way of knowing when someone would notice the grisly thing staring sightlessly at them from the brush. He hadn't heard anything by the time he and Hawk were out of earshot.

They descended from the ridge, crossed the creek, and headed back toward the village, staying under cover as much as they could. They didn't know where more of Tall Bull's warriors might be lurking.

As they got closer, they heard shouts and a quick grin appeared on Preacher's face. "Sounds like somebody spotted that unfortunate fella."

They climbed the bank to take a surreptitious look at the village. A dozen warriors were hurrying across the open ground toward the ridge. They bristled with tomahawks, knives, and bows and arrows.

Behind them, gathered at the edge of the tepees, was a large group of women, children, and old men, along with two warriors left to guard them.

Preacher nodded toward those two warriors as he and Hawk exchanged a grim glance. They pulled themselves over the edge of the creek bank and started toward the village at a run, their moccasin-shod feet making hardly any sound in the grass. Dog bounded behind them.

As they cut through the village, racing between tepees, Preacher saw that the larger group of warriors had reached the brush. More angry shouts went up, signifying that they had found the other bodies.

Several of the women—wives or relatives of the missing men—were wailing. Based on everything they had seen so far, they assumed the men were dead. The commotion helped cover up any sounds Preacher and Hawk made as they closed in on the two warriors left behind in the village.

One of the women spotted them and let out a frightened scream. The warning came too late. Preacher and Hawk were already striking swiftly and savagely with tomahawks in hand.

The Blackfoot twisted desperately, trying to get out of the path of Preacher's attack, but he was no match for the mountain man's lethal speed. The tomahawk smashed against the Blackfoot's jaw with such terrible force it practically tore the bottom half of the man's face off.

The warrior didn't suffer for long. A split second later the tomahawk looped back and shattered his skull, dropping him already dead to the ground.

A few yards away, Hawk broke his man's arm with a stroke of his weapon and then kicked the man in the belly, doubling him over. The tomahawk rose and fell, crushing the back of the warrior's skull and dumping his corpse in the dirt.

With all the women screaming, Preacher knew their hysterics would soon attract the attention of the other warriors and bring them back at a run.

Some of the old men and older boys moved toward Preacher and Hawk, obviously wanting to fight them but made wary by the violent spectacle they had just witnessed.

"Stay back," Preacher told them in the Blackfoot tongue as he and Hawk stood shoulder to shoulder. Dog was in front of them, growling menacingly. "We do not make war on women, children, and old men."

"You are the Ghost Killer!" an old man said in a voice that quavered with age. "Why have you come among us?"

"To seek revenge for the spirits of the cruelly slain Absaroka!"

"Tall Bull said they had to be slain. He said they were not like the Blackfeet, so they must die."

"Tall Bull was wrong, and now all the Blackfeet will pay for his evil arrogance." Preacher's voice rose. "The Ghost Killer swears this! The woman and children will cry and be left alone to mourn their husbands and fathers because of Tall Bull alone!"

He and Hawk backed away. It would have been nice to kill all the warriors Tall Bull had left in the village, but Preacher figured they had sent a pretty potent message already by killing five more men and penetrating the village in broad daylight.

Preacher knew the words he had spoken would infuriate Tall Bull even more when the war chief heard them. Not only that, but he would have to respond to the challenge Preacher had flung in his face, otherwise his grip on the tribe would slip even more than it must have already.

The old men and the boys didn't press them as they retreated toward the creek. Preacher glanced toward the ridge and saw some of the warriors starting back to find out why the crying in the village had grown louder. He and Hawk would have some pursuers on their trail, he knew, but he was confident they could slip away.

Another figure rushed out from the group in the village, and a clear voice cried, "You say you do not make war on women, but you will fight this one or die!"

Winter Wind charged them, her long, buckskin-clad legs flashing over the ground. She had a tomahawk in one hand, a knife in the other, and a killing hate blazed in her eyes.

CHAPTER 28

"Go!" Hawk flung over his shoulder at Preacher as he leaped forward to meet Winter Wind's attack.

Reacting faster than Hawk, Preacher had already pulled one of the pistols from behind his belt. He cocked the hammer, leveled the gun, and squeezed the trigger. It was one of the trickier shots he had ever made in his life, firing past Hawk. With the pistol double-shotted, there was always the chance one of the balls would clip the young man. In the split second before he pulled the trigger, he shaded his aim to the right as much as he dared.

The shot was perfect. Both balls whipped past Hawk without touching him. One missed Winter Wind as well, but the other struck her in the upper left arm. Preacher's intent had been to stop her, not kill her.

She cried out in pain and dropped both weapons as she clutched her wounded arm with her other hand. Her momentum carried her a couple stumbling steps forward before she twisted and collapsed.

"Come on!" Preacher shouted at Hawk. "Let's

go!" The sound of the shot would make the warriors converge faster on the village.

Hawk came to a stop and stared for a second at the fallen Winter Wind, who lay on the ground writhing in pain and shouting angrily, then he whirled and dashed toward Preacher and Dog.

All three of them flew off the creek bank in high, arching leaps that carried them all the way across the stream below and landed them on the lower opposite bank. Dog hit running, but Preacher and Hawk fell and rolled before they were up on their feet again.

Outraged howls lifted from the village behind them. The warriors had found their fallen comrades and discovered that Preacher and Hawk had been inside the village itself.

The two raiders didn't have time to conceal their tracks. Speed was all that mattered, putting as much distance as they could between themselves and the inevitable pursuit. They ran through woods and across meadows. Preacher couldn't hear the Blackfeet anymore, but he knew they were on the trail already.

Neither man wasted any breath talking. They moved at top speed toward Beartooth, taking them in the opposite direction from the isolated canyon where they had left White Buffalo, Charlie Todd, and Aaron Buckley. That was the best way to protect the location of the hideout and keep the old-timer and the two greenhorns safe.

Exhaustion finally forced them to stop and rest for a few minutes. Hawk leaned over and rested his hands on his knees as he breathed heavily. Preacher leaned against a tree trunk. His pulse was galloping madly.

"You . . . you shot that girl," Hawk said after a minute or so.

"You were gonna . . . fight her," Preacher said. "Shootin' was . . . quicker."

"I would have . . . fought them all . . . and given you . . . a better chance to escape."

"Thought you didn't want to . . . throw your life away." Preacher was getting his breath back. "You wouldn't have stood a chance . . . against the whole bunch."

"You did not . . . kill her."

"I just wanted to stop her, and stop you from wastin' time better spent givin' those varmints the slip . . . which is what we're gonna do now. After we came through the pass, I saw an area on the mountain's shoulder where it breaks off in a series of cliffs. They looked rugged enough to climb, and we wouldn't leave no trail goin' up 'em. We'll head for that spot."

Hawk straightened and nodded. "I know the place you mean. I saw it, as well. It will be a hard climb, but we can do it. Then we can work our way over to the pass and up the other side of the valley, back to the canyon where we left the others."

"We ought to make it by sometime tomorrow," Preacher said. "You up to movin' fast again?"

"I will lead the way," Hawk said.

Preacher smiled as the young man moved out on the run. He and Dog followed close behind.

A few times during the long afternoon, they caught sight of the pursuing warriors far behind them, but the Blackfeet never came close enough to start howling in anticipation of catching their quarry.

Preacher and Hawk reached the cliffs in the gloom of twilight. The almost sheer rock walls loomed above them with an air of overpowering menace. Hawk tipped his head back to peer up at them, and Preacher could sense what the young man was thinking.

"We can climb 'em," the mountain man said.

"In the dark." Hawk sounded skeptical.

"If we climb 'em in the dark, ain't no way those fellas who are chasin' us will be able to see us, is there? As far as they're concerned, we'll have vanished into thin air, and that'll spook them Blackfeet even more."

"You are right," Hawk said, but he didn't sound particularly convinced. "What about Dog?"

"He can get back to the canyon on his own. If the Blackfeet spot him, they'll just take him for a wolf." Preacher went down on one knee and curled his fingers in the thick fur on the back of Dog's neck. "You go on back to White Buffalo and those two young fellas, Dog. Hawk and me will see you when we get back to the canyon."

The big cur whined softly.

"I know," Preacher said. "But there ain't no way you can climb these cliffs. You'd have to be a mountain goat, and you ain't. Now skedaddle, and we'll see you tomorrow."

Dog turned and trotted off, but he paused once and looked back before he disappeared into a thicket of trees.

"Perhaps White Buffalo is not the only one who can talk to animals," Hawk said when Dog was gone.

"Anybody can, if they just pay attention." Preacher started toward the base of the first cliff.

"Wait," Hawk said. "I will go first. If you fall, you will not knock me off, too."

"All right, then," Preacher replied with a chuckle. "Up you go."

The climb was a harrowing one. Preacher and Hawk had to move extremely slowly, working by feel to find each new handhold and foothold before they entrusted their weight to it. They measured their progress in inches, but it was steady.

The darkness that closed in around them had another advantage. As they climbed higher and higher, they couldn't see how far it was to the ground below them. All that existed for them was the small area of rock face to which they clung.

When they came to the top and rolled over onto level ground, both men just lay there for long minutes as their muscles quivered with relief.

When Preacher finally sat up, he said quietly, "Well, that wasn't so bad. Now we just got to do it two or three more times."

Hawk groaned. "Are you made of the white man's iron, Preacher? Or the red man's flint?"

"I'd say some o' both, but that's a better description of you, I reckon."

Hawk sat up and rested his arms on his drawn-up knees. "How can a man as old as you keep going like this?"

"I've found the years don't matter as much if you just don't let yourself feel 'em." Preacher tapped a fist lightly against his chest. "In my heart, I'm still the kid who came out here more 'n twenty years ago to see what was on the other side of the mountain. The body's bound to slow down some as time goes by, but if you can keep that kid alive inside of you, you can always do more than you think you can."

Hawk thought about that and nodded slowly. "Those are good words. I will remember them."

"I wasn't actually tryin' to teach you a lesson or nothin' like that. You asked me a question and I just answered it, that's all."

"I do not mind you teaching me things. My mother said you were the smartest man she ever knew."

Preacher snorted. "I never claimed to be no genius. My little pard Audie might be, but I ain't."

"But you have much wisdom to impart."

"Aw, hell, you're just havin' sport with me now!" Preacher jerked a thumb upward. "You've lollygagged around enough for a while. Get up that cliff!"

In the starlight, he thought he caught a glimpse of Hawk grinning as the young man stood up and trotted toward the base of the next cliff rising above them.

The climb took all night. When they finally reached the top of the last cliff they were high above the valley of the Blackfeet, even though Beartooth itself still towered dizzyingly above them. Confident they had escaped any pursuit from Tall Bull and his warriors, they stretched out on the ground and slept. Preacher relied on his instincts and keen senses to rouse him if any sort of threat came near them.

Utterly exhausted, they slept for several hours. Preacher woke first, stood up and stretched stiff muscles, then took a look around to make sure everything was all right. They seemed to be the only ones on the side of the mountain except for the birds in the trees, a few small animals rustling in the brush, and some goats higher still on the bare, rocky sides of the peak above the tree line, like the ones he had mentioned to Dog.

"Rattle your hocks, son," he said in English to Hawk.

The young man sat up, yawned hugely, and said in the same tongue, "What is . . . rattle hocks?"

"Shake a leg. Get movin'. We got places to go. White Buffalo and Charlie and Aaron are probably startin' to get a mite worried by now, since we didn't show up yesterday."

"We did not tell them when we would be back," Hawk pointed out.

"No, but I'll bet they're gettin' restless anyway, and it'll still take us most o' the day to get back from here. That is, if we don't run into any more trouble. I don't want those fellas wanderin' off and gettin' theirselves into some tight spot."

Hawk nodded and pushed himself to his feet. "You are right—" He broke off as Preacher suddenly stiffened.

He'd caught a whiff of a rank, distinctive odor. The mountain man wheeled around swiftly—

Just in time to see the huge, shaggy figure of a grizzly bear burst out of some nearby brush and charge them.

CHAPTER 29

The most dangerous creature on the frontier, other than man himself, was the grizzly—Old Ephraim, as some of the mountain men referred to the beasts. Eight feet and sometimes more than a thousand pounds of furred, ferocious, bad-tempered fury.

Worst of all was a mama with cubs nearby. Preacher didn't know if that was the case and didn't care. This bear was mad as hell, and the reason didn't matter.

He didn't want to fire his pistols. The sound of shots could travel a long way in the thin air and would serve as a beacon to any Blackfoot warriors still searching for them. He didn't really have much of a choice, though.

He jerked out both pistols, which were already loaded and primed, cocked them, and pulled the triggers. In the mountain stillness, the double boom was as loud as a peal of thunder. He knew he hadn't missed a target as tall and wide as the grizzly. All four balls had gone into that incredibly powerful body . . . but they didn't slow the attacking bear.

It continued charging toward Preacher and Hawk.

At first glance the massive creature's gait appeared lumbering, but the bear covered ground with surprising speed.

Preacher knew it was almost impossible to outrun a grizzly on open ground. Sometimes, if a man scampered fast enough, he might reach a tree in time to climb it and get out of the bear's reach that way. Then he could hang on for dear life and pray the bear would get bored and wander off.

Sometimes the bear just pushed the tree down and got the unlucky fella anyway.

There weren't any trees big enough and close enough for Preacher and Hawk to even attempt that. Preacher knew he had only one option.

He dropped the empty pistols, yanked his knife from its sheath, and leaped ahead to meet the bear's charge.

"Preacher, no!" Hawk cried, but it was too late to stop the mountain man.

Anyway, there was nothing Hawk could do. His arrows would have even less effect on the grizzly than Preacher's pistol shots had.

Preacher yelled and waved his arms. Bears couldn't see very well, although they had keen senses of smell and hearing, so it took quite a bit to distract them. This grizzly slowed as Preacher continued hopping and waving right in front of him. A huge paw tipped with razor-sharp claws slashed at the mountain man with blinding speed.

The blow could have knocked Preacher's head right off his shoulders or ripped his chest open to the spine, depending on where it landed. He made sure it didn't land at all by ducking under it and then whipping the knife around in a stroke that cut through the underside of the bear's front leg.

As the grizzly bellowed, Preacher darted closer. The blade flickered in and out as he thrust it several times into the bear's body. He jerked back, trying to get out of reach, but a swipe of the grizzly's other paw caught him on the shoulder.

Luckily it was the back of the paw that struck him. Instead of having his flesh ripped open, Preacher was just knocked off his feet. He landed hard but managed to roll. As he came upright again, he saw a couple arrows sprouting as if by magic from the thick carpet of the bear's chest. Hawk had planted the shafts there, Preacher knew. The grizzly swung toward the young man, searching for the new source of irritation.

That put the bear's back toward Preacher and gave the mountain man a chance to try something else. He raced forward and bounded onto the grizzly's back. His legs locked around the muscular body, and he buried his left hand in the shaggy pelt and hung on. He reached around the bear's shoulder with his right hand and drove the knife into the animal's throat again and again.

The bear tried to roar, but the sound was choked and bubbling as blood poured from the gaping wounds in its neck. It reached futilely for Preacher but the fumbling paws couldn't find him.

Preacher switched his attack, thrusting the knife into the bear's side, trying for its heart. Again and again he struck.

The bear lurched forward and fell. Preacher realized too late the grizzly wasn't collapsing on the verge of death. The canny beast was trying to roll over and crush the annoying varmint clinging to its back.

Preacher let go and flung himself out of the way but wasn't able to avoid all the terrible weight. Some of it pinned his leg, and for a second it felt as if every bone was going to be ground to powder.

The bear's momentum carried it off Preacher, freeing the mountain man, but when he tried to spring to his feet, he couldn't. His leg was just a useless lump of unfeeling flesh. He didn't know if it was broken or if the nerves were just stunned, but either way, it wouldn't respond to his commands.

The bear was up again, in bad shape from its wounds but still full of rage and ready to rend and kill. Its beady little eyes looked around, but before it could spot Preacher, another arrow flew through the air and lodged its flint head in the bear's right eye.

The grizzly threw its head back and tried to bellow in pain, but more blood gushed from the wounds in its throat. It stood high on its hind legs and pawed at the air, striking out instinctively.

Hawk threw the bow aside, dashed around behind the bear, and leaped onto the grizzly's back as Preacher had done. Instead of using his knife, he reached around and grabbed the arrow protruding from the animal's eye. With a savage shout, Hawk rammed it home, driving the flint head all the way into the grizzly's brain.

Hawk dropped to the ground and stumbled back away from the flailing beast. The grizzly was dead, but its body hadn't realized that yet. Within moments, the bear began staggering back and forth.

Hawk raced to Preacher's side, caught hold of the

mountain man under the arms, and dragged him well clear of the grizzly. After they had survived the desperate battle, it wouldn't do to have the huge varmint fall on Preacher and crush him to death.

Preacher pushed himself into a sitting position as Hawk hunkered down beside him. Together they watched as mortality finally caught up to the bear. The grizzly let out one more gurgling groan, then pitched forward, slamming to the ground like a falling tree. Preacher and Hawk felt the vibration from the impact.

"How badly are you hurt?" Hawk asked.

"Don't matter," Preacher replied. "We got to get movin'. Tall Bull's men are liable to have heard those shots."

"But a moment ago you could not walk."

"I still can't, not without help. Hurry and find a branch I can use as a crutch."

"It will be faster if you lean on me, or let me carry you if I have to."

"Can't do that because you're goin' on ahead of me and gettin' out of here while you got the chance. I'll go on by myself."

"No," Hawk said. "I will stay with you."

"Damn it, boy—"

"We are wasting time." Hawk rose to his feet and extended a hand to Preacher. "As you said, we need to move."

Preacher frowned at him for a couple seconds, then growled in frustration, reached up, and clasped Hawk's wrist. He was no lightweight, but Hawk lifted him easily.

Preacher balanced on one leg and gingerly put

some weight on the other. It buckled underneath him, but the lack of any sharp pain made him think no bones were broken.

"Put your arm around my shoulder," Hawk said as he looped an arm around Preacher's waist.

"This is gonna be like a damn three-legged race at a fair," Preacher said, "except the stakes are a lot higher than a pie or whatever would go to the winner."

"I do not know what you are talking about," Hawk said, "but I suggest we leave."

"Yeah, yeah."

They started off awkwardly but soon fell into a rhythm of sorts.

As they walked, Preacher added, "By the way, thanks for killin' that griz. He'd have settled my hash if you hadn't done for him, I reckon."

"We both killed him. He would have died from the wounds you inflicted on him. I just . . . hurried him along, as you might say."

"Now and then, we make pretty good partners."

"Do not become accustomed to it," Hawk said.

Within an hour, most of the feeling had returned to Preacher's leg and he was able to walk on his own, although his gait was slower and more awkward than he liked. The leg hurt like blazes once the numbness wore off. He figured he'd be bruised from hip to sole by the next day.

Several times, Preacher urged Hawk to go on ahead and not allow him to slow him down. Hawk refused.

They had left the canyon together, and they would return together, he insisted.

Even hobbled, Preacher could move as fast through the wilderness as most men were able to when they were healthy. He and Hawk caught sight of what appeared to be a Blackfoot war party about half a mile away on the other side of a high, broad mountain meadow. They laid low in a gully until the warriors were gone, then resumed their trek.

They reached the pass and descended into the foothills on the other side of the valley, staying well above the valley floor as they worked their way north. They were still high enough that some of the drop-offs were fairly dizzying.

Their course came to an abrupt halt when they found themselves facing a stretch of talus—rocks that had fallen from the cliff in ages past and piled up below—that sloped down from left to right in front of them. At the top of that slope was a sheer rock face a good fifty yards wide. At the bottom of the slope was another precipitous drop-off.

Preacher stared at the loose rocks with disgust. They ranged in size from that of a fist to stones larger than a man's head. "We didn't run into this the first time we came through here. Must've gone around somehow and never saw it."

"We will have to go around now," Hawk said. "We cannot cross those rocks or climb that cliff."

"We'd have to double back a mile or more. That'll slow us down. Not only that, we'd be goin' right back toward those Blackfeet we saw earlier. If they've given up lookin' for us and turned back toward the village, we'd be liable to run right smack dab into 'em."

"Then how do you suggest we get across those loose rocks?"

Preacher grunted. "Mighty careful-like. Make sure wherever you step is stable before you put much weight on it. It'll be slow goin', but still faster than doublin' back."

Hawk frowned as he studied the talus slope for a long moment. Then he said, "I will go first."

"So I won't fall and knock you off? I don't reckon that's likely to happen here, since I'd be behind you, not above you."

"You argue as much as an old man like White Buffalo."

"Well, go on, then," Preacher said. "I ain't stoppin' you."

Hawk moved out onto the talus. As he carefully eased across them, testing each step before he committed to it, he dislodged pebbles that bounced down the slope. A few larger rocks slid as well, and when they dropped off the end of the slope, Preacher listened to find out how long it took them to hit the ground below. The interval before the thuds drifted back up was longer than he liked to think about.

From several yards out onto the slope, Hawk paused and turned his head to look back at Preacher. "Stay there until I get across. That way you will know where it is safe."

In turning his head, his body had moved slightly. His right foot twisted, and so did the stone upon which it rested. Suddenly, that rock shot out from under him, and so did his foot. He let out an involuntary shout as he fell. He scrambled, clutching at the rocks, but all of them were shifting. He could find nothing sturdy and stable enough to grab.

With a great clatter, Hawk and a whole section of the talus began to slide swiftly toward the drop-off at the bottom of the slope.

CHAPTER 30

Without pausing to think about what he was doing, Preacher lunged forward, bounding from rock to rock and throwing himself after Hawk. The soreness in his leg was forgotten.

The talus slid under him, as well, just not as much. He spotted an outcropping that didn't seem to be moving and slapped his left hand at it.

At the same time, he stretched out his right arm as far as it would go and reached for Hawk's flailing hands.

A couple things happened at once. Preacher's left hand closed over the outcropping and his right hand caught hold of the fingers on Hawk's right hand. Both were precarious grips. He grimaced when Hawk's out-of-control weight hit his right hand and arm. Bones and muscles strained to hang on.

Preacher knew if the rock he had hold of gave way, it wouldn't matter. He and Hawk would go over the edge and plummet to their deaths. The lower half of Hawk's body was already hanging in midair.

The fingers of Preacher's left hand slipped a tiny bit, but the rock itself didn't budge. It wasn't part of the talus but rather an outcropping from the underlying surface, he realized as he bore down and held on tighter.

The loose rock washed around Hawk like a wave and went over the edge to fall far below. As the clattering and grinding settled down, Hawk gasped, "Let me go . . . or you will fall, too!"

"I ain't . . . lettin' go," Preacher said through clenched teeth. "See if . . . you can grab on somewhere . . . with your other hand!"

Hawk was lying spread-eagled on the slope, both of his arms stretched out as far as they could go in opposite directions. Preacher was the only lifeline keeping Hawk from falling to his death, and it felt as if any second his shoulder sockets were going to pop loose.

Hawk fumbled around, searching for someplace stable to hold with his left hand. Every rock he grasped moved in his grip. Again he said, "Let me fall!"

"Not . . . hardly. See if you can . . . get hold of my arm . . . farther up. You can . . . climb up that way."

"You cannot hold me!"

"I'm your pa, boy! Don't you be tellin' me . . . what I can't do!"

Hawk reached up and grasped the end of Preacher's sleeve. With a grunt of effort, he heaved himself a little higher on the slope. Preacher closed his eyes. He didn't know what was going to give out first, his bones or his muscles.

"A little more . . . and then maybe . . . you can wedge a foot in somewhere."

Hawk shifted his grip and pulled himself up another couple inches. While he clung to Preacher's forearm, Preacher shifted his grip and clasped Hawk's wrist while Hawk took hold of his. That was a more secure grip, but it didn't relieve the weight on Preacher's joints.

Hawk bent his knee and pulled his right leg up. He searched for a place to wedge his toe and after minutes that seemed like hours, he found one. He pushed against the rocks, and they didn't move. As he increased the pressure and took some of the weight, Preacher almost groaned with relief.

"That's it," the mountain man urged. "Keep climbin'."

Painfully slowly, Hawk crawled up the slope away from the brink. More rocks came loose, tumbled down, and shot out into empty space, but eventually, he was spread out on the slope like Preacher was.

The imminent danger was over, but they still had to climb up and across the rest of the talus before they would be safe.

"If you stay here," Hawk said to Preacher, panting as he tried to catch his breath after that terrifying close call, "I can climb up and throw something back down to you."

"You mean like a rope? You gonna conjure one out of thin air?"

"I can cut my shirt into strips and tie them together."

That might actually work, Preacher thought. He nodded. "All right, but take it slow and careful-like.

If you fall again, I doubt if I can catch you a second time."

"I will not fall," Hawk promised. His voice was grim with determination.

Inch by painstaking inch, Hawk angled toward the top of the talus slope. Preacher clung to the outcropping that had saved them and watched, occasionally calling out a suggestion as to where Hawk might place a hand or foot next.

Finally, Hawk pulled himself onto solid ground again. Preacher had no idea how long the nerve-wracking journey had taken, but the sun was well into the afternoon sky by then.

It was a good thing none of the Blackfeet had come along while they were stuck out there. Those blood-thirsty varmints would have had a high old time feathering them full of arrows, Preacher thought.

Hawk was trembling slightly from exhaustion and the strain of making that climb, but he set to work immediately fashioning the rope made from his buckskin shirt. He tied all the knots tight and tested them, then tossed one end down the slope toward Preacher.

The makeshift rope fell short, so Hawk had to pull it up and add more. The next time he threw it, Preacher was able to grab hold of the end. He wrapped it around his wrist and tied it in place.

"Let me brace myself, then you use the rope to pull yourself up," Hawk called.

Preacher waited until the young man gave him a curt nod, then he rose to his knees and carefully stood up. He had hold of the rope with both hands. With it to steady him, he was able to find rocks that didn't shift under his feet and made the climb much more quickly than Hawk had. He sprawled on the ground next to the young man and lay there with his chest rising and falling deeply.

"Well," Preacher said at last, "that's somethin' I'd just as soon not do every day."

After they had rested a while, they set off again. The terrain was still rugged, but they didn't encounter any more obstacles as daunting as the ones they had already overcome.

"Seems like we're sort of gettin' in the habit of savin' each other's lives," Preacher commented as they traveled through a dense stretch of pines and firs.

"We are allies against the Blackfeet," Hawk said. "Those who fight side by side do what they can to help each other."

"Yeah, I know, but it seems to me it's a mite more than that."

Hawk glanced over at the mountain man. "You mean because we are father and son?" He shrugged. "It is hard to deny the bond that exists between blood, but I cannot forget how my mother spent her life hoping you would return to her . . . and knowing that you would not."

"Blast it. If I'd known Birdie and I had a son—"

"We have talked about this. If you had known, it is still likely you never would have come back to her."

"Likely, maybe, but we can't ever know for sure, can we? Folks like to say, oh, if such-and-such a thing was to happen, I'd do this or I'd do that, but when you

come right down to it, they don't *know*." Preacher
paused, then added, "Folks never know for sure what
they're gonna do until life's problems are starin' 'em
right square in the face. That's what tells the tale, and
nothin' else."

Hawk didn't say anything, but after a moment he
shrugged again, although he remained silent. Preacher
figured that was as close to agreement as he was going
to get from the youngster.

Preacher's injured leg kept trying to stiffen up, but
the way they kept moving, he didn't give it much of a
chance to. He would be glad for the opportunity to
rest it once they got back to the canyon.

It was late afternoon before Preacher recognized
various landmarks near their destination. He was
about to say something to Hawk about it when he
heard something that made him stiffen as his forehead creased in a frown.

Hawk had heard it, too. "Those sound like gun-
shots."

"They damn sure do. Comin' from the direction of
where we left White Buffalo and those greenhorns."

As far as Preacher knew, Charlie Todd and Aaron
Buckley were the only ones in the area who had
firearms, other than him. Of course, it was possible
another group of trappers had drifted into the valley,
but that wasn't very likely. Most experienced mountain men knew to give the Blackfeet plenty of room.
Crowding them was just asking for bad trouble.

The shots were irregular and spaced out considerably. They didn't sound like a battle was going on, but
he could tell whoever was doing the shooting wasn't

just hunting for game. Todd and Buckley wouldn't have done that, anyway. They would have been too afraid of attracting unwanted attention, and rightly so.

"That's trouble, sure enough," Preacher went on. "Those boys are puttin' up a fight. We'd best go see if we can give 'em a hand before it's too late."

It wasn't easy to pick up the pace with his leg hurting like it did, but Preacher ignored the pain and hustled on with Hawk at his side. The shots grew louder as they approached the canyon, giving Preacher no doubt that was where they were coming from.

They came in sight of the tall rock face with the cleft in it leading to the canyon and knelt behind some boulders to study the situation.

Scattered around in a half circle facing the cleft were a dozen or more Blackfoot warriors. Using rocks and brush and gullies for cover, they fired arrows toward the opening. A shot boomed somewhere inside the cleft and Preacher saw a spurt of powder smoke.

A couple warriors were sprawled unmoving on the ground near the cleft. The defenders had scored at least twice with their shots.

Preacher frowned again as he waited for a second shot from the cleft. It finally came, but not until enough time had passed for a man to reload his rifle.

"I think there's only one fella in there puttin' up a fight," he said quietly to Hawk.

"One of the white men must have been killed or wounded."

"That's what I figure," Preacher said. "Or—" Just then the other possibility that had occurred to him was shown to be right, as two warriors pushed out of some brush holding a struggling figure between them.

Charlie Todd was a prisoner, and he didn't stop trying to get loose until one of the Blackfeet held a knife to his throat. The young white man was only a second away from death.

CHAPTER 31

The other warrior hanging on to Todd shouted toward the cleft, "Come out, white man, or we will kill your friend!"

He spoke in the Blackfoot tongue, of course, which Aaron Buckley wouldn't understand at all. White Buffalo would, though, so he could translate for the greenhorn . . . assuming White Buffalo was still alive in the canyon.

Todd didn't wait for a response. He shouted, "Whatever he's saying, don't listen to him, Aaron! Shoot the sons of bitches!"

The man with the knife responded by taking it away from Todd's throat, then slamming a fist against the young man's head. The blow knocked Todd to his knees. The man with the knife grabbed him by the hair and jerked his head back, drawing the skin of his throat tight. A quick, hard slash with the blade would open Todd's throat all the way to his spine. The knife hovered there, ready to strike.

"Wait!" Buckley shouted from the cleft. "Don't kill him!"

"Damn it," Preacher muttered. "Don't come outta there, boy. They'll just kill you both."

"We can try to help them." Hawk didn't sound like he thought that was the best idea in the world, since he didn't really know the two young white men and didn't have much use for them, but Preacher could tell Hawk would go along with whatever he wanted to do.

"Get an arrow ready. Reckon you can hit the fella with the knife from here?"

"I can," Hawk said with the simple confidence of a man who didn't feel any need to boast. He nocked an arrow into his bow.

"Take him down first, then, when the time comes."

"When will that be?"

"I want to see what Aaron's gonna do first." Preacher pulled out his pistols, checked the loads, and made sure they were ready to fire. The range was a little long for pistols, but he had left his rifle in the canyon, knowing what he and Hawk were setting out to do would require a great deal of stealth and close-up killing. A rifle wasn't good for those things.

"I surrender!" Buckley shouted from the cleft. "I'm coming out!"

Hawk understood enough of that to grasp Buckley's meaning. "The fool. Does he think to bargain with Blackfeet? One might as well try to strike a deal with the lowliest of carrion eaters!"

"I reckon he don't know no better."

"They will fill him with arrows as soon as he steps into the open."

"Maybe, maybe not. They might just take him prisoner so they can haul both of 'em back to the village and torture 'em to death." A grim chuckle came from the mountain man's lips. "I happen to know they're right fond of burnin' fellas at the stake."

A stir of excitement went through the Blackfeet as Aaron Buckley appeared in the opening to the cleft. Both hands were empty as he held them up level with his head.

"Where is White Buffalo?" Hawk wondered.

"If he's alive, he's still in there, and he ain't comin' out," Preacher said. "If they want that old man, they'll have to go in there and drag him out by his heels. He'll probably make them kill him instead of surrenderin'."

"That might be wise," Hawk said quietly. "If they saw he was Absaroka, they would subject him to even greater horrors than they will those two white men." He paused, then went on, "The Blackfeet should not even be here! We are far from their village."

"Reckon that's probably a search party lookin' for us. Tall Bull's sendin' 'em out far and wide now, after what happened this mornin'. They've had time to get here from the village whilst we was takin' the long way around. It must've been just bad luck they stumbled over Charlie."

"He should not have left the canyon. You warned them not to."

"Yeah, we'll have to have a talk about that . . . assumin' any of us come through this alive."

Half a dozen Blackfoot warriors swarmed out of their cover and rushed toward Buckley as he walked slowly away from the cleft. The other six, including the two who had hold of Todd, hung back.

"They're gonna grab him," Preacher said. "They don't want to kill him right off, just like I thought."

Buckley suddenly stopped as the warriors approached him. His right hand dropped and pulled something from his belt, just behind his hip. Preacher saw sparks shooting in the air and said, "What the hell?"

Buckley tossed the object toward the Blackfeet. As it flew through the air, Preacher recognized it as a powder horn. The sparks came from the narrow end of it. Instinctively, one of the warriors reached up and caught it as it came toward him.

A split second later, the powder horn blew up.

The unexpected explosion mangled the hand and arm of the man holding the powder horn and flung him backwards, knocking the two men closest to him off their feet, as well.

Buckley reached behind his back again and brought out two pistols, cocking the hammers as he raised them. Too close to the Blackfeet to miss, he fired the weapons simultaneously. Two more men fell as the heavy lead balls smashed into their chests.

"Now!" Preacher told Hawk.

Rising from his concealment, Hawk drew back the bowstring and let fly with the arrow he had nocked a few moments earlier. It drove into the back of the man holding the knife to Todd's throat, catching him squarely between the shoulder blades. He dropped the knife as he collapsed.

Todd twisted and butted his head into his other captor's belly, driving the warrior backwards.

Pistols in hand, Preacher charged the remaining Blackfeet. The explosion, followed by the two shots from Buckley's guns, had created thunderous echoes from the tall rock face split by the cleft. He added to the din by firing his pistols and cutting down two more warriors.

Hawk whipped arrows from his quiver and fired twice more. One shaft skewered a warrior in the belly as the man turned. The other struck its target in the side of the neck with such force the flint head went all the way through and burst out the other side of the man's neck in a bloody wound.

All the Blackfeet were down, either dead or mortally wounded, except the two with whom Buckley and Todd were now engaged in hand-to-hand struggles. The young men battled with desperation on their side, but they were no match for experienced fighters like the Blackfoot warriors.

White Buffalo darted out of the cleft with a large rock clutched in both hands. Buckley's opponent had him down on the ground and was about to gut him with a knife when White Buffalo brought the rock crashing down on his head from behind.

With a tomahawk throw, Preacher took care of the warrior about to choke Todd to death. It struck the man in the back of the head and shattered his skull. He dropped loosely to the side, allowing Todd to sit up and gasp for breath.

Buckley pushed the dead man off him and crawled away a few feet before he sat up, as well.

Hawk moved quickly among the fallen Blackfeet, checking to make sure they were dead. The three who weren't, he dispatched with swift, efficient knife slashes across the throat.

Preacher went to Todd's side and helped the young man to his feet.

"Preacher!" Todd said. "I . . . I'm sorry—"

"I reckon you mean about gettin' caught outside the canyon," the mountain man interrupted him. "We'll talk about that later. Right now let's go make sure Aaron's all right."

Buckley was visibly shaken but appeared to be uninjured. He clasped his friend's shoulders and asked, "Are you all right, Charlie?"

"Yeah, I . . . I guess so. What the hell happened? Was that a *bomb*?"

"I was sort of wonderin' the same thing myself," Preacher said.

Buckley smiled sheepishly. "I didn't know if it would work or not. It seemed to me like it ought to. An explosive shell is basically just gunpowder under compression that's ignited. All I had to do was rig a fuse that would burn at the right rate of speed and not blow *me* up before I could get it among the Blackfeet." He shook his head. "I almost cut it too close."

"Aaron was always better than me in our classes at the university," Todd said with a note of pride in his voice. "I could drink more ale, though."

Buckley turned to the old-timer. "Thank you, White Buffalo. You saved my life."

Preacher translated.

White Buffalo shrugged. "It was a good chance to kill a Blackfoot. I could not waste the opportunity."

"He says you're welcome," Preacher said. "Now we got to figure out what to do with all them carcasses. We're far enough away from Tall Bull's village they might not have heard the shots or that powder horn blowin' up, but somebody is bound to notice a whole flock o' buzzards circlin' over a feast."

Preacher found a bluff not far off where they were able to stack the bodies like cordwood at the base. They piled rocks on the corpses and then collapsed part of the bluff on them. A determined search might be able to locate the dead men, but more than likely they would never be found.

Night had fallen by the time he and Hawk returned to the cleft, and as they approached they were greeted by a happy bark. Dog bounded out of the opening and jumped on Preacher, resting his front paws on the mountain man's shoulders.

With Preacher's bad leg, that was almost enough to make him fall down, but he wasn't going to scold the big cur. He was happy to see Dog, too. "Figured you'd be back before now, old son. You must've found plenty of game to chase and interestin' smells to sniff."

"He arrived shortly after you and Hawk dragged off the last of those vermin," White Buffalo said as he emerged from the opening. "He wanted to go and look for you, but I told him you would be back soon."

"Well, I'm obliged to you for that. Those two greenhorns inside where they're supposed to be?"

White Buffalo grunted in agreement.

"Dog, stay and guard," Preacher told the big cur.

"He will let us know if anyone approaches," White Buffalo said.

"Yeah, I figured as much," Preacher said, "since I been dependin' on him to do that for a long time now. Come on. I want to talk to those two."

Todd and Buckley were sitting next to a tiny fire tucked back in a corner of the canyon where it wouldn't be visible from outside. They scrambled to their feet as Preacher, Hawk, and White Buffalo approached them.

Todd began. "Preacher, listen, this was all my fault—"

"No, I was the one who told Charlie he could go outside the canyon," Buckley broke in. "He thought he could find another rabbit and we'd have a good meal waiting for you and Hawk when you got back."

"I didn't just think I could find a rabbit. I *saw* one while I was standing guard, and I knew where it went."

"But you found a Blackfoot war party instead," Preacher said.

Todd grimaced. "Yeah. I thought sure they were gonna kill me, but they didn't. They must have seen me come out of the cleft and figured somebody else was in there. They tried to sneak up on the place, but Aaron spotted them and fought them off."

Preacher looked at Buckley. "When you came up with that trick with the powder horn, you didn't know me and Hawk were close by to lend you a hand. What did you figure on doin' with the ones you *didn't* blow up?"

"I was going to kill as many of them as I could before they killed me. I figured it would give Charlie a chance to put up a fight, too, and I knew he'd want to do that."

"Damn right I did," Todd said. "We've been dodging and ducking those bastards for a while now, and I'm tired of it. It's time to fight back."

Preacher studied the two young men in the dim light of the fire for a moment, then smiled. "Reckon we've got another couple o' allies in our little army, Hawk."

Hawk just grunted skeptically. White Buffalo rolled his eyes.

Preacher grew more serious as he went on. "But you two are still greenhorns, which means that from now on, you do what I say and nothin' else, understand?"

"You have our word on that," Buckley said.

"Good. I sorta like the way you think, mister. Maybe you can come up with some new ways to help us kill Blackfeet."

CHAPTER 32

For the next three days, all eight members of the party—counting Dog, Horse, and The Mule With No Name—stayed close to the canyon. Hawk was the only one who ventured out, and then only to bring down a deer with an expertly placed arrow and carry the carcass draped over his shoulder back to their camp so they would have fresh meat.

The respite served two purposes. It gave Preacher's injured leg time to recover from having the bear fall on it. Given his iron constitution, he was able to get around quite well after the rest, although the leg itself was still colorful with bruises.

The other benefit from staying holed up was giving Tall Bull time to stew in his own juices, knowing that something had happened to the missing search party. Preacher and Hawk had been striking at the village on a regular basis, and most of its inhabitants had to be pretty nervous, even the bravest of warriors. Their tormentors seemed to have the ability to show up without warning, deal out death, and then disappear. Anyone who went out to look for them stood a good chance of never coming back.

Preacher was willing to bet nobody in the village was sleeping much. That weariness would make them more on edge and more likely to question Tall Bull's leadership.

On the evening of the third day, Aaron Buckley came to Preacher and said, "I have an idea."

"About how to kill more Blackfeet, you mean?"

"That's right. I've been thinking about it, as you asked me to do, and I believe we should build a catapult."

Preacher frowned at him. "A what?"

"A catapult. It's an ancient weapon of war. The Greeks used it in their siege of Troy."

Preacher scratched his ear. "I reckon I've heard a little somethin' about that, somewhere along the line. Audie probably told me about it."

"We can build a small-scale version, assembling the framework out of tree branches. The original catapults were designed to hurl large rocks hundreds of yards through the air. We don't need anything powerful enough to do that. You said there's a ridge overlooking the Blackfoot village?"

"That's right," Preacher said.

"I propose we use the catapult to lob incendiary rounds into the village and set it on fire."

"Incinder . . . What?"

"We can form rounds out of dried mud and fill them with shavings we set on fire before we launch them. They will crack open on impact and burst open, the flames spreading and setting the tepees on fire."

Preacher rubbed his chin and thought over the

idea for a moment. Then he said, "Well, that *might* work . . . but couldn't Hawk just shoot some flamin' arrows into the tepees and wind up doin' the same thing?"

"Oh." Buckley looked crestfallen. "That *would* be a lot simpler, wouldn't it?"

"Yeah, but you came up with the general idea," Preacher said with a grin as he slapped Buckley on the back. "Let's go talk to Hawk."

After Preacher had explained about the flaming arrows to Hawk, the young man nodded solemnly. "I can do that. We can strike in the middle of the night, and I can launch at least five or six arrows into the village before any of the Blackfeet know what is going on, perhaps more."

"That's what I figured," Preacher said.

"But does that not mean we will be waging war on women and children, which you said we should not do?"

"They'll all have time to get out. We're destroyin' their homes but not killin' 'em. It'll be a mite rough on 'em, but they can rebuild the village . . . especially if they go somewheres else to do it."

"You mean to make them flee, instead of killing all the warriors?"

Preacher sighed. "How many of 'em you reckon we've killed so far? Forty? Fifty? I've lost count, but it's a whole heap, I know that. There's gotta be an end to the killin' sooner or later."

"There will be . . . when Tall Bull and his warriors are all dead," Hawk insisted.

"Tall Bull needs to die," Preacher said with a nod. "I ain't shied away from killin' any of his warriors we've come up against, neither. But if we kill Tall Bull and the rest of his people turn tail and light a shuck outta these parts, I reckon I'll be satisfied with that."

Hawk glared at him. "You grow weak! I should have expected as much from a white man!"

"Damn it, boy, I ain't gonna put up with that talk. I'll fight them bastards as long as I got breath in my body. I'm just sayin' my idea of avengin' your people is startin' to be a little different."

"They were *my* people. I will decide when they have been avenged." Hawk's voice was cold as ice.

"Suit yourself," Preacher said. "Spend the rest of your life killin' Blackfeet if you want. They ain't never been friends to me. I'm just sayin' that when Tall Bull's dead, I'll be movin' on."

Hawk made no response other than to turn on his heel and stalk away.

Aaron Buckley cleared his throat. "From everything I've heard about what happened to his people, he has a right to be vengeful, you know."

"Yeah, but there comes a time when enough's enough. I don't want a bunch of women and kids and old folks starvin' to death on my conscience."

"I've never seen anyone who can fight like you, Preacher . . . but it appears you have a gentle side as well."

Preacher grunted. "Don't go countin' on that."

Nothing else was said about the brief argument between Preacher and Hawk, and the next morning Hawk began preparing the arrows he would use for their next assault on the village. He wrapped dry grass around the heads of the arrows and tied it in place with strips of rawhide. When he had eight of them, he slid them into his quiver with the heads up so they wouldn't be disturbed when he pulled them out.

"We'll go tonight," Preacher said. "Hit 'em in the middle of the night."

"They will be on guard," Hawk warned.

"Why, sure they will." Preacher grinned. "Lucky for us we're mighty stealthy. It wouldn't surprise me if Tall Bull's posted guards up on that ridge, so we may have to deal with them first."

"What do you want Charlie and me to do?" Buckley asked.

"You're stayin' here with White Buffalo."

Todd said, "We told you we want to fight, Preacher. I know we're new out here on the frontier . . . greenhorns, you call us, and I can't deny it's true . . . but we can follow orders and we want to help."

"I told you before to stay inside the canyon, out of sight, and you didn't do it," Preacher reminded them. "That could have worked out mighty bad."

Buckley sighed and nodded. "You're right, of course. We made a mistake. But we've learned from it, haven't we, Charlie?"

"Absolutely," Todd declared. "We'll follow your orders to the letter, Preacher."

White Buffalo said in his tongue, "The foolish young white men want to fight the Blackfeet, yes?"

"Yeah, that's right," Preacher told the old-timer.

"You should let them." White Buffalo shrugged. "No doubt they will die, but perhaps they will accidentally kill one or two of Tall Bull's warriors before they do."

"They might surprise us all and turn out to come in handy."

"A white man doing something well?" White Buffalo let out a snort of disbelief. "Yes, that *would* be a surprise."

Todd said, "I can't tell exactly what he's saying, but I think White Buffalo believes you should let us come along, Preacher." He smiled at the old man. "Thanks for being on our side, White Buffalo."

"Yeah, about that . . ." Preacher began, then stopped and shook his head. "Never mind. If you two are bound and determined to come along, then I reckon I won't stop you. But you do everything I say without hesitatin' or questionin', and if you get yourselves in trouble anyway, I may not be able to save your hides."

"That's fair enough," Buckley said. "We just want to do our part."

"Just make sure all your guns are loaded. Once things start hoppin', we're liable to be a mite busy."

Late that afternoon, Hawk scouted the immediate area and reported there were no Blackfeet around the canyon. As dusk gathered, the four men set out on their mission, accompanied by Dog. White Buffalo remained behind.

Preacher's leg felt almost back to normal. He limped only slightly as he and Hawk led the way on a roundabout route toward the Blackfoot village. Preacher had warned Buckley and Todd to stay close to them. If they got separated once darkness fell, the two greenhorns might not be able to find them again.

"No talkin' if it ain't absolutely necessary, either," Preacher said quietly just before the last of the light faded. "Voices carry at night, and you won't be able to see if any of those varmints are lurkin' around. You'll need to rely on Hawk and Dog and me for that."

Both young men nodded silently, which made Preacher smile.

At the slow, deliberate pace the group was taking, it would be well after midnight before they reached the ridge overlooking the Blackfoot village. That was all right with Preacher. Nearly everyone would be asleep by then.

Behind the ridge were several more crests in a gradually ascending series. Preacher and his companions worked their way high above the valley and then, when they reached the right spot, started down again.

Hawk and Dog took the lead, both eager to sniff out—literally—any guards posted on the ridge. Preacher whispered to Todd and Buckley, "You boys stay right here. Don't move from this spot. One of us will be back to fetch you."

He took their silence to mean they understood.

He caught up to Hawk and Dog, and the three of them spread out to cover the ridge. Preacher didn't have to tell Hawk to make as little noise as possible in disposing of any sentries. The young warrior knew that.

Preacher stopped as he smelled a hint of bear grease in the air. Since the Blackfeet rubbed that in their hair, he knew someone was close by. Standing absolutely motionless and silent, he waited until he heard a faint noise, as if someone had just shifted a foot. He eased in the direction of the sound, and a moment later his keen eyes spotted a man-shaped patch of deeper darkness in the shadows.

Patiently, Preacher waited until the man moved again, which told him which way the warrior was facing. Like the ghost the Blackfeet called him, he glided behind the sentry, clapped a hand over his mouth, and cut his throat. The man collapsed as blood welled hotly from his neck.

With that obstacle taken care of, Preacher moved farther to his right along the ridge. Hawk was checking the left flank, while Dog held down the middle. The big cur wouldn't attack any of the Blackfeet unless it was absolutely necessary, since that might make enough racket to attract attention from the village.

Preacher came across another guard and dispatched him with a swift knife thrust in the back. He ventured farther until finally he was satisfied there were no more warriors posted on his part of the ridge. He started backtracking toward the center.

He stopped when he heard a soft bird call. He responded in kind, and a moment later Hawk materialized out of the shadows with Dog at his side.

"There were three in that direction," the young man whispered, pointing to the left.

Preacher knew exactly what he meant by *were*. Those sentries were dead, just like the ones Preacher had encountered.

The moon was only a sliver in the sky, but the light from millions of stars filtered down on the valley and the tepees clustered along the creek bank.

"Can you see well enough to hit what you're aimin' at?" Preacher asked.

Hawk just made a disgusted noise in his throat, as if to indicate the question was ridiculous.

"I'll go get Aaron and Charlie," the mountain man whispered. "Don't start the ball until we get back."

"Do not waste any time," Hawk said.

"I don't plan to. Dog, stay with Hawk."

Preacher crossed the level ground and went up the next slope to the spot where he and Hawk had left Todd and Buckley. A quick, "Hsst! Boys!" brought them to his side.

"Is everything all right?" Buckley asked.

"Yeah. Hawk and me got rid of the guards, and he's gettin' ready to light them arrows. Come on. Quiet as you can, now."

They hurried back to join Hawk. The two greenhorns made some noise, but not too much, Preacher thought. They were learning.

When they reached Hawk's position, they found he had made a small fire pit out of rocks and kindled a tiny blaze inside the ring that was unlikely to be visible from the village below. He took all eight of the special arrows from his quiver and handed them to Preacher, keeping one that he fitted to his bowstring.

"Cock your rifles, boys," Preacher said to Todd and Buckley. "We're just about ready."

Hawk held the arrowhead in the fire. The dry grass caught instantly. He raised the bow, drew back the string, paused for a heartbeat, and then let fly.

The flaming arrow arched up and out before curving downward to fly with perfect aim toward the village. It struck the side of a tepee and lodged there. A couple tense seconds went by, then more flames erupted as the hide caught fire.

By that time, Preacher had handed Hawk another arrow, and its tip was blazing. With a *twang* of the bowstring, the second flaming missile soared toward the village.

The attack was on.

CHAPTER 33

"Get ready," Preacher told Todd and Buckley as he handed another special arrow to Hawk, who let it fly. "Those fellas will be tumblin' out of their tepees any second now. Hell's about to break loose down there, and when it does they'll be scurryin' around like ants. Make sure you've got good targets before you fire. We won't have enough time to waste shots."

While he was telling them this, he had given the fourth arrow to Hawk. All of the young warrior's shots had been perfect so far. Three tepees were ablaze in different parts of the village.

As Preacher had predicted, warriors flung aside the hide flaps over the entrances to the tepees and raced outside. Shouts of alarm rang back and forth in the village.

"Take your shots whenever you're ready," Preacher told Todd and Buckley as he raised his rifle to his shoulder and squinted over the weapon's long barrel. He settled the sights on a large warrior who was slapping at one of the fires with a robe, trying to put out the flames.

Preacher squeezed the trigger.

The rifle boomed and kicked hard against his shoulder. Smoke and sparks flew from the muzzle.

Down in the village, the man Preacher had drawn a bead on jerked his head back in shock and pain as the heavy lead ball smashed into his body. He took a couple staggering steps and then plunged facedown on the ground.

A few yards away, Todd and Buckley fired, too, a couple seconds after Preacher did. The mountain man was already reloading, his movements so automatic he didn't have to watch what he was doing in order to accomplish his goal. He kept his eyes on the village and saw another warrior grab at his arm in obvious pain. One of the greenhorns' shots had winged him. Preacher had no doubt whichever of the young men had fired the shot had been aiming at the Blackfoot's body, but still, that wasn't bad shooting at that range.

The other ball, as far as Preacher could see, missed entirely, but he wasn't too worried about that. He was counting on Todd and Buckley to help keep the Blackfeet spooked, whether they hit anything or not.

Hawk continued his barrage with the flaming arrows.

With all the commotion going on in the village, people shouting and running around as flames crackled fiercely, it was possible that nobody had noticed the shots and arrows were coming from the ridge. Preacher lifted his reloaded rifle, took aim at a warrior who had stopped to gaze in shock at one of the burning tepees, and fired again.

His target went over backwards as if punched in the

chest by a giant fist, which was about what it amounted to. The man didn't get up.

Todd had reloaded more quickly and smoothly than Buckley. He squeezed off his second shot while Buckley was still tamping down his second load with the ramrod.

Preacher saw a warrior stumble and fall. "Nice shootin', Charlie."

A grin flashed across Todd's bearded face. "I always had a good eye when we were playing darts in the tavern, didn't I, Aaron?"

Buckley had finished reloading and lined up his shot. "I'm glad to see all that practice is coming in handy for you, Charlie." He fired, then exclaimed, "Drat! Why can't I seem to get the hang of this? I managed to shoot those Indians back at the canyon."

"That was a lot closer range," Preacher told him. "Just keep tryin'. We're makin' those varmints duck for cover, if nothin' else."

That was true. Some of the warriors had noticed their fallen comrades and realized the village was under attack with more than fire arrows.

Hawk had reached the end of his supply of such arrows, having sent all eight of them streaking down into different parts of the village. All of them had started fires, and those flames were spreading.

The rifle shots had forced some of the warriors to retreat toward the creek, herding the women and children and old ones with them.

A group of a dozen men headed toward the ridge at a run, though. They had finally spotted the place where the shots and the flaming arrows were coming from.

"One more volley, and then we'll pull back,"

Preacher said as he finished reloading again. He settled his sights on the warrior leading the charge and pulled the trigger. As the rifle blasted, the warrior's torso went backwards while his legs kept running forward for a second before he went down in an ungainly sprawl.

The two greenhorns' weapons boomed again. Two more warriors went down.

"That's more like it!" Buckley said.

Preacher didn't tell the young man he had spotted an arrow sprouting from the chest of one of the warriors. Hawk was raining the deadly missiles down among the Blackfeet. The attack suddenly fell apart as the warriors scattered.

"Come on," Preacher said. "Let's git while the gittin's good."

They withdrew from the ridge and started climbing higher in the foothills. It was unlikely the Blackfeet would be able to trail them in the darkness, although once the warriors realized they weren't being shot at anymore and regrouped, they might cast back and forth on the ridge for a while, looking for any sign of the men who had wreaked havoc on the village.

For all Preacher knew, Tall Bull might have been one of the men killed in the attack. The Blackfeet might pack up what few belongings they could from their destroyed village and leave that part of the country.

If that happened, Preacher knew his vengeance quest might be over. He would have to make his own decision about that, as would Hawk.

But as they moved through the night with the orange glow from the burning tepees lighting up the sky behind them, Preacher's instincts told him it wasn't over yet.

The sun was about to peek over the mountains in the east when they got back to the canyon. There had been no pursuit they were aware of, but Preacher had set a pretty fast pace anyway, and everyone was tired from the long, strenuous night.

Despite that weariness, Todd and Buckley were still excited from their participation in the attack. When White Buffalo asked what had happened, Todd especially bubbled over with details as Preacher translated the young man's enthusiastic response and toned it down a mite.

White Buffalo nodded solemnly, then asked, "And what of Tall Bull?"

"Don't know," Preacher said. "He might've died, or he might not have. No way to tell."

White Buffalo gazed off into the distance. "I saw him, you know. When he and his men wiped out our village. When I lay as if dead, under the bodies of my friends. He came walking through the slaughter with his subchiefs following him. He carried a war club, and when he saw an Absaroka still drawing breath, he crushed their skull with that club. He is a tall man, as you would guess from his name, and has the horns of several bull buffalo hung on his chest by a thong around his neck."

Preacher's eyes narrowed. "You're just now thinkin' to describe him to us, when you know we been tryin' to kill him for a couple weeks?"

The old-timer blew out a haughty breath. "No one

asked White Buffalo if he knows what Tall Bull looks like, did they?"

Hawk had been listening intently. "I do not recall seeing a warrior like that among any we have killed."

Preacher's fingertips rasped over the salt-and-pepper bristles on his chin as he frowned in thought. "No, I don't reckon I've laid eyes on the rascal, either. Of course, we were a pretty good distance away from those fellas last night, and he might've taken off that buffalo horn necklace when he turned in. I didn't see anybody carryin' a big ol' war club, though."

"He is alive, and I know it," Hawk snapped. "My belly tells me he is alive. I think yours does as well, Preacher, if you will admit it."

Preacher trusted his own instincts completely, and he had come to trust Hawk's during the time they had been fighting side by side. He had thought earlier that their battle wasn't over yet and was more convinced than ever.

"Excuse me," Aaron Buckley said in English. "This seems to be a pretty intense conversation the three of you are having, and I just wondered what it's about. Is there some sort of trouble Charlie and I aren't aware of?"

"Not really," Preacher said. "Turns out White Buffalo knows what Tall Bull, the Blackfoot war chief, looks like, and Hawk and I agree that we haven't killed him yet."

"So you're going to keep on fighting them?" Todd asked.

"The job ain't finished. I don't figure on walkin' away until it is."

"Then we're still with you," Buckley declared without hesitation. "Right, Charlie?"

"Damn right," Todd said.

"I appreciate that, boys. Right now, though, I reckon we all need some rest." Preacher turned to the old-timer. "White Buffalo, will you keep watch while the rest of us sleep?"

"Of course," White Buffalo answered. "Dog and I have much to talk about. Horses and mules . . ." He blew out a disgusted breath. "A man could go mad with boredom talking to them."

Preacher chuckled. "Dog may want to get some shut-eye, too, but I'll leave it up to the two o' you to work that out." He turned to the two greenhorns. "We're gonna rest and lie low for a while, then maybe tomorrow we'll go take a look at the village again."

"What do you expect to find?" Buckley asked.

"That's a good question."

They took it easy until the next day, as Preacher had said, then he and Hawk set out for the village again.

"We're just doin' some scoutin'," Preacher told Todd and Buckley when the two greenhorns wanted to join them. "No reason for you fellas to go along this time."

"What if you run into trouble?" Buckley asked, then before Preacher could answer, he shook his head and went on. "Of course, if anything is bad enough for the two of you to be in trouble, I doubt Charlie and I could do anything to help you."

"I don't know that I'd go that far," Preacher said. "Charlie's a pretty fair shot, and you're good at figurin' things out and comin' up with ideas. I reckon we'll be fine this time. You fellas just stay here and keep White Buffalo company."

"I don't know about that," Todd said with a dubious frown. "Sometimes I catch that old man looking at me like he's thinking about slitting my throat."

"Don't worry. He ain't as fierce as he makes himself out to be."

"We don't understand a word of what he's saying to us. I'm sure he doesn't understand us, either."

"Well, just smile and nod a lot," Preacher advised. "I don't reckon you can go wrong with that."

The two young men waved uneasily as Preacher and Hawk set off for the village. Preacher's leg was completely healed, and they were able to move fast, like streaking shadows.

Instead of approaching from the ridge side, they circled wide again and came up along the creek. The smell of ashes lingered in the air as they drew closer.

As they crouched in some brush about a quarter mile away from the village location, they saw that the dwellings left standing were gone, taken down, packed up, and carried away.

All that remained were the charred ruins of the tepees that had burned.

"The Blackfeet are gone," Hawk said.

"Yep. They've pulled up stakes and headed for the tall and uncut. I had a hunch they might if we made it too hot for 'em around here."

"Tall Bull thought to drive the Absaroka away and destroy those who would not leave. He would have done the same to any other tribe that got in his way. And yet now . . . he and his people are the ones who are gone."

"White folks have a sayin' about what happens when a fella gets too big for his britches. I reckon ol' Tall Bull is livin' proof of that."

Hawk looked over at Preacher. "But he *is* living. You are right about that. Our work is not done."

Preacher drew in a deep breath. He had mulled over what he would do if the Blackfoot village was abandoned. A part of him wanted to put this whole ugly war behind him and get on with the fur trapping that had brought him to the mountains in the first place.

He wasn't exactly weary of killing—he didn't figure he would ever get tired of killing evil bastards who had it coming—but a man's hands could get so covered with blood that he wanted to put it all aside for a while.

At the same time, he had promised Hawk he wouldn't stop fighting until Tall Bull was dead. He thought about Bird in the Tree and Little Pine and all the other Absaroka who had been slain because of Tall Bull's lust for power.

Hawk got tired of waiting for his father's response and said, "What will you do, Preacher, now that Tall Bull is gone?"

The mountain man took a deep breath. "Why, I reckon you and me will just have to go hunt the son of a bitch down and kill him."

CHAPTER 34

They carried the news back to the canyon.

"That's good, isn't it?" Charlie Todd asked. "I mean, the Blackfeet are gone. We won."

Hawk scowled and said in English, "Tall Bull is alive. We . . . have not . . . won."

Buckley said, "You have to kill him to properly avenge all the Absaroka he slaughtered."

Preacher nodded. "I reckon that's about the size of it."

Buckley looked over at his friend. "I understand. We feel the same about those fellows who were with us, don't we, Charlie?"

"We didn't really know them all *that* well," Todd said. "We just joined their company to come out here and trap furs." He saw the way Preacher and Buckley were looking at him and went on hurriedly. "But yeah, sure. They won't rest easy until Tall Bull is dead, and neither will we."

Buckley clapped a hand on his friend's shoulder. "That's the spirit." He nodded to the mountain man.

"We're with you, Preacher, as long as you want our help."

"I ain't sure what comes next, but we'll be glad to have you along, boys."

White Buffalo folded his arms across his scrawny chest. "So Tall Bull ran like the cowardly snake he is."

"You cannot call him cowardly," Hawk said. "He fights, or he never would have become a war chief. But he is evil and must be destroyed."

"Did the craven Blackfeet flee northward, back to the lands that spawned them?" White Buffalo asked Preacher.

"That's what we'll have to find out. We'll go back to the village and pick up the trail tomorrow."

"All of us?" Buckley asked.

"Yeah, I reckon we'll be travelin' together, at least for now. Once we find Tall Bull, we may have to split up again, dependin' on where he is and how we'll need to get at him."

"Just tell us what you need us to do," Buckley said. "We're at your command, Preacher."

"You're our general," Todd added. "General Preacher."

Preacher narrowed his eyes and shook his head. "I don't much cotton to the sound o' that. I ain't been in no army since I fought for Andy Jackson at the Battle o' New Orleans."

"I, uh, meant no offense—"

"It's all right, Charlie." Preacher held up a hand to forestall Todd's apology. "Army or not, we're all on the same side, after the same thing."

"Killing Tall Bull," Hawk said, and the others all nodded solemnly.

* * *

All five men left the canyon hideout the next day and traveled to the foothills above the former location of the Blackfoot village. Arriving at a high ridge, Preacher told White Buffalo, Buckley, and Todd to remain in the thick trees while he, Hawk, and Dog descended to look for a trail.

Along the creek, Preacher's eyes searched the trees, but he didn't see any shrouded forms placed among the branches. The Blackfeet had taken their dead with them to lay them to rest elsewhere.

Hawk noticed that, too. "They were afraid we would return to desecrate the bodies if they left them here."

"But we wouldn't have," Preacher said.

"No, we would never have done such a thing. We are better than the Blackfeet."

"Now you're startin' to catch on."

They walked among the burned tepees. Nothing was left except ashes and some rubble—the remains of clay pots, charred pieces of bearskin robes, and the like. Even though the Blackfeet were his enemies, Preacher thought, it was sad to see their lives reduced to destruction.

All of that misfortune could be laid at the feet of Tall Bull. It was his lust for power that had led to it.

Hawk pointed to the ground. "I can see the marks left by the travois they used to carry their belongings. We should be able to follow the trail without any trouble."

Preacher tugged at his earlobe and frowned in thought. "Yeah," he agreed, "but is that what they want us to—"

A soft growl from Dog interrupted him. Preacher turned to look at the big cur as Dog suddenly leaped toward Hawk and crashed into the young warrior's back.

Something flashed through the air, and Dog let out a yelp.

The arrow that had clipped him—the arrow that would have landed in the middle of Hawk's back if not for Dog's swift action—flew on past, fluttering a little from the impact with Dog's hip, where a bloody streak stood out.

Preacher finished his pivot and dropped to a knee as another arrow whipped over his head. He raised his rifle to his shoulder but couldn't find a target. More arrows slashed through the air.

"Stay down!" he called to Hawk, who had started to get up.

Hawk went flat on the ground. So did Preacher, and Dog hunkered low, as well.

They couldn't stay that way. It wouldn't take long for the hidden archers to adjust their aim and send their arrows high in the sky to arch back down at their targets.

The arrows came from the direction of the creek, where some of the Blackfoot warriors were concealed under the edge of the bank. They'd been left behind when the others pulled out, and Preacher and Hawk had walked right into the trap.

Preacher snarled in anger directed more at himself than his enemies. Tall Bull was canny, and it wouldn't pay to underestimate him.

At the moment, it was more important to figure out a way to deal with the new threat. The devastated village didn't offer any cover, and if Preacher and Hawk tried to dash back to the trees along the base of the ridge, they would be easy targets for the Blackfoot bowmen.

Knowing the warriors had to reveal themselves a little in order to launch their arrows, Preacher watched for any sign of movement. When he saw a flicker of it, he squeezed the rifle's trigger.

The ball smashed into the forehead of a Blackfoot warrior who had just pulled back his bowstring. His head exploded like a ripe melon, and the arrow flew wildly as the man toppled backwards off his perch just below the rim of the creek bank. Angry shouts came from his companions.

"The Blackfeet are cowards!" Preacher yelled back at them. "They hide themselves from their enemies! They fight like women!" He set the empty rifle aside and drew both pistols. The range was a little long . . . but the solution to that was to bring the Blackfeet closer.

"The Blackfeet cower like dogs! Brave warriors will wipe them from the face of the earth!"

Arrows soared into the sky. Preacher saw the angle at which they flew and knew the Blackfeet had figured out what they needed to do. "Move!" he told Hawk. "Roll the other way!"

They split apart, rolling desperately in opposite directions. The deadly rain of arrows fell all around them, and it was pure luck neither man was skewered. An arrow pinned one of Preacher's trouser legs to the ground for a second, but he ripped it free and kept moving.

He saw that Hawk was all right for the moment and

that Dog had sprung up and outraced the falling arrows, getting clear of the ruined village. The big cur stopped, turned back, and would have returned to Preacher, but the mountain man called, "No, Dog! Get outta here!"

Dog hesitated, clearly reluctant to leave his trail partner, but then turned and raced toward the ridge, limping only slightly from his arrow wound.

"Again the Blackfeet fail!" Preacher shouted toward the creek. "Your enemies live and spit in your face!"

"You cannot defeat the Absaroka!" Hawk added to the taunting. "The spirits of the slain are with us and will bring down bloody vengeance on your heads!"

Preacher figured the Blackfeet didn't outnumber them by too much, or the warriors would have already rushed and overrun them. Tall Bull's forces had been whittled down considerably, and he wouldn't strip all his remaining warriors away from the fleeing band.

Preacher was willing to take his chances against the enemy and knew Hawk was, too. It was just a matter of getting the fight out in the open. He called out, "The Great Spirit has abandoned the Blackfeet! Your medicine is gone!"

That did it. Shouting and howling, five warriors boiled over the edge of the bank and charged toward Preacher and Hawk, firing arrows on the run as they attacked.

Preacher came up on one knee, thrust the pistols out in front of him, and pulled the triggers. The thunderous double boom of their reports was deafening. The shots scythed two of the warriors off their feet as blood flew from their wounds.

Hawk rose from the ground, leaning to the side to

let an arrow slash through the air only inches from his right ear. The next instant, his bowstring twanged. The shaft he fired found its target, burying its flint head deep in the guts of an onrushing Blackfoot. The warrior doubled over in agony and collapsed.

That left the odds even, two against two. Too close for arrows, the Blackfeet cast their bows aside and yanked out their tomahawks. Preacher and Hawk surged to their feet and met that assault with tomahawks of their own.

The weapons slashed back and forth, striking and blocking almost too fast for the eye to follow. All four fighters were fast and skilled. The slightest hesitation or miscalculation might well be followed by instant death. They twisted around, giving ground and then retaking it. They all knew it was a fight to the finish.

As often happened, luck played a part in the outcome. As Hawk backed away from his opponent, hard put to block a flurry of swings launched by the Blackfoot, he came within reach of the man he'd shot in the belly with an arrow.

Gasping in pain, the warrior looked up, saw the source of his agony close by, and lunged out to grab Hawk's right ankle. With the last of his fading strength, the man jerked that foot out from under Hawk, robbing him of his balance and making him topple to the side before the dying man collapsed again.

Hawk's opponent seized the opportunity, leaping in and swinging his tomahawk as the young Absaroka's guard dropped. Hawk jerked his head, but the tomahawk struck him a glancing blow and stunned him. The Blackfoot raised the weapon again, ready to bring it crashing down on Hawk's skull.

In the split second that separated Hawk from death, a rifle boomed. The Blackfoot pitched to the side as a chunk of his skull flew into the air, blown apart by the lead ball that struck it. Blood and brains splattered Hawk's face, but he was alive and the man who'd been about to kill him was not.

A few yards away, Preacher was still battling fiercely. The remaining Blackfoot was several inches shorter but had the longest arms the mountain man had ever seen. His tomahawk whipped back and forth, but he couldn't seem to get inside that long reach.

If he couldn't get to the varmint one way, he would try another way, Preacher decided. He bided his time, and when he had an opening, he suddenly leaped into the air and kicked out with both feet, driving his heels into the warrior's solar plexus. The Blackfoot flew backwards like a puppet jerked at the end of a string.

Preacher caught himself with his free hand as he fell. He pushed into a roll and came up swinging the tomahawk. The Blackfoot was gasping for breath but managed to block the mountain man's tomahawk as it came sweeping down at his face.

That was the last resistance he was able to muster. The next second Preacher rammed a knee into the Blackfoot's belly and weakened him even more. Preacher knocked the warrior's tomahawk aside, and then with a backhanded swing of his own weapon, he shattered the Blackfoot's skull. Another blow crunched more bone to make sure.

Preacher stood up and looked around in time to see Hawk pushing a corpse off himself. Blood trickled down the side of Hawk's face from a wound in his hair, near his left temple. He didn't appear to be badly hurt, however, so Preacher checked the other Blackfeet first and made sure they were all dead. Satisfied the threat was over, at least for the moment, the mountain man turned to his son. "How bad is it?"

"This is nothing," Hawk said as he climbed to his feet, but his eyes seemed to be a little unfocused. "The Blackfoot dog barely struck me." As soon as those words were out of his mouth, Hawk's knees buckled and he started to fall.

Preacher sprang forward to grab him and hold him up. "We'd best clean that wound and see how bad it really is. Come on. I'll help you down to the creek."

Before he could do that, he heard his name being called. He looked around and saw Charlie Todd and Aaron Buckley running across the open ground toward the destroyed village. Dog was with them. A considerable distance behind them, White Buffalo followed at a more deliberate pace as he led Horse and the pack mule.

They appeared to be all right, so Preacher resumed helping Hawk down to the creek. Half-leading, half-carrying Hawk, they took one of the paths the Blackfoot women had worn into the bank.

The body of the first man Preacher had shot bobbed limply in the water a short distance downstream where it had floated up against a log.

Hawk stretched out on the grass while Preacher took a rag from his possibles bag and got it wet in the creek. He swabbed the blood away and found a long but shallow gash in Hawk's hair. A poultice would fix that up, he decided. In the meantime, Hawk's head would hurt like hell and his vision might be a little fuzzy, but it wouldn't take him long to shake off those effects.

After all, he was Preacher's son, wasn't he?

"You're gonna be all right," Preacher told him.

From the top of the bank, Aaron Buckley asked, "How badly is he hurt?"

"Not too bad," Preacher said. "Got a wallop to the noggin with a tomahawk, that's all."

"That's all, he says," Charlie Todd commented, "like it's something that happens every day."

Hawk's eyes focused on the two young white men as they peered down at him, and he pushed himself up on an elbow. "You! One of you . . . shot that Blackfoot . . ."

"That was Charlie," Buckley said with a grin as he pointed a thumb at his friend. "We were too far away to be sure, but it looked like he was about to kill you, and . . . well, we had to do something."

"I am . . . in your debt . . . Charlie."

"I'm just glad I was able to make the shot," Todd said.

"I have some salve that might help that head wound," Buckley added.

"I can make a poultice from some herbs that'll fix it right up," Preacher said, "but I'm obliged for the offer. And I'm obliged for that shot you made, Charlie. Looks like askin' you fellas to throw in with us was a mighty good idea."

Both young men looked pleased at the mountain man's praise.

Buckley said, "Tall Bull left his men behind to ambush anybody who came to take a look around the village, didn't he?"

"Yeah, it was a trap, all right. I didn't give the varmint enough credit." Preacher paused, then added grimly, "I won't make that mistake a second time, you can bet a brand-new beaver hat on that."

CHAPTER 35

Preacher helped Hawk back up the path and then the young man sat on the ground while Preacher went to look for the herbs he needed for the poultice.

"You fellas scout around a mite while I'm tendin' to Hawk," he told Buckley and Todd. "Make sure no more Blackfeet are lurkin' in these parts."

"You'd trust us to do that?" Buckley asked.

"Yep. Just keep your eyes and ears open, and don't mess up any tracks you find." Preacher was pretty sure all the warriors Tall Bull had left behind were already dead, but having a look around would give the two greenhorns something to do.

He was going to have to stop thinking of them as greenhorns, he told himself. They were far from being seasoned frontiersmen, but they were learning more and gaining confidence every day.

During the next hour, Preacher found the plants he needed, mashed and soaked them into a poultice, and then tied it into place on Hawk's head with strips of rawhide. "You'll be good as new in a day or two," he told the young warrior.

"I am good enough to hunt and kill Blackfeet right now," Hawk said.

"Best not get too far ahead o' yourself. You wasn't too steady on your feet the last time you tried to stand up."

"I will not delay our revenge," Hawk declared as he started to get to his feet. He didn't make it very far before his suddenly sickened expression made it clear the world had started spinning crazily. He sank back, bracing himself with a hand against the ground, and groaned.

"White Buffalo, watch over the boy," Preacher said. "Make sure he don't do nothin' foolish, like tryin' to get up and run around."

White Buffalo folded his arms. "I can do nothing except offer him the wise counsel of my years."

"I reckon that'll have to be enough, then." Preacher pointed a finger at Hawk. "Stay right there."

"I am not Dog," Hawk said with a surly frown. "You cannot command me as you would the cur."

"Dog is more reasonable than a young man filled with the hot blood of hatred and pride," White Buffalo said.

Hawk scowled even more.

Trying not to chuckle, Preacher left them there and followed Buckley and Todd, who had headed up the creek toward the north.

It didn't take him long to catch up with them. Buckley pointed toward marks in the grass where things had been dragged through it. "Are those the tracks you were talking about?"

"Yeah," Preacher said. "You know what a travois is?"

"I've heard the word," Todd replied, looking puzzled. "But I'm not exactly sure . . ."

"It's a long pair of poles with hide stretched between them. The Indians use some of the tepee poles once they've taken it down. Indians don't have a lot, so they make use of everything they've got. Each family piles all their possessions on their travois and then drags it behind 'em. That way, all they have to do when they get where they're goin' is unload and set up the tepees again. You could say they carry their homes with 'em. That way, wherever they are . . . they're home."

"That seems like a really primitive way to live," Buckley said.

"Well, if you was to ask them, they'd say that livin' in houses and wearin' uncomfortable duds and goin' out to do work for somebody else every day in the hope you'll get paid for it is a crazy way to live." Preacher smiled. "I ain't sure I'd argue too much with 'em about that, neither."

They studied the tracks for a while. Preacher estimated at least thirty families were in the band. Most of the people left had to be women and children and old ones. He and Hawk had killed enough warriors that Tall Bull might not have more than two dozen men left to follow him into battle.

That left the war chief with a dilemma. Should he protect his people . . . or should he go after the men who had caused so much trouble and caused the proud Blackfeet to flee?

Either way, there had to be grumbling in the tribe. That thought pleased Preacher. He didn't want Tall Bull to ever rest easy again. He wanted the war chief stirred up and worried . . . until the time finally came for Tall Bull to die.

When Hawk was steady enough on his feet to travel, Preacher said, "I want all four of you fellas to pull back west a ways and then head north along the edge of the valley. Stay out of sight. Hawk, you know what I'm talkin' about. I'm countin' on you to guide the other three, even with that head wallopin' you got."

"And what are you going to do?"

"Dog and me will follow the creek," Preacher said as he gestured toward the stream. "That's what the Blackfeet are doin', and I intend to stay on their trail."

"You would push me aside now, after everything that has happened?"

Preacher could tell Hawk wanted to argue, so he said sharply, "That ain't it at all, and you know it. Right now, all I'm doin' is a mite of scoutin'. I want to know where the Blackfeet are headed and what they're gonna do once they get there. When I've found that out, I'll hunt you fellas up, and we'll make our plans for what we're gonna do next."

He didn't care much for explaining himself, but he knew how strong-willed Hawk was. Preacher was nothing if not a practical man, so taking a moment to lay out his thoughts would save time later on.

Hawk still wore a reluctant frown, but he nodded. "It is not a bad idea."

"It will give your injury time to heal," White Buffalo said.

That turned Hawk's scowl darker. "My head is fine. The world no longer spins around me."

"We need to keep it like that," Preacher said. "Anyway, like I said, you're gonna be in charge, and I'm countin' on you to watch out for these two fellas." He nodded toward Buckley and Todd, who hadn't been able to follow the conversation in the Absaroka tongue.

Both young men smiled hopefully at Preacher's gesture.

"We're ready to do whatever you say, Preacher," Buckley said.

"I was just tellin' Hawk and White Buffalo the four of you are gonna head north along the edge of the valley while I follow the creek and the trail Tall Bull's bunch left. I'll scout out where they are then find you fellas and we'll figure out what we're doin' next."

"You're going by yourself?" Todd asked.

"Not exactly. Dog'll be with me."

The big cur was worth at least two good fighting men, Preacher knew. He'd put some of the poultice he'd made for Hawk on the arrow wound on Dog's hip. That leg seemed to be a little stiff and sore, but it wouldn't slow Dog down much.

If there was a fight, Preacher figured it wouldn't slow him down at all.

"It may be a few days 'fore you see me again," the mountain man went on. "Don't worry, just keep headin' north. I'll find you when the time comes." He looked at Hawk. "For what it's worth, I've gotten used to havin' you fightin' with me, boy. It's gonna seem a mite odd, you not bein' there, but you got a more important job to do right now."

"Who will save your life when your ancient senses betray you?"

"Well, who's gonna save *your* life when you do somethin' foolish 'cause you don't know no better?" Preacher didn't wait for a response. He just clapped a hand on Hawk's shoulder for a second, then jerked his head. "Come on, Dog."

They started off, following the creek. With the twists and turns and the thick stands of trees and brush that grew in the valley, it wasn't long before Preacher's companions were out of sight behind him. He didn't look back. He was leaving them in Hawk's hands and knew if anyone could keep them safe, it was the young warrior.

It was natural for a man to be proud of his son. Preacher had discovered he had that pride in his heart, after all. He and Hawk might not ever be as close as some fathers and sons, but that bond was between them and always would be, he thought.

The Blackfeet had abandoned their village the day before, but the entire band couldn't move very fast. Preacher figured they were less than ten miles ahead of him. He could make up that much ground fairly quickly. He didn't expect to catch up with them by the end of the day, but it was entirely possible he might the next day.

As he and Dog walked along the creek bank, his eyes were always on the move, searching for signs of anything out of the ordinary. He knew Dog's senses were alert, too. It wasn't likely they would walk into an ambush, but anything was possible. All of Preacher's guns were loaded and primed.

The Blackfeet hadn't gone to any pains to conceal their trail. Even Buckley and Todd could have followed it without much trouble.

They weren't trying to hide, Preacher thought. They didn't care if anybody followed them. They just wanted to get away from the scene of their disastrous encounters with the legendary Ghost Killer, where so many of their husbands and brothers and sons had died.

Once they had settled into a new, semipermanent camp—no Indian camp was truly permanent—Tall Bull would deal with the white devil and his allies. Preacher could imagine the war chief's blustery boasting about what he was going to do. Tall Bull would have to *talk* big to keep his people's loyalty. His actions sure hadn't accomplished much lately.

In fact, since the attack on the Absarokas, just about everything had gone badly for Tall Bull. He really had to be questioning whether his medicine had deserted him.

By late afternoon, Preacher could tell from the tracks of the Blackfeet that he had closed the gap between them by quite a bit. They were still a good distance ahead of him, but he didn't intend to close in on them. When they chose a place to settle down for a while, he could go find Hawk and the others and lead them back for the next phase of the war.

General Preacher, Todd had called him, the mountain man mused as night fell and he settled down with Dog under a tree. He gnawed some pemmican from his possibles bag. The quest for vengeance he and Hawk and White Buffalo had set out on had taken on the characteristics of a war, sure enough. Maybe he *was* a general after all. A general in command of a very small army . . .

Preacher dozed off.

CHAPTER 36

Dog's quiet growl roused Preacher from sleep. Instantly, he was wide awake and ready to fight.

Dog didn't sound like the threat was imminent, however. Preacher slitted his eyes and listened intently for whatever sound had disturbed the big cur. He sniffed the air, although his sense of smell couldn't hope to match Dog's, then reached over and rested his hand on the back of the animal's neck. Dog's hair was standing up, a sure sign something had bothered him.

After a moment, Preacher heard something. Soft sounds he recognized as men moving quietly through the night, trying not to make any noise.

Even seasoned Blackfoot warriors couldn't move in complete silence. That required a man to glide through the shadows like a . . . ghost.

Preacher sat with his back against a tree trunk about twenty yards from the creek. Along that stretch, a man could hunker down on the shallower bank, reach out, and cup a handful of the cold, crystal-clear water.

The three men who emerged from the darkness

did just that. They knelt at the edge of the creek to drink.

Preacher watched them in the starlight. As keen as his eyes were, he couldn't make out too many details. He could tell they were Indians, though, and had no doubt they were Blackfoot warriors sent by Tall Bull to scout the band's back trail.

A moment later, he heard the soft murmur of their voices as they talked to each other, and although he couldn't make out all the words, he caught enough to be sure they were speaking the Blackfoot tongue.

Well, he thought, since Fate dropped this little *present* in his lap—

Interrupting his thought, a memory flashed through his brain, the recollection of a night when he, Audie, Nighthawk, and some other trappers had been sitting around a campfire and Audie had been telling them about a war between two bunches of men in the old days.

Audie talked about the Trojans and Greeks: "The Greeks made a giant wooden horse and left it in front of the gates of Troy, then their army lit a shuck out of there.

"Only they didn't, really. They just got out of sight so the Trojans would think they were gone and haul in that fool horse, believing it to be some sort of tribute from a vanquished foe.

"Greeks were hiding in it, of course. Once they were inside they gate they came out of the horse that night, opened the gates, and let in the rest of their army. The real massacre quickly commenced. That's why folks sometimes say, 'Don't look a gift horse in the mouth.'"

Audie pointed out that was actually foolish advice. "As the Trojans learned, the smart thing was to take a good long look in that gift horse's mouth and make sure there wasn't more in it than what a fella might expect."

All that went through Preacher's mind in a heartbeat. What Audie had said on that long-ago night made sense. Because of that, Preacher waited to see if more warriors showed up before he made a move.

Several minutes passed as the Blackfeet quenched their thirst and talked in complaining tones. They straightened, stretched, and generally acted like men who were tired and doing a job they didn't particularly want to do.

One of them turned and ambled toward the trees where Preacher and Dog waited in the shadows. He fumbled with his buckskin leggings, clearly intent on answering the call of nature.

That pretty well made up Preacher's mind. "Now, Dog!"

The big cur sprang out of the darkness like a spring uncoiling.

The luckless warrior barely had time to open his mouth and try to scream before massive jaws full of sharp teeth closed on his face. Dog's weight bore him backwards.

Preacher charged right behind Dog, plucking his tomahawk from his belt. Shots from guns would carry too far. He brought his arm back, then whipped it forward. The tomahawk made a whispering sound as it revolved through the air, then landed with a meaty *thunk!* as the head sunk into a warrior's shoulder.

That man yelled in pain and staggered to the side, out of the fight for the moment. Preacher bore down on the other warrior, who was trying to get an arrow out of his quiver and fit it to his bow. Preacher left his feet in a diving tackle, crashed into the warrior, and drove him off his feet into the creek.

Water rose high around them in a huge splash. Preacher landed on top and groped for the Blackfoot's throat as the man thrashed around underneath him. He caught hold of it and bore down, trying to hold him under the surface so the water would rush into the man's lungs and finish him off.

Preacher glanced over his shoulder to make sure the man he had wounded hadn't recovered enough to charge into the creek after him. That warrior was still stumbling around on the bank, trying to wrench the tomahawk's head out of his flesh.

One of the desperately flailing arms belonging to the Blackfoot in the creek clipped Preacher on the jaw. It wasn't much of a blow, but it was enough to make his grip slip for an instant. The warrior tore loose and broke the surface, gasping for air. He didn't get much before Preacher's left hand shot out and grabbed him by the throat again.

Preacher took a second look at the bank. The warrior there had gotten the tomahawk loose but was bleeding heavily, the blood black and oily in the starlight.

"Hell with this," Preacher muttered. He drew his knife and plunged it into the chest of the man he was holding, ramming the blade into his heart. He pulled it free and let go of the man's throat, allowing his already dead body to collapse into the stream.

Preacher turned toward the bank with the bloody knife in his hand.

The wounded Blackfoot tried to run, but Dog took him down from behind. Slashing teeth opened the warrior's throat and finished him off.

With water dripping off him, Preacher stepped up onto the bank and told the big cur, "I reckon if Hawk was here, he'd be keepin' count and takin' great pleasure in pointin' out I killed one of the varmints while you got two."

Dog just made a little chuffing sound as he shook drops of blood from his muzzle.

"Yeah, it don't make no never mind to me, neither," Preacher said. "Let me drag these fellas into the brush so they won't be found so easy if anybody comes lookin' for 'em. Then maybe we can finish our night's sleep."

They were up before the sun in the morning, as usual. For some reason, Preacher had a hankering for a cup of coffee, but of course there was none to be had. He had some in his supply packs on The Mule With No Name, but that critter, along with the other members of Preacher's motley little army, was miles away.

He settled for gnawing on pemmican again, washed it down with creek water, and then took up the trail with Dog padding along beside him.

Neither of them even cast a glance at the thicket where Preacher had left the bodies of the three Blackfoot warriors. That violent incident was over and done with, and he wasn't the sort to brood over such things any more than Dog was.

Wouldn't have been natural for either one of them.

Mid-afternoon found them kneeling atop one of the small hills that cropped up here and there on the valley floor. Preacher wanted to take advantage of its height to study the landscape ahead of them. His eyes spotted movement about a mile away.

Dog growled.

"You see 'em, too, eh? That's them, all right, the whole bunch of 'em. We don't need to get no closer than this. Tall Bull's likely to send more men back to make sure nobody's followin' 'em. Although, since those three last night didn't come back, he's liable to have a devil of a time gettin' anybody to step up and volunteer."

Dog ignored the mountain man's musings and kept his gaze fastened on the tiny figures in the distance as they struggled along, dragging their travois and all their worldly possessions behind them.

Preacher waited until the Blackfeet were out of sight again before he and Dog resumed their trek. Knowing they were close to their quarry, they used all the stealth at their command to stay out of sight as they followed the Blackfoot pilgrims.

That night they crept closer to study the camp Tall Bull's people made. The Blackfeet had built cooking fires, but they didn't set up their tepees. It was just a stopping place for one night. They hadn't found their new "home" yet.

Preacher counted the warriors he could see and came up with the number twenty-seven, including Tall Bull himself. Preacher might have laid eyes on

the bastard during some of the many confrontations
he and Hawk had had with the Blackfeet, but it was the
first time he was certain he was looking at the war
chief. Tall Bull was like White Buffalo had described
him, tall and burly and brutal, wearing a necklace of
buffalo horns and carrying a wicked-looking war club.

From where Preacher was stretched out in some
brush a hundred yards away, he could have put a rifle
ball in Tall Bull's head. He was sure of it. He was
equally certain he and Dog could get away without
any of the Blackfoot warriors ever coming close to
them.

For a long moment, he gave the idea serious consideration. Finally, he decided against it. One reason
was personal, the other strategic.

If he killed Tall Bull, the Blackfeet would come up
with a new chief and continue their pilgrimage to
wherever they were going. That wouldn't be enough
to satisfy Hawk. The youngster would continue fighting them all by himself if he had to, and Preacher
wasn't sure Hawk was up to that challenge yet. That
was the strategic reason.

The personal one was that he carried Birdie's image
in his mind and the warmth he felt for her in his heart.
He didn't want to kill Tall Bull from a distance. If
things had worked out that way in battle, fine. But
given a choice . . .

Preacher wanted to be looking right in that son of
a bitch's eyes, nice and close, when Tall Bull died.

CHAPTER 37

The Blackfeet pulled out at dawn the next morning and continued trudging northward. The mountain called Beartooth and the valley of the Absaroka on the other side of it were far behind them.

They couldn't leave their actions behind them, though. The consequences of Tall Bull's ruthlessness and cruelty followed them, in the forms of a man and a dog.

Preacher kept his distance for the next two days, until the Blackfeet stopped at a mountain lake formed where the creek flowed down into a bowl between some hills. Except for occasional open areas, tall green pines and firs surrounded the lake, which was an incredibly deep blue. It was a beautiful spot, Preacher thought as he and Dog watched from one of the hills while the Blackfeet began setting up their new village in one of those meadows along the shore.

It was better than they deserved, he decided, but he was willing to let them live there in peace . . . once Tall Bull and most of the remaining warriors were dead.

The lake would be teeming with fish and plenty

of game was in the area, too. Preacher saw deer and antelope every day. The Blackfoot women and children wouldn't have much trouble surviving, even without warriors to go out and hunt.

The boys would grow up to be warriors, but maybe they would remember what had happened during the long, bloody season and realize it wasn't wise to slaughter other tribes just because they weren't Blackfoot. Maybe the memory of Preacher's vengeance would remain with them.

Preacher looked around, studying the terrain. They were near the head of the valley. Snowcapped peaks rose in a solid line to the east and north, closing in to pinch off the valley. To the west was an area of ridges and gullies and spires of rock, a broken land.

A land made for ambushes, Preacher thought as his eyes narrowed.

Knowing the Blackfeet weren't going anywhere, he turned and descended from the hill, taking Dog with him. They headed west, toward the badlands. Somewhere in that direction they would find Hawk, White Buffalo, and the two young white men.

From time to time, Preacher stopped and gave the call of a loon. It was the signal he and Hawk had agreed on to help them find each other.

Night had almost fallen before he heard an answering call a good distance off to the southwest. He and Dog headed toward it, and when, after a while, Preacher tried the loon call again, the response was louder and clearer. They loped toward a wooded ridge that loomed darkly in the dusk.

"Preacher!"

The mountain man heard his name called softly. He said, "Here," and Hawk came out of the gathering shadows. Preacher put his right hand on the young man's left shoulder for a moment, and Hawk returned the gesture.

"How are you doin'?" Preacher asked.

"The wound on my head is much better," Hawk replied. "The world no longer spins without warning. Have the Blackfeet made a new camp?"

The boy believed in getting right down to business, Preacher thought. He pointed to the northeast. "Yeah, they're settin' up their village beside a lake about five miles yonderways, I'd say. It's a mighty nice place. Better even than where they were before, I reckon."

Hawk's mouth twisted bitterly in the gloom. "They should have no home. They should be condemned to wander in squalor and misery for the rest of their lives."

"And for all the generations to come?"

"It would be justice," Hawk insisted.

"Maybe so, but you go to holdin' grudges like that for long, sooner or later nobody really knows why all the killin' and the hatin' is goin' on. It's just somethin' they do . . . and that ain't no way to live."

"You are not one of our people. You do not know."

Preacher let it go. Hawk would figure out that he had to let go of his hate sometime . . . or he wouldn't, and in the end it would consume him.

Either way it was up to the boy—No, it was up to the *man* Hawk had become, Preacher corrected silently. "The rest of the bunch all right?" he asked.

"Yes. White Buffalo never stops complaining."

Preacher grinned. "I might worry about him if he did. What about Aaron and Charlie?"

"They have done well," Hawk said with a note of grudging respect in his voice. "I can speak to them only so much in their white man's tongue, but they listen and try to do as I say. They have caused no trouble."

"I'm glad to hear it. Where's your camp?"

Hawk turned to point. "Back there in those trees, along the base of the ridge." He paused. "We have a haunch of deer cooking."

Preacher's grin widened. After several days of living on pemmican and creek water, that sounded mighty good to him.

"So they've stopped and plan to stay where they are for a while," Aaron Buckley said as the five men sat around a small fire and gnawed on roasted venison. "What do we do?"

"They've come a pretty far piece," Preacher said. "They didn't waste any time doin' it, neither. That won't sit well with Tall Bull and the other warriors. It'll feel too much like runnin' away from a fight."

"Well, that's what they did, isn't it?" Todd asked.

"Yeah. Tall Bull probably told everybody they were doin' it to protect the women and young'uns, but it'll stick in their craw anyway. There's one more thing to remember . . . we haven't hurt any of the women or kids." Preacher glanced at Hawk. "*That's* why you try not to make war on anybody except the warriors. Keep the hostilities between fightin' men, and in the end they can't use what you done to stir up even more hard feelin's."

Buckley said, "Some military strategists claim that to win, you have to completely annihilate the enemy."

"Well, I reckon that would do the job, too. Wipe 'em out and sow salt so nothin' ever grows there again. I heard tell about a fella name of Hannibal who did that. You know where Hannibal is today?"

"Why, he's, uh, dead, I suppose," Buckley said with a frown.

"Yep. Ever' bit as dead as the folks he conquered. I wonder if he's restin' easy in his grave, though." Preacher shrugged. "Reckon we'll never know."

Hawk made a disgusted noise. "You are too . . . soft in the heart," he told Preacher in English.

"That's somethin' I ain't often been accused of. I reckon the twenty or thirty Blackfoot warriors I've sent over the divide in recent weeks would dispute it, too." The mountain man's voice hardened. "I'll kill whoever's in need of a killin', and don't you ever forget it."

A strained silence hung over the camp for a moment, then Buckley asked, "So what's our next move?"

"We need to draw Tall Bull and his men outta the village. They've come all this way. They're hopin' they're safe now and that their troubles are behind 'em." Preacher smiled. "We'll show 'em that ain't true. I figure that'll make Tall Bull so mad he'll decide to hunt us down once and for all, even if it takes every last one of his warriors to do it."

"Uh . . . how many did you say there are?" Todd asked.

"Twenty-seven. Might be a few more I didn't see that night."

"So we could be facing as many as thirty blood-thirsty warriors . . . and there's five of us. That's, uh, six-to-one odds." Todd shook his head. "Not very promising."

"Five-to-one. You didn't count Dog. I never said we'd kill 'em all at once, neither. What we'll do is, Hawk and me will pay the Blackfeet a visit in their new village, and when we light a shuck outta there, we'll make sure they see which way we're goin'."

"And which way will we be going?" Hawk asked in English.

"Toward the badlands west of that lake. If we can get Tall Bull to follow us in there with all of his men, we'll be waitin' for 'em . . . and either they'll come out . . . or we will."

"A desperate plan," Buckley said, nodding slowly. "One that sounds like it might work . . . but even though they've fled, Preacher, they'll be on their guard, especially since those men you told us about never came back. They may hope otherwise, but they'll be expecting trouble."

"Sure," the mountain man agreed, "but I don't figure they'll be expectin' it from the direction I plan to come at 'em."

Night lay thick and dark over the lake. On the shore, fires blazed high and warriors stood around the outer edge of the village holding bows or tomahawks as they stood sentinel. Preacher counted eight of them as he stroked through the water with his face barely above the surface, as sleek and smooth and silent as an otter.

A few feet away, Hawk swam the same way, cutting almost noiselessly through the lake. They had entered on the far side, holding on to a log and kicking to propel themselves toward the Blackfoot village. When they were close enough, Preacher had signaled for Hawk to let go of the log and start swimming, so their approach would be quieter. He had done likewise.

All the guards were facing away from the lake. The idea of someone attacking them from that side of the new village hadn't occurred to them. Preacher was glad to see his hunch had been correct.

All he and Hawk had to do was make it ashore before they froze to death.

Fed by springs and snowmelt, the mountain lake was icy enough to chill a man all the way to his bones in a matter of minutes. He was stripped down to the bottoms of a pair of long underwear, and Hawk wore only a loincloth. They had tomahawks and knives slung around their necks on rawhide thongs.

Preacher paused and pointed right. In the starlight that glittered on the water, he saw Hawk nod in understanding. They split up, Hawk going right, Preacher heading toward the left side of the village as they looked at it from the water.

Preacher hadn't thought it was possible to be any colder than he was in the lake, but when he pulled himself onto the bank and a night breeze hit him, an even deeper chill coursed through him. He ignored it, clenching his jaw so his teeth didn't chatter. There would be plenty of time to warm up later, when the night's work was done.

Being careful not to let the tomahawk and knife clatter together, he took them from around his neck. He was out of reach of the glow from the fires, but he was concerned he might be spotted anyway, since so much of his pale skin was on display in the darkness. He stayed in the shadows as much as possible as he seemingly floated toward the nearest guard like a ghostly phantasm.

On the other side of the village, Hawk should be doing the same thing, Preacher knew.

His first target was on edge, pacing back and forth for a short distance as his head kept turning from side to side. He peered nervously at the woods.

The knife first, Preacher decided. Nice and quiet-like . . .

The guard died a moment later, with Preacher's left arm clamped around his neck and the mountain man's knife buried in his back. Preacher pulled the blade free and lowered the body to the ground.

The plan was for him and Hawk to kill as many of the sentinels as they could before being discovered. It was unlikely they would be able to dispose of all the warriors Tall Bull had posted to watch over the village, but however many they sent over the divide, it was that many fewer for the war chief to bring with him when he pursued the two stealthy killers.

Those odds Charlie Todd worried about got better with every Blackfoot that died.

Preacher closed in on the next guard on his side of the village. The man was more stolid than the first one, standing still with his arms crossed over his broad chest. He gripped a tomahawk in one hand, a war club in the other.

The warrior was big and looked strong. Best to put him down quick, Preacher thought. A stroke with the tomahawk to the back of the head would crush his skull without him ever knowing he was in danger. It would be noisier—couldn't stave in a fellow's head without a pretty good thud—but Preacher figured it was worth the risk. As he moved a silent step closer, he raised the tomahawk.

At that moment, somewhere behind him, a woman let out a piercing scream.

CHAPTER 38

Preacher and Hawk had waited late enough to launch their attack that Preacher hoped everyone in the village would be asleep except the guards.

Clearly, that wasn't the case.

Such things couldn't be planned for, only dealt with as they came up. Preacher dealt with that one by leaping forward and striking swiftly as the broad-shouldered sentinel in front of him started to turn around.

Another shrill scream from the woman ripped through the night as Preacher's tomahawk slammed down on the warrior's head. He felt bone crunch under the impact, and from the way the Blackfoot dropped like a rock, he knew some of those bone shards had driven deep into the man's brain.

A screeching wildcat landed on his back an instant later. More than likely, the woman was married to the guard and had been sneaking out to see him when she spotted Preacher. She was attacking him out of sheer fury at seeing her man struck down.

Her fingers clawed him like an eagle's talons. He

felt the rough nails rake over his skin. She went for his eyes, but he twisted his face away from her groping hands.

Preacher grabbed the woman, bent forward, and flung her over his head. He wasn't trying to hurt her, necessarily, but he wasn't going out of his way to be gentle with her, either. He figured she had called the tune, and she could dance to it.

He heard shouting and the rapid slap of footsteps on the ground. As he turned in that direction he saw one of the other guards rushing at him, tomahawk in hand.

The man was already close enough to swing his tomahawk at Preacher's head. Preacher blocked the blow with his own weapon and lashed out with his left fist at the same time, crossing a sharp blow to the guard's solar plexus. The punch knocked the warrior back a step and caused him to lower his tomahawk. Preacher's backhanded slash crushed his jaw and sent him moaning to the ground.

Preacher put the Blackfoot out of his misery an instant later with a two-handed stroke that buried the tomahawk in the man's brain. He wrenched it free and whirled to meet a new attack from two more sentries drawn by the commotion.

The rest of the village would be waking up. Preacher knew he couldn't afford to waste any time. He dropped to the ground, caught himself with his free hand, and swung his right leg in a sweeping move that took the legs of both men out from under him. That took them by surprise, and they were unable to stay upright.

Preacher pushed himself up, lunged, and chopped

down at the nearest of the fallen men. The tomahawk took him in the throat and ripped it open, at the same time crushing his windpipe. He gurgled and thrashed as blood spouted like one of those geysers down in Colter's Hell.

The other man recovered quickly enough to slash at Preacher with a knife. The mountain man broke his wrist with little more than a glancing blow. The man scrambled after the knife he had dropped, reaching for it with his other hand, but Preacher kicked him in the jaw. The heel of his foot struck with such force the Blackfoot's neck broke with a sharp crack.

All sorts of yelling was going on. Preacher leaped to his feet and looked around to see warriors boiling out of the tepees.

Time to go.

He let loose with another loon call. It worked as a signal to Hawk, and the crazy-sounding, high-pitched racket might well unnerve the Blackfeet, too. Preacher raced for the trees.

He heard feet slapping swiftly on the ground behind him and looked over his shoulder to see Hawk's familiar shape catching up to him.

"You are slow . . . old man!" Hawk said.

"Ain't always the fastest . . . who wins the race," Preacher replied as Hawk drew even with him.

Arrows began to whip through the air around them and strike the ground near their racing feet. Howls of outrage pursued them as well. They could still hear the yelling as they entered the trees, but the trunks and the thickly woven branches provided cover for them where the arrows were concerned.

"Leave plenty o' sign!" he called to Hawk. "We don't

want 'em to have any trouble . . . followin' us!" He
wondered if Tall Bull was canny enough to figure out
that his enemies were trying to lead him into a trap.

The war chief might be so desperate to destroy
them that he wouldn't care about the risks. In fact,
that was pretty much what Preacher was counting on.

A pair of rocks some fifty feet tall stood at the edge
of the badlands. Preacher had noticed them when
he was scouting the day before and had described
them to his companions. Made of red sandstone, the
massive rocks would look like flame when the sun
came up in the morning.

"Sounds like the gates to Hell," Aaron Buckley had
commented.

"Reckon that's about right," Preacher had said,
"because what's beyond 'em don't exactly look pleasant,
either. Lots of sharp rocks and sticker bushes that'll
claw you like a panther."

Those rocks were big enough to be seen even at
night, and as they approached the badlands, they
were what Preacher and Hawk steered for. Their flight
from the new Blackfoot village had finally warmed
them up after their midnight swim in the cold lake. In
fact, both men were covered with a fine sheen of sweat
from their run.

They paused before they reached the rocks and
Preacher gave another loon call. Another such call answered. It didn't sound as real as the one Preacher
had given voice to, but it was the best Charlie Todd
could do. Buckley hadn't been able to master the call
at all when Preacher tried to teach them.

"They wait for us, just as they said they would," Hawk said.

"I didn't doubt they would."

The two of them trotted on into the gap between the rocks. The shadows were thick, but Preacher was able to spot Buckley and Todd when the two young men stepped out to greet them.

"Preacher!" Buckley said. "Are the Blackfeet right behind you?"

"Naw, they wouldn't have been able to follow us in the dark," the mountain man said. "But we left a trail they can follow when the sun comes up, and it'll lead 'em right here."

"How many of them did you kill tonight?" Todd asked.

"A few. Don't reckon the number matters. Tall Bull still has enough warriors to make things plenty hot for us if he catches us . . . which same I don't reckon on lettin' happen."

"We have your clothes and the rest of your gear," Buckley said. "White Buffalo and the animals are waiting on top of a little mesa about half a mile away. I took careful notice of the landmarks between here and there so we can find it again."

"Yeah, it wouldn't do to get lost while we're waitin' for the Blackfeet to show up."

Preacher took his buckskins from Buckley and pulled them on. Hawk got dressed as well.

Preacher felt good about getting his guns back. He stuck the pistols behind his belt and cradled the rifle in his left arm. "Lead on, Aaron. We'll go back to the camp and get some rest, and then tomorrow mornin' . . . the last part o' this war gets started."

* * *

The mesa where White Buffalo, Dog, Horse, and the pack mule waited was a shallow one, and the slope of its sides was gentle enough it could be climbed without much trouble. White Buffalo greeted them with his customary reserve, but Preacher could tell the old-timer was glad to see them.

They all gathered around a small fire. It was a special occasion of sorts, so Preacher brewed some coffee. Hawk and White Buffalo weren't interested in it, but Buckley and Todd were quite appreciative.

"This seems like the first coffee I've had in a year," Todd said after he took a sip of the strong black brew and sighed.

Buckley said, "I take it this is a council of war, Preacher?"

"Reckon you could call it that," the mountain man replied. "Here's what I'm thinkin'. Tomorrow mornin' we'll pull back farther into the badlands, makin' sure to leave enough sign so Tall Bull can follow us without it bein' too obvious we're leadin' him on. Now, this is the important part for you two fellas. We're gonna be on the lookout for someplace where we can draw 'em in and then bottle 'em up from behind. That'll be your job. You block their retreat, and we'll have 'em trapped between us."

"We can do that, can't we, Charlie?" Buckley said, nodding.

"Sure," Todd replied, but he didn't sound as confident about it as his friend did.

In English, Hawk asked, "What do we do when Tall Bull and his men are all dead?"

"Then it's over," Preacher said. "Leastways, it is for me. I came out here after beaver plews, and I intend to get some. So did Aaron and Charlie, but they lost their outfits." He turned his head to look at the two young white men. "There's a tradin' post southwest o' here. Take about a week to get there. If you want, I'll take you there. The fella who runs it might be willin' to stake you to new outfits in return for a share of whatever you make."

"That's very generous of you, Preacher," Buckley said. "It sounds like the best course of action for us."

Todd nodded. "We'd be obliged to you if you did that, Preacher."

The mountain man looked at Hawk and asked, "How about you? You and White Buffalo'd be welcome to come along, too."

"You seem to think we will all live through this battle," Hawk said.

"I don't see no reason to think otherwise."

Hawk scowled. It was a familiar expression, even though Preacher hadn't seen it as much lately.

"The rest of the Blackfeet will still live."

"We've talked about this," Preacher said. "I'll be damned if I help massacre a whole village. I wouldn't be no better 'n Tall Bull if I did that."

"You will regret leaving them alive."

"Maybe . . . but even if I do regret it one of these days, I'll sleep a whole hell of a lot better between now and then."

Hawk sighed. "You are right. White Buffalo will not like it. He has so much hate in his heart he would see all the Blackfeet dead. But alone there is nothing he can do."

"You ain't said whether or not you're gonna go with me and Aaron and Charlie."

"What else is left?" Hawk asked. "White Buffalo and I are the last of our band of Absaroka. We will travel with you to the trading post, and from there . . . I do not know."

"Fair enough," Preacher said. "Let's get some sleep. I don't reckon there's much chance o' Tall Bull showin' up tonight, but just in case, we'd best have some guards."

"Charlie and I can do that," Buckley said. "You and Hawk have done your share for now. Let us handle it. You can trust us."

"You know," Preacher said, nodding slowly, "I reckon I can."

When the sun came up the next morning, Preacher was sprawled atop one of the big rocks he had dubbed the Gates of Hell. Behind him, a mile back in the badlands, Hawk and the others would be breaking camp and heading farther west into the broken land. Hawk would make sure Preacher could follow their trail.

Preacher's gaze was turned toward the lake, which was a dark blue smudge among the trees in the distance. He watched patiently, waiting for the inevitable pursuit.

When he spotted movement, he concentrated on it until he was able to make out the group of men striding toward him, led by a tall figure that had to be the Blackfoot war chief. The warriors were too far away to make an exact count, but he could tell there had to be fewer than two dozen.

Given what he had learned the day before, he knew he had finally accomplished his goal. Tall Bull was leading all of his remaining warriors on the trail of their enemies. However it turned out, it would be the final showdown with the Blackfeet. The only ones to leave the badlands would be the victors.

Or the survivors, depending on how you wanted to look at it.

Preacher slid down from the rock and grinned at Dog waiting on the ground behind it. "Come on. Let's go find the others and get this over with."

CHAPTER 39

To Preacher's experienced eye, the trail leading to the mesa where he and his companions had camped the night before was plain to see. Maybe not as plain as a line on a map, but he knew the Blackfeet would be able to follow it without a lot of effort.

Setting out from the mesa to penetrate deeper into the broken land, he saw overturned pebbles, faint scrapes on rocks, even the occasional scuffed footprint. Those were the kinds of marks inexperienced frontiersmen like Buckley and Todd might leave anyway, but Preacher knew Hawk was making sure the Blackfeet would have sign to follow.

The trail led him to a ridge with a trail zigzagging up its face. As Preacher climbed, he spotted a head peeking out from behind a rock on top of the ridge, near the head of the trail. "Howdy, Charlie," he called.

"Blast it," Todd said as he stepped out into the open. "I was trying to be stealthy."

"You'll have to try a mite harder," Preacher said when he reached the top of the trail. "Start by takin' your hat off when you're tryin' to sneak a look around somethin'. Don't make any jerky movements, neither. That'll draw the eye quicker 'n just about anything. Whatever you do, keep it smooth."

Todd sighed and nodded. "I'll try to remember that for next time."

"If you don't, the enemy's liable to remind you. Of course, you won't like the reminder."

Todd let out a nervous laugh.

"Where are the rest of the bunch?" Preacher asked.

"Aaron and White Buffalo are in a gully on the other side of this ridge with Horse and the mule. Hawk said he was going to scout on ahead. I guess you saw Tall Bull and his warriors, or you wouldn't be back yet."

The mountain man nodded. "They're on their way. Best I could tell, it's the whole lot of 'em, too, which is just what we wanted."

"So . . . bad odds."

"It's what we need to finish this, Charlie."

The two of them went to join the others. Again Preacher took note of the tracks they had left and nodded in approval. Following the trail would be just enough of a challenge to convince Tall Bull he wasn't being led into a trap . . . Preacher hoped.

By the time they reached the gully where Buckley and White Buffalo were waiting, Hawk had returned, as well.

"There is a canyon about two miles from here that will serve our purpose," the young warrior reported. "It is narrow with cliffs on both sides stretching as far as the eye can see, so the canyon is the only way through that tableland. Not far inside the mouth of the canyon on both sides are ledges where brush grows, so Aaron and Charlie will be able to hide there while Tall Bull and his men go past. Preacher, you and I will wait ahead of them, around a bend in the canyon. Once a stream flowed there, so it twists like a snake. When we open fire on them, Aaron and Charlie can shoot any who try to flee."

Preacher nodded. "Sounds like you put some thought into it. But you know Tall Bull and his men. Most of 'em ain't likely to turn tail and run. Fact is, there's a good chance they'll try to stampede right over us. And since we'll be outnumbered quite a bit . . ."

"We will be ready for them. Once there were trees growing on the rim of the canyon. They have died and fallen, and several of them are in one place just above the spot where we will ambush the Blackfeet. White Buffalo can go on through the canyon and then double back with the horse and the mule. There is a trail he can follow. It will not be easy, but they can make it to the rim, and when the time comes White Buffalo can use the animals to push the deadfall off the edge and down onto the Blackfeet. That will kill some of the warriors and scatter the others."

"Damn, boy, you *have* been doin' some plannin'," Preacher said, clearly impressed. "Settin' all this up is gonna take some work, though, and I figure Tall Bull and his bunch will be here about an hour from now, so we'd best get busy."

Once they arrived at the canyon where the ambush would take place, Hawk went over White Buffalo's part of the plan with the old-timer while Preacher showed Buckley and Todd the ledges where they would position themselves. Even though he hadn't seen the place until then, all Preacher had to do was glance at the layout to know what needed to be done.

"There's just one problem," Todd said as he tipped his head back to look up at the ledges about thirty feet above the ground. "How are we going to get up there?"

"You'll have to climb," Preacher said.

"Climb? But those walls are sheer!"

"Not really. Not when you look close at 'em. See that rock stickin' out?" Preacher pointed. "You can grab hold of that. And that little crack? You can get your toe in there. Just look for the kinds of places like that. The walls ain't as straight up and down as they look. They've got a little slope to 'em. Not much, but you'd be surprised how much even a little bit can help when you're climbin'."

Buckley looked nervous, too, but he said, "I'm willing to give it a try."

"Of course you are," Todd said. "You've always been braver than me as well as smarter than me."

"You can do it, Charlie. I have faith in you."

"Those ledges aren't very wide, either. And we're supposed to hide behind those little bushes? The Indians will see us and fill us full of arrows!"

"No, the brush is thick enough to hide you if you get down on your belly and don't move or make any noise," Preacher assured them.

Todd sighed "I guess we can give it a try."

"The worst they can do is kill us," Buckley told him.

"If you're trying to encourage me, Aaron, you're failing."

Preacher rigged slings for them so they could carry

their rifles over their shoulders while they climbed. Each young man picked a side of the canyon and started his ascent while Preacher watched and called out suggestions and encouragement to them.

Buckley climbed fairly quickly, hauling himself up from handhold to foothold and vice versa. The more rotund Charlie Todd had a harder time of it, grunting and sweating as he struggled to lift himself along the slope. Buckley reached his ledge first and rolled over the rim onto it. He turned and called to Todd, "Come on, Charlie, you can do it."

Todd cast a despairing glance over his shoulder, but he kept climbing.

Red-faced and puffing by the time he finally reached the ledge on his side of the canyon, he sat there for several moments, breathing heavily as he tried to recover, then abruptly he let out a groan.

"What's wrong?" Preacher asked.

"I just realized something," Todd said. "When this is all over, I have to climb *down*!"

Preacher tried not to laugh, but he couldn't hold back a soft chuckle. "You'll do fine," he told Todd. "You fellas get behind that brush, now. Hunker down good. Make sure your rifles are loaded, and don't fire unless some o' the Blackfeet try to get back past you."

"If none of them attempt to retreat, we won't have anything to do," Buckley said.

"You can count yourselves lucky, then." Preacher waved to the young men and then turned to trot up the canyon and rendezvous with Hawk.

The canyon had a number of twists and turns, as Hawk had said, and as Preacher rounded one of them, he saw the young warrior coming toward him.

Preacher stopped to wait and looked up at the rim to his left, having spotted the deadfall up there. The fallen trees were close to the rim. If White Buffalo could get Horse to cooperate, the stallion could knock the deadfall loose and send those logs plummeting into the canyon.

Looked like the old-timer's ability to talk to animals was going to come in handy, Preacher thought with a smile.

"You are pleased?" Hawk asked as he came up to the mountain man.

"You picked a good spot. If we have a little luck on our side to even the odds, I'd say we've got a chance against Tall Bull and his bunch."

"Whether I live or not, as long as Tall Bull dies, my mother and Little Pine will have been avenged. As for the rest of my people"—Hawk paused—"a man can do no more than to give up his life for a cause."

"That's true enough, I reckon." Preacher looked around. "This is where we're gonna take 'em?"

"It seems like a good place to me."

Preacher nodded. He had trusted Hawk with the responsibility of picking the spot for the ambush, knowing it might do him some good. On the other hand, Preacher wouldn't go ahead with the attack unless he thought it stood a good chance of working.

Strategically, that canyon was fine, he decided. They needed close quarters to have a chance, and there they could strike at the Blackfeet from three directions. The first few minutes of the battle would tell the story. They needed to kill enough of the warriors right away to be able to tackle on fairly even terms the ones who were left.

Preacher looked at the sides of the canyon lined with rocks and scrub brush. He told Hawk, "Pick your spot and find some cover. They ought to be here before too much longer."

"Aaron and Charlie are in position?"

"Yep. White Buffalo will be where he needs to be in time?"

"He is already there," Hawk said.

Preacher looked up at the deadfall again. White Buffalo stood beside the logs. The old-timer raised one arm in a solemn gesture that Preacher returned with a wave and a grin.

"Seems like we're ready," he said. "All we need now is some Blackfeet for the killin'."

CHAPTER 40

Preacher positioned himself in a thicket of brush on one side of the canyon while Hawk stood behind a boulder across from him. The mountain man had taken the extra pistols from his saddlebags and loaded them. He checked the rifle and all four pistols to make sure they were ready to fire. Satisfied they were, he went down on one knee and waited for the Blackfoot warriors to arrive.

"Preacher!" Hawk called across to him.

Preacher frowned. They needed to be quiet. He wasn't sure how close the Blackfeet were, and voices might echo and carry in the canyon. "What?"

"Tall Bull is mine to kill."

Preacher's frown deepened. He hadn't told Hawk about it, but his plan had been to go ahead and put a rifle ball in the war chief's head with his first shot. That went against what he had thought earlier, his desire to kill Tall Bull close-up and personal-like, but on reflection Preacher had decided it was the best thing to do. Killing their chief right away would dishearten the rest of the warriors. Preacher didn't expect them to give up, but they might not fight quite as hard.

"Preacher?" Hawk prodded him.

Preacher thought about Bird in the Tree and Little Pine, and he jerked his head in a curt nod. Maybe it wasn't the smartest thing to do, but he knew what was in Hawk's heart. The rage that burned there would never subside if Hawk didn't get the chance to face the man responsible for the deaths of the two women he loved.

Hawk returned the nod, then focused his attention on the nearest bend of the canyon. That was where the Blackfeet would appear.

Some men found waiting for a fight worse than the battle itself, but Preacher never had. He possessed the ability to clear his thoughts and concentrate solely on the matter at hand. Once he was satisfied he had done everything he could to get ready for the trouble that was coming, he was content and able to wait in a cool, calm state.

He felt that way as he waited, but when he looked across the canyon at his son, he could tell Hawk was nervous. A part of him wished there was something he could do to help, but that time had passed. The two of them weren't father and son at the moment. They were fellow fighting men.

A few minutes later, Preacher's instincts as much as his senses warned him the moment had come. He heard low-pitched voices approaching. They sounded like they were arguing.

Maybe some of Tall Bull's warriors didn't cotton to the idea of following the trail into the canyon. Maybe they thought Tall Bull's angry heart was getting the best of his brain.

A lone Blackfoot warrior appeared. He wasn't Tall Bull. Preacher figured the war chief had sent the man around the bend to scout what was up ahead in the canyon. The warrior looked nervous but determined as he stalked forward, bow and arrow held at the ready.

Preacher held his fire and so did Hawk. Either of them could have killed the scout without any trouble, but to do so would have warned Tall Bull of the ambush. They waited. Not that patiently on Hawk's part, maybe, but they waited.

The warrior turned and called in the Blackfoot tongue, "There is nothing here."

The others came in sight, led by Tall Bull. It was the best look Preacher had gotten at the big war chief. The lines of brutal arrogance in his face were easy to see. He strode forward, holding his favorite weapon, the war club that had known the blood of many of his enemies. The necklace of buffalo horns draped across his chest rattled.

Preacher glanced across the canyon at Hawk. He could see the eagerness that gripped the young warrior. With an arrow nocked and the bowstring drawn back halfway, it would take only a second for him to step out, line up his shot, and fire.

Tall Bull let out an ugly laugh and turned his head to address the remaining warriors following closely behind him. "You see, our enemies still flee. They are too cowardly to stand and face us. They can only strike at night, when they have the cover of the shadows. One is a white man, one is an Absaroka, and both are craven dogs! Soon they will all be wiped out, and this land will belong only to the Blackfeet!"

That was more boasting than Hawk could take. With the Blackfeet in range, the young warrior made his move. In little more than the blink of an eye, he stepped out and let fly with his arrow.

Preacher figured Hawk was aiming at Tall Bull's broad chest, and the missile might have found its target if the scout, whose back was to Hawk, hadn't taken a step just then that unwittingly brought him into the path of the arrow. The head struck him in the middle of the back with such force it ripped all the way through his body and emerged from his chest, along with several inches of the bloody shaft.

The scout let out a cry of pain, arched his back, and stood there like that for a split second before flopping forward on his face.

By the time he hit the ground, the ball was wide-open.

Preacher had lined up his shot and took aim through the brush concealing him. The rifle's sights were on the man standing just behind Tall Bull to the war chief's right. The long-barreled flintlock boomed and kicked against Preacher's shoulder as it spewed flame and black smoke from its muzzle.

The Blackfoot warrior went over backwards as the heavy lead ball smashed into his chest.

Preacher set the rifle down and picked up two of the pistols he had ready. He rose to his feet and fired both guns into the mass of Blackfoot warriors, which had already surged forward, led by a furiously shouting Tall Bull.

At the same time, Hawk whipped arrows into their

ranks as fast as he could draw the shafts from his quiver and fit them to the bowstring.

Arrows flew from the charging Blackfeet in return. Preacher heard their deadly whispers as they sliced through the air around him. He saw two more warriors go down as the pistol balls scythed into the ranks of the Blackfeet.

A cry came from above, and when Preacher glanced up he spotted White Buffalo holding Horse's reins and urging the stallion around in a tight turn. Horse's rump slammed into the deadfall, and the four logs slid off the rim and plummeted into the canyon.

The men caught in their path shouted and tried to get out of the way. Most of them made it, but three warriors didn't. The logs fell on them with crushing force. The air inside the canyon was already getting thick with dust and powder smoke, but he didn't expect those warriors to be getting up again any time soon, if ever.

The falling logs had scattered and disoriented the remaining warriors, so Preacher was able to grab his other pistols and blow two more of them into eternity. Another pair fell, skewered by Hawk's arrows.

Preacher bounded into the open, knowing he couldn't allow the Blackfeet to regroup and launch another concerted charge. He and Hawk wouldn't be able to stand up to that. As far as the mountain man could tell, none of the Blackfeet had fled from the ambush, so he and Hawk still faced plenty of foes.

Tomahawk in one hand, knife in the other, Preacher went among them like a whirlwind, moving almost too fast for the eye to follow. A slash of the knife opened a warrior's throat. A swift strike with the tomahawk shattered another man's skull.

Hawk had run out of arrows by now and joined the desperate hand-to-hand battle. His tomahawk landed with such force on the side of one man's neck that the warrior's head was almost sheared off his shoulders. Hawk kicked the corpse aside and leaped toward another man.

Preacher saw that from the corner of his eye and figured Hawk was trying to find Tall Bull in the confusion. Preacher had been looking for the war chief, too, but he'd lost sight of him with so much dust in the air. He buried his knife in the chest of another man, ripped it free, and turned to meet his next foe.

He felt the fiery touch of an arrow tearing across his ribs but it didn't penetrate, just left a bloody scrape behind. Preacher ignored the wound, blocked a tomahawk stroke coming at his head, and kicked the man wielding it in the belly. When the warrior bent over, Preacher crushed the back of his skull with a blindingly fast blow.

A deafening bellow made Preacher glance up. Tall Bull had closed with Hawk. The war chief was evil, but he was also a hell of a fighter. He seemed almost twice Hawk's size as he loomed over the younger man. The war club flashed around with a speed no normal man could have achieved with such a heavy weapon and batted the tomahawk out of Hawk's hand.

Hawk tried to dart in and strike with his knife, but Tall Bull twisted aside. He let go of the war club with one hand and grabbed Hawk's arm while the young warrior was off balance.

Preacher lunged toward them. He knew he was turning his back on the rest of the Blackfeet, but he had to help Hawk.

Before the mountain man could reach them, Tall Bull pivoted, turning and heaving on Hawk's arm, and in a prodigious display of strength, he lifted the young man off his feet and literally flung him into Preacher.

The collision was hard enough to stun both of them and send them sprawling to the ground. Preacher dropped his knife but managed to hang on to his tomahawk. As he gathered his wits, he tried to push Hawk off himself and get up in time to continue the fight.

Just as Preacher got clear, Tall Bull's foot slammed down on his chest, pinning him to the ground. The war club knocked the tomahawk from his hand, seemingly with just a flick of the chief's wrist.

Preacher expected to die as the next stroke would surely crush his skull, but Tall Bull held off as his surviving warriors thronged around. "Wait!" he shouted as his men lifted knives and tomahawks. "A quick death is more than dogs like these deserve! They must pay for the suffering they have inflicted on the noble Blackfeet!"

Preacher knew what that meant. Tall Bull intended to torture him and Hawk to death, or burn them at the stake, or some other fate equally as horrible. The only question was whether he would do it there or take them back to the village.

Either way, although they had fought a good fight against overwhelming odds, their luck had finally run out and they were doomed.

CHAPTER 41

Hawk was still a little stunned from slamming into Preacher. As the Blackfeet took hold of them and hauled them roughly to their feet, Hawk shook his head and peered around groggily.

The sight of his Blackfoot captors surrounding him cleared the cobwebs from the young warrior's brain. His lips twisted in a snarl, and he tried to pull free from the strong hands holding him.

The effort was futile. The Blackfeet weren't going to let either of the prisoners escape. After all the misery Preacher and Hawk had dealt out to them in the past couple weeks, it was all Tall Bull could do to keep his men from gutting the two of them and using tomahawks to pound them into something only vaguely resembling humans.

Tall Bull swaggered up in front of them and sneered at Preacher. "The fearsome Ghost Killer. You are now helpless in the hands of the Blackfeet."

"Ain't the first time I been took prisoner," Preacher

said. "And as long as I'm drawin' breath, I ain't helpless."

"You will not be drawing breath much longer." With that threat, Tall Bull turned his attention to Hawk. "This young one is of the Absaroka. You must be all that is left of that pathetic band south of Beartooth."

Hawk strained against the men holding him. "Tell your men to let me go," he said as he bared his teeth at Tall Bull. "Fight me if you dare, Blackfoot! Man-to-man!"

Tall Bull threw back his head and laughed. "You are mad," he told Hawk. "I could have killed you before with a mere swing of my war club. You are like a tiny mountain lion cub, hissing and spitting at a grizzly bear. A swipe of my hand would destroy you! You are a sad little boy, nothing more." Tall Bull paused, then said, "But I would know why you and this white man wage war on me and my people."

"To avenge our loved ones! Your men killed the woman who gave birth to me, as well as the woman I intended to marry. The spirits of the slain cry out for justice!"

"Death is justice for the filthy Absaroka." Tall Bull spat at Hawk's feet to demonstrate his contempt, then made a curt gesture to his men. "Take them back to the village, so the women can spit on them and the children can throw stones at them. Tonight we will teach them the folly of attacking the Blackfeet, and then . . . they will *burn*."

Their captors used rawhide thongs to bind their wrists behind their backs then prodded Preacher and Hawk out of the canyon.

As they passed the brushy ledges where Aaron Buckley and Charlie Todd lay hidden, Preacher gave a tiny shake of his head in the hope the two young men would see it and understand he was telling them not to open fire. They wouldn't stand much of a chance by themselves against the warriors, and tied up like Preacher and Hawk were, there wouldn't be anything they could do to help.

Tall Bull's arrogance had led him to make what Preacher hoped might be a fatal mistake. He had assumed Preacher and Hawk had acted on their own and had no allies. He hadn't even sent any of his warriors to see why those logs had fallen from the rim when they did. It was possible he assumed Preacher had somehow rigged them to fall.

While he and Hawk were being tied up, the mountain man had glanced up at the rim and been relieved White Buffalo was nowhere to be seen. The old-timer was still on the loose, too.

As they left the canyon, Preacher thought there was a chance White Buffalo would rejoin Buckley and Todd.

What those three could accomplish against the Blackfeet, Preacher didn't know, but he suspected they would try *something*.

He and Hawk would have to be ready whenever that happened.

The women and children howled with glee when they saw the prisoners being herded into the village beside the lake. Preacher had learned a long time ago it was better to be killed in battle than to be captured and turned over to the women. They took more pleasure in torturing captives than their men did. The children could be almost as vicious.

As Tall Bull had predicted, the young ones began pelting Preacher and Hawk with rocks and sticks as soon as they entered the village. The prisoners did their best to ignore the assault. Preacher was proud to see the way Hawk kept his head up with an emotionless mask on his face, even when one of the rocks clipped him on the forehead and left a scratch from which a trickle of blood welled.

They were taken to a pair of trees near the lake and tied there with their wrists still bound behind their backs. Strands of rawhide were passed around their bodies, lashing them to the rough trunks so they faced the village.

Throwing things at them was less of a challenge now that they were tied to the trees, so the children quickly grew bored and went back to doing other things. The women gathered around, though, cackling with laughter as they talked about what they would do to the prisoners. Although Hawk had to be hearing the grisly details as well as Preacher was, his face remained expressionless.

The women, too, tired of the verbal torment and wandered off. The actual torture wouldn't begin until evening, when the Blackfeet would build a large fire near the prisoners to illuminate their bloody sport.

When they could speak without being overheard, Hawk said bitterly, "I wish we had been able to kill Tall Bull before they captured us. Now nothing has changed. My mother, Little Pine, the rest of my people . . . have not been avenged."

"We've killed dozens of the sons o' bitches,"

Preacher pointed out. "The Blackfeet have paid a price for what they did. There's got to be some discontent among the warriors about how many of them Tall Bull's gotten killed."

"But now he has captured us, and once we are dead, the others will soon forget," Hawk said. "Tall Bull will remain their war chief, and their ranks will be restored and grow. His plans have been delayed, but not stopped."

What Hawk said was true, but he wasn't taking into account everything Preacher was. "Maybe it ain't over yet," the mountain man said.

Hawk glanced sharply at him. "What do you mean? What can we do—" He stopped short and frowned at Preacher. "You cannot mean you place any faith in White Buffalo and those two white men?"

"They're still out there somewhere, on the loose."

"Right now they are fleeing as fast as they can, trying to get as far away from this place as possible."

"You really believe that?"

Hawk hesitated before answering, then said, "Perhaps not White Buffalo. He hates the Blackfeet so much he may not be able to abandon his hopes of revenge. But he is an old man, full of words and little else. What can he do?"

"You said yourself Aaron and Charlie were learnin' a lot. Maybe they learned not to turn their backs on their friends."

"But alone . . . or even with White Buffalo's help . . . they are no match for Tall Bull and his warriors."

"There are only a handful of 'em left. The odds ain't *that* bad."

Hawk just shook his head with a bleak, fatalistic look on his face.

"And if the two of us could get loose somehow, the odds wouldn't be bad at all," Preacher added.

"The Blackfeet will never be careless enough to let that happen."

"Unless they think it's their idea."

Hawk's forehead creased in a confused frown, but Preacher didn't offer any explanations and Hawk didn't press the issue.

They simply stood there, waiting for night to fall and their ordeal to begin.

Darkness descended swiftly on the rugged landscape once the sun plunged behind the western mountains. As night fell, the women of the village built a large fire not far from the trees where the prisoners were tied, as Preacher had expected.

He had dozed a little during the day. Like most veteran frontiersman, he had developed the ability to snatch some sleep whenever he had the chance, even under arduous conditions. He was pretty sure Hawk had remained awake. The boy couldn't relax enough to sleep, and under the circumstances, Preacher couldn't really blame him for that.

Since there were no Blackfeet near them at the moment other than two guards standing about twenty feet away, watching them, Preacher asked from the side of his mouth, "You seen any sign of our friends?"

"No. I told you, they have fled."

"Could be. Can't hardly blame 'em if they did, can you?"

"The white men had no reason to remain. They care nothing for the red men and see us only as savages."

"You might be wrong about that, but I reckon we'll have to wait and see."

After a moment, Hawk said, "I tried to free myself from my bonds, but I failed. All I did was tear the skin of my wrists until they bled."

"I figured as much, so I didn't try. I can tell when I'm tied up good an' proper. Like I told Tall Bull, this ain't the first time I've been in such a pre-dicament."

"And how did you save yourself those other times?"

Preacher thought back to when he'd first been captured by the Blackfeet. He didn't figure going on a preaching spree would do him any good. Tall Bull hated him so much the war chief wouldn't care whether Preacher was touched in the head. He wanted the mountain man dead.

"Reckon we'll have to come up with some other way," he said quietly.

Hawk just let out a disgusted grunt.

A few minutes later, a group of warriors emerged from one of the largest tepees. Preacher figured it belonged to Tall Bull, who led the delegation as they strode toward the lake. More than likely, the men had been in council, deciding exactly what to do with the prisoners who had caused so much trouble for the tribe. The Blackfoot women and children followed, making plenty of noise to show they were eager for whatever was going to happen next.

Tall Bull carried his war club as usual. The buffalo horns clattered against each other as he came to a stop in front of Preacher and Hawk and sneered. "You are as powerless as infants. Beg for mercy, and perhaps I will kill you quickly instead of letting the women have you and then burning what is left when next the sun rises."

"Beggin' ain't exactly in my line," Preacher said, "but I might strike a bargain with you."

Tall Bull frowned in surprise and repeated, "A bargain? You have nothing to bargain with, Ghost Killer!"

"Don't I?" Preacher asked calmly. "How about givin' you the chance to boast about how you killed the legendary Ghost Killer in single combat?"

"Preacher . . ." Hawk said in a warning tone.

Tall Bull laughed. "Why would I worry about such a thing?"

"Because after all the Blackfoot warriors I've killed lately, some o' these other fellas must've got to wonderin' just how good an idea it is to keep you on as war chief."

Tall Bull wasn't laughing any longer. As several of the men behind him stirred, obviously in acknowledgment of what Preacher had just said, rage darkened Tall Bull's face and he stepped closer to Preacher, raising the war club. "I could crush your skull—"

"Hell, I'm tied up! Anybody in the village who's strong enough to lift that blasted club could do the same, even some of the women. Probably even some o' the kids!"

Tall Bull looked like he understood exactly what Preacher was doing, but at the same time, he couldn't allow the mountain man to compare him to women and children and get away with it.

Through clenched teeth, the war chief said, "Your so-called *bargain* is a lie. You are only trying to force me to kill you quickly."

Preacher shook his head. "Oh, no, I need better stakes than that. My bargain is this. You and I battle it out, man-to-man. If you kill me . . . well, there's nothin' I can do about whatever happens next. But if I kill you . . . you let this Absaroka boy go."

He didn't want Tall Bull to know Hawk was his son. That might change everything.

"And what of you, if you kill me?" Tall Bull demanded. "Not that there is any chance of that!"

Preacher shrugged as best he could, tied to the tree the way he was. "Then your warriors can do whatever they want to me. I ask only for freedom for Hawk That Soars."

"Preacher, no!" Hawk yelled. "You cannot—"

"How about it, Tall Bull?" Preacher said, overriding Hawk's protest. "I'll fight you any way you want. War clubs, tomahawks, knives . . . hell, I'll even take you on hand-to-hand, if you want."

"With freedom for this filthy Absaroka alone at stake, nothing for you?"

"That's the deal," Preacher said.

Hawk said, "Preacher, please—"

"Hush up, boy. And you know how I'm sayin' that." Father to son, Preacher meant, and he saw that Hawk indeed knew it. Even though he didn't have much right to be issuing parental commands, not after they had lived nearly all of Hawk's life apart, Preacher was going to put his foot down . . . for whatever that was worth.

Hawk didn't say anything else, but he stared at Preacher with a mixture of anger and sorrow and regret in his eyes.

"You allow me to set the terms of our battle," Tall Bull said, "and so I say I will fight with my war club . . . and you will fight with your bare hands."

Preacher saw the looks some of the other warriors exchanged and played on that reaction, saying, "Ain't hardly fair . . . but you got a deal."

Tall Bull grunted and brandished the club toward Preacher. "Turn the Ghost Killer loose."

CHAPTER 42

One of the warriors cut the rawhide strips holding Preacher to the tree, then sawed through the thongs around his wrists. It was a relief to Preacher's muscles when he brought his arms around in front of him again. Since his hands had gone partially numb, he flexed the long, strong fingers to get feeling back in them again.

"Preacher, you do not have to do this," Hawk said. "I can endure whatever torment they want to inflict on me—"

"Well, maybe I can't. I reckon I could stand the pain, but I always figured I'd go out fightin'. This is my chance to do that, son."

Tall Bull had hold of the club with both hands, swinging it lightly back and forth.

Hawk turned to him. "Wait! *I* will fight you, Tall Bull. It is my right. My people are the ones you wiped out."

Tall Bull blew out a contemptuous breath. "Who are you?" he asked, then answered his own question. "A puny Absaroka! There would be no glory in crushing the life from you. But this man"—he pointed the club at Preacher—"this is the Ghost Killer. The White Wolf. Our women use tales of this man to frighten our children into their sleeping robes at night. When I kill him, the fame of Tall Bull will spread to all the lands west of the Father of Waters I have heard of but never seen."

"Even if it ain't strictly a fair fight," Preacher gibed with a grin.

Tall Bull snarled and raised the war club. "Are you ready to die, white man?"

"I was born ready, but I reckon I'll put it off as long as I can."

"Your time has come!" Tall Bull sprang at Preacher, launching a mighty swing with the war club.

The other warriors, without being told to, had arranged themselves in a semicircle around the two trees, making sure Preacher couldn't attempt a dash for freedom.

Escape was the last thing on his mind. He didn't know if the Blackfeet would honor the deal he had made with Tall Bull, but it was the only chance for life Hawk seemed to have.

As the club in Tall Bull's hands swept through the air toward Preacher's head, the mountain man dived under the devastating blow, somersaulted, and came up with a double kick that planted both feet in Tall Bull's stomach. The impact caused the war chief to double over and sent him flying backwards. The women, watching from beyond the circle of warriors, wailed in despair.

Preacher leaped to his feet and went after Tall Bull, knowing he couldn't afford to waste even the slightest advantage. Kicking the war club out of Tall Bull's hand would go a long way toward evening the odds. As he dove toward Tall Bull, the war chief swung the club from the ground. Preacher's momentum carried him into its arc, and the head of the club struck him a glancing blow in the ribs. It spun him around and knocked him off his feet. The women screamed in appreciation.

Preacher rolled and came right back up, ignoring the ache in his side. He was pretty sure no ribs were broken, but it still hurt like blazes where Tall Bull had swatted him. He couldn't allow himself to pay any attention to that.

Tall Bull was up, too. He lunged at Preacher and brought the club down like a man using a maul to split wood. Preacher darted aside. The club missed him by inches and slammed into the ground.

Tall Bull felt the impact shivering all the way up his arms. During the split second while the war chief was off balance, Preacher hammered his fists into Tall Bull's face, first the left and then the right. The powerful punches rocked Tall Bull's head back, but he didn't go down. He didn't even appear to be fazed.

Another charge with the club slashing back and forth had Preacher scrambling to get out of the way. He knew if any of those strokes connected, it might knock his head right off his shoulders. As he was backing and darting, movement along the lakeshore caught his eye.

Taking his attention off Tall Bull for even an instant could prove fatal, but his instincts told him he needed to find out what he had spotted from the corner of his eye. As soon as he could, he glanced that way again.

A dark shape crouched there, easing closer an inch at a time, using the sparse brush for cover. The sticklike figure and the white hair told Preacher who it was.

White Buffalo.

Preacher didn't know why the old-timer was trying to sneak up, but he could make a guess. If White Buffalo reached the tree where Hawk was tied, he might be able to free the young warrior.

Instantly, Preacher reversed course in his efforts to avoid Tall Bull's club. One of the blows clipped him on the left shoulder, making his arm go completely numb.

He scrambled away from Hawk, drawing Tall Bull after him. As the battle shifted along the shore, the attention of the Blackfoot warriors moved with it. None of them were watching Hawk as closely, which meant they weren't as likely to notice White Buffalo.

Preacher swung his left arm wildly to force sensation back into it. Seconds that seemed like minutes passed as he leaped out of the way of those crushing blows and darted in to pepper a swift jab to Tall Bull's face whenever he could. Blood trickled from the war chief's nose, and his mouth was dark with blood.

Preacher could tell the war chief was getting frustrated. He'd figured the mountain man would be dead quickly. Instead, Preacher had taken some damage but was dealing out punishment, as well. Tall Bull growled like an animal and leaped at Preacher again.

Too late, Preacher realized his opponent was trying strategy instead of just raw power. Tall Bull pulled up short. His charge had been a feint, and as Preacher tried to avoid that false charge, the war club flicked at him and took him on the left hip.

Preacher's left leg buckled and he went down. Tall Bull could have killed him at that moment, but instead of continuing to attack with the war club, he tried to kick Preacher in the head. Preacher got his hands up in time to grab Tall Bull's foot and heave.

Not expecting that, Tall Bull wasn't braced for it. He went over backwards and crashed to earth like a tree falling.

Preacher tried to get up, but his leg wouldn't cooperate. The same one the bear had fallen on, it went out from under him. He had believed the injury was fully healed, but obviously that leg wasn't quite as strong as the other one yet.

As he fell, his head was turned toward the tree where Hawk was tied. He caught a hint of movement on the other side of the trunk, just enough to tell him White Buffalo had reached the tree and was trying to free the young warrior.

Preacher wondered fleetingly if Aaron Buckley and Charlie Todd were somewhere nearby, too, or if the old-timer was the only one determined to continue the war against the Blackfeet.

Tall Bull rolled over, pushed himself to his feet, and bellowed in rage. "This ends now! The Ghost Killer dies!"

A shot blasted through the echoes of the words.

Preacher saw blood fly in the air and one of the warriors collapsed as a rifle ball tore off his jaw. A second shot rang out, and another warrior stumbled, pawing at his chest as crimson suddenly began to well between his fingers.

Tall Bull's head jerked around at the sound of the shots, giving Preacher time to force his leg to work well enough to come up on his knees. He threw himself forward in a diving tackle at the war chief's legs.

At the same time, Hawk leaped away from the tree where he had been bound. With no chance to work any feeling back into his limbs, his movements were a little awkward, but he was faster than the warriors who weren't expecting any trouble from him. He lowered his shoulder and rammed into the closest of the Blackfeet. As the man stumbled back several steps, Hawk tore the tomahawk from the man's hand and backhanded it across his face. Blood spurted and bone crunched under the terrible impact.

Tall Bull fell again as Preacher yanked his legs out from under him. Preacher pushed himself up and sledged a punch into the war chief's belly. It was almost like hitting a stone wall.

Even lying on his back, Tall Bull was dangerous. He swung the war club clutched in his fist at the end of his long arm. The mountain man lowered his head so the blow went over him and clambered up Tall Bull's massive body, hammering punches along the way. With all the feeling back in Preacher's left arm, he was at full strength . . . in his upper body, anyway.

Hawk darted aside from an arrow fired at him, crashed into the man who had loosed the shaft, and knocked the bow aside. Hawk's knee rose into the man's groin, and as the warrior doubled over and gasped in agony, Hawk brought the tomahawk down on the back of his neck with stunning force. The Blackfoot's face met the ground hard as he collapsed.

Another warrior had drawn a bead on Hawk and was about to let fly when a rifle shot tore through his throat. Charlie Todd, who stood at the edge of the village, lowered his weapon and began reloading. Hawk's eyes met his for a second, and both men nodded.

On the other side of the village, Aaron Buckley's second shot screamed harmlessly past its intended target. The warrior turned with a screech of rage and charged Buckley, brandishing a tomahawk. Buckley acted like he was going to turn and run, then stopped short and lunged to meet his foe, thrusting out the rifle barrel like a spear. It sank deeply into the warrior's belly.

Hawk arrived at that moment to cave in the Blackfoot's skull with a swift stroke of the tomahawk.

"Thanks!" Buckley yelled.

"You should learn to shoot better!" Hawk replied as he twisted away to continue fighting.

With a desperate spring, Preacher caught hold of Tall Bull's club. The war chief tried to wrench it free, but Preacher hung on for dear life. Both men grunted with effort as they struggled and strained against each other.

From the corner of his eye, Preacher saw a gray streak flash past. Dog was getting in on the fight, too. The big cur brought down one of the remaining warriors and ripped his throat out with a single slash of sharp teeth.

Hawk traded blows with a tomahawk-wielding

warrior. The weapons clashed, leaped apart, came together again as each man blocked his opponent's strokes. The action was too fast for the eye to follow, and whoever slipped first was going to lose.

That turned out to be the Blackfoot warrior. He was a fraction of a second too slow, allowing Hawk's tomahawk to dart past and crash down on his shoulder. The man yelled in pain, a shout cut short when Hawk's backhand struck him in the temple and splintered his skull.

Several yards away, Preacher and Tall Bull still wrestled over the war club. The war chief was massive and powerful, but Preacher packed an incredible amount of strength into his rangy frame. It began to appear that the struggle might go on indefinitely, as neither man could overpower the other.

Slowly, slowly, Preacher began to force his opponent's arms to the side. Tall Bull's eyes widened in shock. No one had ever defeated him before, certainly not in a contest of strength and will.

But he had never battled the man called Preacher.

Suddenly, as he straddled Tall Bull's broad chest, Preacher jackknifed and butted the war chief in the face. Tall Bull's grip loosened enough for Preacher to rip the club out of his hands. The club rose and fell with blinding speed. Preacher struck again and again and again, turning Tall Bull's own weapon against him, until there was nothing left of the man's head except a grisly mess of blood, bone, and brain. Gore was splattered all over Preacher's face and the front of his buckskin shirt.

He paused with the club lifted to strike another

blow, when he heard Hawk say, "Tall Bull is dead. All the Blackfeet are dead."

Preacher gave a little shake of his head and blinked blood out of his eyes. He looked around and saw Hawk, White Buffalo, and the two greenhorns standing there . . . except he couldn't think of them as *greenhorns* anymore. They had achieved the look of seasoned fighters.

The bodies of the slain Blackfoot warriors were scattered around on the ground. A short distance away, the women of the village stood in stunned silence. There would be plenty of wailing and mourning later on, but at the moment they were struggling to understand that all their men were dead, led to that unfortunate fate by the power-mad Tall Bull.

"I wished to kill him myself," Hawk said, "but I see now it was fitting for you to do so, Preacher. Each blow you struck was for my mother."

Preacher dragged the back of a hand across his mouth and nodded. "I reckon," he said, thinking of Bird in the Tree. "But he had it comin' for a lot of reasons."

White Buffalo waved a gnarled hand toward the women and children and old ones from the village. "What of these?"

Preacher came to his feet, looked for a second at the blood-smeared war club in his hand, and then cast it aside. "What of them? I told you all along, I don't make war on women and young'uns."

"I don't, either," Buckley said. "Charlie?"

"Yeah, I think there's been enough killing." Todd looked a little sick.

Preacher fastened his gaze on his son. "Hawk?"

For a long moment, Hawk didn't say anything. Then he took a deep breath, sighed, and said in his native tongue, "The spirits of Bird in the Tree and Little Pine are at rest, as are those of the other Absaroka." Then he added in English, "Let's get the hell out of here."

A weary smile touched Preacher's lips as he said, "Best idea anybody's had in a long time."

CHAPTER 43

Charlie Todd lifted the tin cup, threw back the whiskey it contained, licked his lips, and sighed. "I can't tell you just how much I needed that."

Hawk let out a disdainful grunt. White Buffalo just looked above it all as he sat at the round, rough-hewn table with his arms folded. Aaron Buckley sipped his whiskey rather than guzzling it down like his friend had.

With Dog at his feet, Preacher stood at the bar in the trading post and smiled as he looked at his friends. He had been talking idly with Ben Crandall, the proprietor of the trading post. Although acquainted with Crandall, Preacher didn't know him all that well.

The door opened and a stooped figure shuffled into the low-ceilinged room and headed for a corner. The newcomer's head was down and a thick buffalo robe enveloped the evidently frail figure. With a tired sigh, the individual sank down to the hard-packed dirt floor and huddled against the wall not far from the fireplace.

Crandall glanced over and frowned. "Damn redskins." He caught himself and added hastily, "Not your friends, of course, Preacher. They're always welcome here. You know that. Some of those old-timers slink in here and try to cadge drinks from me, and we can't have that. You know how Injuns are with firewater."

Preacher didn't respond to that. Some Indians were his best friends, others were his bitterest enemies. Like every other bunch of folks, there were all sorts of them.

"So you ain't run into any trouble so far this season?" Crandall went on.

"None to speak of," Preacher said.

That was true. The story of the long, bloody war he and Hawk had carried out against Tall Bull's band of Blackfeet would probably get around sooner or later, but Preacher was damned if he was going to add to the yarns people already spun about him.

Anyhow, the way folks dressed up those stories, by the time they were done they'd have him killing five or six hundred Blackfoot warriors all by himself . . . instead of the fifty or sixty he and Hawk had sent across the divide with a little help from their friends.

"Where are you bound from here?" Crandall asked.

"Thought we'd drift south and west a ways, over into the Tetons, maybe," Preacher said. "Do a little trappin'."

Crandall leaned his elbows on the bar. "The way I heard it, you usually play a lone hand, Preacher. It ain't common for you to travel with a group."

"Well," Preacher said, "they ain't exactly a common group."

There had been much discussion of the future during the week's journey from the Blackfoot village on the shore of that nameless mountain lake. Somewhat to his own surprise, he had found himself hoping Hawk would want to throw in with him for a while. He wouldn't mind getting to know the boy better. And of course, where Hawk went, White Buffalo was likely to go, as well. They were, after all, the last of the Absaroka—that particular band, anyway.

And Hawk was the last link to a time of fond memories for Preacher, a time he wasn't willing to let go of just yet.

As for Buckley and Todd, the two of them had expressed a desire to partner up with Preacher for a while, if he would have them.

"We might be able to make it on our own," Buckley had said next to the campfire one night, "but I think our odds will be a lot better with you, Preacher. There's still so much we can learn from you."

"How to shoot better," Hawk had said with a touch of dry humor, unusual for him.

"Yes, definitely," Buckley agreed. "But if we're going to be mountain men, who better to teach us?"

Preacher had agreed to let them come along. Maybe, with any luck, the rest of the season would pass peacefully. He wasn't going to bet a brand-new felt hat on it, though. Not the way trouble seemed to follow him around wherever he went.

As he stood in the trading post, Preacher felt his restlessness growing. He had been under a roof long enough. They had replenished their supplies, and he was ready to be gone from that outpost of civilization.

He walked over to the table and said, "You fellas about ready to go?"

"To set out on a new adventure?" Buckley said. "I certainly am. What about you, Charlie?"

Todd frowned and asked, "Are people going to try to kill us where we're going next, Preacher?"

"That's hard to say," the mountain man replied. "But I reckon there's nigh on to a million ways to die out here on the frontier, so it don't pay to lose any sleep worryin' about 'em. You just deal with 'em as they come."

"I suppose you're right. And we *did* come west in search of excitement . . ."

White Buffalo said, "Next time we should kill *all* of our enemies. Dog agrees with me on this."

"How about Horse?" Preacher asked.

"One does not ask for a horse's opinion on important matters, and certainly not that of a mule." White Buffalo blew out a breath that indicated just how ridiculous he considered the mountain man's question.

"All right," Preacher said as the others got to their feet. "Let's go see the elephant."

"Wait a minute . . . There are elephants where we're going?" Charlie Todd asked as they went out the door into the sunlight.

A short time later, Ben Crandall frowned and came out from behind the bar. He walked over to the huddled figure dozing against the wall and kicked it.

"Damn it, redskin, you're gonna have to haul your filthy carcass outta here—"

That was as far as Crandall got. The figure cast the robe aside and uncoiled like a striking snake. Lantern light flashed on a blade as the buckskin-clad figure pressed a knife against his throat. His eyes widened in shock. He had just enough time to hear a woman's voice say, "No one speaks to a Blackfoot warrior that way!"

The blade bit deep and Crandall began to make a gurgling sound as he staggered back. He clutched at his throat with both hands but couldn't stop the crimson flood over his shirt and apron. He fell to his knees and then toppled onto his side, still twitching as death claimed him.

His killer strode out of the trading post and stood slim and straight, peering toward distant snowcapped peaks visible far to the southwest.

"When the time is right, I will see you again, Preacher," Winter Wind said with hate burning brightly in her eyes.

Keep Reading for a special preview of
the next thrilling book from
WILLIAM W. and J. A. JOHNSTONE.

SAVAGE TEXAS
Seven Days to Hell

*From national bestselling authors William W. Johnstone
and J. A. Johnstone comes the epic tale of Hangtree
County, Texas, where a gunslinger and a lawman work to
bring peace to the most dangerous town in the West . . .*

TO SAVE A KILLER, A GUNMAN BLASTS
HIS WAY ACROSS TEXAS

On the trail to Hangtree, a gang of bandits give
chase to a teenage gunslinger. Young Bill is
bracing for the end when the crack of a Winchester
scatters the bandits. Sam Heller, Hangtree lawman,
has saved another life. And Bill will beg
Heller to save one more . . .

Bill rode in from East Texas, where Cullen Baker,
the original quick-draw artist, fights a life-and-death
battle with a corrupt robber baron for control of the
Torrent River. Bill came seeking help from Cullen's
old pal Johnny Cross, who agrees to ride east to lend
a bullet or two. It's a trek across a desert held by
brutal outlaws just waiting to kill. But with Sam
Heller at Cross's side, the odds are better. And when
the ammo's loaded for an all-out gun battle, the
Torrent will flow red—with blood . . .

Coming soon from Pinnacle Books!

CHAPTER 1

Spud Barker went to the Sunrise Café in Weatherford, Texas, to chow down on his daily breakfast feed. He didn't know it but his regular routine was about to be rudely interrupted. He was heavyset with a face like a fresh-dug potato: gnarly, lumpy, and none too clean, thus giving rise to his handle, "Spud." He dressed like a businessman and wore no gun in plain view. He was trailed by two bodyguards, Vic Terrill and Chubb Driscoll. Terrill had a face like a horse's clean-picked skull, long, bony, and dead-white. Driscoll was an un-jolly fat man with the permanent expression of a colicky baby.

The Sunrise Café was the best eatery in town, in the county for that matter. Which wasn't saying much. To be a regular there meant one had arrived, was an insider. It gave one prestige—so Spud Barker reckoned. He liked to see and be seen there. The food was good, too. Spud was a big eater.

Sunrise Café at weekday breakfast time was the last place he expected to find trouble. This morning trouble would find him.

It was about eight in the morning and the breakfast rush was over. Westerners were early risers generally and Weatherford folk were no exception. About a dozen patrons were scattered among the tables on both sides of the central aisle.

Among them but not of them was Sam Heller, no citizen of Weatherford he. He sat alone at a front table facing a window, which gave him a view of the entrance and beyond to the town square.

He was laying for Spud Barker, and when he saw him coming he rose from his chair and quietly sidled over to the front door, standing to one side of it.

Sam Heller was a yellow-haired and bearded well-armed titan in buckskins and denim. A Yankee born and bred, he was Texas sized, standing several inches above six feet, broad-shouldered, rawboned, long-limbed.

A Northerner who stood alone in Texas 1867, when the War Between the States was recent history and Yankee-hating by the populace was the rule rather than the exception, had to be able to take care of himself.

Sam Heller was such a man.

No one in the café knew him. They didn't know he was a Yankee, didn't know him from Adam. They were blissfully unaware he was about to set in motion a chain of events guaranteed to generate considerable bad feelings.

Sam felt good about the prospect.

Spud Barker came in first, then Terrill, then Driscoll. None of them spared more than a passing glance at the big galoot gawking at the picture on the wall. Their minds were on their bellies, for they were hungry. More, they assumed they were safe on home ground. Spud's bodyguards had perhaps grown too comfortable in the seeming security of familiar everyday surroundings.

They moved toward Spud's usual table on the left-hand side of the dining room, comfortably set back from the strong morning sunlight filtering through red-and-white-checked curtains that covered the pair of windows bracketing the front door.

The first warning Spud Barker had that something was amiss was a sudden sense of rushing motion in the immediate vicinity. That was the sound of Sam Heller coming up fast behind Terrill and Driscoll.

He grabbed each of them by the back of the collar and slammed their heads together, making a loud thumping noise. Chubb Driscoll took the brunt of the hit, eyes rolling up in his head as he went down, hitting the floor.

Vic Terrill went wobbly at the knees but stayed on his feet, stunned, seeing stars. He went for his gun more by instinct than anything else, groping blindly for it, but before he could find it Sam grabbed his gun hand by the wrist. Terrill struggled but could make no headway against Sam's iron grip.

Sam used the arm as a handle to swing the bodyguard hard against the wall on the left. Terrill hit an empty table along the way, rocking it but not knocking it over, upending several chairs.

Terrill slammed into the wall, crying out. Sam closed in on him, powering a pile-driving right uppercut that connected square on the point of Terrill's chin. Terrill's head snapped back, hitting the wall. His eyes showed their whites, his face went senselessly slack.

Sam's fist was cocked, ready to deliver a follow-up blow, but it was unneeded. Terrill was out cold. He folded at the knees, sliding down the wall with his back to it, falling in a crumpled heap at Sam's feet.

Spud Barker's bodyguards had been put out of commission in less than thirty seconds.

Sam turned, bearing down on Spud. It had all happened so fast that Spud hadn't had time to react. Now he did. He felt the Fear.

Spud's mouth went cotton-dry and his belly felt like the bottom dropped out of it. His hands flew up in front of him in a warding gesture: "No! Don't—"

Chubb Driscoll stirred on the floor, groggy, glassy eyed. Getting on hands and knees and trying to rise.

Sam swerved from his path toward Spud to kick Driscoll in the head. Driscoll flopped down and out.

The distraction gave Spud time to recover some of his wits. He started to reach toward his right-side jacket pocket for an object inside that made a suspicious bulge.

Before he could put a hand in his pocket, he was the recipient of a punch in the face that rocked him back on his heels, sending him hurtling backward. Sam crowded Spud, giving him no time to recover.

Sam grabbed Spud by the lapels, holding him upright and giving him a good shaking.

"W-what are you p-p-icking on me for? I don't even know you—"

"But I know you, Spud," Sam Heller interrupted.

Sam had set his attack inside the café to maximize the element of surprise, hitting his targeted men where and when they would least expect it.

He now wanted to take the action outside where there was less chance of innocent bystanders being hurt.

The windows flanking the front door caught his eye—and Sam was a direct actionist.

He grabbed Spud's collar by the scruff of the neck, his other hand gripping the top of the man's belt and waistband at the small of Spud's back.

Sam heaved upward, lifting Spud until only the toes of his boots were touching the floor, hustling him toward the front of the building.

Sam was giving Spud Barker the "bum's rush," a technique well known to bartenders and bouncers for ejecting belligerent drunks and troublemakers from the premises with a maximum of haste and a minimum of fuss.

"No!—What're you doing? Stop! You loco? Stop, stop!—" came Spud's wailing cries as he was swept forward toward a window to one side of the entrance.

"No, *don't*—!"

Sam stopped short, using his momentum to help heave Spud headfirst into the window.

It was closed.

Sam manhandled Spud Barker like pitching a hay bale into a wagon. A clean toss!

Spud hit the window in a tremendous explosion of shattered glass, splintered wood, red-and-white-checked curtains, and brass curtain rods—gone, now.

He spewed through the window frame into the outer air, landing with a bone-jarring thud on the boardwalk porch fronting the café.

Spud lay still, unmoving. After a pause he started groaning and twitching.

Sam grinned. He wasn't done with Spud Barker yet, not hardly. But first he had to make sure his rear lines were secure. That meant ensuring the bodyguards were still out of commission and stayed that way.

Sam turned, facing inward to the café. The customers were townsfolk mostly, judging by their clothes, and a few ranchers. They seemed a fairly prosperous lot.

Now they looked like a bomb had gone off. Sam's sudden outburst of violence had come as unexpectedly as a thunderbolt crashing out of a clear blue sky.

Customers and staffers alike tried to make themselves very still and small to avoid drawing Sam's notice. They looked away, not meeting his eyes.

Well and good. Part of the reason for Sam's shock tactics was to cow them into submission so none would be minded to interfere. Which took some doing with stiff-necked Texas men but so far it seemed to be working.

Vic Terrill lay sprawled on the floor, inert, unconscious. But Chubb Driscoll was showing signs of life.

Driscoll had managed to drag himself to an upright support pillar. The side of his face where Sam had kicked him was bruised with an eye swollen shut. His good eye glared hatefully, rolling this way and that. Sam started toward him. Chubb Driscoll went for his gun, pawing at it. Sam came on, not breaking stride. He grabbed a table chair and threw it at Driscoll. Driscoll had his gun in hand, he opened his mouth to shout—

The chair hit hard, breaking apart, silencing his outcry. Chubb Driscoll didn't break, but the hit didn't do him any good, either. He went limp, slumping to the floor.

Busting up the café was one thing, but a shoot-out was a horse of a different color. Sam took his chances as they came, but he'd hate like hell for some luckless breakfaster to catch a bullet right in the middle of his or her ham and eggs.

He took a look at Chubb Driscoll. Driscoll's eyes were closed, his smashed nose and lips bleeding. Was he alive or dead?

Sam didn't know. In any case the first thing to do was disarm him. Driscoll's gun was clutched in a closed fist but hadn't been fired.

Sam stepped on Driscoll's wrist, pinning his gun hand to the floor. Driscoll moaned, wincing and flinching like a dog having bad dreams.

"Alive, eh?" Sam said to himself. "But he won't be getting up any time soon."

He broke Driscoll's gun, emptying it and throwing the rounds out the broken window. He let the empty gun fall to the floor.

Sam absently rubbed the top of his big right hand, where he had skinned a couple of knuckles. He crossed to Terrill to give him the once-over. Terrill lay facedown, motionless in the spot where he'd been knocked out.

Sam grabbed a handful of Terrill's hair and raised his head off the floor to see what condition he was in. Terrill didn't so much as twitch.

Sam liked it when they stayed down after he hit them. He let go of the hair, Terrill's head flopping down.

Sam emptied Terrill's gun anyway. He wouldn't be getting a bullet in the back from either of the body-guards any time soon.

Now he could do his business with Spud Barker undisturbed.

Sam Heller took a last look at the people in the dining room, a long hard look. Had any been minded to show fight, that steely eyed gaze stifled any fleeting impulse toward combativeness.

Sam went out. Unlike Spud Barker, he used the door.

CHAPTER 2

Weatherford town was the capital of the same-named county. It lay in North Central Texas roughly along the same east-west latitude line as Dallas and Hangtree.

Dallas was a money town, Hangtree was a frontier cowtown, and Weatherford was . . . what, exactly?

Weatherford town and county was a good locale for ranching and farming. It was a good locale for lawlessness, too, far enough away from Dallas to avoid attracting unwanted attention from Federal troops yet close enough to be within ready reach of the U.S. Cavalry when CMN raiders were on the prowl.

In the war's aftermath Weatherford had attracted a bumper crop of outlaws who preyed on Hangtree, Dallas, and all points in between . . . The gangs raided neighboring communities, killing and plundering.

No lonely ranch house was too small, no settlement too large to escape their depredations. Travelers and wayfarers were prime targets. Many stagecoaches, freight haulers, and wagon trains had left their burned-out hulks scattered about the countryside.

And the sun-bleached bones of their passengers, too.

Weatherford was a clearinghouse for stolen goods. Outlaws from nearby counties disposed of their loot in town. Rustlers, robbers, bandits, and brigands, all came knowing their plunder would find a ready market in the merchants of Weatherford. They paid pennies on the dollar but it added up.

People being people and times being hard, buyers and sellers alike were none too fussy about little things like titles and bills of sale for goods and livestock that changed hands.

Any fool could see that the newcomers thronging Weatherford were outlaws dealing in stolen goods, but only a bigger fool would call them on it. Such great fools tend to be short-lived.

That was Weatherford: a lot of folks doing all right by doing wrong. Making it of interest to Sam Heller, a soldier of fortune, bounty hunter, and more. Much more.

A class of men, and some women, too, had sprung up who served as contacts linking town merchants with the bandit chiefs.

These middlemen—or fences, to call them by their right name—insulated the merchants from the tricky and dangerous business of dealing directly with the outlaws in the field, providing much-needed protection for the townsmen to avoid being robbed and killed while trying to exchange money for stolen goods.

The fences took a fat cut of the profits from buyers and sellers in exchange for brokering the deals.

One such middleman was Spud Barker, making him of interest to Sam Heller.

Sam was even more interested in Loman Vard, Spud's partner. Spud took care of business in town but it was Vard who had the contacts with the outlaws. Spud was a businessman and politician, and Vard was an outlaw and killer.

Sam very much wanted to get his hands on Loman Vard, but Vard was a tough man to corner. To get at him, Sam needed a middleman: Spud Barker.

Spud Barker didn't know what hit him. Literally.

He came crashing through the café window into the fresh clean brightness of a spring morning, one he was unable to appreciate at the moment. Somehow he managed to rise to his hands and knees, head hanging down. Pieces of broken glass that had gotten stuck to his clothes fell off, making little chiming tones when they hit the wooden plank board sidewalk.

His vision swam in and out of focus. He raised his hands to his aching head. The backs of his hands and forearms were all cut up, covered with hairline bleeding scratches—his face, too. His hat was lost somewhere along the way between café and sidewalk, but that was the least of his worries.

He made quite a sight in that heretofore-quiet street scene, though there weren't too many people around to see it.

The Sunrise Café stood on the west side of the town's central square, which was lined along the sides by some of Weatherford's leading establishments.

There was a bank, a hotel, the town hall, a dry goods emporium, a feed store, and so on. Also a couple of more or less respectable saloons and various shops and stores.

A few people were out on the street, mostly townsfolk running errands or doing some early shopping. They stopped what they were doing when Spud Barker exploded out the café window onto the boardwalk sidewalk. They paused to see what it was all about, staying a safe distance away.

A fancy two-wheeled buggy drawn by one horse rolled north, its driver slowing it to a halt when he came abreast of the café. The driver had a long bushy beard reaching to his collarbone. He wore a white shirt, black vest, and dark pants. He stared openmouthed, goggling at Spud Barker.

Spud stood on his knees, gingerly feeling around at the top of his head for damage and in the process dislodging more pieces of broken glass. He winced as his fingers discovered a goose egg–sized bump atop his aching noggin. The pain brought tears to his eyes. He blinked away the wetness until he could see clearly again.

Spud didn't like what he saw. A pair of boots had stepped into his field of vision. His gaze traveled upward, taking in the figure of the man looming over him—the wildman who had knocked eight bells out of his bodyguards and thrown him through the window.

Seeing Sam Heller come out of the café to hover over Spud Barker, the driver of the two-wheeled cart snapped the reins to get his horse moving up the street and away.

Sam Heller cut an impressive, even formidable, figure.

Beneath a dark, battered slouch hat his yellow hair fell to his shoulders in the go-to-hell style favored by certain U.S. Cavalry scouts, one of which he had once been. That long hair taunted hostile Indians, "*Take this scalp if you dare!*"

By contrast Sam's beard was close cut, neatly trimmed.

He wore a gun, a .36 Navy Colt tucked handle out into his waistband over his left hip. But that was not his main weapon. That was a Winchester 1866 repeating rifle, chopped down at barrel and stock. A weapon commonly known as a mule's leg. It rested in a custom-made leather holster on his right hip.

Sam also carried a Green River knife with an eighteen-inch blade, secured on his left side in a belt-sheath low-slung enough to avoid blocking access to the Navy Colt. Like the famed bowie knife, the Green River model was also balanced for throwing.

His blue eyes were as cold as polar seas.

Sam didn't like standing with his back to the café, his broad back a tempting target for anybody inside wanting to take a shot at him.

"Let's have some privacy, Spud," he said, grabbing the other by the back of his collar and hauling him to his feet.

Spud Barker's face swelled above the choking collar, reddening under Sam's tight grip. Sam hustled him away from the café to the south end of the wooden sidewalk. The sidewalk and building fronts were raised three feet above the ground. A short flight of three wooden steps with no railing angled down to solid ground.

Sam booted Spud Barker down the stairs. Spud's too-solid flesh clattered and banged on the stairs, counterpointed by his howls of pain and outrage. He hit the ground sprawling.

"You trying to kill me?" he demanded.

"If I do, you won't have to ask, you'll know it," Sam said. His ready boot toe none too gently prodded Spud to his feet.

"Stay on your feet, Spud. I'm getting tired of picking up your sorry carcass. If I have to do it much more you might just as well stay down permanently," Sam said.

An alley mouth opened at the bottom of the steps. The passageway stood crosswise to the street and ran between two blocks of wooden frame buildings.

Sam muscled Spud fifteen feet deeper into the alley, propping him up and slamming his back against the wall.

"That's better. Now we can have a nice private talk," Sam said.

"I've got nothing to say to you!" Spud Barker blustered.

"No?" Sam said, chuckling.

"No! . . . Why, I know what you are! You're a Yankee, a damned Yankee!" Spud Barker accused, his fleshy jowls quivering with indignation as he stabbed a pointing forefinger at Sam.

"How'd you figure that out?"

"You talk funny," Spud spat. "You know what's good

for you, you'll hightail it out of town quick and don't look back. We don't rightly care for your kind in Weatherford, Billy Yank. It's none too healthy for outsiders of the Northern persuasion."

"Not for the sons and daughters of Old Dixie, either, going by all the burned-out wagon trains and stagecoaches I've seen scattered around the county," Sam said.

"Northerners, every last one of them," Spud declared, chin outthrust defiantly.

"Lots of Southerners packing up and heading for California and points west these days. Anyway, how would you know if the missing wayfarers are Yankees or Rebs?"

"The devil must have a special sauce for Yankees, to make them so mean."

"Probably, but we'll get to that later. First, I want to make sure you're defanged." Sam reached into Spud's right-hand jacket pocket, pulling out a four-barreled pepperbox derringer. "Standard issue for the well-dressed Weatherford businessman," he said. "This little beauty can make a real mess. Too much gun for you, Spud—you might hurt yourself. I'll put it away for safekeeping."

He dropped it into a pocket of his buckskin vest. A further pat-down search yielded a set of spiked brass knuckles, a penknife, and a wad of greenback bills. Sam tossed the knuckle-duster and the penknife farther back into the alley and held on to the greenbacks.

"Enough frogskins here to choke a horse," Sam said, thumbing through the wad. "Big bills all the way through, with no little ones to pad it out. It'll go toward covering my expenses."

Sam pocketed the bills while Spud Barker sputtered with impotent outrage.

"Damn you! This is robbery! Robbery in broad daylight, no less!"

Sam tsk-tsked. "Makes you wonder what the town is coming to, eh?"

"You must be mad. The marshal's office is straight across the square and he's probably on his way here right now with his deputies. If you value your skin you'll give me back my money and make tracks out of here as fast as you can—"

"Not to worry, Marshal Finn and company are otherwise engaged. I'm afraid he's going to be a no-show."

"How can you know that?"

Weatherford's notoriously corrupt town marshal, Skeates Finn, upheld the law with sterling even-handed impartiality, allowing every outlaw who cut him in on the take the right to sell stolen goods in town.

He and his deputies were equally merciless to any badmen who refused to pay, or cheated the lawman out of what he regarded as his fair share. Such offenders were usually shot dead out of hand.

Sam said, "While you and the rest of Weatherford's good citizens were sleeping, Chuck Ramsey's bunch was making a predawn run of stolen goods into town for delivery at Banker Drysdale's warehouse off Town Square. Real first-class merchandise, from what I heard—this ring any bells for you, Spud?"

"Not a bit; I don't know what you're talking about." But Spud did know, if the flicker of recognition in his sick eyes was any indication, and Sam Heller reckoned it was so.

"Here's something you don't know. The Ramsey gang ran into an ambush and got shot to pieces, every last man jack of them, dead," Sam said.

Spud Barker looked even sicker, face wrenched out of shape by a spasm of strong emotion, as if he'd taken a bite out of an apple to find half a worm.

"It's a sin and a scandal how cheap these owlhoots hold human life," Sam went on. "Maybe they figure such killers and scavengers ain't really human . . . or maybe it takes one to know one, as the saying goes.

"Now here's the part that'll really gall you, Spud. After going to all that trouble of bushwhacking the Ramseys, the hijackers set fire to the wagons and burned up all the goods."

"*They burned them up?!*" Spud Barker said every word carefully and distinctly.

"Burned them up," Sam repeated cheerfully. "All those plundered goods, turned into a heap of ashes. It's like burning up money, don't you think? A lot of money, I heard."

"You hear a lot," Spud said, looking daggers at him. "Too much."

"I get around," Sam said modestly. "Some good Samaritan passing through stopped by the warehouse to give them the bad news. Banker Drysdale being one of the big men in town, there was nothing for it but for Marshal Finn and deputies to saddle up and gallop pronto out to Hansen's Pass where the ambush went down.

"Now just between the two of us, Spud, and don't let on where you heard it, but I suspicion that when Finn gets to the pass, he's going to find some clues and a set of tracks that lead right straight to Lem Buckman's camp on the far side of the ridge."

"Buckman!" Spud said, startled into angry vehemence. "Buckman would never cross Ramsey, they've been stringing together since the war! They're like brothers! It's all a put-up job to point the finger at Buckman and away from whoever really did the job—"

"Buckman didn't do it, eh, Spud? You would know."

"I don't know a thing," the other said dully.

"Lord, I hope Finn doesn't go off half-cocked and ride into Buckman's camp shooting! A lot of fellows could get hurt . . . Here's a puzzlement: If Buckman and his bunch didn't jump the Ramsey gang and burn the wagons, who did?"

"You tell me," Spud said in flat, clipped tones.

"Loman Vard," Sam suggested brightly. "Why not? Who better? Vard could be going behind your back and everybody else's, trying to take over the town—"

"You madman!" Spud Barker had reached the breaking point where fear gave way to rage, greed, and frustration. "It's not Vard who's sneaking around doing the back shooting and burning, it's you! You lowdown no-account good-for-nothing Yankee jackanapes! Who are you? What do you want? What're you trying to do to this town, destroy it?" Spud Barker was all but shrieking.

"I'll do that and more if that's what it takes to get what I want," Sam Heller said quietly.

"If it's money you're after, I'll pay you to go away

and leave me alone. I'll pay you one hundred—no, five hundred dollars in gold!"

"Glad you upped the ante, because there's more than two hundred dollars' worth of greenbacks in your billfold alone, Spud."

"Five hundred dollars in gold, in your hand within the hour, if you'll leave me alone and ride out."

"Sure, let's take a stroll over to the bank and you'll take it out of the petty cash drawer. What could go wrong? I trust you. Who wouldn't trust a receiver of stolen goods plundered from robbed and murdered travelers and emigrants, men, women, and children?" Sam mocked.

"We'll work out a way to get you the money that doesn't put you at risk," Spud insisted.

"I like money as well as anyone else, Spud, but it's just incidental. What I want is information."

"You won't get it from me; it'll take more than a lunatic lone Yankee storming into town, beating innocent people within an inch of their lives, and slandering blameless businessmen like myself to make me betray my sacred trusts!"

"I'll make you talk, Spud."

"I've had a bellyful of your damned cat-and-mouse games—"

"Cat and rat, more like."

"Blast you, speak plainly and say who you are and what you want!"

"The name's Heller, Sam Heller, if that means anything to you."

It did. Blood drained away from Spud Barker's florid complexion, leaving it a sallow white. His eyes narrowed, calculating. He chewed tiny flecks of skin from his quivering lower lip.

Spud felt quite the fool. Had he not been so intimidated by his assailant, the mule's leg on his hip should have been a dead giveaway to his identity. The notoriety of the Yankee bounty man with the chopped-down Winchester was widespread throughout North Central Texas and beyond.

"The Yankee bounty hunter who kills for gold," Spud said. He tried to speak forcefully but his voice cracked, causing him to finish with a near-whisper.

"Guilty as charged," Sam said.

"Y-you're wasting your time sniffing around here, Bluebelly. There's no price on my head!"

"That's because you haven't got caught yet. You may not be a wolf in sheep's clothing but you're no lamb, either . . . A polecat in sheep's clothing, maybe."

"Quit name-calling and tell me what you want."

"Loman Vard, that's who I want."

Spud Barker waited a long time before replying. "Never heard of him."

"Stop it. If you're going to lie—you might as well put some feeling into it. There's not a man, woman, or stray dog in Weatherford who doesn't know who Loman Vard is," Sam said. "Loman Vard, your partner in the stolen goods and livestock business. Ring any bells yet?"

"Oh, *that* Vard!"

"Uh-huh, that one. Loman Vard—there's only one," Sam pressed.

"Sure I know him, er, ah, that is I mean I've heard of him, certainly, yes," Spud said, stalling for time. "I got confused for a minute—who wouldn't be, after getting beaten up, thrown through a window, and terrorized by a maniac Yankee? But you've got the wrong man, mister. I'm not partnered up with Vard or anyone else in the stolen goods business. I'm an honest dealer in used and secondhand merchandise—*oof!*"

This last reaction was occasioned by a sharp stiff jab that Sam Heller popped into Spud's soft belly. It was not a particularly hard hit, for Sam wanted the other to be able to talk. But Spud still staggered under the blow.

Some color had been returning to Spud's face, but the jab turned it pasty white again.

Sam grabbed a fistful of Spud's shirtfront, tearing cloth and sending buttons popping. "Better talk while you can, Spud. If Johnny Cross gets hold of you, your life won't be worth a Confederate dollar," he snapped.

"*Johnny Cross!*—What's he got to do with me?!" Spud Barker was near-hysterical. White rings circled his eyes, fear-dilated pupils swollen to black disks.

"Vard sent Terrible Terry Moran to kill him— You're Vard's partner! Cross'll kill Vard but he won't stop there, he'll clean up on the whole gang and everybody tied in with Vard, then he'll burn down Vard's house to warm his hands by!

"The only chance you've got of coming out of this alive is to give me Vard first. If I get him before Johnny does, I can keep you out of it. But if Johnny gets to Vard first, you're a dead man. You can start running now, but no matter how far and how fast you go, some fine day you'll find yourself looking at Cross from the wrong side of a gun."

"This is madness! You've got the wrong man, I

tell you." Spud Barker's shoulders heaved and he knuckled his eyes as though wiping away tears.

Sam noticed that Spud's eyes were both dry and that Spud was peeking at him over the tops of his hands, looking to see if Sam was buying his story.

"It's no good, Spud. I'm not guessing, I *know*. I tracked down Fly Norvine, the only member of Moran's gang to escape the gundown. He spilled his guts by the time I was through with him. He told about Moran and all the rest of it, how you and Vard were thick as thieves with Jimbo Turlock in the run-up to the Marauder raid on Hangtree . . ."

Sam's voice trailed off. Something had changed. A moment ago, Spud Barker had been panting for breath as if he'd just run a mile. Now his breathing had slowed almost to normal.

"You overplayed your hand, Billy Yank," Spud said, smirking. "You had me going there for a while, I'll give you that. But you made a mistake."

"Oh, really?" Sam said.

"Yes, really," Spud returned with hateful mockery of Sam's words and tone. He actually seemed to be enjoying himself now. "If you had Fly Norvine, you could have taken him to Fort Pardee, sworn out a warrant, and come here with the Army to crush this town. But you being here all by your lonesome tells me that you've got nothing, nothing at all."

"That's a horse on me, I reckon," Sam said in a conversational tone, after a pause. "But you know, Spud, there's also such a thing as being too damned smart to live."

Spud tried to put across a reasonable tone.

"See here, Heller, I can hardly tell you what I don't know—"

Sam drew his knife and held it up to Spud Barker's face.

Spud's stream of words came to a dead stop. The formidable Green River knife with its eighteen-inch blade tended to have a chilling effect on conversation. Rays of morning sunlight set the blade ablaze with a white-hot glinting. The knife bore the seal of authenticity, the Green River maker's mark stamped into the metal of the blade near the hilt.

Spud Barker stared at the blade as if hypnotized. "W-wuh-wuh—what're that for?!"

"You would have it this way, Spud." Sam sighed. He played with the knife, turning it this way and that, causing its glaring reflected light to shine directly in Spud's eyes, dazzling them.

"Funny thing about nicknames, they get right straight to the heart of the matter," Sam began. "You get a fellow called Shorty and he's going to be short. Man they call Long Nose will have a long nose, and so on. You get the idea. Now what do they call you?— '*Spud.*' That's right on the money because your head does look like a potato. All lumpy, skin rough and patchy like a potato skin, eyes that're little black holes like a 'tater's eyes . . ."

"What're you going on about, Heller?" Spud Barker's words were brittle with rising hysteria.

"I'm through playing with you, Spud. Tell me where Vard is or I'll peel you like a potato."

"You're crazy!"

Sam didn't answer, he just kept playing with the knife, throwing the sun-dazzle into Spud's eyes.

"You can't get away with this!"

"I'm getting away with it, Spud. The law's out of town so there's no help for you there. Your fellow citizens are famously minding their own business, so they won't interfere. You can't stop me. So what's it to be, Spud? Talk? Or get peeled?"

Sam's free hand shot out, grabbing a fistful of Spud Barker's greasy hair, holding his head upright for the knife.

The sudden action caused Spud to cry out in fear. He started wriggling.

"Hold still, Spud, you'll do yourself a mischief," Sam warned. He touched the other's taut neck not with the sharp end of the blade but rather with the squared-off edge running along the top of the knife.

Spud stopped wriggling.

"There's more than one way to peel a potato. I'm going to scalp you, Spud."

Too undone by terror to speak, Spud could only make a croaking gasp by way of protest.

"Scalping won't kill you. It'll put you in a world of hurt, but it won't kill you," Sam said brightly. "Every now and then you run into a fellow that's been scalped. More than you might think. They get left for dead and don't die. Scalped man usually keeps his head covered all the time with a hat or head scarf or whatever. For good reason: The top of the head is a mess of scars from crown to ears. It ain't pretty.

"Back when I was fighting Sioux up on the North Range I got to be a pretty fair hand at taking scalps. They made a practice of lifting the hair of our people, men and women both, so we scouts figured turnabout was fair play. Now this Green River blade is no scalping knife but it'll do the job right handily—"

"No, no! . . . Don't!"

"Ah, you can speak after all, Spud. Thought the cat got your tongue, you were so quiet for a while. Long as you can talk, why not tell me where Vard is and save yourself a heap of grief?"

"I can't tell what I don't know!"

"Shh! Not so loud. You'll startle me. If my hand slips I might put out your eye by mistake. Lord knows you'll have misery enough without adding to your troubles."

"Oh, why won't you believe me when I tell you I don't know where Vard is? Why, why?"

"Because you're a liar, Spud."

"I'm not lying—"

"What else would a liar say?" Sam asked reasonably.

"But so would a man telling the truth!" Spud insisted.

"Vard would have given up and thrown you over as soon as I started leaning on him, but you're too dumb to do it to him first," Sam said.

"Vard will kill me if I talk," Spud whispered, wringing his hands. "Not that I know where he is," he added quickly.

"If that's your song, you're stuck with it. Too bad for you," Sam said, touching the knife blade tip to the right-hand corner of Spud's forehead where the hairline met.

"Now I'll tell you what I'm going to do," he went on. "First, I'll mark out the area to be cut along the hairline, down around the ears and then across the back of the neck at the collar. Done right, I can just sort of slip the flat of the knife under the top layers of skin, working it in deep, back toward the crown. Work loose a nice flap of scalp big enough to get a good grip on and, with a bit of luck, I'll peel the whole scalp right off the top of the skull all in one piece!"

Sam pressed the knife blade tip a bit harder against Spud's flesh, pricking it. A tear-sized, ruby droplet beaded at the surface.

Spud Barker shrieked. He went limp, eyes closed, head bowed. Sam thought the man had fainted but Spud was still on his feet. He slapped Spud's jowly cheeks several times, trying to rouse him.

"*Oww!* That hurts," Spud complained.

"You won't even notice it once the scalping starts," Sam said.

"To hell with that, I'll talk!"

"Ah, now you're showing good sense."

"First you've got to promise me something."

"You're sorely trying my patience, Spud. We're not horse-trading here. Tell me where I can find Vard and you won't get scalped. That's the only deal on tap today."

"No conditions here, no strings attached. This is something you'll want," Spud Barker said, gripping Sam's arm—not his knife arm. "You've got to kill Loman Vard first chance you get."

"I'm looking forward to it," Sam said, taking Spud's hand off his arm. No need to tell him that Sam meant to take Vard alive. Vard was a storehouse of information about outlaw alliances and criminal conspiracies in Texas and throughout the Southwest. Sam Heller would squeeze him dry of all he knew before sending him on to swing on a rope in Hangtree.

"Vard will know I've talked, and if you don't kill him he'll kill me."

"You'll be safe enough, Spud."

Spud Barker nervously gnawed on a knuckle. "Vard's hard enough to kill man-to-man, but he won't be alone. He surrounds himself with top guns: Big Taw, the tinhorn they call Acey-Deucy, Kurt Angle and his cousin—they're a pair of right bastards—Ginger Culhane, the Mex. Every one a killer and that's not the half of them. Are you sure you can take him? What can you do? One lone man . . ."

"Chuck Ramsey had a five-man gang of stone killers siding him. They went down in a couple minutes shooting at Hansen's Pass," Sam said. "With a rifle you don't have to work close."

"I know you're a sharpshooter, you can pick off Vard at a distance. You don't even have to show yourself. That must be nice," Spud said, not trying to hide the envy in his voice.

Color was coming back to his cheeks as he took heart. "You side Johnny Cross, a one-man army all by himself! If you could bring him in on this thing, Heller."

"Better if Johnny doesn't get involved . . . better for you," Sam said. "Don't forget that bit with Terry Moran. If Johnny finds out you had a hand in that, he'll skin you alive.

"Which is what I'm going to do to you, Spud, if you don't quit stalling and steer me to Loman Vard—and quick!"

"All right, I'll tell you. Between you and Johnny Cross, Vard is finished. If you don't get him Cross surely will."

Sam Heller heaved a sigh of relief when Spud Barker wasn't looking. He'd been afraid he'd really have to start scalping to get him to talk.

Spud Barker opened his mouth to speak but before he could do so a voice demanded:

"Let Spud go!"

ABOUT THE AUTHOR

WILLIAM W. JOHNSTONE was the author of over 220 *USA Today* and *New York Times* bestselling books, including *The First Mountain Man, MacCallister, Eagles, Savage Texas, Matt Jensen, The Last Mountain Man, The Family Jensen,* and *The Kerrigans: A Texas Dynasty,* as well as the stand-alone thrillers *Suicide Mission, The Bleeding Edge, Home Invasion, Stand Your Ground,* and *Tyranny.*

Visit his website at www.williamjohnstone.net.